Praise for the Immortals Series by Alyson Noël

"*Evermore* is addictive. When I wasn't reading, I was thinking about how I could sneak away to read some more. I couldn't put it down. I dreamt about this book. And when I was finished, I couldn't get it out of my head. This book was simply breathtaking." —*Teens Read Too*

"Teen angst and the paranormal make a combustible mix as Noël utilizes typical themes and gives them a dangerous and eerie twist. Getting hooked on this new series, The Immortals, is guaranteed."
—*RT Book Reviews* (4 stars)

"*Evermore* will thrill many teen fantasy–suspense readers, especially fans of Stephenie Meyer's Twilight series. . . . Noël creates a cast of recognizably diverse teens in a realistic high school setting, along with just the right tension to make Ever's discovery of her own immortality—should she choose it—exciting and credible."
—*Booklist*

"Readers who enjoy the works of P. C. Cast and Stephenie Meyer will love this outstanding paranormal teen-lit thriller."
—*Midwest Book Review*

"Get ready for a wild ride that is filled with twisting paths and mystery, love, and fantasy. . . . The writing style, story, and characters are a bit like Meyer's and Marr's popular books, but written with a new twist and voice. And after reading the book, you too will probably want your own Damen, even if it means making the ultimate sacrifice." —*The Book Queen* (5 stars)

"I found myself unwilling to put the book down, even though I had to at some points, because I wanted to know what was going to happen. . . . Ever was so real and her emotions were so believable that it was a little creepy. It's like Alyson Noël is actually a grieving, love-struck teenager. She got Ever completely perfect. And by perfect, I mean delightfully flawed and deep."

—*Frenetic Reader*

"Evermore is a wonderful book that I believe would be a lovely addition to any library . . . a book that fans of Stephenie Meyer and Melissa Marr should add to their collections. Definitely engaging and will catch your attention the minute you open to the first page!"

—*Mind of a Bibliophile*

"Alyson Noël creates a great picture of each and every character in the book. I am a fan of the Twilight series and I recommend this book to those who like the series as well. It is a very quick read, with all the interesting twists and turns."

—*Flamingnet* book reviews

"I loved this book. It really keeps your attention throughout the story, because the puzzle gets pieced together bit by bit, but you don't know exactly what happened until the end. . . . I would definitely recommend this to my friends."

—*Portsmouth Teen Book Review*

"This is the first installment of the Immortals series. Ms. Noël pens a well-detailed story that makes it easy for the reader to visualize both the characters and the world around them. *Evermore* has a familiar theme that attracts readers, but inside this book you'll find that the author has added some unique details that sets it apart."

—*Darque Reviews*

"*Evermore*'s suspense, eerie mystery, and strange magic were interestingly entertaining. . . . I found Ever to be a character I could really respect. . . . Recommended."

—*The Bookworm*

"Beautiful main characters, tense budding romance, a dark secret, mysterious immortals—what more could you ask from this modern gothic romance?"

—*Justine* magazine

"*Evermore* was a great way to lighten my reading load this winter and provided me with a creative, magical story that I really enjoyed. This is the first in a series for Noël and I think she may have a hit on her hands. . . . *Evermore* has good and evil, likable characters, vivid descriptions, and a good story."

—*Planet Books*

"I fell into it easily, and loved the world Noël created. . . . The fact that Ever had psychic powers was truly interesting. They flowed neatly through the book and I felt Ever's pain. . . . Trust me, this book was really good. I couldn't put it down. Alyson Noël created an amazing new world, and after this book I am so curious to see where it heads because, honestly, I have no idea."

—*Reading Keeps You Sane*

"Ever is an easy character to like. I really felt for her because of all she lost and what she struggled with daily. . . . *Evermore* was a really fast, engaging read with some great characters. It is the first in a series, so I'm eager to see if we will learn more about Ever, Damen, and friends in the next one. . . . It's sure to be a great read."

—*Ninja* reviews

"The writing here is clear, the story well defined, and narrator Ever has an engaging voice that teens should enjoy."

—*January Magazine*

also by alyson noël

Everlasting
Night Star
Dark Flame
Shadowland
Whisper
Dreamland
Shimmer
Radiance
Cruel Summer
Saving Zoë
Kiss & Blog
Fly Me to the Moon
Laguna Cove
Art Geeks and Prom Queens
Faking 19
Fated
Echo
Mystic
Horizon

alyson noël

The Immortals
The Beginning

Evermore
and
Blue Moon

st. martin's griffin new york

This is a work of fiction. All of the characters, organizations, and events portrayed in this novel are either products of the author's imagination or are used fictitiously.

 Printed in the United States of America. For information, address St. Martin's Press, 175 Fifth Avenue, New York, N.Y. 10010.

www.stmartins.com

Library of Congress Cataloging-in-Publication Data Available Upon Request

ISBN 978-1-250-03728-2

St. Martin's Griffin books may be purchased for educational, business, or promotional use. For information on bulk purchases, please contact Macmillan Corporate and Premium Sales Department at 1-800-221-7945 extension 5442 or write specialmarkets@macmillan.com.

First Edition: July 2013

10 9 8 7 6 5 4 3 2 1

evermore

aura color chart

Red: Energy, strength, anger, sexuality, passion, fear, ego

Orange: Self-control, ambition, courage, thoughtfulness, lack of will, apathetic

Yellow: Optimistic, happy, intellectual, friendly, indecisive, easily led

Green: Peaceful, healing, compassion, deceitful, jealous

Blue: Spiritual, loyal, creative, sensitive, kind, moody

Violet: Highly spiritual, wisdom, intuition

Indigo: Benevolence, highly intuitive, seeker

Pink: Love, sincerity, friendship

Gray: Depression, sadness, exhaustion, low energy, skepticism

Brown: Greed, self-involvement, opinionated

Black: Lacking energy, illness, imminent death

White: Perfect balance

The only secret people keep / Is immortality.

—Emily Dickinson

one

"Guess who?"

Haven's warm, clammy palms press hard against my cheeks as the tarnished edge of her silver skull ring leaves a smudge on my skin. And even though my eyes are covered and closed, I know that her dyed black hair is parted in the middle, her black vinyl corset is worn over a turtleneck (keeping in compliance with our school's dress-code policy), her brand-new, floor-sweeping, black satin skirt already has a hole near the hem where she caught it with the toe of her Doc Martens boots, and her eyes appear gold but that's only because she's wearing yellow contacts.

I also know her dad isn't really away on "business" like he said, her mom's personal trainer is way more "personal" than "trainer," and her little brother broke her Evanescence CD but he's too afraid to tell her.

But I don't know any of this from spying or peeking or even being told. I know because I'm psychic.

"Hurry! Guess! The bell's gonna ring!" she says, her voice hoarse, raspy, like she smokes a pack a day, even though she only tried smoking once.

I stall, thinking of the last person she'd ever want to be mistaken for. "Is it Hilary Duff?"

"Ew. Guess again!" She presses tighter, having no idea that I don't have to *see* to *know*.

"Is it Mrs. Marilyn Manson?"

She laughs and lets go, licking her thumb and aiming for the tarnish tattoo she left on my cheek, but I raise my hand and beat her to it. Not because I'm grossed out by the thought of her saliva (I mean, I *know* she's healthy), but because I don't want her to touch me again. Touch is too revealing, too exhausting, so I try to avoid it at all costs.

She grabs the hood of my sweatshirt and flicks it off my head, then squints at my earbuds and asks, "What're you listening to?"

I reach inside the iPod pocket I've stitched into all of my hoodies, concealing those ubiquitous white cords from faculty view, then I hand it over and watch her eyes bug out when she says, "What *the*? I mean, can it *be* any louder? And who is that?" She dangles the iPod between us so we can both hear Sid Vicious screaming about anarchy in the UK. And the truth is, I don't know if Sid's for it or against it. I just know that he's almost loud enough to dull my overly heightened senses.

"Sex Pistols," I say, clicking it off and returning it to my secret compartment.

"I'm surprised you could even hear me." She smiles at the same time the bell rings.

But I just shrug. I don't need to *listen* to *hear*. Though it's not like I mention that. I just tell her I'll see her at lunch and head toward class, making my way across campus and cringing when I sense these two guys sneaking up behind her, stepping on the hem of her skirt, and almost making her fall. But when she turns and makes the sign of evil (okay, it's not really the sign of evil, it's just something she made up) and glares at them with her yellow eyes, they immediately back off and leave her alone. And I breathe a sigh of relief as I push into class, knowing it won't be long before the lingering energy of Haven's touch fades.

I head toward my seat in the back, avoiding the purse Stacia Miller has purposely placed in my path, while ignoring her daily serenade of *"Looo-ser!"* she croons under her breath. Then I slide onto my chair, retrieve my book, notebook, and pen from my bag, insert my earpiece, pull my hood back over my head, drop my backpack on the empty seat beside me, and wait for Mr. Robins to show.

Mr. Robins is always late. Mostly because he likes to take a few nips from his small silver flask between classes. But that's only because his wife yells at him all the time, his daughter thinks he's a loser, and he pretty much hates his life. I learned all of that on my first day at this school, when my hand accidentally touched his as I gave him my transfer slip. So now, whenever I need to turn something in, I just leave it on the edge of his desk.

I close my eyes and wait, my fingers creeping inside my sweatshirt, switching the song from screaming Sid Vicious to something softer, smoother. All that loud noise is no longer necessary now that I'm in class. I guess the small student/teacher ratio keeps the psychic energy somewhat contained.

I wasn't always a freak. I used to be a normal teen. The kind who went to school dances, had celebrity crushes, and was so vain about my long blond hair I wouldn't dream of scraping it back into a ponytail and hiding beneath a big hooded sweatshirt. I had a mom, a dad, a little sister named Riley, and a sweet yellow Lab named Buttercup. I lived in a nice house, in a good neighborhood, in Eugene, Oregon. I was popular, happy, and could hardly wait for junior year to begin since I'd just made varsity cheerleader. My life was complete, and the sky was the limit. And even though that last part is a total cliché, it's also ironically true.

Yet all of that's just hearsay as far as I'm concerned. Because ever since the accident, the only thing I can clearly remember is dying.

I had what they call an NDE, or "near death experience." Only *they* happen to be wrong. Because believe me, there wasn't anything "near" about it. It's like, one moment my little sister Riley and I were sitting in the back of my dad's SUV, with Buttercup's head resting on Riley's lap, while his tail thumped softly against my leg, and the next thing I knew all the air bags were blown, the car was totaled, and I was observing it all from outside.

I gazed at the wreckage—the shattered glass, the crumbled doors, the front bumper clutching a pine tree in a lethal embrace—wondering what went wrong as I hoped and prayed everyone had gotten out too. Then I heard a familiar bark, and turned to see them all wandering down a path, with Buttercup wagging her tail and leading the way.

I went after them. At first trying to run and catch up, but then slowing and choosing to linger. Wanting to wander through that vast fragrant field of pulsating trees and flowers that shivered, closing my eyes against the dazzling mist that reflected and glowed and made everything shimmer.

I promised myself I'd only be a moment. That soon, I'd go back and find them. But when I did finally look, it was just in time to catch a quick glimpse of them smiling and waving and crossing a bridge, mere seconds before they all vanished.

I panicked. I looked everywhere. Running this way and that,

but it all looked the same—warm, white, glistening, shimmering, beautiful, stupid, eternal mist. And I fell to the ground, my skin pricked with cold, my whole body twitching, crying, screaming, cursing, begging, making promises I knew I could never ever keep.

And then I heard someone say, "Ever? Is that your name? Open your eyes and look at me."

I stumbled back to the surface. Back to where everything was pain, and misery, and stinging wet hurt on my forehead. And I gazed at the guy leaning over me, looked into his dark eyes, and whispered, "I'm Ever," before passing out again.

two

Seconds before Mr. Robins walks in, I lower my hood, click off my iPod, and pretend I'm reading my book, not bothering to look up when he says, "Class, this is Damen Auguste. He just moved here from New Mexico. Okay Damen, you can take that empty seat in the back, right next to Ever. You'll have to share her book until you get your own copy."

Damen is gorgeous. I know this without once looking up. I just focus on my book as he makes his way toward me since I know way too much about my classmates already. So as far as I'm concerned, an extra moment of ignorance really is bliss.

But according to the innermost thoughts of Stacia Miller sitting just two rows before me—*Damen Auguste is totally smoking hot*.

Her best friend, Honor, completely agrees.

So does Honor's boyfriend, Craig, but that's a whole other story.

"Hey." Damen slides onto the seat next to mine, my backpack making a muffled thud as he drops it to the floor.

I nod, refusing to look any further than his sleek, black, motorcycle boots. The kind that are more *GQ* than Hells Angels.

The kind that looks very out of place among the rows of multicolored flip-flops currently gracing the green-carpeted floor.

Mr. Robins asks us all to turn our books to page 133, prompting Damen to lean in and say, "Mind if I share?"

I hesitate, dreading the proximity, but slide my book all the way over until it's teetering off the edge of my desk. And when he moves his chair closer, bridging the small gap between us, I scoot to the farthest part of my seat and hide beneath my hood.

He laughs under his breath, but since I've yet to look at him, I have no idea what it means. All I know is that it sounded light and amused, but like it held something more.

I sink even lower, cheek on palm, eyes on the clock. Determined to ignore all the withering glances and critical comments directed my way. Stuff like: *Poor hot, sexy, gorgeous new guy, having to sit next to that freak!* That emanates from Stacia, Honor, Craig, and just about everyone else in the room.

Well, all except for Mr. Robins, who wants class to end almost as much as me.

By lunch, everyone's talking about Damen.

Have you seen that new kid Damen? He's so hot—So sexy—I heard he's from Mexico—No I think it's Spain—Whatever, it's some foreign place—I'm totally asking him to Winter Formal—You don't even know him yet—Don't worry I will—

"Omigod. Have you seen that new kid, Damen?" Haven sits beside me, peering through her growing-out bangs, their spiky tips ending just shy of her dark red lips.

"Oh please, not you too." I shake my head and bite into my apple.

"You would so not be saying that if you'd been privileged

enough to actually *see* him," she says, removing her vanilla cupcake from its pink cardboard box, licking the frosting right off the top in her usual lunchtime routine, even though she dresses more like someone who'd rather drink blood than eat tiny little sweet cakes.

"Are you guys talking about Damen?" Miles whispers, sliding onto the bench and placing his elbows on the table, his brown eyes darting between us, his baby face curving into a grin. "*Gorgeous!* Did you see the boots? So *Vogue.* I think I'll invite him to be my next boyfriend."

Haven gazes at him with narrowed, yellow eyes. "Too late, I called dibs."

"I'm sorry, I didn't realize you were into non-goths." He smirks, rolling his eyes as he unwraps his sandwich.

Haven laughs. "When they look like that I am. I swear he's just so freaking smoldering, you *have* to see him." She shakes her head, annoyed that I can't join in on the fun. "He's like—*combustible*!"

"You haven't seen him?" Miles grips his sandwich and gapes at me.

I gaze down at the table, wondering if I should just lie. They're making such a big deal I'm thinking it's my only way out. Only I can't. Not to them. Haven and Miles are my best friends. My only friends. And I feel like I'm keeping enough secrets already. "I sat next to him in English," I finally say. "We were forced to share a book. But I didn't really get a good look."

"Forced?" Haven moves her bangs to the side, allowing for an unobstructed view of the freak who'd dare say such a thing. "Oh that must have been awful for you, that must've really sucked." She rolls her eyes and sighs. "I swear, you have no idea how lucky you are. And you don't even appreciate it."

"Which book?" Miles asks, as though the title will somehow reveal something meaningful.

"*Wuthering Heights.*" I shrug, placing my apple core on the center of my napkin and folding the edges all around.

"And your hood? Up or down?" Haven asks.

I think back, remembering how I raised it right as he moved toward me. "Um, up," I tell her. "Yeah, definitely up." I nod.

"Well thank you for that," she mumbles, breaking her vanilla cupcake in half. "The last thing I need is competition from the blond goddess."

I cringe and gaze down at the table. I get embarrassed when people say things like that. Apparently, I used to live for that kind of thing, but not anymore. "Well, what about Miles? You don't think he's competition?" I ask, diverting the attention away from me and back on someone who can truly appreciate it.

"Yeah." Miles runs his hand through his short brown hair and turns, gracing us with his very best side. "Don't rule it out."

"Totally moot," Haven says, dusting white crumbs from her lap. "Damen and Miles don't play for the same team. Which means his oh-so-devastating, model-quality looks don't count."

"How do you know which team he's on?" Miles asks, twisting the cap off his VitaminWater and narrowing his gaze. "How can you be so sure?"

"Gaydar," she says, tapping her forehead. "And trust me, this guy does not register."

Not only is Damen in my first-period English class, and my sixth-period art class (not that he sat by me, and not that I looked, but the thoughts swirling around the room, even from our teacher,

Ms. Machado, told me everything I needed to know), but now he'd apparently parked next to me too. And even though I'd managed to avoid viewing anything more than his boots, I knew my grace period had just come to an end.

"Omigod, there he is! Right directly next to us!" Miles squeals, in the high-pitched, singsongy whisper he saves for life's most exciting moments. "And check out that ride—shiny black BMW, extra-dark tinted windows. Nice, very nice. Okay, so here's the deal, I'm going to open my door and *accidentally* bump it into his, so then I'll have an excuse to talk to him." He turns, awaiting my consent.

"Do *not* scratch my car. Or his car. Or any other car," I say, shaking my head and retrieving my keys.

"Fine." He pouts. "Shatter my dream, whatever. But just do yourself a favor and *check him out*! And then look me in the eye and tell me he doesn't make you want to freak out and faint."

I roll my eyes and squeeze between my car and the poorly parked VW Bug that's angled so awkwardly it looks like it's trying to mount my Miata. And just as I'm about to unlock the door, Miles yanks down my hood, swipes my sunglasses, and runs to the passenger side where he urges me, via not-so-subtle head tilts and thumb jabs, to look at Damen who's standing behind him.

So I do. I mean, it's not like I can avoid it forever. So I take a deep breath and look.

And what I see leaves me unable to speak, blink, or move.

And even though Miles starts waving at me, glaring at me, and basically giving me every signal he can think of to abort the mission and return to headquarters—I can't. I mean, I'd like to, because I know I'm acting like the freak everyone's already convinced that I am, but it's completely impossible. And it's not just because Damen is undeniably beautiful, with his shiny dark hair that hits just shy of his shoulders and curves around his high-sculpted cheekbones, but when he looks at me, when he lifts his dark sunglasses and meets my gaze, I see that his almond shaped eyes are deep, dark, and strangely familiar, framed by lashes so lush they almost seem fake. And his lips! His lips are ripe and inviting with a perfect Cupid's bow. And the body that holds it all up is long, lean, tight, and clad in all black.

"Um, Ever? Hel-*lo*? You can wake up now. *Please.*" Miles turns to Damen, laughing nervously. "Sorry about my friend here, she usually has her hood on."

It's not like I don't know I have to stop. I need to stop right now. But Damen's eyes are fixed on mine, and their color grows deeper as his mouth begins to curve.

But it's not his complete gorgeousness that has me so transfixed. It has nothing to do with that. It's mainly the way the entire area surrounding his body, starting from his glorious head and going all the way down to the square-cut toes of his black motorcycle boots, consists of nothing but blank empty space.

No color. No aura. No pulsing light show.

Everyone has an aura. Every living being has swirls of color emanating from their body. A rainbow energy field they're not even aware of. And it's not like it's dangerous, or scary, or in any way bad, it's just part of the visible (well, to me anyway) magnetic field.

Before the accident I didn't even know about things like that. And I definitely wasn't able to see it. But from the moment I woke in the hospital, I noticed color everywhere.

"Are you feeling okay?" The red-haired nurse asked, gazing down anxiously.

"Yes, but why are you all pink?" I squinted, confused by the pastel glow that enveloped her.

"Why am I *what*?" She struggled to hide her alarm.

"Pink. You know, it's all around you, especially your head."

"Okay, sweetheart, you just rest and I'll go get the doctor," she'd said, backing out of the room and running down the hall.

It wasn't until after I'd been subjected to a barrage of eye exams, brain scans, and psych evals that I learned to keep the color-wheel sightings to myself. And by the time I started hearing thoughts, getting life stories by touch, and enjoying regular visits with my dead sister, Riley, I knew better than to share.

I guess I'd gotten so used to living like this, I'd forgotten there was another way. But seeing Damen outlined by nothing more than the shiny black paint job on his expensive cool car is a vague reminder of happier, more normal days.

"Ever, right?" Damen says, his face warming into a smile, revealing just another one of his perfections—dazzling white teeth.

I stand there, willing my eyes to leave his, as Miles makes a show of clearing his throat. And remembering how he hates to be ignored, I motion toward him and say, "Oh, sorry. Miles, Damen, Damen, Miles." And the whole time my eyes never once waver.

Damen glances at Miles, nodding briefly before focusing back on me. And even though I know this sounds crazy, for the split second his eyes moved away, I felt strangely cold and weak.

But the moment his gaze returns, it's all warm and good again. "Can I ask a favor?" He smiles. "Would you lend me your copy of *Wuthering Heights*? I need to get caught up and I won't have time to visit the bookstore tonight."

I reach into my backpack, retrieve my dog-eared copy, and dangle it from the tips of my fingers, part of me yearning to brush the tips against his, to make contact with this beautiful stranger, while the other part, the stronger, wiser, psychic part cringes—dreading the awful flash of insight that comes with each touch.

But it's not until he's tossed the book into his car, lowered his sunglasses, and said, "Thanks, see you tomorrow," that I realize that other than a slight tingle in the tips of my fingers, nothing happened. And before I can even respond, he's backing out of the space and driving away.

"Excuse me," Miles says, shaking his head as he climbs in beside me. "But when I said you'd *freak out* when you saw him, it wasn't a *suggestion,* it wasn't supposed to be taken *literally.* Seriously Ever, what *happened* back there? Because that was some mega tense awkwardness, a real *Hello, my name is Ever and I'll be your next stalker* kind of moment. I'm so serious, I thought we were gonna have to *resuscitate* you. And believe me, you are extremely lucky our good friend Haven was not here to see that, because I hate to remind you, but she did call dibs . . ."

Miles continues like that, yammering on and on, the entire way home. But I just let him talk it out as I navigate traffic, my finger absently tracing the thick red scar on my forehead, the one that's hidden under my bangs.

I mean, how can I explain how ever since the accident, the only people whose thoughts I can't hear, whose lives I can't know, and whose auras I can't see, are already dead?

three

I let myself into the house, grab a bottle of water from the fridge, then head upstairs to my room, since I don't have to poke around any further to know Sabine's still at work. Sabine's always at work, which means I get this whole huge house to myself, pretty much all the time, even though I usually just stay in my room.

I feel bad for Sabine. I feel bad that the life she worked so hard for was forever changed the day she got stuck with me. But since my mom was an only child and all of my grandparents had passed by the time I was two, it's not like she had much of a choice. I mean, it was either live with her—my dad's only sibling and twin—or go into foster care until I turned eighteen. And even though she doesn't know anything about raising kids, I wasn't even out of the hospital before she'd sold her condo, bought this big house, and hired one of Orange County's top decorators to trick out my room.

I mean, I have all the usual things like a bed, a dresser, and a desk. But I also have a flat-screen TV, a massive walk-in closet, a huge bathroom with a Jacuzzi tub and separate shower stall, a balcony with an amazing ocean view, and my own private den/game room, with yet another flat-screen TV, a wet bar, microwave, mini fridge, dishwasher, stereo, couches, tables, beanbag chairs, the works.

It's funny how before I would've given anything for a room like this.

But now I'd give anything just to go back to before.

I guess since Sabine spends most of her time around other lawyers and all those VIP executives her firm represents, she actually thought all of this stuff was necessary or something. And I've never been sure if her not having kids is because she works all the time and can't schedule it in, or if she just hasn't met the right guy yet, or if she never wanted any to begin with, or maybe a combination of all three.

It probably seems like I should know all of that, being psychic and all. But I can't necessarily see a person's motivation, mainly what I see are events. Like a whole string of images reflecting someone's life, like flash cards or something, only more in a movie-trailer format. Though sometimes I just see symbols that I have to decode to know what they mean. Kind of like with tarot cards, or when we had to read *Animal Farm* in Honors English last year.

Though it's far from foolproof, and sometimes I get it all wrong. But whenever that happens I can trace it right back to me, and the fact that some pictures have more than one meaning. Like the time I mistook a big heart with a crack down the middle for heartbreak—until the woman dropped to the floor in cardiac arrest. Sometimes it can get a little confusing trying to sort it all out. But the images themselves never lie.

Anyway, I don't think you have to be clairvoyant to know that when people dream of having kids they're usually thinking in terms of a pastel-wrapped, tiny bundle of joy, and *not* some five-foot-four, blue-eyed, blond-haired teenager with psychic powers and a ton of emotional baggage. So because of that, I try to stay quiet, respectful, and out of Sabine's way.

And I definitely don't let on that I talk to my dead little sister almost every day.

The first time Riley appeared, she was standing at the foot of my hospital bed, in the middle of the night, holding a flower in one hand and waving with the other. I'm still not sure what it was that awoke me, since it's not like she spoke or made any kind of sound. I guess I just felt her presence or something, like a change in the room, or a charge in the air.

At first I assumed I was hallucinating—just another side effect of the pain medication I was on. But after blinking a bunch and rubbing my eyes, she was still there, and I guess it never occurred to me to scream or call for help.

I watched as she came around to the side of my bed, pointed at the casts covering my arms and leg, and laughed. I mean, it was silent laughter, but still, it's not like I thought it was funny. But as soon as she noticed my angry expression, she rearranged her face and motioned as though asking if it hurt.

I shrugged, still a little unhappy with her for laughing, and more than a little freaked by her presence. And even though I wasn't entirely convinced it was really her, that didn't stop me from asking, "Where are Mom and Dad and Buttercup?"

She tilted her head to the side, as though they were standing right there beside her, but all I could see was blank space.

"I don't get it."

But she just smiled, placed her palms together, and tilted her head to the side, indicating that I should go back to sleep.

So I closed my eyes, even though I never would've taken orders from her before. Then just as quickly I opened them and said, "Hey, who said you could borrow my sweater?"

And just like that, she was gone.

I admit, I spent the rest of that night angry with myself for asking such a stupid, shallow, selfish question. Here I'd had the opportunity to get answers to some of life's biggest queries, to possibly gain the kind of insight people have been speculating about for ages. But instead, I wasted the moment calling out my dead little sister for raiding my closet. I guess old habits really do die hard.

The second time she appeared, I was just so grateful to see her, I didn't make any mention of the fact that she was wearing not just my favorite sweater, but also my best jeans (that were so long the hems puddled around her ankles), and the charm bracelet I got for my thirteenth birthday that I always knew she coveted.

Instead I just smiled and nodded and acted as though I didn't even notice, as I leaned toward her and squinted. "So where're Mom and Dad?" I asked, thinking they'd appear if I just looked hard enough.

But Riley just smiled and flapped her arms by her sides.

"You mean they're angels?" My eyes went wide.

She rolled her eyes and shook her head, clutching her waist as she bent over in fits of silent laughter.

"Okay, fine, whatever." I threw my body back against the pillows, thinking she was really pushing it, even if she was dead. "So tell me, what's it like over there?" I asked, determined not to fight. "Are you, well, do you like, live in heaven?"

She closed her eyes and raised her palms as though balancing an object, and then right out of nowhere, a painting appeared.

I leaned forward, gazing at a picture of what was surely paradise, matted in off-white and encased in an elaborate gold frame. The ocean was deep blue, the cliffs rugged, the sand golden, the trees flowering, and a shadowy silhouette of a small distant island could be seen in the distance.

"So why aren't you there now?" I asked.

And when she shrugged, the picture disappeared. And so did she.

I'd been in the hospital for more than a month, suffering broken bones, a concussion, internal bleeding, cuts and bruises, and a pretty deep gash on my forehead. So while I was all bandaged and medicated, Sabine was burdened with the thankless task of clearing out the house, making funeral arrangements, and packing my things for the big move south.

She asked me to make a list of all the items I wanted to bring. All the things I might want to drag from my perfect former life in Eugene, Oregon, to my scary new one in Laguna Beach, California. But other than some of my clothes, I didn't want anything. I just couldn't bear a single reminder of everything I'd lost, since it's not like some stupid box full of crap would ever bring my family back.

The whole time I was cooped up in that sterile white room, I received regular visits from a psychologist, some overeager intern with a beige cardigan and clipboard, who always started our sessions with the same lame question about how I was handling my "profound loss" (his words, not mine). After which he'd try to convince me to head up to room 618, where the grief counseling took place.

But no way was I taking part in that. No way would I sit in a circle with a bunch of anguished people, waiting for my turn to share the story of the worst day of my life. I mean, how was that supposed to help? How could it possibly make me feel better to confirm what I already knew—that not only was I solely responsible for what happened to my family, but also that I was stupid enough, selfish enough, and lazy enough to loiter, dawdle, and procrastinate myself right out of eternity?

Sabine and I didn't speak much on the flight from Eugene to John Wayne Airport, and I pretended it was because of my grief and injuries, but really I just needed some distance. I knew all about her conflicting emotions, how on the one hand she wanted so desperately to do the right thing, while on the other she couldn't stop thinking: *Why me?*

I guess I never wonder: *Why me?*

Mostly I think: *Why them and* not *me?*

But I also didn't want to risk hurting her. After all the trouble she'd gone to, taking me in and trying to provide a nice home, I couldn't risk letting her know how all of her hard work and good intentions were completely wasted on me. How she could've just dropped me off at any old dump and it wouldn't have made the least bit of difference.

The drive to the new house was a blur of sun, sea, and sand, and when Sabine opened the door and led me upstairs to my room, I gave it a quick cursory glance then mumbled something sounding vaguely like *thanks*.

"I'm sorry I have to run out on you," she'd said, obviously anxious to get back to her office where everything was organized, consistent, and bore no resemblance to the fragmented world of a traumatized teen.

And the moment the door closed behind her, I threw myself on my bed, buried my face in my hands, and started bawling my eyes out.

Until someone said, "Oh please, would you look at yourself? Have you even seen this place? The flat-screen, the fireplace, the tub that blows bubbles? I mean, Hel-*lo*?"

"I thought you couldn't talk?" I rolled over and glared at my sister, who, by the way, was dressed in a pink Juicy tracksuit, gold Nikes, and a bright fuchsia china doll wig.

"Of course I can talk, don't be ridiculous." She rolled her eyes.

"But the last few times—" I started.

"I was just having a little fun. So shoot me." She stalked around my room, running her hands over my desk, fingering the new laptop and iPod Sabine must have placed there. "I cannot believe you have a setup like this. This is so freaking unfair!" She placed her hands on her hips and scowled. "And you're not even appreciating it! I mean, have you even seen the balcony yet? Have you even bothered to check out the view?"

"I don't care about the view," I said, folding my arms across my chest and glaring. "And I can't believe you tricked me like that, pretending you couldn't speak."

But she just laughed. "You'll get over it."

I watched as she strode across my room, pushed the drapes aside, and struggled to unlock the french doors. "And where are you getting all these clothes?" I asked, scrutinizing her from head to toe, reverting right back to our normal routine of bickering and grudge holding. "Because first you show up in my stuff, and now you're wearing Juicy, and I know for a fact that Mom never bought you those sweats."

She laughed. "Please, like I still need Mom's permission when

I can just head over to the big celestial closet and take whatever I want. *For free,*" she said, turning to smile.

"Serious?" I asked, my eyes going wide, thinking that sounded like a pretty sweet deal.

But she just shook her head and waved me over. "Come on, come check out your cool new view."

So I did. I got up off the bed, wiped my eyes with my sleeve, and headed for my balcony. Brushing right past my little sister as I stepped onto the stone tile floor, my eyes going wide as I took in the scenery before me.

"Is this supposed to be funny?" I asked, gazing out at a view that was an exact replica of the gilt-framed picture of paradise she'd shown me in the hospital.

But when I turned back to face her, she'd already gone.

four

It was Riley who helped me recover my memories. Guiding me through childhood stories and reminding me of the lives we used to live and the friends we used to have, until it all began to resurface. She also helped me appreciate my new Southern California life. Because seeing her get so excited by my cool new room, my shiny red convertible, the amazing beaches, and my new school, made me realize that even though it wasn't the life I preferred, it still had value.

And even though we still fight and argue and get on each other's nerves as much as before, the truth is, I live for her visits. Being able to see her again gives me one less person to miss. And the time we spend together is the best part of each day.

The only problem is, she knows it. So every time I bring up the subjects she's declared strictly off limits, things like: *When do I get to see Mom, Dad, and Buttercup?* And, *where do you go when you're not here?* She punishes me by staying away.

But even though her refusal to share really bugs me, I know better than to push it. It's not like I've confided my new aura-spotting/mind-reading abilities, or how much it's changed me, including the way I dress.

"You're never gonna get a boyfriend dressed like that," she says, lounging on my bed as I rush through my morning routine, trying to get ready for school and out the door—more or less on time.

"Yeah, well, not all of us can just close our eyes and *poof,* have an amazing new wardrobe," I say, shoving my feet into worn-out tennis shoes and tying the frayed laces.

"Please, like Sabine wouldn't hand over her credit card and tell you to have at it. And what's with the hood? You in a gang?"

"I don't have time for this," I say, grabbing my books, iPod, and backpack, then heading for the door. "You coming?" I turn to look at her, my patience running big-time thin as she purses her lip and takes her time to decide.

"Okay," she finally says. "But only if you put the top down. I just love the feel of the wind in my hair."

"Fine." I head for the stairs. "Just make sure you're gone by the time we get to Miles's. It creeps me out to see you sitting in his lap without his permission."

By the time Miles and I get to school, Haven is already waiting by the gate, her eyes darting frantically, scanning the campus as she says, "Okay, the bell's gonna ring in less than five minutes and still no sign of Damen. You think he dropped out?" She looks at us, yellow eyes wide with alarm.

"Why would he drop out? He just started," I say, heading for my locker as she skips alongside me, the thick rubber soles of her boots bouncing off the pavement.

"Uh, because we're not worthy? Because he really is too good to be true?"

"But he has to come back. Ever leant him her copy of

Wuthering Heights, which means he has to return it," Miles says, before I can stop him.

I shake my head, and spin my combination lock, feeling the weight of Haven's glare when she says, "When did this happen?" She puts her hand on her hip and stares at me. "Because you know I called dibs, right? And why didn't I get an update? Why didn't anyone tell me about this? Last I heard you hadn't even seen him yet."

"Oh, she saw him alright. I almost had to dial nine-one-one she freaked out so bad." Miles laughs.

I shake my head, shut my locker, and head down the hall.

"Well, it's true." He shrugs, walking alongside me.

"So let me get this straight; you're more of a liability than a threat?" Haven peers at me through narrowed, heavily lined eyes, her jealousy transforming her aura into a dull puke green.

I take a deep breath and look at them, thinking how if they weren't my friends, I'd tell them how ridiculous this all is. I mean, since when can you call dibs on another person? Besides, it's not like I'm all that datable in my current voice-hearing, aura-seeing, baggy-sweatshirt-wearing condition. But I don't say any of that. Instead I just say, "Yes, I'm a liability. I'm a huge uninsurable disaster waiting to happen. But I'm definitely not a threat. Mainly because I'm not interested. And I know that's probably hard to believe, with him being so gorgeous and sexy and hot and smoldering and combustible or whatever it is that you call him, but the truth is, *I don't like Damen Auguste,* and I don't know how else to say it!"

"Um, I don't think you need to say anything else," Haven mumbles, her face frozen as she stares straight ahead.

I follow her gaze, all the way to where Damen is standing, all shiny dark hair, smoldering eyes, amazing body, and knowing smile, feeling my heart skip two beats as he holds the door open and says, "Hey Ever, after you."

I storm toward my desk, narrowly avoiding the backpack Stacia has placed in my path, as my face burns with shame, knowing Damen's right there behind me, and that he heard every horrifying word I just said.

I toss my bag to the floor, slide onto my seat, lift my hood, and crank my iPod, hoping to drown out the noise and deflect what just happened, assuring myself that a guy like that—a guy so confident, so gorgeous, so completely amazing—is too cool to bother with the careless words of a girl like me.

But just as I start to relax, just as I've convinced myself not to care, I'm jolted by an overwhelming shock—an electric charge infusing my skin, slamming my veins, and making my whole body tingle.

And it's all because Damen placed his hand upon mine.

It's hard to surprise me. Ever since I became psychic, Riley's the only one who can do so, and believe me, she never tires of finding new ways. But when I glance from my hand to Damen's face, he just smiles and says, "I wanted to return this." Then he gives me my copy of *Wuthering Heights.*

And even though I know this sounds weird and more than a little crazy, the moment he spoke, the whole room went silent. Seriously, like one moment it was filled with the sound of random thoughts and voices, and the next:_______.

Yet knowing how ridiculous that is, I shake my head and say, "Are you sure you don't want to keep it? Because I really don't need it, I already know how it ends." And even though he removes his hand from mine, it's a moment before all the tingling dies down.

"I know how it ends too," he says, gazing at me in a way so intense, so insistent, so intimate, I quickly look away.

And just as I'm about to reinsert my earbuds, so I can block out the sound of Stacia and Honor's continuous loop of cruel commentary, Damen places his hand back on mine and says, "What're you listening to?"

And the whole room goes quiet again. Seriously, for those few brief seconds, there were no swirling thoughts, no hushed whispers, nothing but the sound of his soft, lyrical voice. I mean, when it happened before, I figured it was just me. But this time I *know* that it's real. Because even though people are still talking and thinking and engaging in all of the usual things, it's completely blocked by the sound of his words.

I squint, noticing how my body has gone all warm and electric, wondering what could possibly be causing it. I mean, it's not like I haven't had my hand touched before, though I've yet to experience anything remotely like this.

"I asked what you're listening to." He smiles. A smile so private and intimate, I feel my face flush.

"Oh, um, it's just some goth mix my friend Haven made. It's mostly old, eighties stuff, you know like the Cure, Siouxsie and the Banshees, Bauhaus." I shrug, unable to avert my gaze as I stare into his eyes, trying to determine their exact color.

"You're into goth?" he asks, brows raised, eyes skeptical, taking inventory of my long blond ponytail, dark blue sweatshirt, and makeup-free, clean scrubbed skin.

"No, not really. Haven's all into it." I laugh—a nervous, cackling, cringe-worthy sound—that bounces off all four walls and right back at me.

"And you? What are you into?" His eyes still on mine, his face clearly amused.

And just as I'm about to answer, Mr. Robins walks in, his cheeks red and flushed, but not from a brisk walk like everyone thinks. And then Damen leans back in his seat, and I take a deep breath and lower my hood, sinking back into the familiar sounds of adolescent angst, test stress, body image issues, Mr. Robin's failed dreams, and Stacia, Honor, and Craig all wondering what the hot guy could possibly see in me.

five

By the time I make it to our lunch table Haven and Miles are already there. But when I see Damen sitting beside them, I'm tempted to run the other way.

"You're free to join us, but only if you promise *not* to stare at the new kid." Miles laughs. "Staring is very rude. Didn't anyone ever tell you that?"

I roll my eyes and slide onto the bench beside him, determined to show just how blasé I am about Damen's presence. "I was raised by wolves, what can I say?" I shrug, busying myself with the zipper on my lunch pack.

"I was raised by a drag queen and a romance novelist," Miles says, reaching over to steal a candy corn off the top of Haven's pre-Halloween cupcake.

"Sorry, that wasn't you, sweetie, that was Chandler on *Friends.*" Haven laughs. "I, on the other hand, was raised in a coven. I was a beautiful vampire princess, loved, worshiped, and admired by all. I lived in a luxurious, gothic castle, and I have no idea how I ended up at this hideous fiberglass table with you losers." She nods at Damen. "And you?"

He takes a sip of his drink, some iridescent red liquid in a glass bottle, then he gazes at all three of us and says, "Italy, France, England, Spain, Belgium, New York, New Orleans, Oregon, India, New Mexico, Egypt, and a few other places in between." He smiles.

"Can you say 'military brat'?" Haven laughs, picking off a candy corn and tossing it to Miles.

"Ever lived in Oregon," Miles says, placing the candy on the center of his tongue before chasing it down with a swig of VitaminWater.

"Portland." Damen nods.

Miles laughs. "Not a question, but okay. What I meant was, our friend Ever here, well, she lived in Oregon," he says, eliciting a sharp look from Haven, who, even after my earlier blunder, still views me as the biggest obstacle in her path to true love, and doesn't appreciate any attention being directed my way.

Damen smiles, his eyes on mine. "Where?"

"Eugene," I mumble, focusing on my sandwich instead of him, because just like in the classroom, every time he speaks it's the only sound I hear.

And every time our eyes meet I grow warm.

And when his foot just bumped against mine, my whole body tingled.

And it's really starting to freak me out.

"How'd you end up here?" He leans toward me, prompting Haven to scoot even closer to him.

I stare at the table, pressing my lips together in my usual nervous habit. I don't want to talk about my old life. I don't see the point in relaying all the gory details. Of having to explain how even though it's completely my fault that my entire family died, I somehow managed to live. So in the end I just tear the crust from my sandwich, and say, "It's a long story."

I can feel Damen's gaze—heavy, warm, and inviting—and it makes me so nervous my palms start to sweat and my water bottle slips from my grip. Falling so fast, I can't even stop it, all I can do is wait for the splash.

But before it can even hit the table, Damen's already caught it and returned it to me. And I sit there, staring at the bottle and avoiding his gaze, wondering if I'm the only one who noticed how he moved so fast he actually blurred.

Then Miles asks about New York, and Haven scoots so close she's practically sitting on Damen's lap, and I take a deep breath, finish my lunch, and convince myself I imagined it.

When the bell finally rings, we all grab our stuff and head toward class, and the second Damen's out of earshot I turn to my friends and say, "How did he end up at our table?" Then I cringe at how my voice sounded so shrill and accusing.

"He wanted to sit in the shade, so we offered him a spot." Miles shrugs, depositing his bottle in the recycling bin and leading us toward the building. "Nothing sinister, no evil plot to embarrass you."

"Well, I could've done without the staring comment," I say, knowing I sound ridiculous and overly sensitive. I'm unwilling to express what I'm really thinking, not wanting to upset my friends with the very valid, yet unkind question: *Why is a guy like Damen hanging with us?*

Seriously. Out of all the kids in this school, out of all the cool cliques he could join, why on earth would he chose to sit with us—the three biggest misfits?

"Relax, he thought it was funny." Miles shrugs. "Besides, he's coming by your house tonight. I told him to stop by around eight."

"You what?" I gape at him, suddenly remembering how all through lunch Haven was thinking about what she was going to wear, while Miles wondered if he had time for a spray tan, and now it all makes sense.

"Well, apparently Damen hates football as much as we do, which we happened to learn during Haven's little Q and A that took place just moments before you arrived." Haven smiles and curtseys, her fishnet-covered knees bowing out to either side. "And since he's new, and doesn't really know anyone else, we figured we'd hog him all to ourselves and not give him the chance to make other friends."

"But—" I stop, unsure how to continue. All I know is that I don't want Damen coming over, not tonight, not ever.

"I'll swing by sometime after eight," Haven says. "My meeting's over by seven, which gives me just enough time to go home and change. *And,* by the way, I call dibs on sitting next to Damen in the Jacuzzi!"

"You can't do that!" Miles says, shaking his head in outrage. "I won't allow it!"

But she just waves over her shoulder as she skips toward class, and I turn to Miles and ask, "Which meeting is it today?"

He opens the classroom door and smiles. "Friday is for overeaters."

Haven is what you'd call an anonymous-group addict. In the short time I've known her, she's attended twelve-step meetings for alcoholics, narcotics, codependents, debtors, gamblers, cyber addicts, nicotine junkies, social phobics, pack rats, and vulgarity lovers. Though as far as I know, today is her first one for overeaters. But then again, at five foot one with the slim, lithe body of a music box ballerina, Haven is definitely not an overeater. She's also not an alcoholic, a debtor, a gambler, or any of those other things. She's just terminally ignored by her self-involved parents, which makes her seek love and approval from just about anywhere she can get it.

Like with the whole goth thing. It's not that she's really all that into it, which is pretty obvious by the way she always skips instead of skulks, and how her Joy Division posters hang on the pastel pink walls of her not-so-long-ago ballerina phase (that came shortly after her J. Crew catalog preppy phase).

Haven's just learned that the quickest way to stand out in a town full of Juicy-clad blondes is to dress like the Princess of Darkness.

Only it's not really working as well as she hoped. The first time her mom saw her dressed like that, she just sighed, grabbed her keys, and headed off to Pilates. And her dad hasn't been home long enough to really get a good look. Her little brother, Austin, was freaked, but he adjusted pretty quickly. And since most of the kids at school have grown so used to the outrageous displays of behavior brought on by the presence of last year's MTV cameras, they usually ignore her.

But I happen to know that beneath all the skulls, and spikes, and death-rocker makeup is a girl who just wants to be seen, heard, loved, and paid attention to—something her earlier incarnations have failed to produce. So if standing before a room full of people, creating some sob story about her tormented struggle with that day's fill-in-the-blank addiction makes her feel important, well, who am I to judge?

In my old life I didn't hang with people like Miles and Haven. I wasn't connected with the troubled kids, or the weird kids, or the kids everyone picked on. I was part of the popular crowd, where most of us were cute, athletic, talented, smart, wealthy, well liked, or all of the above. I went to school dances, had a best friend named Rachel (who was also a cheerleader like me), and I even had a boyfriend, Brandon, who happened to be the sixth boy I'd ever kissed (the first was Lucas, but that was only because of a dare back in sixth grade, and trust me, the ones in between are hardly worth mentioning). And even though I was never mean to anyone who wasn't part of our group, it's not like I really noticed them either. Those kids just didn't have anything to do with me. And so I acted like they were invisible.

But now, I'm one of the unseen too. I knew it the day Rachel and Brandon visited me in the hospital. They acted so nice and supportive on the outside, while inside, their thoughts told a whole other story. They were freaked by the little plastic bags dripping liquids into my veins, my cuts and bruises, my cast-covered limbs. They felt bad for what happened, for all that I'd lost, but as they tried not to gape at the jagged red scar on my forehead, what they really wanted to do was run away.

And I watched as their auras swirled together, blending into the same dull brown, knowing they were withdrawing from me, and moving closer to each other.

So on my first day at Bay View, instead of wasting my time with the usual hazing rituals of the Stacia and Honor crowd, I headed straight for Miles and Haven, the two outcasts who accepted my friendship with no questions asked. And even though we probably look pretty strange on the outside, the truth is, I don't know what I'd do without them. Having their friendship is one of the few good things in my life. Having their friendship makes me feel almost normal again.

And that's exactly why I need to stay away from Damen. Because his ability to charge my skin with his touch, and silence the world with his voice is a dangerous temptation I cannot indulge.

I won't risk hurting my friendship with Haven.

And I can't risk getting too close.

six

Even though Damen and I share two classes, the only one where we sit next to each other is English. So it's not until I've already put away my materials and am heading out of sixth-period art that he approaches.

He runs up beside me, holding the door as I slink past, eyes glued to the ground, wondering how I can possibly uninvite him.

"Your friends asked me to stop by tonight," he says, his stride matching mine. "But I won't be able to make it."

"Oh!" I say, caught completely off guard, regretting the way my voice just betrayed me by sounding so happy. "I mean, are you sure?" I try to sound softer, more accommodating, like I really do want him to visit, even though it's too late.

He gazes at me, eyes shiny and amused. "Yah, I'm sure. See you Monday," he says, picking up his pace and heading for his car, the one that's parked in the red zone, its engine inexplicably humming.

When I reach my Miata, Miles is waiting, arms crossed, eyes narrowed, his annoyance clearly displayed in his signature smirk. "You better tell me what just happened back there, because that did not look good," he says, sliding in as I open my side.

"He cancelled. Said he couldn't make it." I shrug, glancing over my shoulder as I shift in reverse.

"But what did *you* say that made him cancel?" He glares at me.

"Nothing."

The smirk deepens.

"Seriously, I'm not responsible for wrecking your night." I pull out of the parking lot and onto the street, but when I feel Miles still staring I go, "What?"

"Nothing." He lifts his brows and stares out the window, and even though I know what he's thinking, I focus on driving instead. So then of course he turns to me and says, "Okay, promise you won't get mad."

I close my eyes and sigh. *Here we go.*

"It's just that—I so don't get you. It's like, nothing about you makes any sense."

I take a deep breath and refuse to react. Mostly because it's about to get worse.

"For one thing, you're completely knock-down, drag-out gorgeous—at least I think you might be, because it's really hard to tell when you're always hiding under those ugly stretched-out hoodies. I mean, sorry to be the one to say it, Ever, but the whole ensemble is completely tragic, like camouflage for the homeless, and I don't think we should have to pretend otherwise. Also, I hate to be the one to break it to you, but making a point to avoid the completely hot new guy, who is so obviously into you, is just weird."

He stops long enough to give me an encouraging look, as I brace for what's next.

"Unless—of course—you're gay."

I make a right turn and exhale, grateful for my psychic abilities for probably the first time ever, since it definitely helped lessen the blow.

"Because it's totally cool if you are," he continues. "I mean, obviously, since I'm gay, and it's not like I'm gonna discriminate against you, *right*?" He laughs, a sort of nervous, we're-in-virgin-territory-now kind of laugh.

But I just shake my head and hit the brake. "Just because I'm not interested in Damen doesn't mean I'm gay," I say, realizing I sounded far more defensive than I intended. "There's a lot more to attraction than just looks, you know."

Like warm tingling touch, deep smoldering eyes, and the seductive sound of a voice that can silence the world—

"Is it because of Haven?" he asks, not buying my story.

"No." I grip the steering wheel and glare at the light, willing it to change from red to green so I can drop Miles off and be done with all this.

But I know I answered too quickly when he goes, "Ha! I *knew* it! It *is* because of Haven—because she called dibs. I can't believe you're actually honoring dibs! I mean, do you even realize you're giving up a chance to lose your virginity to the hottest guy in school, maybe even the *planet,* all because Haven called dibs?"

"This is ridiculous," I mumble, shaking my head as I turn onto his street, pull into his driveway, and park.

"What? You're not a virgin?" He smiles, obviously having a wonderful time with all this. "You been holding out on me?"

I roll my eyes and laugh in spite of myself.

He looks at me for a moment, then grabs his books and heads for his house, turning back long enough to say, "I hope Haven appreciates what a good friend you are."

As it turns out, Friday night was cancelled. Well, not the night, just our plans. Partly because Haven's little brother, Austin, got sick and she was the only one around to take care of him, and partly because Miles's sports-loving dad dragged him to a football game and forced him to wear the team colors and act like he cared. And as soon as Sabine learned I'd be home by myself, she left work early and offered to take me to dinner.

Knowing she doesn't approve of my fondness for hoodies and jeans, and wanting to please her after everything she's done, I slip on this pretty blue dress she recently bought me, slide my feet into the heels she got to go with it, slick on some lip gloss (a relic from my old life, when I cared about things like that), transfer my essentials from my backpack to the little metallic clutch that goes with the dress, and trade my usual ponytail for loose waves.

And just as I'm about to walk out the door, Riley pops up behind me and says, "It's about time you started dressing like a girl."

And I nearly jump out of my skin.

"Omigod, you scared the heck out of me!" I whisper, shutting the door so Sabine can't hear.

"I know." She laughs. "So where you going?"

"Some restaurant called Stonehill Tavern. It's in the St. Regis hotel," I say, my heart still racing from the ambush.

She raises her brows and nods. "Chichi."

"How would you know?" I peer at her, wondering if she's been. I mean, it's not like she ever tells me where she spends her free time.

"I know lots of things." She laughs. "Way more than you." She jumps onto my bed and rearranges the pillows before she leans back.

"Yeah, well, not much I can do about that, huh?" I say, annoyed to see how she's wearing the exact same dress and shoes as I am. Only since she's four years younger and quite a bit shorter, she looks like she's playing dress-up.

"Seriously though, you should dress like that more often. Because I hate to say it, but your usual look is *so* not working for you. I mean, you think Brandon ever would've gone for you if you'd dressed like that?" She crosses her ankles and gazes at me, her posture as relaxed as a person, living or dead, could ever be. "Speaking of, did you know he's dating Rachel now? Yep, they've been together five months. That's like, even longer than you guys, huh?"

I press my lips and tap my foot against the floor, repeating my usual mantra: *Don't let her get to you. Don't let her—*

"And omigod, you're never gonna believe this but they almost went all the way! Seriously, they left the homecoming dance early, they had it all planned out, but then—well . . ." She pauses long enough to laugh. "I know I probably shouldn't repeat this, but let's just say that Brandon did something very regrettable and extremely embarrassing that turned out to be a major mood breaker. You probably had to be there, but I'm telling you, it was *hilarious*. I mean, don't get me wrong, he misses you and all, even accidentally called her by your name once or twice, but as they say, life goes on, right?"

I take a deep breath and narrow my eyes, watching as she lounges on my bed like Cleopatra on her litter, critiquing my life, my look, virtually everything about me, giving me updates on former friends I never even asked for, like some kind of prepubescent authority.

Must be nice to just drop in whenever you feel like it, to not have to get down here in the trenches and do all the dirty work like the rest of us!

And suddenly I feel so annoyed with her little pop-in visits that are really just glorified sneak attacks, wishing she'd just leave me in peace and let me live whatever's left of my crummy life without her constant stream of bratty commentary, that I look her right in the eye and say, "So when are you scheduled for angel school? Or have they banned you because you're so evil?"

She glares at me, her eyes squeezing into angry little slits as Sabine taps on my door and calls, "Ready?"

I stare at Riley, daring her with my eyes to do something stupid, something that will alert Sabine to all the truly strange goings on around here.

But she just smiles sweetly and says, "Mom and Dad send their love," seconds before disappearing.

seven

On the ride to the restaurant all I can think about is Riley, her snide remark, and how completely rude it was to just let it slip and then disappear. I mean, I've been begging her to tell me about our parents, pleading for just one smidgen of info this whole entire time. But instead of filling me in and telling me what I need to know, she gets all fidgety, acts all cagey, and refuses to explain why they've yet to appear.

You'd think being dead would make a person act a little nicer, a little kinder. But not Riley. She's just as bratty, spoiled, and awful as she was when she was alive.

Sabine leaves the car with the valet and we head inside. And the moment I see the huge marble foyer, the outsized flower arrangements, and the amazing ocean view, I regret everything I just thought. Riley *was* right. This place really is chichi. Big-time, major chichi. Like the kind of place you bring a date—and *not* your sullen niece.

The hostess leads us to a cloth-covered table adorned with flickering candles and salt and pepper shakers that resemble small silver stones, and when I take my seat and gaze around the room,

I can hardy believe how glamorous it is. Especially compared to the kind of restaurants I'm used to.

But just as soon as I think it, I make myself stop. There's no use examining the before and after photos, of reviewing the *how things used to be* clip stored in my brain. Though sometimes being around Sabine makes it hard not to compare. Her being my dad's twin is like a constant reminder.

She orders red wine for herself and a soda for me, then we look over our menus and decide on our meals. And the moment our waitress is gone, Sabine tucks her chin-length blond hair back behind her ear, smiles politely, and says, "So, how's everything? School? Your friends? All good?"

I love my aunt, don't get me wrong, and I'm grateful for everything that she's done. But just because she can handle a twelve-man jury doesn't mean she's any good at the small talk. Still, I just look at her and say, "Yep, it's all good." Okay, maybe I suck at the small talk too.

She places her hand on my arm to say something more, but before she can even get to the words, I'm already up and out of my seat.

"I'll be right back," I mumble, nearly knocking over my chair as I dart back the way we came, not bothering to stop for directions since the waitress I just brushed against took one look at me and doubted I'd make it out the door and down the long hallway in time.

I head in the direction she unknowingly sent me, passing through a hall of mirrors—gigantic gilt-framed mirrors, all lined up in a row. And since it's Friday, the hotel is filled with guests for a wedding that, from what I can *see,* should never take place.

A group of people brush past me, their auras swirling with alcohol-fueled energy that's so out of whack it's affecting me too, leaving me dizzy, nauseous, and so light-headed that when I glance in the mirrors, I see a long chain of Damens staring right back.

I stumble into the bathroom, grip the marble counter, and fight to catch my breath. Forcing myself to focus on the potted orchids, the scented lotions, and the stack of plush towels resting on a large porcelain tray, I begin to feel calmer, more centered, contained.

I guess I've grown so used to all of the random energy I encounter wherever I go, I've forgotten how overwhelming it can be when my defenses are down and my iPod's at home. But the jolt I received when Sabine placed her hand on mine was filled with such overwhelming loneliness, such quiet sadness, it felt like a punch in the gut.

Especially when I realized I was to blame.

Sabine is lonely in a way I've tried to ignore. Because even though we live together it's not like we see each other all that often. She's usually at work, I'm usually at school, and nights and weekends I spend holed up in my room, or out with my friends. I guess I sometimes forget that I'm not the only one with people to miss, that even though she's taken me in and tried to help, she still feels just as alone and empty as the day it all happened.

But as much as I'd like to reach out, as much as I'd like to ease her pain, I just can't. I'm too damaged, too weird. I'm a freak who hears thoughts and talks to the dead. And I can't risk getting found out, can't risk getting too close, to anyone, not even her. The best I can do is just get through high school, so I can go away to college, and she can get back to her life. Maybe then she can get together with that guy who works in her building. The one she doesn't even know yet. The one whose face I saw the moment her hand touched mine.

I run my hands through my hair, reapply some lip gloss, and head back to the table, determined to try a little harder and make her feel better, all without risking my secrets. And as I slip back onto my seat, I sip from my drink, and smile when I say, "I'm fine. Really." Nodding so that she'll believe it, before adding, "So tell me, any interesting cases at work? Any cute guys in the building?"

After dinner, I wait outside while Sabine gets in line to pay the valet. And I'm so caught up in the drama unfolding before me, between tomorrow's bride-to-be and her so-called maid of "honor," that I actually jump when I feel a hand on my sleeve.

"Oh, hey," I say, my body flooding with heat and tingling the second my eyes meet his.

"You look amazing," Damen says, his gaze traveling all the way down my dress to my shoes, before working their way back to mine. "I almost didn't recognize you without the hood." He smiles. "Did you enjoy your dinner?"

I nod, feeling so on edge I'm amazed I could even do that.

"I saw you in the hall. I would've said hello, but you seemed in such a rush."

I gaze at him, wondering what he's doing here, all alone, at this swanky hotel on a Friday night. Dressed in a dark wool blazer, a black open-neck shirt, designer jeans, and those boots—an outfit that seems far too slick for a guy his age, yet somehow looks just right.

"Out-of-town visitor," he says, answering the question I hadn't yet asked.

And just as I'm wondering what to say next, Sabine appears. And while they're shaking hands I say, "Um, Damen and I go to school together."

Damen's the one who makes my palms sweat, my stomach spin, and he's pretty much all I can think about!

"He just moved here from New Mexico," I add, hoping that'll suffice until the car arrives.

"Where in New Mexico?" Sabine asks. And when she smiles I can't help but wonder if she's flooded with that same wonderful feeling as me.

"Santa Fe." He smiles.

"Oh, I hear it's lovely. I've always wanted to go there."

"Sabine's an attorney, she works a lot," I mumble, focusing in the direction that the car will be coming from in just ten, nine, eight, sev—

"We're headed back home, but you're more than welcome to join us," she offers.

I gape at her, panicked, wondering how I failed to see that coming. Then I glance at Damen, praying he'll decline as he says, "Thanks, but I have to head back."

He hooks his thumb over his shoulder, and my eyes follow in that direction, stopping on an incredibly gorgeous redhead, dressed in the slinkiest black dress and strappy high heels.

She smiles at me, but it's not at all kind. Just pink glossy lips slightly lifting and curving, while her eyes are too far, too distant to read. Though there's something about her expression, the tilt of her chin, that's so visibly mocking, as though the sight of us standing together could be nothing short of amusing.

I turn back to face him, startled to find him looming so close, his lips moist and parted, mere inches from mine. Then he brushes his fingers along the side of my cheek, and retrieves a red tulip from behind my ear.

Then the next thing I know, I'm standing alone as he heads back inside with his date.

And I gaze at the tulip, touching its waxy red petals, wondering where it could've possibly come from—especially two seasons past spring.

Though it's not until later, when I'm alone in my room, that I realize the redhead was auraless too.

I must've been in a really deep sleep because the moment I hear someone moving around in my room, my head feels so groggy and murky I don't even open my eyes.

"Riley?" I mumble. "Is that you?" But when she doesn't answer, I know she's up to her usual pranks. And since I'm too tired to play, I grab my other pillow and plop it over my head.

But when I hear her again, I say, "Listen Riley, I'm exhausted, okay? I'm sorry if I was mean to you, and I'm sorry if I upset you, but I really don't feel like doing this now at—" I lift the pillow and open one eye to peer at my alarm clock. "At three forty-five in the morning. So why don't you just go back to wherever it is that you go and save it for a normal hour, okay? You can even show up in that dress I wore to the eighth grade graduation and I won't say a word, scout's honor."

Only, the thing is, now that I've said all of that, I'm awake. So I toss the pillow aside and glare at her shadowy form lounging on the chair by my desk, wondering what could possibly be so important it can't keep until morning.

"I said I'm sorry, okay? What more do you want?"

"You can see me?" she asks, pushing away from the desk.

"Of course I can see—" Then I stop in midsentence when I realize the voice isn't hers.

eight

I see dead people. All the time. On the street, at the beach, in the malls, in restaurants, wandering the hallways at school, standing in line at the post office, waiting in the doctor's office, though never at the dentist. But unlike the ghosts you see on TV and in movies, they don't bother me, they don't want my help, they don't stop and chat. The most they ever do is smile and wave when they realize they've been seen. Like most people, they like being seen.

But the voice in my room definitely wasn't a ghost. It also wasn't Riley. The voice in my room belonged to Damen.

And that's how I know I was dreaming.

"Hey." He smiles, slipping into his seat seconds after the bell rings, but since this is Mr. Robins's class it's the same as being early.

I nod, hoping to appear casual, neutral, not the least bit interested. Hoping to hide the fact that I'm so far gone I'm now dreaming of him.

"Your aunt seems nice." He looks at me, tapping the end of his pen on his desk, making this continuous *click click click* sound that really sets me on edge.

"Yeah, she's great," I mumble, mentally cursing Mr. Robins for lingering in the faculty bathroom, wishing he'd just stow the flask and come do his job already.

"I don't live with my family either," Damen says, his voice quieting the room, quieting my thoughts, as he spins the pen on the tip of his finger, twirling it around and around without faltering.

I press my lips together and fumble with the iPod in my secret compartment, wondering how rude it would seem if I turned it on and blocked him out too.

"I'm emancipated," he adds.

"Seriously?" I ask, even though I was firmly committed to keeping our conversations to an absolute minimum. It's just, I've never met anyone who was emancipated, and I always thought it sounded so lonely and sad. Though from the looks of his car, his clothes, and his glamorous Friday nights at the St. Regis hotel, he doesn't seem to be doing so badly.

"Seriously." He nods. And the moment he stops talking I hear the heightened whispers of Stacia and Honor, calling me a freak, and a few other things much worse than that. Then I watch as he tosses his pen in the air, smiling as it forms a series of slow lazy eights before landing right back on his finger. "So where's your family?" he asks.

And it's so weird how all the noise just stops and starts, starts and stops, like some messed up game of musical chairs. One where I'm always left standing. One where I'm always *it*.

"What?" I squint, distracted by the sight of Damen's magic pen now hovering between us, as Honor makes fun of my clothes, and her boyfriend pretends to agree even though he's secretly wondering why she never dresses like me. And it makes me want to lift my hood, crank my iPod, and drown it all out. Everything. Including Damen.

Especially Damen.

"Where does your family live?" he asks.

I close my eyes when he speaks—silence, sweet silence, for those fleeting few seconds. Then I open them again and gaze right into his. "They're dead," I say, as Mr. Robins walks in.

"I'm sorry."

Damen gazes at me from across the lunch table as I scan the area, eager for Haven and Miles to show. I just opened my lunch pack to find a single red tulip lying smack between my sandwich and chips—*a tulip!* Just like the one from Friday night. And even though I've no idea how he did it, I'm sure Damen's responsible. But it's not so much the strange magic tricks that bother me, it's more the way he looks at me, the way he speaks to me, the way he makes me feel—

"About your family. I didn't realize . . ."

I gaze down at my juice, twisting the cap back and forth, forth and back, wishing he'd just let it go. "I don't like to talk about it." I shrug.

"I know what it's like to lose the people you love," he whispers, reaching across the table and placing his hand over mine, infusing me with a feeling so good, so warm, so calm, and so safe—I close my eyes and allow it. Allow myself to enjoy the peace of it. Grateful to hear what he says and not what he thinks. Like an average girl—with a much better than average boy.

"Um, excuse me."

I open my eyes to find Haven leaning against the edge of the table, her yellow eyes narrowed and fixed on our hands. "So sorry to interrupt."

I pull away, shoving my hand in my pocket like it's something shameful, something no one should have to see. Wanting to explain how what she saw was nothing, how it meant nothing, even though I know better. "Where's Miles?" I finally say, not knowing what else to say.

She rolls her eyes and sits beside Damen, her hostile thoughts transforming her aura from bright yellow to a very dark red. "Miles is texting his latest Internet crush, hornyyoungdingdong307," she says, avoiding my eyes as she as she busies herself with her cupcake. Then gazing at Damen, she adds, "So, how was everyone's weekend?"

I shrug, knowing she wasn't really addressing me, watching as she taps the frosting with the tip of her tongue, performing her usual test lick, even though I've yet to see her reject one. And when I glance at Damen, I'm shocked to see him shrug too, because from what I saw, he was poised for a much better weekend than me.

"Well, as you can probably guess, my Friday night sucked. Big-time. I spent most of it cleaning up Austin's vomit, since the housekeeper was in Vegas and my parents couldn't be bothered to come home from wherever the hell they were. But Saturday totally made up for it. I mean, it *rocked*! Like, seriously, it was probably the best night of my entire life. And I totally would've invited you guys if it hadn't been so last minute." She nods, deigning to look at me again.

"Where'd you go?" I ask, trying to sound casual even though I just envisioned a dark scary place.

"This totally awesome club that some girl from my group took me to."

"Which group?" I sip from my water.

"Saturday is for codependents." She smiles. "Anyway, this girl, Evangeline? She's like a hardcore case. She's what they call a donor."

"What who calls a donor?" Miles asks, placing his Sidekick on the table and sitting down beside me.

"The codependents," I say, bringing him up to speed.

Haven rolls her eyes. "No, not them, the *vampires*. A donor is a person who allows other vamps to feed off them. You know, like suck their blood and stuff, whereas I'm what they call a *puppy*, because I just like to follow them around. I don't let anyone feed. Well, not yet." She laughs.

"Follow who around?" Miles asks, lifting his Sidekick and flipping through his messages.

"Vampires! Jeez, try to keep up. Anyway, what I was saying is this codependent donor chick, Evangeline, which, by the way, is her vampire name, not her real name—"

"People have vampire names?" Miles asks, setting his phone on the table where he can still peek at it.

"Totally." She nods, poking her finger deep into the frosting, then licking the tip.

"Is that like a stripper name? You know, like your first childhood pet plus your mom's maiden name? Because that makes me Princess Slavin, thank you very much." He smiles.

Haven sighs, striving for patience. "Uh, no. It's nothing like that. You see, a vampire name is serious. And unlike most people, I don't even have to change mine, because Haven is like an *organic* vamp name, one hundred percent natural, no additives or preservatives." She laughs. "I told you I'm a dark princess! Anyway, we went to this really cool club somewhere up in L.A. called Nocturnal, or something like that."

"Nocturne," Damen says, gripping his drink as his eyes focus on hers.

Haven sets down her cupcake and claps. "Yay! Finally, someone cool at this table," she says.

"And did you run into any *immortals*?" he asks, still gazing at her.

"Tons! The place was packed. There was even a VIP coven room, which I totally snuck into and hung out at the blood bar."

"Did they card you?" Miles asks, his fingers racing over his Sidekick as he partakes in two conversations at once.

"Laugh all you want, but I'm telling you it was way cool. Even after Evangeline sort of ditched me for some guy she met, I ended up meeting this other girl, who was even cooler, and who also, by the way, just moved here. So we'll probably start hanging out and stuff."

"Are you breaking up with us?" Miles gapes at her in mock alarm.

Haven rolls her eyes. "Whatever. All I know is that it was better than your guys' Saturday night—well, maybe not yours, Damen, since you seem to be up on these things, but definitely those two," she says, pointing at Miles and me.

"So how was the game?" I elbow Miles, trying to get his attention back on us and away from his electronic boyfriend.

"All I know is there was *way* too much team spirit, somebody won, somebody lost, and I spent most of it in the bathroom text-messaging this guy who's apparently a *big fat liar*!" He shakes his head and shows us the screen. "Look, right there!" He stabs it with his finger. "I've been asking for a picture all weekend because no way am I meeting up without getting a solid visual. And *this* is what he sends. Stupid phony poseur!"

I squint at the thumbnail, not quite getting what he's so angry about. "How do you know it's not him?" I ask, glancing at Miles.

And then Damen says, "Because it's me."

nine

Apparently Damen modeled for a short time, back when he lived in New York, which is why his image is out there, floating around cyberspace, just waiting for someone to download and claim that it's them.

And even though we passed it around and had a good solid laugh at the whole weird coincidence, there's still one thing I can't quite get past: If Damen just moved here from New Mexico and *not* New York, well, doesn't it seem like he should've looked a little bit younger in that picture? Because I can't think of anyone who looks exactly the same at seventeen as they did at fourteen, or even fifteen, and yet, that thumbnail on Miles's Sidekick showed Damen looking exactly the same as he does right now.

And it just doesn't make any sense.

When I get to art, I beeline for the supply closet, grab all my stuff, and head for my easel, refusing to react when I notice how Damen is set up right next to mine. I just take a deep breath and go about the business of buttoning my smock and selecting a brush, stealing the occasional glance at his canvas and trying not to gawk at his masterpiece in the making—a seriously perfect rendition of Picasso's *Woman with Yellow Hair*.

Our assignment is to emulate one of the great masters, to choose one of those iconic paintings and attempt to re-create it. And somehow I got the idea that those simple Van Gogh swirls would be a sure thing, a cinch to reproduce, an easy A. But from the looks of my chaotic, hectic strokes, I completely misjudged it. And now it's so far gone, I can't possibly save it. And I've no idea what to do.

Ever since I became psychic, I'm no longer required to study. I'm not even required to read. All I have to do is place my hands on a book, and the story appears in my head. And as far as tests go? Well, let's just say there's no more "pop" in the quiz. I just brush my fingers over the questions and the answers are instantly revealed.

But art is totally different.

Because talent cannot be faked.

Which is why my painting is pretty much the exact opposite of Damen's.

"*Starry Night*?" Damen asks, nodding at my drippy, pathetic, blue mottled canvas, as I cringe in embarrassment, wondering how he could've made such an accurate guess from such a poorly realized mess.

Then just to torture myself even further, I take another glance at his effortless, curving brushstrokes, and add it to the never-ending list of things he's amazingly good at.

Seriously, like in English, he can answer all of Mr. Robins's questions, which is kind of weird since he only had one night to skim all three hundred and some odd pages of *Wuthering Heights*. Not to mention how he usually goes on to include all manner of random historical facts, talking about those long-ago days as though he was actually there. He's ambidextrous too, which might not sound like all that big a deal, until you watch him write with one hand and paint with the other, with neither project seeming to suffer. And don't even get me started on the spontaneous tulips and magic pen.

"Just like Pablo himself. Wonderful!" Ms. Machado says, smoothing her long glossy braid as she stares at his canvas, her aura vibrating a beautiful cobalt blue, as her mind performs cartwheels and somersaults, jumping in glee, racing through her mental roster of talented former students, realizing she's never had one with such innate, natural ability—until now.

"And Ever?" On the outside she's still smiling, but inside she's thinking: *What on earth could it possibly be?*

"Oh, um, it's supposed to be Van Gogh. You know, *Starry Night*?" I cringe in shame, my worst suspicions confirmed by her thoughts.

"Well—it's an honorable start." She nods, struggling to keep her face neutral, relaxed. "Van Gogh's style is much more difficult than it seems. Just don't forget the golds, and the yellows! It is a starry, starry night after all!"

I watch her walk away, her aura expanding and glowing, knowing she dislikes my painting, but appreciating her effort to hide it. Then without even thinking I dip my brush in yellow, before wiping off the blue, and when I press it to my canvas it leaves a big blob of green.

"*How* do you do it?" I ask, shaking my head in frustration, gazing from Damen's amazingly good painting to my amazingly bad one, comparing, contrasting, and feeling my confidence plummet.

He smiles, his eyes finding mine. "Who do you think taught Picasso?" he says.

I drop my brush to the floor, sending mushy globs of green paint splattering across my shoes, my smock, and my face, holding my breath as he leans down to retrieve it, before placing it back in my hand.

"Everyone has to start somewhere," he says, his eyes dark and smoldering, his fingers seeking the scar on my face.

The one on my forehead.

The one that's hidden under my bangs.

The one he has no way of knowing about.

"Even Picasso had a teacher." He smiles, withdrawing his hand and the warmth that came with it, returning to his painting, as I remind myself to breathe.

ten

The next morning as I'm getting ready for school, I make the mistake of asking Riley's help in choosing a sweatshirt.

"What do you think?" I hold up a blue one, before replacing it with a green.

"Do the pink one again," she says, perched on my dresser, head cocked to the side as she considers the options.

"There is no pink one." I scowl, wishing she could just be serious for a change, stop making everything into such a big game. "Come on, help me out, clock's ticking."

She rubs her chin and squints. "Would you say that's more of a *cerulean* blue or a *cornflower* blue?"

"That's it." I toss the blue one and start yanking the green over my head.

"Go with the blue."

I stop, eyes visible, nose, mouth, and chin sheltered in fleece.

"Seriously. It brings out your eyes." I squint at her for a moment, then I toss the green one and do as she says. Rummaging for lip gloss and stopping just short of applying it when she goes,

"Okay, what gives? I mean, the sweatshirt crises, the sweaty palms, the makeup, what's going on?"

"I'm not wearing makeup," I say, cringing as my voice nears a shout.

"Not to fault you on a technicality, Ever, but lip gloss counts. It definitely qualifies as makeup. And you, dear sister, were just about to apply it."

I drop it back in the drawer and reach for my usual ChapStick instead, smearing it across my lips in a waxy dull line.

"Um, hello? Still waiting for an answer over here!"

I press my lips, heading out the door and down the stairs.

"Fine, play that way. But don't think you can stop me from guessing," she says, trailing behind me.

"Whatever," I mumble, going into the garage.

"Well, we know it's not Miles, since you're not really *his* type, and we know it's not Haven since she's not really *your* type, which leaves me with—" She slips right through the closed and locked car door and onto the front seat while I try not to cringe. "Well, I guess that's pretty much it for your circle of friends, so tell me, I give up."

I open the garage door and climb in my car the old-fashioned way, then rev up the engine to drown out her voice.

"I know you're up to something," she says, talking over the roar. "Because excuse me for saying so, but you're acting just like you did right before you hooked up with Brandon. Remember how nervous and paranoid you were? Wondering if he liked you back, and bippidy-blah-blah. So come on, tell me. Who's the unlucky guy? Who's your next victim?"

And the second she says that, an image of Damen flashes before me, looking so gorgeous, so sexy, so smoldering, so palpable, I'm tempted to reach out and claim it. But instead I just clear my throat, shift into reverse, and say, "No one. I don't like anyone. But trust me, that's the last time I'll ever ask you to help."

By the time I get to English, I'm as giddy, nervous, sweaty palmed, and anxious as Riley accused me of being. But when I see Damen talking to Stacia, I add *paranoid* to the already long list.

"Um, excuse me," I say, blocked by Damen's gloriously long legs, which are taking the place of her usual booby trap.

But he just ignores me and remains perched on her desk, and I watch as he reaches behind her ear, and comes away with a rosebud.

A single white rosebud.

A fresh, pure, glistening, dewy, white rosebud.

And when he hands it to her, she squeals so loud you'd think he just gave her a diamond.

"Oh-my-*gawd*! No *way*! *How'd* you do that?" She shrieks, waving it around so everyone can see.

I press my lips and gaze down at the ground, fiddling with my iPod and cranking the sound until I can no longer hear her.

"I need to get by," I mumble, my eyes meeting Damen's, catching the briefest flash of warmth before his gaze turns to ice and he moves out of my way.

I storm toward my desk, my feet moving like they're supposed to, one in front of the other, like a zombie, a robot, some dense numb thing just going through its preprogrammed motions, unable to think on its own. Then I settle onto my chair and continue the routine, retrieving paper, books, and a pen, pretending I don't notice how reluctant Damen is, how he drags his feet when Mr. Robins makes him return to his seat.

"What the *fug*?" Haven says, moving her bangs to the side and staring straight ahead, her profanity ban the only New Year's resolution she's ever been able to keep, but only because she thinks *fug* is funny.

"I knew it wouldn't last." Miles shakes his head and gazes at Damen, watching him wow the A-list with his natural charm, magic pen, and stupid fugging rosebuds. "I knew it was too good to be true. In fact, I said exactly that the very first day. Remember when I said that?"

"No," Haven mumbles, still staring at Damen. "I don't remember that at all."

"Well, I did." Miles swigs his VitaminWater, and nods. "I said it. You just didn't hear me."

I gaze down at my sandwich and shrug, not wanting to get into the whole "who said what when" debate, and definitely not willing to look anywhere near Damen, Stacia, or anyone else at that table. I'm still reeling from English, when Damen leaned toward me, right in the middle of roll call, so he could pass me a note.

But only so I could pass it to Stacia.

"Pass it yourself," I'd said, refusing to touch it. Wondering how a single piece of notebook paper, folded into a triangle, could possibly cause so much pain.

"Come on," he said, flicking it toward me so it landed just shy of my fingers. "I promise you won't get caught."

"It's not about getting caught." I glared at him.

"Then what is it about?" he asked, dark eyes on mine.

It's about not wanting to touch it! Not wanting to know what it says! Because the moment my fingers make contact, I'll see the words in my head—the whole, sexy, adorable, flirty, unfiltered message. And even though it'll be bad enough to hear it in her thoughts, at least then I can pretend that it's compromised, diluted by her dimwitted brain. But if I touch that piece of paper, then I'll know the words are true—and I just can't bear to see them—

"Pass it yourself," I finally said, tapping it with the tip of my pencil and sending it off the edge of my desk. Hating the way my heart slammed against my chest as he laughed and bent down to retrieve it.

Hating myself for the flood of relief when he slid it into his pocket instead of passing it to *her.*

"Um, hel-*lo,* earth to Ever!"

I shake my head and squint at Miles.

"I asked what happened? I mean, not to point fingers or anything, but you *are* the last one who saw him today . . ."

I gaze at Miles, wishing I knew. Remembering yesterday in art, the way Damen's eyes sought mine, the way his touch warmed my skin, so sure we'd shared something personal—*magical* even. But then I remember the girl before Stacia, the gorgeous haughty redhead at the St. Regis, the one I conveniently managed to forget. And I feel like a fool, for being so naïve, for thinking he just might've liked me. Because the truth is, that's just Damen. He's a player. And he does this all the time.

I gaze across the lunch tables, just in time to see Damen compile an entire bouquet of white rosebuds from Stacia's ear, sleeve, cleavage, and purse. Then I press my lips and avert my gaze, sparing myself the gratuitous hug that soon follows.

"I didn't *do* anything," I finally say, as confused by Damen's erratic behavior as Miles and Haven, only far less willing to admit it.

I can hear Miles's thoughts, weighing my words, trying to decide if he should believe me. Then he sighs and says, "Do you feel as dejected, jilted, and heartbroken as me?"

I look at him, wanting to confide, wishing I could tell him *everything,* the whole sordid jumble of feelings. How just yesterday I was sure something significant had passed between us, only to wake up today and be presented with *this.* But instead I just shake my head, gather my things, and head off to class, long before the bell even rings.

All through fifth-period French, I think of ways to get out of art. Seriously. Even as I'm participating in the usual drills, lips moving, foreign words forming, my mind is completely obsessed with faking a stomachache, nausea, fever, a dizzy spell, the flu, whatever. Any excuse will do.

And it's not just because of Damen. Because the truth is, I don't even know why I signed up for that class in the first place. I have no artistic ability, my project's a mess, and it's not like I'm going to be an artist anyway. And yeah, I guess if you throw Damen into that already full mix, you end up not only with a seriously compromised GPA, but fifty-seven minutes of awkwardness.

But in the end, I go. Mostly because it's the right thing to do. And I'm so focused on gathering my supplies and donning my smock, that at first I don't realize he's not even there. And as the minutes tick by with still no sign of him, I grab my paints and head for my easel.

Only to find that stupid triangle note balanced on the edge.

I stare at it, focusing so intensely that everything around me grows dark and out of focus. The entire classroom reduced to one single point. My entire world consisting of a triangle-shaped letter resting on a thin wooden ledge, the name *Stacia* scrawled on its front. And even though I've no idea how it got there, even though a quick survey of the room reaffirms Damen's not there, I don't want it anywhere near me. I refuse to participate in this sick little game.

I grab a paintbrush and flick it as hard as I can, watching as it soars through the air before tumbling to the ground, knowing I'm acting childish, ridiculous, especially when Ms. Machado comes by and swoops it up in her hand.

"Looks like you dropped something!" she sings, her smile bright and expectant, having no idea that I put it there on purpose.

"It's not mine," I mumble, rearranging my paints, figuring she can get it to Stacia herself, or better yet, throw it away.

"So there's another *Ever* I'm not aware of?" She smiles.

What?

I take the note she dangles before me, *Ever* clearly scrawled across its front, and written in Damen's unmistakable hand. Having no idea how this happened, no logical explanation. Because I know what I saw.

My fingers tremble as I begin to unfold it, opening all three corners and smoothing the crease, gasping when a small detailed sketch is unveiled—a small detailed sketch of one beautiful red tulip.

eleven

Halloween is just a few days away and I'm still working on the final touches for my costume. Haven's going as a vampire (duh), Miles is going as a pirate—but that's only after I talked him out of going as Madonna in her cone-breast phase, and I'm not telling what I'm going as. But only because my once great idea has morphed into an overly ambitious project I'm quickly losing faith in.

Though I have to admit I was pretty surprised Sabine even wanted to throw a party to begin with. Partly because she never really seems interested in stuff like that, but mostly because I figured that between the two of us we'd be lucky to come up with five guests max. But apparently Sabine's a lot more popular than I realized, as she quickly filled two and a half columns, while my list was pathetically shorter—consisting of my only two friends and their possible plus ones.

So while Sabine hired a caterer to handle the food and drink, I put Miles in charge of audio/visual (which means he'll dock his iPod and rent some scary movies), and asked Haven to provide the cupcakes. Which pretty much left Riley and me as the sole members of the decorations committee. And since Sabine handed me a catalog and a credit card with specific instructions to "don't hold back," we've spent the last two afternoons transforming the house from its usual look of semicustom Tuscan track home to spooky, scary, crypt-keeper's castle. And it's been so much fun, reminding me of when we used to decorate our old house for Easter, Thanksgiving, and Christmas. Not to mention how staying busy and focused has really helped curb some of our bickering.

"You should go as a mermaid," Riley says. "Or as one of those kids from those OC reality shows."

"Oh jeez, don't tell me you still watch that stuff?" I say, balancing precariously on the second to last rung, so I can string up yet another faux spiderweb.

"Don't blame me, Tivo's got a mind of its own." She shrugs.

"You have Tivo?" I turn, desperate for any information I can get since she's always so stingy with the afterlife details.

But she just laughs. "I swear, you are so gullible—the things you believe!" She shakes her head and rolls her eyes, reaching into a cardboard box and retrieving a string of fairy lights. "Wanna trade?" she offers, unraveling the cord. "I mean, it's ridiculous the way you insist on climbing up and down that ladder when I can just levitate and get the job done."

I shake my head and frown. Even though it might be easier, I still like to pretend my life is somewhat normal.

"So what are you going as?"

"Forget it," I say, attaching the web to the corner, before climbing down the ladder to get a good look. "If you can have secrets, then I can too."

"No fair." She crosses her arms and pouts in the way that always worked on Dad, but never on Mom.

"Relax, you'll see it at the party," I tell her, picking up a glow-in-the-dark skeleton and untangling the limbs.

"You mean, I'm invited?" she asks, her voice squeaky, eyes wide with excitement.

"Like I could stop you?" I laugh, propping Mr. Skeleton near the entryway so he can greet all our guests.

"Is your boyfriend coming too?"

I roll my eyes and sigh. "You know I don't have a boyfriend," I say, bored with this game before it's even begun.

"Please. I'm not an idiot." She scowls. "It's not like I've forgotten the great sweatshirt debate. Besides, I can't wait to meet him, or I guess I should say, *see* him, since it's not like you'd ever introduce me. Which is really pretty rude if you think about it. I mean just because he can't see me doesn't mean—"

"Jeez, he's not invited, okay?" I shout, not realizing I've stumbled into her trap until it's too late.

"Ha!" She looks at me, eyes wide, brows raised, lips curving with delight. "I *knew* it!" She laughs, tossing the fairy lights and jumping in glee, spinning and thrusting and pointing at me. "I *knew* it, I *knew* it, I *knew* it!" she sings, punching her fists in the air. "Ha! I *knew* it!" She twirls.

I close my eyes and sigh, chiding myself for falling into her poorly concealed trap. "You don't *know* anything." I glare at her and shake my head. "He was never my boyfriend, okay? He—he was just some new kid, who at first I thought was kind of cute, but then, when I realized what a total player he is, well, let's just say that I'm over it. In fact, I don't even think he's cute anymore. Seriously, it lasted like ten seconds, but only because I didn't know any better. And it's not like I'm the only one who fell for his game, because Miles and Haven were practically fighting over him. So why don't you just stop with all the air punching and hip thrusts, and get back to work, okay?"

And the moment I stop, I know I sounded way too defensive

to ever be believed. But now that it's out there I can't take it back, so I just try to ignore her as she hovers around the room singing, "Yup! I *so so* knew it!"

By Halloween night the house looks amazing. Riley and I taped webs in all of the windows and corners, and stuck huge black widow spiders in their middles. We hung black rubber bats from the ceiling, scattered bloodied, severed (fake) body parts all around, and set up a crystal ball next to a plug-in raven whose eyes light up and roll around when he says, "You'll be sorry! Squawk! You'll be sorry!" We dressed zombies in "blood" covered rags and placed them where you'd least expect to find them. We put steaming cauldrons of witches' brew (really just dry ice and water) in the entry, and scattered skeletons, mummies, black cats and rats (well, fake ones, but still creepy), gargoyles, coffins, black candles, and skulls pretty much everywhere. We even decorated the backyard with jack-o'-lanterns, floating pool globes, and blinking fairy lights. And oh yeah, we placed a life-sized grim reaper out on the front lawn.

"How do I look?" Riley asks, gazing down at her purple shell-covered chest and red hair as she swishes her sparkly, metallic, green fish tail around.

"Like your favorite Disney character," I say, powdering my face until it's very pale, trying to think of a way to get rid of her so I can change into my costume and maybe surprise her for a change.

"I'll take that as a compliment." She smiles.

"As you should." I brush my hair back and pin it close to my head, preparing for the big, blond, towering wig I'll wear.

"So who are you going as?" She gazes at me. "I mean, would

you just tell me already, because the suspense is really killing me!" She clutches her stomach in a fit of laughter, rocking back and forth, and nearly falling off the bed. She loves making death puns. Thinks they're hysterical. But mostly they just make me cringe.

Ignoring the joke, I turn to her and say, "Do me a favor? Sneak down the hall and check out Sabine's costume, and let me know if she tries to wear that big rubber nose with the hairy wart on the end. I told her it's a really great witch's costume, but she needs to ditch the nose. Guys don't usually go for that sort of thing."

"She's got a guy?" Riley asks, clearly surprised.

"Not if she wears the nose," I say, watching as she slips off the bed and heads across the room, mermaid tail dragging behind her. "But don't make any noise, or do anything to scare her, okay?" I add, cringing as she slinks through my closed bedroom door, not even bothering to open it. I mean, just because I've witnessed that like a gazillion times doesn't mean I've gotten used to it.

I head into my closet and unzip the bag I've hidden in the back, removing the beautiful black gown with the low square neckline, the sheer three-quarter-length sleeves, and the super tight bodice that swells into shiny, loose folds—just like the one Marie Antoinette wore to the masked ball (well, as portrayed by Kirsten Dunst in the movie). And after struggling with the zipper in the back, I slip on my very tall platinum blond wig (because even though I'm already blond, I could never get my hair to go that high), apply some red lipstick, fasten a filmy black mask over my eyes, and insert some long, dangly, rhinestone earrings. And when my costume's complete I stand before my mirror twirling and spinning and smiling as my shiny black dress sways all around, and I'm thrilled with how good it turned out.

The second Riley pops back in she shakes her head and says,

"All clear—*finally!* I mean, first she put the nose on, then she took it off, then she put it back on and turned to check out her profile, only to take it back off again. I swear it took all of my will not to just snatch it off her face and chuck it out the window."

I freeze, holding my breath, hoping she didn't do any such thing, because with Riley you just never know.

She plops herself onto my desk chair and uses the tip of her sparkly green fin to propel herself around. "Relax," she says. "Last I saw, she left it in the bathroom, next to the sink. And then some guy called needing directions, and she went on and on about what a great job you did on the house, and how she can hardly believe you handled it all by yourself, and bippidy-blah-blah." She shakes her head and frowns. "You must really love that, huh? Taking all the credit for *our* hard work." She stops spinning and gives me a long, appraising look. "So, Marie Antoinette," she finally says, her eyes taking a tour of my costume. "I never would've guessed. I mean, it's not like you're all that big on cake."

I roll my eyes. "For your information, she never said that about the cake. It was a vicious tabloid rumor, so don't you believe it," I tell her, unable to stop mirror gazing, as I recheck my makeup and pat my wig, hoping it will all stay where it's supposed to. But when I catch Riley's reflection, something about the way she looks makes me stop and move toward her. "Hey, you okay?"

She closes her eyes and bites her lip. Then she shakes her head and says, "Jeez, would you look at us? You're dressed as a tragic teen queen, and I'd do anything just to *be* a teen."

I start to reach for her, but my hands fumble at my sides. I guess I'm so used to having her around that I sometimes forget how she's not *really* here, how she's no longer part of this world, and how she'll never grow any older, never get the chance to be thirteen. And then I remember how it's all my fault to begin with, and I feel a million times worse. "Riley, I—"

But she just shakes her head and waves her tail around. "No worries." She smiles, floating up from the chair. "Time to greet the guests!"

Haven came with Evangeline, her codependent donor friend, who, big surprise, is dressed like a vampire too, and Miles brought Eric, some guy he knows from his acting class who looks like he might actually be pretty cute beneath that black satin Zorro mask and cape.

"I can't believe you didn't invite Damen," Haven says, shaking her head and skipping right past *hello*. She's been mad at me all week, ever since she learned he didn't make the list.

I roll my eyes and take a deep breath, tired of defending the obvious, of having to point out yet again how he's clearly ditched us, becoming a permanent fixture not just at Stacia's lunch table but also her desk. Procuring rosebuds from all manner of places, and how his art project, *Woman with Yellow Hair* is beginning to look suspiciously like her.

I mean, excuse me for not wanting to dwell on the fact of how despite the red tulips, the mysterious note, and the intimate gaze we once shared, he hasn't spoken to me in almost two weeks.

"It's not like he would've come anyway," I finally say, hoping she won't notice how my voice just cracked in betrayal. "I'm sure he's out somewhere with Stacia, or the redhead, or—" I shake my head, refusing to continue.

"Wait—*redhead?* There's a redhead too?" She squints at me.

I shrug. Because the truth is, he could be with just about anyone. All I know is that he isn't here with me.

"You should see him." She turns to Evangeline. "He's *amazing*. Gorgeous like a movie star—sexy like a rock star—he even does illusions." She sighs.

Evangeline raises her brows. "Sounds like he *is* an illusion. No one's that perfect."

"Damen is. Too bad you can't see for yourself." Haven frowns at me again, her fingers fiddling with the black velvet choker she wears around her neck. "But if you do happen to meet him, don't forget that he's mine. I called it way before I knew you."

I gaze at Evangeline, taking in her dark murky aura, fishnet stockings, tiny black boy shorts, and mesh T-shirt, knowing she has no intention of keeping any such promise.

"You know I could lend you some fangs and fake blood for your neck and you could be a vampire too," Haven offers, looking at me, her mind flip-flopping back and forth, wanting to be my friend, convinced I'm her foe.

But I just shake my head and steer them to the other side of the room, hoping she'll move on to something else and soon forget about Damen.

Sabine's talking to her friends, Haven and Evangeline are spiking their drinks, Miles and Eric are dancing, while Riley plays with the tail of Eric's whip, swinging the fringe up and down and back and forth, then looking around to see if anyone notices. And just as I'm about to give her the signal, the one that means she better cut it out if she wants to stick around, the doorbell rings, and we race each other to get it.

And even though I beat her to it, when I open the door I forget to gloat, because Damen is there. Flowers in one hand, gold-tipped hat in the other, with his hair gathered into a low ponytail, his usual sleek black clothes replaced with a frilly white shirt, a coat with gold buttons, and what can only be described as breeches, tights, and pointy black shoes. And just as I'm thinking how Miles is going to be completely envious of that costume, I realize who he's dressed as, and my heart skips two beats.

"Count Fersen," I mumble, barely managing the words.

"Marie." He smiles, offering a deep, gallant bow.

"But . . . it was a secret . . . and you weren't even invited," I whisper, peering past his shoulder, searching for Stacia, the redhead, anyone at all, knowing he couldn't possibly be here for me.

But he just smiles and hands me the flowers. "Then it must be a lucky coincidence."

I swallow hard and turn on my heel, leading him through the entry, past the living and dining rooms, and into the den, my cheeks burning as my heart beats so hard and so fast I fear it might burst through my chest. Wondering how this possibly could've happened, searching for some logical explanation for Damen's showing up at my party dressed as my perfect other half.

"Omigod, Damen's here!" Haven squeals, arms waving, face all lit up—well, as much as a heavily powdered, fang-wearing, blood-dripping, vampire face can light up. But the moment she sees his costume, realizing he came as Count Axel Fersen, the not-so-secret lover of Marie Antoinette, her entire face dims, and her eyes turn to me, glaring accusingly.

"So, when'd you two arrange it?" she asks, advancing on us, trying to keep her voice light, neutral, but more for Damen's benefit than mine.

"We didn't," I say, hoping she'll believe it, yet knowing she won't. I mean, it's such a bizarre coincidence I'm beginning to doubt it myself, wondering if I somehow let it slip, even though I know that I didn't.

"Complete fluke," Damen says, hooking his arm around my waist. And even though he only keeps it there for a moment, it's still long enough to leave my whole body tingling.

"You've *got* to be Damen," Evangeline says, slinking up beside him, fingers plucking at the ruffles on his shirt. "I thought for sure Haven was exaggerating, though apparently not!" She laughs. "And who're you dressed as?"

"Count Fersen," Haven says, voice hard and brittle, eyes narrowed on mine.

"Whoever." Evangeline shrugs, stealing his hat and perching it on top of her head, smiling seductively from under the brim before grabbing his hand and leading him away.

The moment they're gone, Haven turns to me and says, "I can't *believe* you!" Her face is angry, fists clenched, but that's nothing compared to the horrible thoughts that swirl through her head. "You know how much I like him. I *confided* in you, I *trusted* you!"

"Haven, I swear, it wasn't planned. It's just some freaky coincidence. I don't even know what he's doing here, and you know I didn't invite him," I say, wanting to convince her, yet knowing it's useless, she's already made up her mind. "And I don't know if you noticed, but your good friend Evangeline is practically humping his leg over there."

Haven glances across the room then turns back to me, shrugging when she says, "She does that with everyone, she's hardly a threat. Unlike you."

I take a deep breath, striving for patience and trying not to laugh as Riley stands beside her, mimicking every word, reenacting every move, mocking her in a way that's definitely funny though not at all kind. "Listen," I finally say. "I *don't* like him! I mean, how can I convince you of that? Just tell me and I'll do it!"

She shakes her head and looks away, shoulders sinking, thoughts turning dark, redirecting all of that anger back on herself. "Don't." She sighs, blinking rapidly, staving off tears. "Don't say a word. If he likes you then he likes you, and there's nothing I can do. I mean, it's not your fault you're smart and pretty and guys are always going to like you better than me. Especially once they see you without your hood." She tries to laugh, but doesn't quite make it.

"You're making something out of nothing," I say, hoping to convince her, hoping to convince myself. "The only thing Damen and I have in common is our taste in movies and costumes. That's it, I swear." And when I smile, I'm hoping it plays more real than it feels.

She gazes across the room at Evangeline who's taken hold of Zorro's whip and is demonstrating the proper way to use it, then she turns back to me and says, "Just do me a favor."

I nod, willing to do just about anything to put an end to all this.

"Stop lying. You really suck at it."

I watch as she walks away, then I turn to Riley who's jumping up and down, shouting, "Omigod, this has *got* to be your best party ever! Drama! Intrigue! Jealousy! An almost–cat fight! I am *so* glad I didn't miss this!"

And I'm just about to tell her to *shush* when I remember how I'm the only one who can actually hear her and how it might look a little strange for me to do that. And when the doorbell rings again, despite the fish tail flopping behind her, this time, she beats me to it.

"Oh my," says the woman standing on the porch gazing between Riley and me.

"Can I help you?" I ask, noticing how she's not dressed up, unless California casual counts as a costume.

She looks at me, her brown eyes meeting mine when she says, "Sorry I'm late, traffic was a bitc—well you know." She nods at Riley as though she can actually see her.

"Are you a friend of Sabine's?" I ask, thinking maybe it's some weird nervous tic that keeps her eyes darting to where Riley is standing, because even though she has a nice purple aura, for some reason, I can't read her.

"I'm Ava. Sabine hired me."

"Are you one of the caterers?" I ask, wondering why she's wearing a black off-the-shoulder top, skinny jeans, and ballet flats instead of a white shirt and black pants like the rest of the team.

But she just laughs and waves at Riley, who's hiding behind the folds of my dress, like she used to do with our mom whenever she felt shy. "I'm the psychic," she says, brushing her long auburn hair off her face, and kneeling down beside Riley. "And I see you have a little friend with you."

twelve

Apparently Ava the psychic was supposed to be this fun surprise for everyone. But trust me, no one was more surprised than me. I mean, how did I not see it coming? Was I so wrapped up in my own world that I forgot to poke around in Sabine's?

And it's not like I could just send her away, even though I was tempted. But before I could even react to the shock of her seeing Riley, Sabine was at the door, inviting her in.

"Oh good, you made it. And I see you've met my niece," she says, ushering her into the den where a table is set up and waiting.

I hover close by, wondering if Ava the Psychic will try to mention my dead little sister. But then Sabine asks me to fetch Ava a drink, and by the time I return she's giving a reading.

"You should get in line before it gets any longer," Sabine says, her shoulder pressed against Frankenstein, who, with or without the creepy mask, is *not* the cute guy who works in her building. He's also not the big, successful investment banker he pretends to be. In fact, he still lives with his mother.

But I don't want to tell her any of that and destroy her good mood, so I just shake my head and say, "Maybe later."

It's nice to see Sabine enjoying herself for a change, good to know she has a whole network of friends, and from what I can see, a renewed interest in dating. And even though it's fun watching Riley dance with unsuspecting people and eavesdrop on conversations she probably shouldn't hear, I need a break from all of the random thoughts, vibrating auras, swirling energy, but most of all—Damen.

So far I've done my best to keep my distance, to act cool and ignore him when I see him at school, but seeing him tonight, dressed in what is clearly the other half of a couple's costume—well, I'm not sure what to think. I mean, last I saw, he was into the redhead, Stacia, anyone but me. Enchanting them with his charm, good looks, charisma, and inexplicable magic tricks.

I bury my nose in the flowers he brought me, twenty-four tulips, all of them red. And even though tulips aren't exactly known for their scent, somehow these are heady, intoxicating, and sweet. I inhale deeply, losing myself in their fragrant bouquet and secretly admitting I like him. I mean, I *really* like him. I can't help it. I just do. And no matter how hard I try to pretend otherwise, it doesn't make it any less true.

Before Damen came along, I'd resigned myself to a solitary fate. Not that I was thrilled with the idea of never having another boyfriend, of never getting close to another person again. But how can I date when touch feels so overbearing? How can I be in a relationship when I'll always know what my partner is thinking? Never getting the chance to obsess, dissect, and guess at the secret meaning of everything he says and does?

And even though it probably seems cool to read minds and

energy and auras, trust me, it so isn't. I would give anything to get my old life back, to be as normal and clueless as every other girl. Because sometimes even your best friends can think some pretty unflattering things, and not having an *off* switch requires a heck of a lot of forgiveness.

But that's what's so great about Damen. He's like an *off* switch. He's the only one I can't read, the only one who can silence the sound of everyone else. And even though he makes me feel wonderful and warm and as close to normal as I'll ever get to be, I can't help but think that there's nothing normal about it.

I sit on one of the lounge chairs and arrange my full skirt all around, watching the water globes bob and change color as they glide across the pool's shiny surface. And I'm so lost in my thoughts and the amazing view before me, that at first I don't notice when Damen appears.

"Hey." He smiles.

And when I glance at him, my whole body heats.

"It's a good party. I'm glad I crashed." He sits down beside me, as I stare straight ahead, aware that he's teasing but too nervous to respond. "You make a good Marie," he says, his finger tapping the long black feather I stuck in my wig at the very last moment.

I press my lips together, feeling anxious, nervous, tempted to flee. Then I take a deep breath and relax and go with it. Allow myself to live a little—if just for one night. "And you make a good Count Fersen," I finally say.

"Please, call me Axel." He laughs.

"Did they charge extra for the moth hole?" I ask, nodding at the frayed spot near his shoulder, though choosing not to mention its musty scent.

He looks at me, his eyes right on mine when he says, "That's no moth hole. That's the by-product of artillery fire, a real *near miss* as they say."

"Well, if I remember right, in this particular scene you were pursuing a dark-haired girl." I glance at him, remembering a time when flirting came easy, summoning the girl I used to be.

"There's been a last-minute rewrite." He smiles. "Didn't you get the new script?"

I kick my feet up and smile, thinking how nice it feels to finally let go, to act like a normal girl, with a normal crush, just like anyone else.

"And in this new version it's just us. And you, Marie, get to keep your pretty head." He takes his finger, the very tip of his index finger, and slides it across the width of my neck, leaving a trail of warm wonderful sizzle as he lingers just under my ear. "Why didn't you get in line for a reading?" he whispers, his fingers traveling along my jaw, my cheek, tracing the curve of my ear, as his lips loom so close our breaths meet and mingle.

I shrug and press my lips, wishing he'd just shut up and kiss me already.

"Are you a skeptic?"

"No—I just—I don't know," I mumble, so frustrated I'm tempted to scream.

Why does he insist on talking? Doesn't he realize this may be my last remaining shot at a normal boy-girl experience? That an opportunity like this may never present itself again?

"How come you're not in line?" I ask, no longer trying to hide my frustration.

"Waste of time." He laughs. "It's not possible to read minds, or tell the future—*right?*"

I shift my gaze to the pool, blinking at the water globes that have not only turned pink but are forming a heart.

"Have I angered you?" he asks, his fingers cupping my chin, bringing my face back to his.

And that's another thing. Sometimes he uses California surf speak as well as anyone else around here, and other times, he sounds like he just walked straight out of the pages of *Wuthering Heights*. "No. You have not *angered* me," I say, laughing in spite of myself.

"What's so funny?" he asks, his fingers sliding under my bangs, seeking the scar on my forehead and causing me to pull away. "How'd you get that?" he asks, hand back to his side, gazing at me with such warmth and sincerity I almost confide.

But I don't. Because this is the one night of the year when I get to be someone else. When I get to pretend that I'm not responsible for the end of everything I held dear. Tonight I get to flirt, and play, and make reckless decisions I'll probably live to regret. Because tonight I'm no longer Ever, I'm Marie. And if he's any kind of a Count Fersen he'll shut up and kiss me already.

"I don't want to talk about it," I say, blinking at the water globes that are now red and forming into a tulip.

"What do you want to talk about?" he whispers, gazing at me with those eyes, two infinite pools luring me in.

"I don't want to talk," I whisper, holding my breath as his lips meet mine.

thirteen

If I thought his voice was amazing with the way it envelopes me in silence, if I thought his touch was incredible with the way it awakens my skin, well, the way he kisses is *otherworldly.* And even though I'm no expert, having only kissed a few guys before, I'm still willing to bet that a kiss like this, a kiss this complete and transcendent, is a once-in-a-lifetime thing.

And when he pulls away and gazes into my eyes, I close mine again, grab his lapels, and bring him back to me.

Until Haven says, "Jeez, I've been looking all over for you. I should've known you'd be hiding out here."

I pull away, horrified to be caught in the act, not long after swearing that I don't even like him.

"We were just—"

She raises her hand to stop me. "Please. Spare me the details. I just wanted you to know that Evangeline and I are taking off."

"Already?" I ask, wondering how long we've been out here.

"Yeah, my friend Drina stopped by, she's taking us to another party. You guys are welcome to tag along too—though you seem pretty busy." She smirks.

"Drina?" Damen says, standing so fast his whole body blurs.

"You know her?" Haven asks, but Damen's already gone, moving so fast we scramble to follow.

I rush behind Haven, anxious to catch up, desperate to explain, but when we reach the french doors and I grab onto her shoulder I'm filled with such darkness, such overwhelming anger and despair, the words freeze on my tongue.

Then she pulls away and glares over her shoulder, saying, "I told you you suck at lying," before continuing on.

I take a deep breath and follow behind, trailing them through the kitchen, the den, making my way to the door, my eyes fixed on the back of Damen's head, noticing how he moves so fast and sure, it's as though he knows just where to find her. And by the time I step into the foyer, I freeze when I see them together—he in his eighteenth-century splendor—and she dressed as a Marie Antoinette so rich, so lovely, so exquisite, she puts me to shame.

"And you must be . . ." She lifts her chin as her eyes land on mine, two glowing spheres of deep emerald green.

"Ever," I mumble, taking in the pale blond wig, the creamy flawless skin, the tangle of pearls at her throat, watching as her perfect pink lips display teeth so white they hardly seem real.

I turn to Damen, hoping he can explain, provide some logical explanation for how the redhead from the St. Regis ended up in my foyer. But he's too busy gazing at her to even notice my existence.

"What are you doing here?" he asks, his voice nearly a whisper.

"Haven invited me." She smiles.

And as I glance from her to him, my body fills with a cold hard dread. "How do you know each other?" I ask, noting how Damen's entire demeanor has changed, suddenly growing chilly, cold, and distant—a dark cloud where the sun used to be.

"I met her at Nocturne," Drina says, gazing right at me.

"We're headed there now. I hope you don't mind my stealing her away?"

I narrow my eyes, ignoring the twitch in my heart, the pang in my gut, as I struggle to get some kind of read. But her thoughts are inaccessible, sealed off completely, and her aura nonexistent.

"Oh, silly me, you were referring to Damen and I, weren't you?" She laughs, her eyes traveling slowly over my costume, until coming back to meet mine. And when I don't respond she nods when she says, "We knew each other back in New Mexico."

Only, when she says, "New Mexico," Damen says, "New Orleans." Causing Drina to laugh in a way that never quite reaches her eyes.

"Let's just say we go way back." She nods, extending a hand to my sleeve, her fingers trailing its beaded edge, before sliding down to my wrist. "Lovely dress," she says, clasping me tightly. "Did you make it yourself?"

I wrench my arm free, less from the shock of being mocked and more from the chill of her fingers, the frigid scratch of her cold sharp nails freezing my skin and shooting ice through my veins.

"Isn't she the coolest?" Haven says, gazing at Drina with the sort of awe she usually reserves for vampires, goth rockers, and Damen. While Evangeline stands beside her, rolling her eyes and checking her watch.

"We really need to go if we're going to make it to Nocturne by midnight," Evangeline says.

"You're welcome to join us." Drina smiles. "Fully stocked limo."

And when I glance at Haven, I can hear her thinking: *Say no, say no, please say no!*

Drina glances between Damen and me. "Driver's waiting," she sings.

I turn to him, my heart caving when I see how conflicted he is. Then I clear my throat and force myself to say, "You can go if you want. But I need to stay. I can't exactly leave my own party." Then I laugh, attempting to sound light and breezy, when the truth is, I can barely breathe.

Drina glances between us, brows arched, face haughty, betraying just the briefest glimmer of shock when Damen shakes his head and takes my hand instead of hers.

"So wonderful to meet you Ever," Drina says, pausing before climbing into the limo. "Though I'm sure we'll meet again."

I watch as they disappear from the driveway and onto the street, then I turn to Damen and say, "So, who should I expect next, Stacia, Honor, and Craig?"

And the second it's out, I'm ashamed for having said it, for revealing what a petty, jealous, pathetic person I am. It's not like I didn't know better. So I shouldn't feel so surprised.

Damen's a player. Pure and simple.

Tonight just happened to be my turn.

"Ever," he says, smoothing his thumb over my cheek.

And just as I start to pull away, unwilling to hear his excuses, he looks at me and whispers, "I should probably go too."

I search his eyes, my mind accepting a truth my heart would rather refuse, knowing there's more to the statement, words he failed to include—*I should go—so I can catch up with her.*

"Okay, well thanks for coming," I finally say, sounding less like a prospective girlfriend and more like a waitress after a particularly long shift.

But he just smiles, removes the feather from the back of my

wig, and guides it down the length of my neck, tapping the very tip to my nose as he says, "Souvenir?"

And I've barely had a chance to respond before he's in his car and driving away.

I sink down onto the stairs, my head in my hands, wig teetering precariously, wishing I could just disappear, go back in time, and start over. Knowing I never should've allowed him to kiss me, never should've invited him in—

"There you are!" Sabine says, grabbing hold of my arm and pulling me to my feet. "I've been looking all over for you. Ava agreed to stay just long enough to give you a reading."

"But I don't want a reading," I tell her, not wanting to offend, but not wanting to go through with it either. I just want to go to my room, ditch this wig, and fall into a long, dreamless sleep.

But Sabine's been hitting the party punch, which means she's too tipsy to listen. So she grabs my hand and leads me into the den where Ava is waiting.

"Hello, Ever." Ava smiles as I sink onto the seat, grip the table, and wait for Sabine's inebriated energy to fade.

"Take all the time you need." She smiles.

I gaze at the tarot cards laid out before me. "Um, nothing personal, but I don't want a reading," I say, meeting her eyes before averting my gaze.

"Then I won't give you a reading." She shrugs, gathering the cards and beginning to shuffle. "What do you say we just go through the motions so we can make your aunt happy? She worries about you. Wonders if she's doing the right thing—providing enough freedom, providing too much freedom." She looks at me. "What do you think?"

I shrug and roll my eyes. That hardly qualifies as a revelation.

"She's getting married, you know."

I look up, startled, my eyes meeting hers.

"But not today." She laughs. "Not tomorrow either. So don't worry."

"Why would I worry?" I shift in my seat, watching as she cuts the deck in half before spreading the cards into a crescent. "I want Sabine to be happy, and if that's what it takes—"

"True. But you've experienced so many changes this past year already, haven't you? Changes you're still trying to adjust to. It's not easy, is it?" She gazes at me.

But I don't respond. And why should I? She's yet to say anything remotely earth shattering or insightful. Life is full of change, big deal. I mean, isn't that pretty much the point? To grow, and change, and move along? Besides, it's not like Sabine's an enigma. It's not like she's all that complex, or hard to figure out.

"So how are you handling your gift?" Ava asks, turning some cards, while leaving others face down.

"My *what?*" I peer at her, wondering where she could possibly be going with this.

"Your psychic gift." She smiles, nodding as though it's a fact.

"I don't know what you're talking about." I press my lips together and glance around the room, seeing Miles and Eric dance with Sabine and her date, and unbeknownst to them, Riley.

"It's hard at first." She nods. "Believe me, I know. I was the first to know about my grandmother's passing. She came right into my room, stood at the foot of my bed, and waved good-bye. I was only four at the time, so you can imagine how my parents reacted when I ran into the kitchen to tell them." She shakes her head and laughs. "But you understand, because you see them too, right?"

I stare at the cards, my hands clasped together, not saying a word.

"It can feel so overwhelming, so isolating. But it doesn't have to. You don't have to hide under a hood, killing your eardrums with music you don't even like. There are ways to handle it, and I'd be happy to show you because, Ever, you don't have to live like that."

I grip the edge of the table and rise from my seat, my legs feeling shaky, unsure, my stomach unstable. This lady is crazy if she thinks what I have is a *gift*. Because I know better. I know it's just one more punishment for everything that I did, everything that I caused. It's my own personal burden, and I just have to deal with it. "I have no idea what you're talking about," I finally say.

But she just nods, and slides her card toward me. "When you're ready, you can reach me here."

I take her card, but only because Sabine's watching from across the room and I don't want to seem rude. Then I fold it in the palm of my hand, squishing it into a hard, angry ball, as I ask, "Are we done?" anxious to get away.

"One last thing." She slides the deck into a brown leather case. "I'm worried about your little sister. I think it's time she moves on, don't you?"

I look at her, sitting there so smug and knowing, judging my life when she doesn't even know me. "For your information Riley *has* moved on! She's dead!" I whisper, dropping her crumbled-up card on the table, no longer caring who sees.

But she just smiles and says, "I think you know what I mean."

fourteen

That night, long after the party had ended and all of our guests were gone, I was lying in bed, thinking about Ava, what she said about Riley being stuck, and how I was to blame. I guess I'd always assumed Riley *had* moved on and was choosing to visit on her own free will. Since it's not like I *ask* her to drop by all the time, it's just something she chooses to do. And the times she's not with me, well, I figure she's kicking it somewhere in Heaven. And even though I know Ava's only trying to help, offering to stand in as some sort of psychic big sister, what she doesn't realize is that I don't want any help. That even though I yearn to be normal again, go back to the way things were before, I also know that this is my punishment. This horrible *gift* is what I deserve for all the harm that I've caused, for the lives I cut short. And now I just have to live with it—and try not to harm anyone else.

When I finally did fall asleep, I dreamt of Damen. And everything about it felt so powerful, so intense, so urgent, I thought it was real. But by morning, all I had left were fragmented pieces, shifting images with no beginning or end. The only thing I could clearly remember was the two of us running through a cold windswept canyon—rushing toward something I couldn't quite see.

"What's your problem? Why so grumpy?" Riley asks, perched on the edge of my bed, dressed in a Zorro costume identical to the one Eric wore to the party.

"Halloween's over," I say, staring pointedly at the black leather whip she slaps against the floor.

"Duh." She makes a face and continues to punish the carpet. "So I like the costume, big deal. I'm thinking about dressing up every day."

I lean toward the mirror, insert my tiny diamond-chip studs, and scrape my hair into a ponytail.

"I can't believe you're still dressing like that," she says, her nose crinkling in disgust. "I thought you bagged yourself a boyfriend?" She drops the whip and grabs my iPod, her fingers sliding around the wheel as she scrolls through my playlist.

I turn, wondering what exactly she saw.

"Hel-*lo*? At the party? By the pool? Or was that just a hookup?"

I stare at her, my face flushing crimson. "What do you know about hookups? You're only twelve! And why the heck are you spying on me?"

She rolls her eyes. "Please, like I'd waste my time spying on you when there's way better stuff I can see. For your information, I just so happened to go outside at the exact same moment you shoved your tongue down that Damen guy's throat. And trust me, I wish I *hadn't* seen it."

I shake my head and ransack my drawer, transferring my annoyance at Riley onto my sweatshirts. "Yeah, well, I hate to break it to you, but he's hardly my boyfriend. I haven't talked to him since," I say, hating the way my stomach just curled in on itself when I said that. Then I grab a clean gray sweatshirt and yank it over my head, completely destroying the ponytail I just made.

"I can spy on him if you want. Or haunt him." She smiles.

I look at her and sigh. Part of me wanting to take her up on it, the other part knowing it's time to move on, cut my losses, and forget it ever happened. "Just stay out of it, okay?" I finally say. "I'd like just one normal high school experience, if you don't mind."

"Up to you." She shrugs, tossing me the iPod. "But just so you know, Brandon's back on the market."

I grab a stack of books and stuff them into my backpack, amazed at how that bit of news doesn't make me feel any better.

"Yup, Rachel dumped him on Halloween when she caught him making out with a *Playboy* bunny. Only it wasn't really a *Playboy* bunny, it was Heather Watson dressed as one."

"Seriously?" I gape. "Heather Watson? You're joking." I try to picture it in my mind, but it doesn't add up.

"Scouts honor. You should see her, she lost twenty pounds, ditched the headgear, got her hair straightened, and she looks like a totally different person. Unfortunately, she also acts like a totally different person. She's kind of a, well, you know, a *B* with an itch," she whispers, going back to whipping the floor, as I let that bizarre piece of news sink in.

"You know, you really shouldn't be spying on people," I say, more concerned with her spying on me than any of my old friends. "It's kind of rude, don't you think?" I heave my bag onto my shoulder and head for the door.

Riley laughs. "Don't be ridiculous. It's good to keep up with people from the old neighborhood."

"Are you coming?" I ask, turning impatiently.

"Yup, and I call shotgun!" she says, slipping right past me and hopping onto the banister, her black Zorro cape floating on air as she slides all the way down.

By the time I get to Miles's, he's waiting outside, thumbs tapping his Sidekick. "Just—one—second—okay, done!" He slips onto the passenger seat and peers closely at me. "Now—tell me *everything*! Start to finish. I want all the dirty details, leave nothing out!"

"What're you talking about?" I back out of his driveway and onto the street, shooting a warning glance at Riley who's perched on his knee, blowing on his face and laughing when he tries to adjust the air vent.

Miles looks at me and shakes his head. "Hel-*lo*? Damen? I heard you guys were macking in the moonlight, making out by the pool, hooking up under the moon's silvery—"

"Where are you going with this?" I ask, even though I already know, but hoping there's some way to stop him.

"Listen, word's out so don't even try to deny it. And I would've called you yesterday but my dad confiscated my phone and dragged me to the batting cages, so he could watch me swing like a girl." He laughs. "You should've seen me, I totally camped it up and he was *horror-fied*! That'll teach him. But anyway, back to you. Come on, the divulging starts now. Tell me everything," he says, turning toward me and nodding impatiently. "Was it as awesome as we all dreamed it would be?"

I shrug, glancing at Riley and warning her with my eyes to either cease and desist or disappear. "Sorry to disappoint you," I finally say. "But there's nothing to tell."

"That's not what I heard. Haven said—"

I press my lips and shake my head. Just because I already

know what Haven said doesn't mean I want to hear it spoken out loud. So I cut him off when I say, "Okay fine, we kissed. But just once." I can feel him looking at me, brows raised, lips smirked in suspicion. "Maybe twice. I don't know, it's not like I counted," I mumble, lying like a red-faced, sweaty-palmed, shifty-eyed amateur, and hoping he doesn't notice. Because the truth is I've replayed that kiss so many times it's tattooed on my brain.

"And?" he says, impatient for more.

"*And*—nothing," I say, relieved when I glance at him and see Riley's gone.

"He didn't call? Or text? Or e-mail? Or drop by?" Miles gasps, visibly upset, wondering what it means not only for me, but the future of our group.

I shake my head and stare straight ahead, angry with myself for not dealing with it better, hating the way my throat's gone all tight as my eyes start to sting.

"But what did he *say*? When he left the party, I mean? What were his very last words?" Miles asks, determined to find some ray of hope in this bleak and bitter landscape.

I turn at the light, remembering our strange and sudden good-bye at the door. Then I face Miles, swallow hard, and say, "He said, 'souvenir?' "

And the moment it's out, I know it's a really bad sign.

Nobody takes a souvenir from a place they plan to frequent.

Miles looks at me, his eyes expressing the words his lips have refused.

"Tell me about it," I say, shaking my head as I pull into the lot.

Even though I'm fully committed to not thinking about Damen, I can't help but feel disappointed when I get to English and see he's not there. Which, of course, makes me think about him even that much more, until I'm teetering on the edge of obsession.

I mean, just because our kiss seemed like something more than just a random hookup doesn't mean he felt the same way. And just because it felt solid and true and transcendent to me doesn't mean he was in on it too. Because no matter how hard I try, I can't shake the image of him and Drina standing together, a perfect Count Fersen with an idyllic Marie. While I stood on the sidelines all shiny and pouffy like the world's biggest wannabe.

I'm just about to click on my iPod when Stacia and Damen burst through the door. Laughing and smiling, shoulders nearly touching, two single white rosebuds clutched in her hand.

And when he leaves her at her desk and heads toward me, I fumble with some papers and pretend I didn't see.

"Hey," he says, sliding onto his seat. Acting like everything's perfectly normal. Like he didn't pull a grope-and-run less than forty-eight hours before.

I place my cheek on my palm and force my face into a yawn, hoping to come off as bored, tired, worn out from activities he couldn't begin to imagine, doodling on a piece of notebook paper with fingers so shaky my pen slips right out of my hand.

I bend down to retrieve it, and when I come back up I find a single red tulip on top of my desk.

"What happened? You run out of white rosebuds?" I ask, flipping through books and papers, as though I've something important to do.

"I would never give you a rosebud," he says, his eyes searching for mine.

But I refuse to meet his gaze, refuse to get sucked into his sadistic little game. I just grab my bag and pretend to search for something inside, cursing under my breath when I find it stuffed full of tulips.

"You're strictly a tulip girl—a red tulip girl." He smiles.

"How exciting for me," I mumble, dropping my bag to the ground and scooting to the farthest part of my seat, having no idea what any of it could possibly mean.

By the time I get to our lunch table, I'm a sweaty mess. Wondering if Damen will be there, if Haven will be there—because even though I haven't seen or spoken to her since Saturday night, I'm willing to bet she still hates me. But despite spending all of third-period chemistry practicing an entire speech in my head, the second I see her, I've lost all the words.

"Well, look who's here," Haven says, gazing at me.

I slide onto the bench beside Miles who's far too busy texting to even notice my existence, and I can't help but wonder if I should try to find some new friends—not that anyone would have me.

"I was just telling Miles how he totally missed out on Nocturne, only he's determined to ignore me." She scowls.

"Only because I was forced to listen to it all through history, and then you still weren't finished and you made me late to Spanish." He shakes his head and continues thumb thumping.

Haven shrugs. "You're just jealous you missed out." Then looking at me, she tries to retreat. "Not that your party wasn't cool or anything, because it was, *totally cool.* It's just—this was more my scene, you know? I mean, you understand, right?"

I polish my apple against my sleeve and shrug, reluctant to hear any more than I already have about Nocturne, *her scene,* or Drina. But when I finally do look at her, I'm startled to see how her usual yellow contacts have been swapped for a brand-new green.

A green so familiar it robs me of breath.

A green that can only be described as—*Drina green.*

"You should've seen it, there was this huge long line out front, but the second they saw Drina, they let us right in. We didn't even have to pay! Not for *anything,* the whole night was comped! I even crashed in her room. She's staying in this amazing suite at the St. Regis until she finds a more permanent place. You should see it: ocean view, Jacuzzi tub, rockin' minibar, the works!" She looks at me, emerald eyes wide with excitement, waiting for an enthusiastic response I just can't provide.

I press my lips together and take in the rest of her appearance, noticing how her eyeliner is softer, smokier, more like Drina's, and how her bloodred lipstick has been swapped for a lighter, rosier, Drina-like shade. Even her hair, which she's ironed straight for as long as I've known her, is now soft and wavy and styled like Drina's. And her dress is fitted, silky, and vintage, like something Drina might wear.

"So where's Damen?" Haven looks at me as though I should know.

I take a bite of my apple and shrug.

"What happened? I thought you guys hooked up?" she asks, refusing to let it go.

And before I can answer, Miles looks up from his Sidekick and shoots her *the look*—the one with the direct translation of: *Caution all ye who enter.*

She glances from Miles to me, then shakes her head and sighs. "Whatever. I just want you to know that I'm totally cool with it, so no worries, okay? And I'm sorry if I got a little weird on you." She shrugs. "But I'm totally over it now. Seriously. Pinky-swear."

I reluctantly curl my pinky around hers and tune into her energy. And I'm completely amazed to *see* that she really does mean it. I mean, just this weekend she'd pegged me as Public Enemy #1, but now she's clearly not bothered, though I can't really see why.

"Haven—" I start, wondering if I should really do this, but then figuring, *oh, what the hell, I have nothing to lose.*

She looks at me, smiling, waiting.

"Um, when you guys went to—Nocturne, did you maybe—by chance—happen to run into Damen?" I press my lips and wait, feeling Miles give me a sharp look, while Haven just stares at me, clearly confused. "Because the thing is, he left shortly after you guys—so I thought maybe—"

She shakes her head and shrugs. "Nope, never saw him," she says, removing a dab of frosting from her lip with the tip of her tongue.

And even though I know better, I choose that moment to take a visual journey through the lunch table caste system, the alphabetical hierarchy, starting with our lowly table *Z* and working toward *A*. Wondering if I'll find Damen and Stacia frolicking in a field of rosebuds, or engaging in some other sordid act I'd rather not see.

But even though it's business as usual over there, with everyone up to the same old antics, for today at least, it's flower free.

I guess because Damen's not there.

fifteen

I'd just fallen asleep when Damen calls. And even though I'd spent the last two days convincing myself not to like him, the second I hear his voice, I surrender.

"Is it too late?"

I squint at the glowing green numbers on my alarm clock, confirming it is, but answering, "No, it's okay."

"Were you asleep?"

"Almost." I prop my pillows against my cloth-covered headboard, then lean back against them.

"I was wondering if I could come over?"

I gaze at the clock again, but only to prove his question is crazy. "Probably not such a good idea," I tell him, which is followed by such a prolonged silence I'm sure he's hung up.

"I'm sorry I missed you at lunch," he finally says. "Art too. I left right after English."

"Um, okay," I mumble, unsure how to respond, since it's not like we're a couple, it's not like he's accountable to me.

"Are you sure it's too late?" he asks, his tone deep and persuasive. "I'd really like to see you. I won't stay long."

I smile, thrilled with this tiny shift in power, to be calling the shots for a change, and allowing myself a mental high-five when I say, "Tomorrow in English works for me."

"How about I drive you to school?" he asks, his voice nearly convincing me to forget about Stacia, Drina, his hasty retreat, everything—just clean the slate, let bygones be bygones, start all over again.

But I haven't come this far to give up so easily. So I force the words from my lips when I say, "Miles and I carpool. So I'll just see you in English." And knowing better than to risk his changing my mind, I snap my phone shut and toss it across the room.

The next morning when Riley pops in, she stands before me and says, "Still cranky?"

I roll my eyes.

"I'll take that as a *yes.*" She laughs, hopping on top of my dresser and kicking her heels against the drawers.

"So, who are you dressed as today?" I toss a pile of books into my bag and glance at her tight bodice, full skirt, and cascading brown hair.

"Elizabeth Swann." She smiles.

I squint, trying to remember that name. *"Pirates?"*

"Duh." She crosses her eyes and sticks out her tongue. "So what's up with you and Count Fersen?"

I sling my bag over my shoulder and head for the door, determined to ignore the question when I call, "Coming?"

She shakes her head. "Not today. I have an appointment."

I lean against the doorjamb and squint. "What do you mean by 'appointment'?"

But she just shakes her head and hops off the dresser. "None of your beeswax." She laughs, walking straight through the wall and disappearing.

Since Miles was running late, I end up running late too, and by the time we make it to school, the parking lot is completely full. All except for the very best, most sought-after space.

The one on the very end.

The one closest to the gate.

The one that just happens to be right next to Damen's.

"*How* did you do it?" Miles asks, grabbing his books and climbing out of my tiny red car, gazing at Damen like he's the world's sexiest magic act.

"Do what?" Damen asks, gazing at me.

"Save the spot. You have to get here like, way before the school year even begins to snatch this one."

Damen laughs, his eyes searching mine. But I just nod like he's my pharmacist or mailman, *not* the guy I've been obsessing over since the moment I saw him.

"Bell's gonna ring," I say, rushing past the gate and heading toward class, noticing how he moves so quickly he beats me to the door with no visible effort.

I storm toward Honor and Stacia, purposely kicking Stacia's bag when she gazes at Damen and says, "Hey, where's my rosebud?"

Then regretting it the second he answers, "Sorry, not today."

He slides onto his seat and gives me an amused look. "Someone's in a foul mood." He laughs.

But I just shrug and drop my bag to the floor.

"What's the rush?" He leans toward me. "Mr. Robins stayed home."

I turn. "How'd you—" but then I stop before I can finish. I mean, how can Damen possibly know what I know—that Mr. Robins is still at home, still hungover, still grieving the wife and daughter who recently left him?

"I saw the substitute while I was waiting for you." He smiles. "She looked a little lost, so I escorted her to the teachers' lounge, but she seemed so confused she'll probably end up in the science lab instead."

And the second he says it I know that it's true, having just *seen* her entering the wrong class, having mistaken it for our room.

"So tell me. What have I done to anger you so?"

I glance up as Stacia whispers in Honor's ear, watching as they shake their heads and glare at me.

"Ignore them, they're idiots," Damen whispers, leaning toward me and placing his hand over mine. "I'm sorry I haven't been around much. I had a visitor; I couldn't get away."

"You mean Drina?" And the moment it's out, I cringe at how awful and jealous I sound. Wishing I could be cool, calm, and collected, act as though I didn't even notice how everything changed the moment she appeared. But the truth is, that's pretty much impossible for me, since I'm much closer to paranoid than naïve.

"Ever—" he starts.

But since I've already started, I may as well continue. "Have you seen Haven lately? She's like a Drina Mini-Me. She dresses like her, acts like her, even has the same eye color. Seriously, stop by the lunch table sometime, you'll see." I glare at him, as though he's responsible, as though it's his fault. But the moment our eyes meet, I'm right back under his spell, a helpless hunk of steel to his irresistible magnet.

He takes a deep breath then shakes his head as he says, "Ever, it's not what you think."

I pull away and press my lips together. *You have no idea what I think.*

"Let me make it up to you. Let me take you out, somewhere special, please?"

I can feel the warmth of his gaze on my skin, but I won't risk trying to meet it. I want him to wonder, to doubt. I want to drag it out for as long as I possibly can.

So I shift in my seat, glance at him briefly, and say, "We'll see."

When I exit fourth-period history, Damen is waiting outside the door. And assuming he just wants to walk me to the lunch table, I say, "Let me just drop my bag in my locker before we head over."

"No need." He smiles, securing his arm around my waist. "The surprise starts now."

"Surprise?" And when I look into his eyes, the whole world shrinks, until it's just me and him, surrounded by static.

He smiles. "You know, I take you somewhere special—so special you forgive my transgressions."

"And what about our classes? We just blow off the rest of the day?" I fold my arms across my chest, though it's mostly for show.

He laughs and leans toward me, his lips grazing the side of my neck as they form the word—*Yes.*

And as I pull away I'm amazed to hear myself answer with *how* instead of *no.*

"No worries." He smiles, squeezing my hand as he leads me through the gate. "You'll always be safe with me."

sixteen

"Disneyland?" I climb out of my car and gaze at him in shock. Out of all the places I thought we'd end up, this never cracked the list.

"I hear it's the happiest place on earth." He laughs. "Have you been?"

I shake my head.

"Good, then I'll be your guide." He slips his arm through mine and leads me through the gates, and as we wander down Main Street I try to imagine him coming here before. He's so sleek, so sophisticated, so sexy, so smooth—it's hard to imagine him trolling a place where Mickey Mouse rules. "It's always better during the week when it's not so crowded," he says, crossing the street. "Come on, I'll show you New Orleans, it's my favorite part."

"You come here enough to have favorites?" I stop in the middle of the street and stare at him. "I thought you just moved here?"

He laughs. "I did just move here. But that doesn't mean I haven't been," he says, pulling me toward the Haunted Mansion.

After the Haunted Mansion we head for the *Pirates* ride, and when that's over, he looks at me and says, "So which one's your favorite?"

"Um, *Pirates.*" I nod. "I think."

He looks at me.

"Well, they're both pretty cool." I shrug. "But *Pirates* has Johnny Depp, so that kind of gives it an unfair advantage, don't you think?"

"Johnny Depp? So that's what I'm up against?" He raises a brow.

I shrug, taking in Damen's dark jeans, black long-sleeved T-shirt, and those boots, his easy good looks dwarfing every Hollywood actor I can think of, though it's not like I'll admit that.

"Wanna go again?" he asks, dark eyes flashing.

So we do. And then we head back to the Haunted Mansion. And when we reach the part at the end, where the ghosts hitch a ride in your car, I half expect to see Riley scrunched in between us, laughing and waving and clowning around. But instead, it's just one of those cartoon Disney ghosts, and I remember Riley's appointment and figure she must be too busy.

After yet another go on those rides, we end up at a waterfront table in the Blue Bayou, the restaurant inside the *Pirates* ride. And as I sip my iced tea I look at him and say, "Okay, I happen to know this is a really big park with more than two rides. Rides that have nothing to do with pirates or ghosts."

"I heard that too." He smiles, spearing calamari with his fork and offering it to me. "They used to have this one called Mission to Mars. It was known as the make-out ride, mostly because it was very dark inside."

"Is it still here?" I ask, my face turning every shade of crimson when I realize how eager I sound. "Not that I want to ride it or anything. I was just curious."

He looks at me, his face clearly amused. Then he shakes his head and says, "No, it closed a long time ago."

"So you were going on the make-out ride when you were what—two?" I ask, reaching for a sausage-stuffed mushroom and hoping I'll like it.

"Not me." He smiles. "That was way before my time."

Normally I'd do anything to avoid a place like this. A place so congested with the random energy of people, their bright swirling auras, their odd collection of thoughts. But it's different with Damen, effortless, pleasant. Because whenever we touch, whenever he speaks, it's like we're the only ones here.

After lunch, we stroll around the park, going on all the fast rides and avoiding the water rides, or at least the ones where you get soaked. And when it gets dark, he leads me over to Sleeping Beauty Castle, where we stop near the moat and wait for the fireworks show to begin.

"So, am I forgiven?" he asks, arms snaking around my waist, teeth nipping at my neck, my jaw, my ear. The sudden burst of fireworks, their booming crackle and snap, seem faint and far away, as our bodies press together and his lips move against mine.

"Look," he whispers, pulling away and pointing toward the expanse of night sky, a profusion of purple color wheels, golden waterfalls, silver fountains, pink chrysanthemums, and for the grand finale—a dozen red tulips. All of it flaring and blasting, in such quick succession it vibrates the concrete under our feet.

Wait—red tulips?

I glance at Damen, eyes full of questions, but he just smiles and nods toward the sky, and even though the edges are sparking and fading, the memory is solid, imprinted on my mind.

Then he pulls me close, lips to my ear when he says, "Show's over, fat lady sang."

"You calling Tinkerbell fat?" I laugh as he takes my hand and leads me through the gates and back to our cars.

I climb into my Miata and get settled in, smiling as he leans through my window and says, "Don't worry, there'll be more days like this. Next time I'll take you to California Adventure."

"I thought we just had a California adventure." I laugh, amazed by the way he always seems to know just what I'm thinking before I've even had a chance to utter the words. "Should I follow you again?" I slip my key in the ignition and start the engine.

He shakes his head. "I'll follow *you.*" He smiles. "Got to see you home safely."

I pull out of the lot, merge onto the southbound freeway, and head home. And when I check the rearview mirror, I can't help but smile when I see Damen right there behind me.

I have a boyfriend!

A gorgeous, sexy, smart, charming boyfriend!

One who makes me feel normal again.

One who makes me forget that I'm not.

I reach over to the passenger seat and pluck my new sweatshirt from its bag, running my fingers over the Mickey Mouse appliqué on the front, remembering the moment Damen chose it for me.

"Notice how this one doesn't have a hood," he'd said, holding it against me, and estimating the fit.

"What are you trying to say?" I squinted into the mirror, wondering if he hates my look as much as Riley thinks.

But he just shrugged. "What can I say? I prefer you hoodless."

I smile at the memory, the way he kissed me as we stood in line to pay, the warm, sweet feel of his lips on mine—

And when my cell phone rings, I glance in my rearview mirror to see Damen holding his.

"Hey," I say, lowering my voice so that it's husky and deep.

"Save it," Haven says. "Sorry to disappoint you, but it's just little ole me."

"Oh, so what's up?" I ask, signaling my intended lane change so that Damen can follow.

Only he's no longer there.

I glance between my side and rearview mirrors, frantically scanning all four lanes, but still, no Damen.

"Are you even listening to me?" Haven asks, clearly annoyed.

"Sorry, what?" I ease up on the gas and look over my shoulder, searching for Damen's black BMW, as someone in a monster truck passes, honks, and flips me the bird.

"I said Evangeline is missing!"

"What do you mean 'missing'?" I ask, hesitating for as long as I can before merging onto the 133, with Damen still nowhere in sight, even though I'm sure he didn't pass me.

"I called her cell a bunch of times and she didn't pick up."

"And," I say, anxious to get through this call-screening story so I can get back to my own missing person's case.

"*And*, not only does she not answer, not only is she not in her apartment, but nobody's seen her since *Halloween*."

"What do you mean?" I check my side mirrors, my rearview mirrors, and glance over each shoulder, but still come up empty. "Didn't she go home with you guys?"

"Not exactly," Haven says, her voice small, contrite.

And after two more cars honk and give me the finger, I give up. Promising myself that as soon as I'm done with Haven I'll call Damen on his cell and sort it all out.

"Hel-*lo*?" she says, practically shouting. "I mean, jeez, if you're too busy for me, then just say so. I can always call Miles, you know."

I take a deep breath, striving for patience. "Haven, I'm sorry, okay? I'm trying to drive and I'm a little distracted. Besides, you and I both know Miles is still at acting class, which is why you called me." I merge over to the far left lane, determined to punch it and get home as quickly as I can.

"Whatever," she mumbles. "Anyway, I haven't exactly told you this yet, but, well, Drina and I kind of left without her."

"You *what?*"

"You know, at Nocturne. She just sort of—disappeared. I mean, we looked everywhere, but we just couldn't find her. So we figured she met someone, which believe me, is not out of character, and then—well, we sort of—*left.*"

"You left her in L.A.? *On Halloween night?* When every freak in the city is on the loose?" And the second it's out of my mouth, I *see* it—the three of them in some dark, seamy club, Drina leading Haven to the VIP room for a drink, purposely eluding Evangeline. And even though it goes blank after that, I definitely didn't see any guy.

"What were we supposed to do? I mean, I don't know if you know this, but she's eighteen, which means she can pretty much do what she wants. Besides, Drina said she'd keep an eye on her, but then she lost track of her too. I just got off the phone with her, she feels awful."

"Drina feels awful?" I roll my eyes, finding that hard to believe. Drina doesn't seem like the type to feel much of anything, much less remorse.

"What's that supposed to mean? You don't even know her."

I press my lips and accelerate hard, partly because I *know* this strip of road is currently cop-free, and partly because I want to outrun Haven, Drina, Evangeline, and Damen's strange disappearance, everything, all of it—even though I know that I can't.

"Sorry," I finally mumble, lifting my foot and easing into a regular speed.

"Whatever. I just—I feel so awful, and I don't know what to do."

"Did you call her parents?" I ask, even though I just sensed the answer.

"Her mom's a drunk, lives in Arizona somewhere, and her dad skipped out when she was still in the womb. And trust me, her landlord just wants her stuff cleared out so he can turn the apartment. We even filed a police report, but they didn't seem overly concerned."

"I know," I say, adjusting my lights for the dark, canyon route.

"What do you mean *you know*?"

"I mean I *know* how you must feel." I scramble to cover.

She sighs. "So where are you? Why weren't you at lunch?"

"I'm in Laguna Canyon, on my way home from Disneyland. Damen took me." I smile at the memory, though it turns pretty quick.

"Omigod that's *so* bizarre," Haven says.

"Tell me," I agree, still not used to the idea of him kicking it in the Magic Kingdom even after seeing it with my own eyes.

"No, I mean Drina went too. Said she hasn't been in years and wanted to see how it's changed. Isn't that wild? Did you guys run into her?"

"Um, no," I say, trying to sound matter of fact despite my churning stomach, sweaty palms, and overwhelming feeling of dread.

"Huh. Weird. But then again, it is pretty huge and crowded." She laughs.

"Yeah, yeah it is," I say. "Listen, I gotta go, see you tomorrow?" And before she can even respond, I pull to the side of the road and park by the curb, searching my call list for Damen's number, and pounding hard on the wheel when I see it's marked *private.*

Some boyfriend. I don't even have his phone number, much less know where he lives.

seventeen

Last night, when Damen finally called (at least I assumed it was him since the display read *private*), I let it go straight into voice mail. And this morning, while I'm getting ready for school, I delete it without even listening.

"Aren't you at least curious?" Riley asks, spinning around in my desk chair, her slicked-back hair and *Matrix* costume a shiny black blur.

"No." I glare at the Mickey Mouse sweatshirt still in its bag, then reach for one that he *didn't* buy me.

"Well, you could've let me listen, so I could give you the gist."

"Double no." I twist my hair into a bun, then stab it with a pencil to hold it in place.

"Well, don't take it out on your hair. I mean, jeez, what'd it ever do to you?" She laughs. But when I don't respond she looks at me and says, "I don't get you. Why are you always so angry? So you lost him on the freeway, and he forgot to give you his number. Big deal. I mean, when did you get so dang paranoid?"

I shake my head and turn away, knowing she's right. I am angry. And paranoid. And things far worse than that. Just your everyday, garden-variety, easily annoyed, thought-hearing, aura-seeing, spirit-sensing freak. But what she doesn't know is that there's more to the story than I'm willing to share.

Like Drina trailing us to Disneyland.

And how Damen always disappears whenever she's near.

I turn back to Riley, shaking my head as I take in her sleek shiny costume. "How long are you going to play Halloween?"

She folds her arms and pouts. "For as long as I want."

And when I see her bottom lip quiver, I feel like the world's biggest grouch.

"Look, I'm sorry," I say, grabbing my bag and slinging it over my shoulder, wishing my life would just stabilize, find some kind of balance.

"No you're not." She glares at me. "It's so obvious you're not."

"Riley, I am, really. And believe me, I don't want to fight."

She shakes her head and gazes up at the ceiling, tapping her foot against the carpeted floor.

"Are you coming?" I head for the door, but she refuses to answer. So I take a deep breath, and say, "Come on, Riley. You know I can't afford to be late. Please make up your mind."

She closes her eyes and shakes her head and when she looks at me again, her eyes have gone red. "I don't have to be here, you know!"

I grip the door handle, needing to leave yet knowing I can't, not after she's said that. "What're you talking about?"

"I mean, *here*! All of *this*! You and me. Our little visits. I don't have to *do* this."

I stare at her, my stomach curling, willing her to stop, not wanting to hear any more. I've gotten so used to her presence I never considered the alternative, that there might be someplace else she'd rather be.

"But—but I thought you liked being here?" I say, my throat tight and sore, my voice betraying my panic.

"I *do* like being here. But, well, maybe it's not the right thing. Maybe I should be somewhere *else*! Did you ever think of that?" She's looking at me, her eyes full of anguish and confusion, and even though I'm now officially late for school, there's no way I can leave.

"Riley—I—what exactly do you mean?" I ask, wishing I could rewind this whole morning and start over again.

"Well, Ava says—"

"Ava?" My eyes practically bug out of my head.

"Yeah, you know, the psychic, from the Halloween party? The one who could see me?"

I shake my head and open the door, looking over my shoulder to say, "I hate to break it to you, but Ava's a quack. A phony. A charlatan. A con artist! You shouldn't listen to a word she says. She's *crazy*!"

But Riley just shrugs, her eyes on mine. "She said some really interesting things."

And her voice bears so much pain and worry, I'll say anything to make it go away. "Listen." I peer down the hall, even though I know Sabine's no longer here. "I don't want to hear about Ava. I mean, if you want to visit her, even after everything I just told you, then fine, it's not like I can stop you. Just remember that Ava doesn't know us. And she has absolutely no right to judge us or the fact that we like to hang together. It's none of her business. It's *our* business." And when I look at her, I see that her eyes are still wide, her lip still quivering, and my heart sinks right to the floor.

"I really need to leave, so are you coming or not?" I whisper.

"Not." She glares.

So I take a deep breath, shake my head, and slam the door behind me.

Since Miles was smart enough not to hang out and wait, I drive to school alone. And even though the bell already rang, Damen is there, waiting next to his car, in the second best spot next to mine.

"Hey," he says, coming around to my side and leaning in for a kiss.

But I just grab my bag and race for the gate.

"I'm sorry I lost you yesterday. I called your cell but you didn't answer." He trails alongside me.

I grab hold of the cold iron bars and shake them as hard as I can. But when they don't even budge, I close my eyes and press my forehead against them, knowing I'm too late, it's useless.

"Did you get my message?"

I let go of the gate and head for the office, envisioning the awful moment when I'll step inside and get nailed for yesterday's ditching and today's tardy.

"What's wrong?" he asks, grabbing hold of my hand and turning my insides to warm molten liquid. "I thought we had fun. I thought you enjoyed it?"

I lean against the low brick wall and sigh. Feeling rubbery, weak, completely defenseless.

"Or were you just humoring me?" He squeezes my hand, his eyes begging me not to be mad.

And just as I start to fold, just when I've almost swallowed his bait, I drop his hand and move away. Wincing as memories of Haven, our phone call, and his strange disappearance on the freeway rush over me like a tidal wave. "Did you know Drina went to Disneyland too?" I say, and the second I say it, I realize how petty I sound. Yet now that it's out there, I may as well continue. "Is there something I should know? Something you need to tell me?" I press my lips together and brace for the worst.

But he just looks at me, gazing into my eyes as he says, "I'm not interested in Drina. I'm only interested in *you*."

I stare at the ground, wanting to believe, wishing it were only that easy. But when he takes my hand again, I realize it *is* that easy, because all of my doubts just slip right away.

"So now's the part when you tell me you feel the same way," he says, gazing at me.

I hesitate, my heartbeat so severe I'm sure he can hear it. But when I pause for too long, the moment flees, and he slips his arm around my waist and leads me back to the gate.

"That's okay." He smiles. "Take your time. There's no rush, no expiration date." He laughs. "But for now, let's get you to class."

"But we have to go through the office." I stop in my tracks and squint at him. "The gate's locked, remember?"

He shakes his head. "Ever, the gate's not locked."

"Uh, sorry, but I just tried to open it. It's locked," I remind him.

He smiles. "Will you trust me?"

I look at him.

"What's it going to cost you? A few steps? Some additional tardy minutes?"

I glance between the office and him, then I shake my head and follow, all the way back to the gate that is somehow, inexplicably open.

"But I saw it! And you saw it too!" I face him, not understanding how any of this could have happened. "I even shook them, as hard as I could, and they wouldn't budge an inch."

But he just kisses my cheek and ushers me through, laughing as he says, "Go on. And don't worry, Mr. Robins is incapacitated and the sub's in a daze. You'll be fine."

"You're not coming?" I ask, that needy, panicky feeling building inside me again.

But he just shrugs. "I'm emancipated. I do what I want."

"Yeah, but—" I stop, realizing his phone number's not the only thing missing. I barely even know this guy. And I can't help but wonder how he can possibly make me feel so good, so normal, when everything about him is so *abnormal.* Though it's not until I've turned away that I realize he's yet to explain what happened on the freeway last night.

But before I can ask he's right there beside me, taking my hand as he says, "My neighbor called. My sprinklers failed and my yard was flooding. I tried to get your attention but you were on the phone, and I didn't want to bother you."

I gaze down at our hands, bronze and pale, strong and frail, such an unlikely pair.

"Now go. I'll see you after school, I promise." He smiles, plucking a single red tulip from the back of my ear.

Usually, I try not to dwell on my old life. I try not to think about my old house, my old friends, my old family, my old self. And even though I've gotten pretty good at heading off that particular storm, recognizing the signs—the stinging eyes, the shortness of breath, the overwhelming feeling of hollowness and despair—before they can take hold, sometimes it just hits, without warning, without time to prepare. And all I can do when that happens is curl up in a ball and wait for it to pass.

Which is pretty hard to do in the middle of history class.

So while Mr. Munoz is going on and on about Napoleon, my throat closes, my stomach clenches, and my eyes start to sear so abruptly, I bolt from my seat and race for the door, oblivious to the sound of my teacher calling me back, immune to my classmates' derisive laugh.

I turn the corner, blinded by tears, gasping for air, my insides feeling empty, cleaned out, a hollow shell folding in on itself. And by the time I see Stacia it's way too late, and I knock her with such speed and force she crashes to the ground and rips a hole in her dress.

"What *the—*" She gapes at her splayed limbs and torn dress, before leveling her gaze right on me. "You *fucking* ripped it, you *freak!*" She pokes her fist through the tear, displaying the damage.

And even though I feel bad for what happened, there's no time to help. The grief is about to consume me and I can't let her see.

I start to brush past her just as she grabs hold of my arm and struggles to stand, the touch of her skin infusing me with such dark dismal energy it robs me of breath.

"For your information, this dress is *designer*. Which means *you* are going to replace it," she says, fingers squeezing so tight, I fear I might faint. "And trust me, it doesn't stop there." She shakes her head and glares. "You are gonna be so fucking sorry you ran into me, you're gonna wish you *never* came to this school."

"Like Kendra?" I say, my stance suddenly steady, my stomach settling into a much calmer state.

She loosens her grip but doesn't let go.

"You planted those drugs in her locker. You got her expelled, destroyed her credibility so they'd believe you and not her," I say, transcribing the scene in my head.

She drops my arm and takes a step back, the color draining from her face as she says, "Who told you that? You didn't even go here when that happened."

I shrug, knowing that's true, though it's hardly the point. "Oh, and there's more," I say, advancing on her, my own personal storm having passed, my overwhelming grief miraculously cured by the fear in her eyes. "I know you cheat on tests, steal from your parents, clothing stores, your friends—it's all fair game as far as you're concerned. I know you record Honor's phone calls and keep a file of her e-mails and text messages in case she ever decides to turn on you. I know that you flirt with her stepdad, which, by the way, is totally disgusting, but unfortunately it gets much worse than that. I know all about Mr. Barnes—Barnum? Whatever, you know who I mean, your ninth-grade history teacher? The one you tried to seduce? And when he wouldn't bite you tried to blackmail him instead, threatening to tell the school principal and his poor pregnant wife . . ." I shake my head in disgust, her behavior so squalid, so self-serving, it hardly seems real.

And yet, there she is, standing before me, eyes wide, lips trembling, stunned to have all of her dirty little secrets revealed. And instead of feeling bad or guilty for exposing her, for using my *gift* in this way, seeing this despicable person, this awful selfish bully who's taunted me since my very first day, reduced to a shaky, sweaty mess, is more gratifying than I ever would've imagined. And with my nausea and grief now merely a memory, I figure, *what the heck,* I may as well continue.

"Should I go on?" I ask. "Because believe me, I can. There's plenty more, but you already know that, don't you?"

I go after her, me walking forward, her stumbling backward, eager to put as much distance between us as she possibly can.

"What are you? Some kind of witch?" she whispers, eyes scanning the corridor, looking for help, an exit, anything to get away from me.

I laugh. Not admitting, not denying, just wanting her to think twice before she messes with me again.

But just as quickly she stops, finds her footing, and looks me in the eye when she says, "Then again, it's your word against mine." Her lips curve into a grin. "And who do you think people will believe? *Me,* the most popular girl in the junior class? Or *you,* the biggest fucking freak that ever came to this school?"

She has a point.

She fingers the hole in her dress, then shakes her head, and says, "Stay away from me, *freak*. Because if you don't, I swear to God you'll regret it."

And when she steps forward, she slams into my shoulder so hard, I've no doubt she means it.

When I get to the lunch table I try not to gawk, but Haven's hair is purple and I'm not sure if I should mention it.

"Don't even try to pretend you don't see it. It's awful, I know." She laughs. "Right after I hung up with you last night I tried to dye it red, you know, that gorgeous coppery shade like Drina's? Only this is what I ended up with." She grabs a chunk of it and scowls. "I look like an eggplant on a stick. But only for a few more hours, 'cuz after school, Drina's taking me to some big celebrity salon up in L.A. You know, one of those A-list hot spots booked a full year in advance? Only she was totally able to sneak me in last minute. I swear, she is *so* connected, she's amazing."

"Where's Miles?" I ask, cutting her off, not wanting to hear another word about the *amazing* Drina and her velvet rope–crashing abilities.

"Memorizing his lines. Community theater's doing a production of *Hairspray,* and he's hoping for the lead."

"Isn't the lead a girl?" I open my lunch pack, finding half a sandwich, a cluster of grapes, a bag of chips, and more tulips.

She shrugs. "He tried to convince me to try out too, but it's so not my thing. So, where's tall, dark, and hot, a.k.a. your boyfriend?" she asks, unfolding her napkin, and using it as a placemat for her strawberry-sprinkle cupcake.

I shrug, remembering how, yet again, I forgot to secure his number, or find out where he lives. "Enjoying the perks of emancipation I guess," I finally say, unwrapping my sandwich and taking a bite. "Any news on Evangeline?"

She shakes her head. "None. But check this out." She raises her sleeve, showing me the underside of her wrist.

I squint at the beginnings of a small circular tattoo, a rough sketch of a snake eating its tail. And even though it's far from complete, for the briefest moment, I actually see it slither and move. But as soon as I blink, it's stagnant again.

"What is that?" I whisper, noticing how the energy it emanates fills me with dread, though I can't fathom why.

"It's supposed to be a surprise. I'll show you when it's finished." She smiles. "In fact, I shouldn't have even told you." She adjusts her sleeve and glances around. "I mean, I promised I wouldn't. I guess I'm just too excited, and sometimes I suck at keeping secrets. Especially my own."

I look at her, trying to tune into her energy, find some logical reason for why my stomach should feel as awful as it does, but I come up empty. "Promised who? What's going on?" I ask, noticing how her aura is a dull charcoal gray, its edges loose and frayed all around.

But she just laughs and pretends to zip her lips shut. "Forget it," she says. "You'll just have to wait."

eighteen

When I get home from school, Damen is waiting on the front steps, smiling in a way that clears the sky of clouds and erases all doubts.

"How'd you get past the gate guard?" I ask, knowing for a fact that I didn't call him in.

"Charm and an expensive car works every time." He laughs, brushing the seat of his dark designer jeans and following me inside. "So, how was your day?"

I shrug, knowing I'm breaking the most fundamental rule of all—never invite a stranger inside—even if this stranger is supposedly my boyfriend. "You know, the usual routine," I finally say. "The substitute vowed to never return, Ms. Machado asked *me* to never return—" I glance at him, tempted to keep making stuff up since it's clear he's not listening. Because even though he nods like he is, his gaze is preoccupied, distant.

I head for the kitchen, poke my head in the fridge, and ask, "What about you? What'd you do?" Then I hold up a bottle of water in offering, but he shakes his head and sips his red drink.

"Went for a drive, surfed, waited for the bell to ring so I could see you again." He smiles.

"You know you could've just gone to school and then you wouldn't have had to wait for anything," I say.

"I'll try to remember that tomorrow." He laughs.

I lean against the counter, twisting the cap on my bottle around and around, nervous about being alone with him in this big empty house, with so many unanswered questions and no idea where to begin.

"You wanna go outside and hang by the pool?" I finally say, thinking the fresh air and open space might calm my nerves.

But he shakes his head and takes my hand. "I'd rather go upstairs, and check out your room."

"How do you know it's upstairs?" I ask, squinting at him.

But he just laughs. "Aren't they always?"

I hesitate, wavering between allowing this to happen and finding a polite way to evict him.

But when he squeezes my hand and says, "Come on, I promise not to bite," his smile is so irresistible, his touch so warm and inviting, that my only hope as I lead him upstairs is that Riley won't be there.

The moment we reach the top of the stairs, she runs from the den and calls, "Omigod, I am *so* sorry! I so don't want to fight with—*oops!*" She stops short and gapes, her eyes wide as Frisbees, darting between us.

But I just continue toward my room as though I didn't even see her, hoping she'll have the good sense to disappear until later. Much later.

"Looks like you left your TV on," Damen says, going into the den, while I glare at Riley who's skipping alongside him, looking him up and down, and giving him two very enthusiastic thumbs up.

And even though I beg her with my eyes to leave, she

plops right down on the couch and places her feet on his knees.

I storm into the bathroom, furious with her for not taking the hint, for overstaying her visit and refusing to split, knowing it's just a matter of time before she does something crazy, something I can never explain. So I yank off my sweatshirt and race through my routine, brushing my teeth with one hand, rolling deodorant with the other, spitting into the sink just seconds before pulling on a clean white tee. Then I ditch the ponytail, smear on some lip balm, spritz some perfume, and rush out the door, only to find Riley still there, peering into his ears.

"Let me show you the balcony, the view's amazing," I say, anxious to remove him from Riley.

But he just shakes his head and says, "Later." Patting the cushion beside him as Riley jumps up and cheers.

I watch as he sits there, innocent, unaware, trusting he's got the couch to himself, when the truth is, that prick in his ear, that itch on his knee, that chill on his neck, is courtesy of my dead little sister.

"Um, I left my water in the bathroom," I say, looking pointedly at Riley and turning to leave, thinking she'll follow if she knows what's good for her.

But Damen stands up and says, "Allow me."

And I watch as he maneuvers between the couch and table in such a way that clearly *avoids* Riley's dangling legs.

Then she gapes at me, and I gawk at her, and the next thing I know she's disappeared.

"All set," Damen says, tossing me the bottle and moving freely through the space that, just a moment ago, he navigated so carefully. And when he catches me gawking, he smiles and says, "What?"

But I just shake my head and stare at the TV, telling myself it was merely a coincidence. That there's no possible way he could've seen her.

"So would you please just explain how you do it?"

We're sitting outside, curled up on the lounge chair, having just devoured almost an entire pizza, most of which was eaten by me, since Damen eats more like a supermodel than a guy. You know—pick, pick—move the food around—take a bite—pick some more, but mostly he just sipped his drink.

"Do what?" he asks, arms wrapped loosely around me, chin resting on my shoulder.

"Do *everything*! Seriously. You never do homework, yet you know all the answers, you pick up a brush, dip it in paint, and voilà, the next thing you know you've created a Picasso that's even better than Picasso! Are you bad at sports? Painfully uncoordinated? Come on, tell me!"

He sighs. "Well, I've never been much good at baseball," he says, pressing his lips to my ear. "But I am a world-class soccer player, and I'm fairly skilled at surfing, if I say so myself."

"Must be music, then. Got a tin ear?"

"Bring me a guitar and I'll strum you a tune. Or even a piano, violin, or saxophone will do."

"Then what is it? Come on, everyone sucks at something! Tell me what you're bad at."

"Why do you want to know this?" he asks, pulling me closer. "Why do you want to wreck this perfect illusion you have of me?"

"Because I hate feeling so pale and meager in comparison. Seriously, I'm so mediocre in so many ways, and I just want to know that you suck at something too. Come on, it'll make me feel better."

"You're not mediocre," he says, his nose in my hair, his voice far too serious.

But I refuse to give up, I need something to go on, something that'll humanize him, if only a little. "Just one thing, please? Even if you have to lie, it's for a good cause—my self-esteem."

I try to turn so that I can see him, but he grips me tighter and holds me in place, kissing the tip of my ear as he whispers, "You really want to know?"

I nod, my heart beating wildly, my blood pulsing electric.

"I suck at love."

I stare into the firepit, wondering what he could possibly mean. And even though I seriously wanted him to answer, that doesn't mean I wanted him to answer so seriously. "Um, care to elaborate?" I ask, laughing nervously, not sure if I really do want to hear it. Fearing it might have something to do with Drina—a subject I'd rather avoid.

He presses against me, his breath drawn out and deep. And he stays like that for so long I wonder if he's ever going to speak. But when he finally does, he says, "I just always end up—disappointing." He shrugs, refusing to explain any further.

"But you're only seventeen." I move out of his arms and face him.

He shrugs.

"So how many *disappointments* could there be?"

But instead of answering, he turns me back around and brings his lips to my ear, whispering, "Let's go for a swim."

One more sign of how perfect Damen is—he keeps a pair of trunks in his car.

"Hey, this is California, you never know when you'll need them," he says, standing at the edge of the pool and smiling at me. "Got a wet suit in the trunk too; should I get it?"

"I can't answer that," I say, wading in the deep end, steam rising up all around. "You just have to see for yourself."

He inches toward the very edge and pretends to dip his big toe.

"No testing, only jumping," I scold.

"May I dive?"

"Cannonball, belly flop, whatever." I laugh, watching as he executes the most gorgeous arcing dive, before popping up beside me.

"Perfect," he says, his hair slicked back, his skin wet and glistening, as tiny drops of water cling to his lashes. And just when I think he's going to kiss me, he ducks back under the water and swims away.

So I take a deep breath, swallow my pride, and follow.

"Much better," he says, holding me close.

"Scared of the deep end?" I smile, my toes barely touching the bottom.

"I was referring to your outfit. You should dress like this more often."

I gaze down at my white body in my white bikini and try not to feel overly insecure next to his perfectly sculpted, bronzed self.

"Definitely a big improvement over the hoodies and jeans." He laughs.

I press my lips together, unsure of what to say.

"But I guess you gotta do what you gotta do, *right?*"

I search his face. Something about the way he just said that seemed like he meant something more, like he might actually know why I dress the way I do.

He smiles. "Obviously it protects you from the wrath of Stacia and Honor. They're not too keen on competition." He tucks my hair behind my ear and smoothes the side of my face.

"Are we competing?" I ask, remembering the flirting, the rosebud retrieving, our brawl today at school, the threat I've no doubt she'll make good on. Watching as he looks at me for the longest time, so long that my mood has changed, and I move away.

"Ever, there was never any contest," he says, following me.

But I duck underwater and swim toward the ledge, grabbing hold and wriggling out, knowing I need to act fast if I'm going to have my say, because the moment he comes near, the words will evaporate.

"How can I possibly know anything when you run so hot and cold?" I say, my hands trembling, my voice shaky, wishing I could just stop, let it go, reclaim the nice, romantic evening we were having. But knowing this needed to be said, despite whatever consequences it brought. "I mean, one minute you're gazing at me in—in that way that you do—and the next thing I know you're all over Stacia." I press my lips together and wait for him to respond, watching as he climbs out of the pool and moves toward me, so gorgeous, wet, and glistening. I fight to catch my breath.

"Ever, I—" He closes his eyes and sighs. And when he opens them again, he takes another step toward me and says, "It was never my intention to hurt you. Truly. Never." He slides his arms around me and tries to make me face him. And when I do, when I finally give in, he looks into my eyes and says, "Not once did I set out to hurt you. And I'm sorry if you feel that I played with your feelings. I told you I'm not so good at this sort of thing." He smiles, burying his fingers in my wet hair, before coming away with a single red tulip.

I stare at him, taking in his strong shoulders, defined chest, washboard abs, and bare hands. No sleeves for hiding things under, no pockets to stow anything in. Just his glorious half-naked body, dripping-wet swim trunks, and that stupid red tulip in hand.

"How do you do it?" I ask, holding my breath, knowing damn well it didn't come from my ear.

"Do what?" He smiles, his arms encircling my waist, pulling me closer.

"The tulips, the rosebuds, all of it?" I whisper, trying to ignore the feel of his hands on my skin, how his touch makes me warm, sleepy, verging on dizzy.

"It's magic." He smiles.

I pull away and reach for a towel, wrapping it tightly around me. "Why can't you ever be serious?" I ask, wondering what I've gotten myself into, and if there's still time to retreat.

"I am serious," he mumbles, pulling on his T-shirt and reaching for his keys as I shiver in my cold damp towel, watching speechless as he heads for the gate, waves over his shoulder, and calls, "Sabine's home," before blending into the night.

nineteen

The next day, when I pull into the parking lot, Damen's not there. And as I climb out of my car, sling my bag over my shoulder, and head for class, I give myself a pep talk and prepare for the worst.

But the moment I reach the classroom, I'm completely immobile. Staring stupidly at the green painted door, unable to open it.

Since my psychic abilities evaporate wherever Damen's concerned, the only thing I can actually *see* is the nightmare I craft in my head. The one where Damen's perched on the edge of Stacia's desk, laughing and flirting, retrieving rosebuds from all manner of places, as I slump by and head for my seat, the warm sweet flicker of his gaze skimming right over me as he turns his back so he can focus on *her.*

And I just can't go through with it. I seriously can't bear it. Because even though Stacia's cruel, mean, horrible, and sadistic, she happens to be cruel, mean, horrible, and sadistic in a straightforward way. Holding no secrets, cloaking no mysteries, her unkindness is out there, clearly displayed.

While I'm just the opposite: paranoid, secretive, lurking behind sunglasses and a hoodie, and hoarding a burden so heavy there's nothing simple about me.

I reach for the handle again, scolding myself: *This is ridiculous. What are you gonna do—drop out of school? You've got another year and a half to deal with this, so just suck it up and go inside already!*

But my hand starts to shake, refusing to obey, and just as I'm about to make a run for it, this kid comes up from behind, clears his throat, and says, "Uh—you gonna open that?" Completing the question in his head with an unspoken—*You fuckin' freak!*

So I take a deep breath, open the door, and slink right inside. Feeling worse than I ever could've imagined, when I see Damen's not there.

The second I enter the lunch area, I scan all the tables, searching for Damen, but when I don't see him, I head for my usual spot, arriving at the same time as Haven.

"Day six and no word on Evangeline," she says, dropping her cupcake box on the table before her and sitting across from me.

"Have you asked around the anonymous group?" Miles slides in beside me and twists the cap off his VitaminWater.

Haven rolls her eyes. "They're *anonymous,* Miles."

Miles rolls his eyes. "I was referring to her *mentor.*"

"They're called *sponsors.* And yeah, she's no help, hasn't heard a thing. Drina thinks I'm overreacting though, says I'm making way too big a deal."

"She still here?" Miles peers at her.

My eyes dart between them, alerted by the edge in his voice and waiting for more. Since most everything to do with Damen and Drina is psychically off limits, I'm as curious to hear the answer as he is.

"Um, yeah, Miles, she *lives* here now. Why? Is that a problem?" She narrows her eyes.

Miles shrugs and sips his drink. "No problem." Though his thoughts say otherwise and his yellow aura turns dark and opaque as he struggles with saying what he wants, versus not saying anything at all. "There's just . . ." he starts.

"Just what?" She stares at him, eyes narrowed, lips pinched.

"Well . . ."

I stare at him, thinking: *Do it, Miles, say it! Drina's arrogant, awful, a bad influence, pure trouble. You're not the only one who sees it, I see it too, so go ahead and say it—she's the worst!*

He hesitates, the words forming on his tongue as I suck in my breath, anticipating their release. Then he exhales loudly, shakes his head, and says, "Never mind."

I glance at Haven, seeing her enraged face, her aura flaring, the edges sparking and flaming all around, forecasting a major meltdown scheduled to start in just *three-two-one—*

"Excuse me, Miles, but I'm so not buying that. So if you have something to say, then just say it." She glares at him, cupcake forgotten as she drums her fingers against the fiberglass table. And when he doesn't respond, she continues. "Whatever, Miles. You too, Ever. Just because you're not saying anything doesn't make you any less guilty."

Miles peers at me, eyes wide, brow raised, and I know I should say something, do something, make a show of asking just what exactly it is that I'm guilty of. But the truth is, I already know. I'm guilty of not liking Drina. Of not trusting her. Of sensing something suspicious, sinister even. And not doing nearly enough to hide those suspicions.

She shakes her head and rolls her eyes, and she's so upset she practically spits out the words, "You guys don't even know her! And you have no right to judge her! For your information, I happen to like Drina. And in the short time I've known her she's been a way better friend to me than either of you!"

"That's so not true!" Miles shouts, eyes blazing. "That's such total bullsh—"

"Sorry Miles, but it *is* true. You guys tolerate me, you go along with me, but you don't really get me like she does. Drina and I like the same things, we share the same interests. She doesn't secretly want me to change like you do. She likes me just as I am."

"Oh, is that why you changed your entire look, because she accepts you for who you really are?"

I watch as Haven closes her eyes and takes a slow breath, then she looks at Miles and rises from her seat, gathering her things as she says, "Whatever, Miles. Whatever, both of you."

"And now, ladies and gentlemen, behold the big dramatic exit!" Miles scowls. "I mean, are you *kidding*? All I did was ask if she was still here! That's it! And you turn it into this major ordeal. Jeez, sit down, find your happy place, and chillax already, would you?"

She shakes her head and grips the table, the small elaborate tattoo on her wrist now finished, but still red and inflamed.

"What do you call that?" I ask, gazing at the ink rendering of the snake eating its own tail, knowing there's a name for it, that it's some sort of mythical creature, but forgetting which one.

"Ouroboros." And when she rubs it with her finger I swear I saw its tongue flicker and move.

"What does it mean?"

"It's an ancient alchemy symbol for eternal life, creation out of destruction, life out of death, immortality, something like that," Miles says.

Haven and I gaze at him, but he just shrugs. "What? So I'm well read."

Then I look at her and say, "It looks infected. Maybe you should have it looked at."

But as soon as it's out I know it was the wrong thing to say, and I watch as she yanks down her sleeve, as her aura sparks and flames. "My tattoo is fine. I'm fine. And excuse me for saying so, but I can't help but notice how neither one of you is freaking out over Damen, who, by the way, never comes to school anymore. I mean, what's up with that?"

Miles gazes down at his Sidekick, and I just shrug. It's not like she doesn't have a point. And we watch as she shakes her head, snatches her cupcake box, and storms away.

"Can you tell me what just happened?" Miles says, watching her slalom through the maze of lunch tables, in a big hurry to nowhere.

But I just shrug, unable to shake the image of the snake on her wrist, how it turned its head, focused its beady eyes, and looked right at me.

The moment I pull into my drive, I see Damen, leaning against his car, smiling.

"How was school?" he asks, coming around to open my door.

I shrug and reach for my books.

"Ah, so you're still angry," he says, following me to the front door. And even though he's not touching me, I can feel his emanating heat.

"I'm not angry," I mutter, opening the door and tossing my backpack onto the floor.

"Well that's a relief. Because I've made reservations for two, and if you're not angry, then I assume you'll be joining me."

I look at him, my eyes grazing over his dark jeans, boots, and soft black sweater that can only be cashmere, wondering what he could possibly be up to now.

He removes my sunglasses and earbuds and sets them on the entryway table. "Trust me, you really don't need all those *defenses,*" he says, lowering my hood, tucking his arm through mine, and leading me out the front door and over to his car.

"Where are we going?" I ask, settling onto the passenger seat, complacent, spineless, always so eager to go along with whatever he says. "I mean, what about my homework? I have a ton of catching up to do."

But he just shakes his head and climbs in beside me. "Relax, you can do it later, I promise."

"How much later?" I peer at him, wondering if I'll ever get used to his amazing dark beauty, the warmth of his gaze, and his ability to talk me into just about anything.

He smiles, starting the car without even turning the key. "Before the stroke of midnight, I promise. Now buckle in, we're going for a ride."

Damen drives fast. Really fast. So when he pulls into the parking lot and leaves his car with the valet, it seems as though only a few minutes have passed.

"Where are we?" I ask, gazing at the green buildings and the sign marked EAST ENTRANCE. "East entrance to what?"

"Well, this should explain it." He laughs, pulling me toward him as four shiny sweaty Thoroughbreds trot by with their grooms, followed by a jockey in a pink-and-green jacket, thin white pants, and muddy black boots.

"The racetrack?" I gape. Like Disneyland, it's pretty much the last place I expected.

"Not just any racetrack, it's Santa Anita," he nods. "One of the nicer ones. Now come on, we've got a three-fifteen reservation at the FrontRunner."

"The *what*?" I ask, standing my ground.

"Relax, it's just a restaurant." He laughs. "Now, come on, I don't want to miss post."

"Um, isn't this illegal?" I say, knowing I sound like the worst kind of goody-good, but still, he's just so—lawless and reckless and—*random*.

"Eating is illegal?" He smiles, but I can tell his patience is running thin.

I shake my head. "Betting, gambling, whatever, *you know.*"

But he just laughs and shakes his head. "It's horse racing, Ever, not cockfighting. Now come on." He squeezes my hand and leads me to the elevator bank.

"But don't you have to be twenty-one?"

"Eighteen," he mumbles, going inside and pressing *five.*

"Exactly. I'm sixteen and a half."

He shakes his head and leans in to kiss me. "Rules should always be bent, if not broken. It's the only way to have any fun. Now come," he says, leading me down a hall and into a large room decorated in varying shades of green, stopping before the front podium and greeting the maitre d' like a long lost friend.

"Ah, Mr. Auguste, so wonderful to see you! Your table is ready, follow me."

Damen nods and takes my hand, leading me through a room full of couples, retirees, single men, groups of women, a father and his young son—not an empty seat in the house. Eventually stopping at a table just across from the finish line, with a beautiful view of the track and the green hills beyond.

"Tony will be right over to take your orders. Should I bring you champagne?"

Damen glances at me then shakes his head. His face flushing slightly when he says, "Not today."

"Very well then, five minutes 'til post."

"Champagne?" I whisper, raising my brows, but he just shrugs and unfolds his racing program.

"What do you think about Spanish Fly?" He looks at me. Smiling when he says, "The horse, not the aphrodisiac."

But I'm too busy gazing around to answer, struggling to take it all in. Because this room is not only huge, but it's also completely full—in the middle of the week—the middle of the day even. All these people playing hooky and betting. It's like a whole other world I never knew existed. And I can't help but wonder if this is where he spends all his free time.

"So what do you say? You wanna bet?" He glances at me briefly, before making a series of notes with his pen.

I shake my head. "I wouldn't even know where to begin."

"Well, I could give you the whole lowdown on odds, percentages, stats, and who sired who. But since we're short on time, why don't you just look this over, and tell me what you *feel*, which names you're drawn to. It's always worked for me." He smiles.

He tosses me the racing form and I look it over, surprised to find three distinct names jump out at me, in a one-two-three order. "How about Spanish Fly to win, Acapulco Lucy second, and

Son of Buddha third," I say, having no idea how I got there, but feeling pretty confident in my picks.

"Lucy to place, Buddha to show," he mumbles, scribbling it down. "And how much would you like to wager on that? Minimum bet's two, but you can certainly go higher."

"Two's good," I say, suddenly losing confidence and unwilling to empty my wallet on a whim.

"You sure?" he asks, looking disappointed.

I nod.

"Well, I think you've got some sound picks so I'm betting five. No, make that ten."

"Don't bet ten," I say, pressing my lips. "I mean, I just picked 'em, I don't even know why."

"Looks like we're about to find out," he says, standing as I reach for my wallet. But he just waves it away. "You can reimburse me when you collect your winnings. I'm going to post. If the waiter comes by, order whatever you want."

"What should I get for you?" I call, but he moves so fast he doesn't even hear me.

By the time he returns, the horses are all in the gate, and when the shot goes off, they bolt from their stalls. At first appearing like shiny dark blurs, as they take the corner and race for the finish, I spring from my seat, watching as my three favorite picks jockey for position, then jumping and shouting and screaming with glee when they all cross the finish in my perfect one-two-three.

"Omigod, we won! We won!" I say, smiling as Damen leans in to kiss me. "Is it always this exciting?" I gaze down at the track, watching as Spanish Fly trots into the winner's circle and gets draped with flowers, preparing for his photo op.

"Pretty much." Damen nods. "Though there's nothing like that first big win, that's always the best."

"Well, I'm not sure how big it will be," I say, wishing I'd had a little more faith in my abilities, at least enough to broaden the stakes.

He frowns. "Well, since you only bet two, I'm afraid you won somewhere around eight."

"Eight dollars?" I squint, more than a little disappointed.

"Eight hundred." He laughs. "Or, eight hundred and eighty dollars and sixty cents to be exact. You won a trifecta, meaning win, place, and show, in that exact order."

"All that on just two *dollars*?" I say, suddenly knowing why he has a regular table.

He nods.

"What about you? What did you win?" I ask. "Did you bet the same as me?"

He smiles. "As it just so happens I lost. I lost big. I got a little greedy and went for the superfecta, which means I added a pony that didn't quite make it. But don't worry, I plan to make up for it on the next race."

And did he ever. Because when we went to the window, after the eighth and final race, I collected a total of one thousand six hundred and forty-five dollars and eighty cents, while Damen pocketed significantly more, having won the Super High Five, meaning he picked all five horses in the exact order they finished. And since he was the only one to have done so, for the last several days, he won five hundred and thirty-six *thousand* dollars and forty-one cents—all on a ten-dollar bet.

"So what do you think of the races?" He asks, his arm tucked around mine as he leads me outside.

"Well, now I get why you're not all that into school. I guess it can't really compete, can it?" I laugh, still feeling high from my winnings, thinking I've finally found a profitable outlet for my psychic *gift*.

"Come on, I want to buy you something to celebrate my big win," he says, leading me into the gift shop.

"No, you don't have to—" I start.

But he squeezes my hand, his lips on my ear as he says, "I insist. Besides, I think I can afford it. But there's one condition."

I look at him.

"Absolutely no sweatshirts or hoodies." He laughs. "But anything else, just say the word."

After joking around and insisting on a jockey cap, a model horse, and a huge bronze horseshoe to hang on my bedroom wall, we settle on a silver horse-bit bracelet instead. But only after I made sure that the crystal bits were really just crystal, not diamonds, because that would be too much, no matter how much money he won.

"This way, no matter what happens, you'll never forget this day," he says, closing the clasp on my wrist as we wait for the valet to bring us the car.

"How could I possibly forget?" I ask, gazing at my wrist, then at him.

But he just shrugs as he climbs in beside me and there's something so sad, so bereft in his eyes, I hope that's the one thing I do forget.

Unfortunately, the ride home seems even quicker than the one to the track and when he pulls into my driveway, I realize how reluctant I am for the day to end.

"Would you look at that?" he says, motioning to the clock on his dash. "Well before midnight, just like I promised." And when he leans in to kiss me, I kiss him back with so much enthusiasm I practically pull him onto my seat.

"Can I come in?" he whispers, tempting me with his lips as they make their way down my ear, my neck, and all along my collarbone.

And I surprise myself by pushing him away and shaking my head. Not just because Sabine's inside and I have homework to do, but because I need to get a backbone already, stop giving in to him so dang easily.

"I'll see you at school," I say, climbing out of his car, before he can change my mind. "You remember, Bay View? That high school you used to attend?"

He averts his gaze and sighs.

"Don't tell me you're ditching—*again?*"

"School is so dreadfully boring. I don't know how you do it."

"You don't know how *I* do it?" I shake my head and glance toward the house, seeing Sabine peek through the blinds and then pulling away. Then I turn back to Damen and say, "Well, I guess I do it the same way you used to do it. You know, you get up, get dressed, and just go. And sometimes, if you pay attention, you actually learn a thing or two while you're there." But the second it's out of my mouth, I know it's a lie. Because the truth is, I haven't learned a damn thing all year. I mean, it's hard to actually learn anything when you just sort of *know* everything instead. Though it's not like I share that with him.

"There's got to be a better way," he groans, his eyes wide, pleading with mine.

"Well, just for the record, truancy and dropping out? *Not* a better way. Not if you want to go to college, and make something of your life." More lies. Because with a few more days like that at the track, one could live very well. Better than well.

But he just laughs. "Fine. We'll play it your way. For now. See you tomorrow, Ever."

And I've barely made it through the front door when he's already driven away.

twenty

The next morning, as I'm getting ready for school, Riley's perched on my dresser, dressed as Wonder Woman, and spilling celebrity secrets. Having grown bored with watching the everyday antics of old neighbors and friends, she's set her sights on Hollywood, which allows her to dish the dirt better than any supermarket tabloid.

"No *way*!" I gape at her. "I can't believe it! Miles will flip when he hears this!"

"You have no idea." She shakes her head, her black curls bouncing from side to side, looking jaded, world weary, like one who's seen too much—and then some. "*Nothing's* what it seems. Seriously. It's just one big illusion, as fake as the movies they make. And believe me, those publicists work their butts off keeping all of their dirty little secrets—*secret*."

"Who else have you spied on?" I ask, eager to hear more. Wondering why it never occurred to me to try to tune in to their energies while I'm watching TV or flipping through a magazine. "What about—"

I'm just about to ask if the rumors about my favorite actress are true, when Sabine pokes her head in my room and says, "What about what?"

I glance at Riley, seeing she's bent over laughing, and clear my throat as I say, "Um, nothing, I didn't say anything."

Sabine gives me an odd look, as Riley shakes her head and says, "Good one, Ever. *Real* convincing."

"Did you need something?" I ask, turning my back on Riley and focusing on the real purpose behind Sabine's visit—she's been invited away for the weekend and isn't sure how to tell me.

She walks into my room, her posture too straight, her gait unnaturally stiff, then she takes a deep breath and sits on the edge of my bed, her fingers nervously picking at a loose thread on my blue cotton duvet as she considers just how to broach it. "Jeff invited me away for the weekend." She merges her brows. "But I thought I should run it by you first."

"Who's Jeff?" I ask, inserting my earrings and turning to look at her. Because even though I already know, I still feel like I should still ask.

"You met him at the party. He came as Frankenstein." She glances at me, her mind clouded with guilt, feeling like a negligent guardian, a bad role model, though it hasn't affected her aura, which is still a bright happy pink.

I cram my books into my backpack, stalling for time, as I decide what to do. On the one hand, Jeff isn't the guy she thinks. Not even close. Though from what I can *see,* he truly does like her and means her no harm. And it's been so long since I've seen her happy like this, I can't bear to tell her. Besides, how would I even go about it?

Um, excuse me, but that Jeff guy? Mr. Swanky Investment Banker? So not the man you think he is. In fact, he still lives with his mom! Just don't ask how I know what I know—just trust that I know.

No. Uh-uh. Can't do it. Besides, relationships have a way of working themselves out—in their own way—in their own good time. And it's not like I don't have my own relationship issues to deal with. I mean, now that things are starting to stabilize with Damen, now that we're growing closer and I'm feeling more like a couple, I've been thinking that maybe it's time I stop pushing him away. Maybe it's time we take the next step. And with Sabine out of town for the next couple days, well, it's an opportunity that may not come around again.

"Go! Have fun!" I finally say, trusting she'll eventually learn the truth about Jeff and move on with her life.

She smiles, with equal amounts of excitement and relief. Then she gets up from my bed and moves toward the door, pausing as she says, "We're leaving today, after work. He's got a place up in Palm Springs, and it's less than a two-hour drive, so if you need anything, we won't be too far."

Correction, his mom *has a place in Palm Springs*.

"We'll be back Sunday. And Ever, if you want to have your friends over that's fine, though—do we need to talk about that?"

I freeze, knowing exactly where this conversation is headed and wondering if she's somehow read my mind. But realizing she's just trying to be a responsible adult and fulfill her new role as "parent," I shake my head and say, "Trust me, it's all been covered."

Then I grab my bag and roll my eyes at Riley who's dancing on top of my dresser, singing, *"Par-ty! Par-ty!"*

Sabine nods, clearly relieved at having avoided the S-E-X talk almost as much as me. "See you Sunday," she says.

"Yup," I say, heading down the stairs. "See you then."

"Swear to God he's on your team," I say, pulling into the parking lot, feeling the warm, sweet tingle of Damen's gaze long before I actually see him.

"I *knew* it!" Miles nods. "I knew he was gay. I could just tell. Where'd you hear that?"

I stall, knowing there's no way I can divulge my true source, admitting that my dead little sister is now the ultimate Hollywood insider. "Um, I don't remember," I mumble, climbing out of my car. "I just know that it's true."

"What's true?" Damen asks smiling as he brings his lips to my cheek.

"Jo—" Miles starts.

But I shake my head and cut him off, unwilling to display my celebrity-obsessing shallow side so early in the game. "Nothing, we just, um, did you hear Miles is playing Tracy Turnblad in *Hairspray*?" I ask, going into a full-blown discourse of jumbled phrases and disjointed nonsense until Miles finally waves goodbye and heads off to class.

As soon as he's gone, Damen stops and says, "Hey, I have a better idea. Let's go have breakfast."

I shoot him the *you're crazy* look and continue walking, but I don't get very far before he's squeezing my hand and pulling me back.

"Come on," he says, his eyes on mine, laughing in a way that's contagious.

"We can't," I whisper, glancing around anxiously, knowing we're seconds from being late and not wanting it to get any worse. "Besides, I already had breakfast."

"Ever, please!" He drops to his knees, palms pressed together, eyes wide and pleading. "*Please* don't make me go in there. If you have any kindness at all, you won't make me do it."

I press my lips and try not to laugh. Watching my gorgeous, elegant, sophisticated boyfriend begging on his knees is a sight I never thought I'd see. But still, I just shake my head and say, "Come on, get up, bell's about to—" And I don't even finish the sentence before it's already rung.

He smiles, rising to his feet, wiping his jeans, and then tucking his arm around my waist as he says, "You know what they say, better a no-show than a tardy."

"Who's *they*?" I ask, shaking my head. "Sound more like *you*."

He shrugs. "Hmmm, maybe it is me. Nonetheless, I guarantee there are much better ways to spend a morning. Because Ever," he says, squeezing my hand, "we don't have to do this. And, *you* don't have to wear this." He removes my sunglasses and lowers my hood. "The weekend starts now."

And even though I can think of a million good and valid reasons why we absolutely should not ditch, why the weekend should wait until three o'clock just like any other Friday, when he gazes at me, his eyes are so deep and inviting, I don't think twice, I just dive right in.

Barely recognizing the sound of my own voice when I hear myself say, "Hurry before they lock the gate."

We take separate cars. Because even though it went unspoken, it's pretty obvious we have no plans to return. And as I follow Damen up the sweeping curves of Coast Highway, I gaze out at the dramatic stretch of coastline, the pristine beaches, the navy blue waters, and my heart swells with gratitude, feeling so lucky to live here, to call this amazing place home. But then I remember how I ended up here—and just like that, the thrill is gone.

He makes a quick right and I pull into the space beside him, smiling as he comes around to open my door. "Have you been here yet?" he asks.

I gaze at the white clapboard hut and shake my head.

"I know you said you weren't hungry, but their shakes are the best. You should definitely try the date malt, or the chocolate peanut butter shake, or both, it's my treat."

"Dates?" I crinkle my nose and make a face. "Um, I hate to say it, but that sounds *awful.*"

But he just laughs and pulls me toward the counter, ordering one of each, and then carrying them over to the painted blue bench where we take a seat and gaze down at the beach.

"So which one's your favorite?" he asks.

I try them each again, but they're both so thick and creamy, I remove their lids and use a spoon. "They're both really good," I say. "But surprisingly, I think I like the date one best." But when I slide it toward him so he can taste too, he shakes his head and pushes it back. And something about that small simple act pierces straight through me.

There's just something about him, something more than just the strange magic tricks and disappearing acts. I mean, for one thing, this guy *never eats.*

But no sooner have I thought it than he reaches for the straw and takes a long deep pull, and when he leans in to kiss me his lips are icy cold.

"Let's head down to the beach, shall we?"

He takes my hand and we walk along the trail, shoulders bumping into each other, as we pass the milkshakes back and forth, even though I'm doing most all of the slurping. And as we make our way down to the beach, we remove our shoes, roll up our hems, and walk along the shore, allowing the frigid water to wash over our toes and splash on our shins.

"Do you surf?" he asks, taking the empty cups and placing one inside the other.

I shake my head, and step over a pile of rocks.

"Would you like a lesson?" He smiles.

"In this water?" I head toward a bank of dry sand, my toes numb and blue from just that quick dip. "No thanks."

"Well, I was thinking we'd wear wet suits," he says, coming up behind me.

"Only if they're fur lined." I laugh, smoothing the sand with my foot, making a flat space for us to sit.

But he takes my hand and leads me away, all the way past the tide pools, and into a hidden natural cave.

"I had no idea this was here," I say, gazing around at the smooth rock walls, the recently raked sand, and the towels and surfboards piled up in the corner.

"Nobody does." He smiles. "That's why all my stuff is still here. Blends into the rock; most people walk right by without even seeing it. But then, most people live their whole lives without ever noticing what's directly in front of them."

"So how'd you find it?" I ask, settling onto the large green blanket he's laid out in the middle.

He shrugs. "I guess I'm not like most people."

He lies down beside me, then pulls me down too. Resting his cheek on the palm of his hand, he gazes at me for so long, I can't help but squirm.

"Why do you hide under those baggy jeans and hoodies?" he whispers, his fingers stroking the side of my face, pushing my hair behind my ear. "Don't you know how beautiful you are?"

I press my lips together and look away, liking the sentiment but wishing he'd stop. I don't want to go down this road of having to explain myself, defend why I am the way I am. Obviously he'd prefer the old me, but it's too late for that. That girl died and left me in her place.

A tear escapes down my cheek, and I try to turn, not wanting him to see. But he holds me tight and won't let me go, erasing my sadness with a brush of his lips before merging with mine.

"Ever," he groans, voice thick, eyes burning, shifting until he's draped right across me, the weight of his body providing the most comforting warmth that soon turns to heat.

I run my lips along the line of his jaw, the square of his chin, my breath coming in short shallow gasps as his hips press and circle with mine, eliciting all of the feelings I've fought so hard to deny. But I'm tired of fighting, tired of denying. I just want to be normal again. And what could be more normal than *this*?

I close my eyes as he removes my sweatshirt, surrendering, yielding, allowing him to unbutton my jeans and remove them too. Consenting to the press of his palm and push of his fingers, telling myself that this glorious feeling, this dreamy exuberance surging inside me could only be one thing—could only be *Love.*

But when I feel his thumbs anchored in the elastic of my panties, guiding them down, I sit up abruptly and push him away. Part of me wanting to continue, to pull him back to me—only not here, not now, not in this way.

"Ever," he whispers, his eyes searching mine. But I just shake my head and turn away, feeling his warm wonderful body mold around mine, his lips on my ear saying, "It's all right. Really. Now sleep."

"Damen?" I roll over, squinting in the dim light, as my hand explores the empty space beside me. Patting the blanket again and again, until I'm convinced he's truly not there. "Damen?" I call again, glancing around the cave, the distant sound of crashing waves the only reply.

I slip on my sweatshirt and stumble outside, staring into the fading afternoon light, scanning the beach, expecting to find him.

But when I don't see him anywhere, I head back inside, seeing the note he left on my bag, and unfolding it to read:

Gone surfing.
Be back soon.
—D

I run back outside, note still in hand, rushing up and down the shore, scanning for surfers, one in particular. But the only two out there are so blond and pale, it's clear they're not Damen.

twenty-one

When I pull into the driveway I'm surprised to see someone sitting on the front steps, but when I get closer, I'm even more surprised to see that it's Riley.

"Hey," I say, grabbing my bag and slamming the car door, a little harder than planned.

"Sheesh!" she says, shaking her head and staring at me. "I thought you were gonna run me over."

"Sorry, I thought you were Damen," I say heading for the front door.

"Oh no, what'd he do now?" She laughs.

But I just shrug and unlock the door. I'm certainly not going to fill her in on the details. "What happened, you get locked out?" I ask, leading her inside.

"Very funny." She rolls her eyes and heads into the kitchen, taking a seat at the breakfast bar as I drop my bag on the counter and stick my head in the fridge.

"So, what's up?" I glance at her, wondering why she's so quiet, thinking maybe my bad mood is contagious.

"Nothing." She rests her chin in her hand and gazes at me.

"Doesn't seem like nothing." I grab a bottle of water instead of the quart of ice cream I really want, and lean against the granite counter, noticing how her black hair is tangled, and the Wonder Woman costume more than a little droopy.

She shrugs. "So, what are you gonna do?" she asks, leaning back on the stool in a way that makes me cringe, even though she can't possibly fall and get hurt. "I mean, this is like a teen dream come true, right? House to yourself, no chaperones." She wiggles her brows in a way that seems false, like she's trying too hard to put up a good front.

I take a swig of water and shrug, part of me wanting to confide in her, unburden my secrets, the good, bad, and the completely revolting. It would be so nice to get it off my chest, not bear all this weight on my own. But when I look at her again, I remember how half her life was spent waiting to turn thirteen, viewing each passing year as the one that brought her closer to the *important* double digits. And I can't help but wonder if that's why she's here. Since I robbed her of her dream, she's left with no choice but to live it through me.

"Well, I hate to disappoint you," I finally say. "But I'm sure you've already guessed what a colossal failure I am in the teen dream department." I gaze up at her shyly, my face flushing when she nods in agreement. "All that promise I showed back in Oregon? With the friends, and the boyfriend, and the cheerleading? Gone. Kaput. O-V-E-R. And the two friends I managed to make at Bay View? Well, they're not speaking to each other. Which, unfortunately means they're barely speaking to me. And even though through some weird, unexplainable, unimaginable fluke I managed to snag a gorgeous, sexy boyfriend, well the truth is, it's not all it's cracked up to be. Because when he's not acting weird, or vanishing into thin air, well, then he's convincing me to ditch school and bet at the tracks and all sorts of sordid business like that. He's kind of a bad influence." I cringe, realizing too late that I shouldn't have shared any of that.

But when I look at her again, it's clear she's not listening. She's staring at the counter, fingers tracing the black granite swirls, as her mind wanders in some other place.

"Please don't be mad," she finally says, gazing at me with eyes so wide and somber it's like a punch in the gut. "But I spent the day with Ava."

I press my lips, thinking: *I don't want to hear this. I absolutely do not want to hear this!* I grip the counter and brace for what follows.

"I know you don't like her, but she has some good points, and she's really making me think about things. You know, the choices I've made. And, well, the more I think about it, the more I realize she just might be right."

"What could she possibly be right about?" I ask, talking past the lump in my throat, thinking this day's gone from really bad, to extremely bad and it's a long way from over.

Riley looks at me, then glances away, her fingers still tracing those random swirls, as she says, "Ava says I shouldn't be here. That I'm not *supposed* to be here."

"And what do you say?" I suck in my breath, wishing she'd stop talking and take it all back. There's no way I can lose her, not now, not ever. She's all I have left.

Her fingers stop moving as she looks up at me. "I say I like being here. I say that even though I'll never get to be a teenager, at least I can kind of live it through you. You know, vicariously."

And even though her comment makes me feel guilty and horrible, and confirms all my thoughts, I try to lighten the load when I say, "Jeez, Riley, you couldn't have picked a worse example."

She rolls her eyes and groans. "Tell me." But even though she laughs, the light in her eyes is quickly extinguished when she says,

"But what if she's right? I mean, what if it *is* wrong for me to be here all the time?"

"Riley—" I start, but then the doorbell rings, and when I glance at her again, she's gone. "Riley!" I yell, gazing around the kitchen. "Riley!" I shout, hoping she'll reappear. I can't leave it like that. I refuse to leave it like that. But the more I shout, yell, and scream for her to return, the more I realize I'm shouting at air.

And as the doorbell continues to ring, one time, followed by two, I know Haven's outside, and I need to let her in.

"The gate guard waved me through," she says, storming into the house, her face a mess of mascara and tears, her newly red hair a tangled-up mess. "They found Evangeline. She's dead."

"What? Are you sure?" I start to shut the door behind her when Damen drives up, leaps from his car, and runs toward us. "Evangeline—" I start, so shocked by the news I've forgotten I've decided to hate him.

He nods and moves toward Haven, peering at her as he says, "Are you okay?"

She shakes her head and wipes her face. "Yeah, I mean, it's not like I knew her all that well, we only hung out a few times, but still. It's *so* awful, and the fact that I may have been the last one to see her . . ."

"Surely you weren't the *last* to see her."

I gape at Damen, wondering if he meant it as some kind of sick joke, but his face is deadly serious, and his gaze far away.

"I just—I just feel so responsible," she mumbles, burying her face in her hands, groaning *oh God, oh God, oh God,* over and over again.

I move toward her, wanting to comfort her in some way, but then she lifts her head, wipes her eyes, and says, "I—I just thought you should know, but I should get going, I need to get to Drina's." She raises her hand and jangles her keys.

Hearing her say that is like fuel for the fire, and I narrow my eyes at Damen, staring accusingly. Because even though Haven's friendship with Drina seems like a fluke, I'm sure that it isn't. I can't shake the feeling it's somehow connected.

But Damen ignores me as he grabs Haven's arm and peers at her wrist. "Where'd you get that?" he says, his voice tight, controlled, but with an undercurrent of edge, reluctantly letting go as she yanks free and covers it with her hand.

"It's fine," she says, clearly annoyed. "Drina gave me something to put on it, some salve, said it would take about three days to work."

Damen clenches his jaw so tight his teeth gnash together. "Do you happen to have it with you? This—*salve*?"

She shakes her head and moves for the door. "No, I left it at home. I mean, jeez, what's with you guys, anyway? Any more questions?" She turns, her eyes darting between us, her aura a bright flaming red. "Because I don't appreciate being interrogated like this. I mean, the only reason I stopped by in the first place was because I thought you might want to know about Evangeline, but since all you want to do is gawk at my tattoo and make stupid comments, I think I'll just go." She storms toward her car.

And even though I call after her, she just shakes her head and ignores me. And I can't help but wonder what happened to my friend. She's so moody, so distant, and I realize she's been lost to me for a while now. Ever since she met Drina, I feel like I hardly even know her.

I watch as she gets in her car, slams the door, and backs down the drive. Then I turn to Damen and say, "Well, that was pleasant. Evangeline's dead, Haven hates me, and you left me alone in a cave. I hope you at least caught some *killer* waves." I fold my arms across my chest and shake my head.

"As a matter of fact, I did," he says, gazing at me intently. "And when I returned to the cave I saw you had left and I raced right over."

I look at him, my eyes narrowed, my lips pressed together. I can't believe he actually expects me to believe that. "Sorry, but I looked, and there were only two surfers out there. Two *blond* surfers, which pretty much rules out either one of them being you."

"Ever, would you look at me?" he says. "*Really* look at me. How do you think I got this way?"

So I do, I lower my glare to take it all in. Noticing his wet suit that's dripping salt water all over the floor.

"But I checked. I ran up and down the beach, I looked *everywhere*," I say, convinced of what I saw, or in this case, *didn't* see.

But he just shrugs. "Ever, I don't know what to tell you, but I didn't abandon you. I was surfing. *Really.* Now, can you please get me a towel, and maybe another for the floor?"

We head into the backyard so he can hose down his wet suit, while I sit on the lounge chair and watch him. I was so sure he'd ditched me. I looked everywhere. But maybe I did miss him. I mean, it *is* a long beach. And I *was* really angry.

"So how'd you know about Evangeline?" I ask, watching as he drapes his wet suit over the outdoor bar, unwilling to let go of my anger quite so easily. "And what's up with Drina and Haven and that creepy tattoo? And, just for the record, I'm not sure I buy your story about surfing, *seriously.* Because believe me, I checked, and you were *nowhere* in sight."

He looks at me, his deep dark eyes obscured by a rim of lush lashes, his lean, sinuous body wrapped in a towel. And when he moves toward me, his step is so light and sure, he's as graceful as any jungle cat. "This is my fault," he finally says, shaking his head as he sits down beside me, folding my hands into his, but then dropping them just as quickly. "I'm not sure how much . . ." he starts, and when he finally looks at me, his eyes are sadder than I ever could've imagined. "Maybe we shouldn't do this," he finally says.

"Are you—*are you breaking up with me?*" I whisper, the wind rushing right out of me, like an ill-fated balloon. All my suspicions confirmed: Drina, the beach, all of it. *Everything.*

"No, I just . . ." He turns away, leaving both the sentence, and me, to dangle.

And when it's clear he has no plans to continue I say, "You know, it would really be nice if you'd stop talking in code, finish a sentence, and tell me what the heck is going on. Because all I know is that Evangeline is dead, Haven's wrist is a red oozing mess, you ditched me at the beach because I wouldn't go all the way, and now you're breaking up with me." I glare at him, waiting for some confirmation that these seemingly random events are easily explained and not at all related. Even though my gut says otherwise.

He's silent for a while, staring at the pool, but when he finally looks at me he says, "None of it's related."

Though he hesitated for so long I'm not sure I believe him.

Then he takes a deep breath and continues. "They found Evangeline's body in Malibu canyon. I was on my way here when I heard it on the radio," he says, his voice becoming sure, steady, as he visibly relaxes and regains control. "And yes, Haven's wrist does appear to be infected, but sometimes those things happen." He breaks my gaze and I suck in my breath, waiting for the rest, the part about me. Then he grabs my hand and covers it with his, flipping it over and tracing the lines on my palm as he says, "Drina can be charismatic, charming—and Haven's a bit of a lost soul. I'm sure she just likes the attention. I thought you'd be glad she transferred her affections to Drina from me." He squeezes my fingers and smiles. "Now there's no one standing between us."

"But maybe there's *something* standing between us?" I ask, my voice barely a whisper. Knowing I should be more concerned with Haven's wrist and Evangeline's death, but unable to focus on anything other than the planes of his face, his smooth dark skin, his deep narrowed eyes, and the way my heart surges, my blood rushes, and my lips swell in anticipation of his.

"Ever, I didn't ditch you today. And I'd never push you to do anything you weren't ready for. Believe me." He smiles, cradling my face in the palms of his hands as his lips part against mine. "I know how to wait."

twenty-two

Even though Haven refused to answer our calls, we managed to get ahold of Miles. And after convincing him to stop by after rehearsals, he showed up with Eric, and the four of us spent a really fun night eating and swimming and watching bad scary movies. And it was so nice to hang out with my friends in such a nice relaxed way, that it *almost* made me forget about Riley, Haven, Evangeline, Drina, the beach—and all of that afternoon's drama.

Almost made me oblivious to the faraway look Damen got whenever he thought no one was looking.

Almost made me ignore the undercurrent of worry bubbling just under the surface.

Almost. But not quite.

And even though I made it perfectly clear that Sabine was out of town and Damen was more than welcome to stay, he stayed just long enough for me to fall asleep, then he quietly let himself out.

So the next morning, when he shows up on my doorstep with coffee, muffins, and a smile, I can't help but feel a little relieved.

We try to call Haven again, and even leave a message or two, but it's not like it takes a psychic to know she doesn't want to speak to either of us. And when I finally call her house and talk to her little brother, Austin, I can tell he's not lying when he says he hasn't seen her.

So after a full day of lounging outside by the pool, I'm just about to order another pizza when Damen grabs the phone out of my hand and says, "I thought I'd make dinner."

"You can cook?" I ask, though I don't know why I'm surprised, because the truth is, I've yet to find anything he can't do.

"I'll let you be the judge of that." He smiles.

"Do you need help?" I offer, even though my kitchen skills are severely limited to boiling water and adding milk to cereal.

But he just shakes his head and heads for the stove, so I go upstairs to shower and change, and when he calls me down for dinner, I'm amazed to find the dining room table dressed with Sabine's finest china, linens, candles, and a large crystal vase filled with dozens of—big surprise—red tulips.

"Mademoiselle." He smiles and pulls out my chair, his French accent lilting and perfect.

"I can't believe you did this." I gaze at the heaping platters lined up before me, so piled with food I wonder if we're expecting guests.

"It's all for you." He smiles, answering the question I hadn't yet asked.

"Just me? Aren't you going to have any?" I watch as he fills my plate with perfectly prepared vegetables, finely grilled meats, and a sauce so rich and complex I don't even know what it is.

"Of course." He smiles. "But mostly I made it for you. A girl can't live on pizza alone, you know."

"You'd be surprised." I laugh, cutting into a juicy piece of grilled meat.

While we eat, I ask questions. Taking advantage of the fact that he's barely touching his food by asking all of the things I've been dying to know but always seem to forget the moment he looks in my eyes. Things about his family, his childhood, the constant moves, the emancipation—partly because I'm curious, but mostly because it feels weird to be in a relationship with someone I know so little about. And the more we talk, the more surprised I am by how much we share in common. For one thing, both of us are orphaned, though he at a much younger age. And even though he's a little sketchy on the details, it's not like I volunteer to talk about my situation either, so I don't really push it.

"So where'd you like best?" I ask, having just cleaned my plate of every last morsel and feeling the beginnings of a nice languid fullness.

"Right here." He smiles, having barely eaten a thing but making a pretty good show of moving his food all around.

I squinch my eyes, not quite believing it. I mean, sure, Orange County's nice, but it can't possibly compare to all of those exciting European cities, *can it?*

"Seriously. I'm very happy here." He nods, looking right at me.

"And you weren't happy in Rome, Paris, New Delhi, or New York?"

He shrugs, his eyes suddenly tinged with sadness as they drift away from mine and he takes a sip of his strange red drink.

"And what exactly is that?" I ask, peering at the bottle.

"You mean this?" he smiles, holding it up for me to see. "Secret family recipe." He swirls the contents around, and I watch as the color glows and sparks as it runs up the sides and splashes back down. Looking like a cross between lightning, wine, and blood mixed with the tiniest hint of diamond dust.

"Can I try it?" I ask, not entirely sure that I want to, but still curious.

He shakes his head. "You won't like it. Tastes just like medicine. But that's probably because it is medicine."

My stomach sinks as I gape at him, imagining a whole host of incurable diseases, horrible afflictions, grave ailments—*I knew he was too good to be true*.

But he just shakes his head and laughs as he reaches for my hand. "No worries. I just get a little low on energy sometimes. And this helps."

"Where do you get it?" I squint, searching for a label, an imprint, some kind of mark, but the bottle is clear, smooth, and appears almost seamless.

He smiles. "I told you, secret family recipe," he says, taking a long deep swig and finishing it off. Then he pushes away from the table and his still-full plate, as he says, "Shall we go for a swim?"

"Aren't you supposed to wait an hour after eating?" I ask, peering at him.

But he just smiles and reaches for my hand. "Don't worry. I won't let you drown."

Since we spent most of the day in the pool, we decide to hang in the Jacuzzi instead. And when our fingers and toes start to resemble small prunes, we wrap ourselves in oversized towels and head up to my room.

He follows me into my bathroom. I drop my damp towel on

the floor, then he comes up behind me, pulls me to him, and holds me so close our bodies meld right together. And when his lips brush across the nape of my neck, I know I better lay down some ground rules while my brain is still working.

"Um, you're welcome to stay," I mumble, pulling away, my cheeks burning with embarrassment when I meet his amused gaze. "I mean, what I meant to say was, I *want* you to stay. I do. But, well, I'm not sure that we should—*you know*—"

Oh god, what am I saying? Um, hello, like he doesn't know what I mean. Like he wasn't the one getting pushed away in the cave and just about everywhere else. What is with you? What are you doing? Any girl would kill for a moment like this, a long, lazy weekend with no parents or chaperones—and yet, here I am, enforcing some stupid set of rules—for no good reason—

He places his finger under my chin and lifts my face until it's level with his. "Ever, please, we've been over this," he whispers, tucking my hair behind my ear and bringing his lips to my neck. "I know how to wait, really. I've already waited this long to find you—I can wait even more."

With Damen's warm body curled around mine, and his reassuring breath in my ear, I fall right to sleep. And even though I was worried I'd be way too freaked by his presence to get any rest, it's the warm secure feeling of having him right there beside me that helps me drift off.

But when I wake at 3:45 A.M., only to discover he's no longer there, I throw the covers aside and rush to the window, reliving that moment in the cave all over again as I search the drive for his car, surprised to find it's still there.

"Looking for me?" he asks.

I turn to find him standing in the doorway, my heart beating wildly, my face gone crimson. "Oh, I—I rolled over and you weren't there, and—" I press my lips, feeling ridiculous, small, embarrassingly needy.

"I went downstairs for some water." He smiles, taking my hand and leading me back to the bed.

But as I lay down beside him, my hand drifts to his side, brushing across sheets so cold and abandoned, it seems he's been gone for a much longer time.

The second time I wake, I'm alone again. But when I hear Damen banging around in the kitchen, I pull on my robe and head downstairs to investigate.

"How long have you been up?" I ask, gazing at a spotless kitchen, the previous night's mess having vanished, replaced by a lineup of donuts, bagels, and cereals that didn't originate in my cupboard.

"I'm an early riser." He shrugs. "So I thought I'd clean up a bit before running to the store. I may have gone a little overboard, but I didn't know what you'd want." He smiles, coming around the counter and kissing me on the cheek.

I sip from the glass of fresh-squeezed orange juice he sets before me and ask, "Want some? Or are you still fasting?"

"Fasting?" He lifts his brow and gazes at me.

I roll my eyes. "Please. You eat less than anyone I know. You just sip your . . . medicine and push your food all around. I feel like a complete pig next to you."

"Is this better?" He smiles, picking up a donut and biting it in half, his jaw working overtime to break down the glazed, doughy mass.

I shrug and gaze out the window, still unused to this California weather, a seemingly endless succession of warm sunny days, even though soon it will officially be winter. "So, what should we do today?" I ask, turning to look at him.

He gazes at his watch and then back at me. "I need to take off soon."

"But Sabine won't be back until late," I say, hating how my voice sounds so whiny and needy, and the way my stomach curls when he jangles his keys.

"I need to get home and take care of a few things. Especially if you want to see me at school tomorrow," he says, his lips grazing my cheek, my ear, the nape of my neck.

"Oh, school. Do we still go there?" I laugh, having successfully avoided thinking about my recent bout of truancy, and the repercussions to follow.

"You're the one who thinks it's important." He shrugs. "If it was up to me, every day would be Saturday."

"But then Saturday wouldn't be special. It'd all be the same," I say, picking off a piece of glazed donut. "A never-ending flow of long lazy days, nothing to work toward, nothing to look forward to, just one hedonistic moment after another. After a while, it wouldn't be so great."

"Don't be so sure." He smiles.

"So what exactly are these mysterious chores of yours, anyway?" I ask, hoping to get a glimpse into his life, of the more mundane things that occupy his time when he's not with me.

He shrugs. "You know, *stuff*." And even though he laughs when he says it, it's pretty obvious he's ready to leave.

"Well, maybe I can—" But before I can even finish the sentence he's already shaking his head.

"Forget it. You are *not* doing my laundry." He shifts his weight from one foot to the other, as though warming up for a race.

"But I want to see where you live. I've never been in the home of someone who's emancipated, and I'm curious." And even though I tried to sound lighthearted, it came out more whiny and desperate.

He shakes his head and gazes at the door as though it's a potential lover he can't wait to meet.

And even though it's obviously time to wave my white flag and cry *uncle,* I can't keep from giving it one last go when I say, "But *why*?" Then I peer at him, waiting for a reason.

He looks at me, his jaw tense when he says, "Because it's a mess. A horrible filthy mess. And I don't want you to see it like that and get the wrong idea about me. Besides, I'll never be able to straighten it up with you around; you'll only distract me." He smiles, but his lips are stretched tight and his eyes are impatient, and it's clear they're just words meant to fill up the space between now and when he finally gets to leave. "I'll call you tonight," he says, showing me his back as he heads for the door.

"And what if I decide to follow you? What will you do then?" I ask, my nervous laughter halting the second he turns back to me.

"Don't follow me, Ever."

And the way he says it makes me wonder if he said, *Don't follow me ever,* or *Don't follow me, Ever.* But either way, it means the same thing.

When Damen leaves, I pick up the phone and try to call Haven, but when it goes straight into voice mail, I don't bother with leaving another message. Because the truth is, I've left several already, and now it's up to her to call me. So after I head upstairs and shower, I sit at my desk, determined to get through my homework, but not getting very far before my thoughts return to Damen, and all of his weird, mysterious quirks that I can no longer ignore.

Stuff like: How does he always seem to know just what I'm thinking when I can't get the slightest read on him? And how, in just seventeen short years, did he find time to live in all of those exotic places, mastering art, soccer, surfing, cooking, literature, world history, and just about every other subject I can think of? And what's up with the way he moves so fast he actually blurs? And what about the rosebuds and tulips and magical pen? Not to mention how one minute he's talking like a normal guy, and the next he sounds like Heathcliff, or Darcy, or some other character from a Brontë sister's book. Add to that the time he acted like he saw Riley, the fact that he has no aura, the fact that Drina has no aura, the fact that I *know* he's hiding something about how he really knows her—and now he doesn't want me to know where he lives?

After we slept together?

Okay, maybe all we did was *sleep,* but still, I think I deserve answers to at least some (if not all) of my questions. And even though I'm not really up for breaking into the school and searching for his record, I know someone who is.

Only I'm not sure I should involve Riley in this. Not to mention how I don't even know how to summon her since I've never had to before. I mean, do I call out her name? Light a candle? Close my eyes and make a wish?

Since lighting a candle seems a little hokey, I settle for just standing in the middle of my room, eyes shut tight, as I say, "Riley? Riley, if you can hear me I really need to talk to you. Well, actually I kind of need a favor. But if you don't want to do it, then I totally understand, and there will be no hard feelings, since I know it's a little weird, and um, I feel kind of dumb right now, standing here talking to myself, so if you can hear me, could you maybe give me some kind of sign?"

And when my stereo suddenly blasts the Kelly Clarkson song she always used to sing, I open my eyes and see her standing before me, laughing hysterically.

"Omigod—you looked like your were two seconds away from closing the blinds, lighting a candle, and pulling the Ouija board out from under the bed!" She shakes her head and looks at me.

"Oh jeez, I feel like an idiot," I say, my face turning red.

"You kind of looked like an idiot." She laughs. "Okay, so let me get this straight, you want to corrupt your little sister by making her spy on your boyfriend?"

"How'd you know?" I stare at her, amazed.

"Please." She rolls her eyes and plops down on my bed. "You think you're the only one around here who can read minds?"

"And how'd you know *that*?" I ask, wondering what else she might know.

"Ava told me. But please don't be mad, because it really does explain some of your more recent fashion blunders."

"And what about your more recent fashion blunders?" I say, motioning to her *Star Wars* getup.

But she just shrugs. "So you wanna know where to find your boyfriend or not?"

I move to the bed and sit down beside her. "Honestly? I'm not sure. I mean, yeah I want to know, but I don't feel right about involving you."

"But what if I already did it? What if I already know?" she says, wiggling her brows.

"You broke into the school?" I ask, wondering what else she's been up to since we last talked.

But she just laughs. "Even better, I followed him home."

I gape at her. "But when? And how?"

She shakes her head. "Come on, Ever, it's not like I need wheels to get where I want to go. Besides, I know how you're all in love with him, and it's not like I blame you, he is pretty dreamy. But remember that day when he acted like he saw me?"

I nod. I mean, how could I forget?

"Well, it freaked me out. So, I decided to do a little investigation."

I lean toward her. *"And?"*

"*And,* well, I'm not sure how to say this, and I hope you won't take it the wrong way, but—he's a little odd." She shrugs. "I mean, he lives in this big house over in Newport Coast, which is strange enough considering his age and all. I mean where does he get the money? Because it's not like he works."

I remember that day at the track. But decide not to mention it.

"But that's not even the strangest part," she continues. "Because what's really weird is that the house is completely *empty.* Like, no furniture whatsoever."

"Well, he is a guy," I say, wondering why I feel the need to defend him.

She shakes her head. "Yeah, but I'm talking seriously weird. I mean, the only things in there are one of those iPod wall docks and a flat-screen TV. Seriously. That's it. And believe me, I checked the whole house. Well, other than this one room that was locked."

"Since when do locked rooms stop you?" I say, having seen her walk through plenty of walls this past year.

"Believe me, it wasn't the door that stopped me. It was *me* that stopped me. I mean, jeez, just because I'm dead doesn't mean I can't get scared." She shakes her head and scowls at me.

"But, he hasn't really lived here all that long," I say, rushing to make more excuses, like the worst kind of codependent fool. "So maybe he just hasn't gotten around to furnishing it yet. I mean, that's probably why he doesn't want me to come over; he doesn't want me to see it like that." And when I replay my words in my head, I can't help but think: *Oh, God, I'm even worse than I thought.*

Riley shakes her head and looks at me like she's about to let me in on the truth behind the tooth fairy, the Easter bunny, and Santa, all in one sitting. But then she just shrugs and says, "Maybe you should see for yourself."

"What do you mean?" I ask, knowing she's holding something back.

But she gets up from the bed and goes over to the mirror, gazing at her reflection and adjusting her costume.

"Riley?" I say, wondering why she's acting so mysterious.

"Listen," she says, finally turning toward me. "Maybe I'm wrong. I mean, what do I know, I'm just a kid." She shrugs. "And it's probably nothing, but . . ."

"But . . ."

She takes a deep breath. "But I think you should see for yourself."

"So how do we get there?" I ask, already up and reaching for the keys.

She shakes her head. "No way. Forget it. I'm convinced he can see me."

"Well we know he can see *me,*" I remind her.

But she stands firm. "*So* not happening. But I'll draw you a map."

Since Riley's not so great at drawing maps, she settles for making a list of street names instead, indicating their left and right turns, since north, south, east, and west always confuse me.

"Sure you don't want to come?" I offer, grabbing my bag and heading out of my room.

She nods and follows me downstairs. "Hey, Ever?"

I turn.

"You could've told me about all the psychic stuff. I feel bad about making fun of your clothes."

I open the front door and shrug. "Can you really read my mind?"

She shakes her head and smiles. "Only when you're trying to communicate with me. I figured it was just a matter of time before you'd want me to spy on him." She laughs. "But, Ever?"

I turn to look at her again.

"If I don't come around for a while, it's not because I'm mad at you or trying to punish you or anything like that, okay? I promise I'll still look in and make sure you're all right and stuff, but, well, I might be gone for a while. I might be kind of busy."

I freeze, the first hint of panic beginning to stir. "You *are* coming back though, right?"

She nods. "It's just, well . . ." She shrugs. "I promise I'll be back, I just don't know when." And even though she smiles, it's obviously forced.

"You're not leaving me, are you?" I hold my breath, exhaling only when she shakes her head. "Okay, well, good luck then," I say, wishing I could hug her, hold her, convince her to stay, but knowing that's not possible, I head for my car and start the engine instead.

twenty-three

Damen lives in a gated community. A detail Riley failed to reveal. I guess since the presence of big iron gates and uniformed guards could never stop someone like her, it didn't seem very important. Though I guess it doesn't really stop someone like me either, since I just smile at the attendant, and say, "Hi, I'm Megan Foster. I'm here to see Jody Howard." Then I watch as she scrolls down her computer screen, searching for the name I just happen to know is listed as entry number three.

"Leave this in your window, on the driver's side," she says, handing me a piece of yellow paper, the word VISITOR and the date clearly marked on its front. "And no parking on the left side of the street, right side only." She nods, returning to her booth as I drive through the open gate, hoping she won't notice when I pass right by Jody's street as I make my way toward Damen's.

I've almost reached the top of the hill when I see the next street on my list, and after making a left, quickly followed by another, I stop at the end of his block, kill the engine, and realize I've lost all my nerve.

I mean, what kind of psycho girlfriend am I? Who in their

right mind would even think of enlisting their dead little sister to help spy on their boyfriend? But then again, it's not like anything in my life is remotely normal, so why should my relationships be any different?

I sit in my car, focusing on my breath, fighting to keep it slow and steady despite the fact that my heart is pounding like crazy and my palms are slick with sweat. And as I gaze around his clean, tidy, affluent neighborhood I realize I couldn't have picked a worse day to do this.

First of all, it's hot, sunny, and glorious, which means everyone's either riding their bikes, walking their dogs, or working in their gardens, which pretty much makes for some of the worst spying conditions you could ask for. And since I spent the entire drive just concentrating on getting here and not even considering what I'd do once I made it, it's not like I have a plan.

Though it probably doesn't matter much anyway. I mean, what's the worst that can happen? I get caught and Damen confirms I'm a freak? After my clingy, needy, desperate act this morning, he's probably already there.

I climb out of my car and head toward his house, the one at the very end of the cul-de-sac with the tropical plants and manicured lawn. But I don't creep, or skulk, or do anything that will draw unwanted attention, I just stroll right along, as though I have every right to be there, until I'm standing before his large double doors wondering what to do next.

I take a step back and gaze up at the windows, their blinds drawn, drapes closed, and even though I've no idea what I'll say, I bite down on my lip, push the bell, hold my breath, and wait.

But after a few minutes pass with no answer, I ring again. And when he still doesn't answer, I turn the handle, confirm that it's locked, then I head down the walk, making sure none of the neighbors are watching as I slip through the side gate and slink around back.

I stay close to the house, barely glancing at the pool, the plants, and the amazing white water view, as I go straight for the sliding glass door, which, of course, is locked too.

Then just as I'm ready to cut my losses and head home, I hear this voice in my head urging—*the window, the one by the sink.* And sure enough, I find it cracked just enough to slip my fingers under and open the rest of the way.

I place my hands on the ledge and use all of my strength to hoist myself in. And the second my feet hit the floor I've officially crossed over the line.

I shouldn't continue. I have no right to do this. I should climb right back out and make a run for my car. Get back to my safe quiet house while I still can. But that little voice in my head is urging me on, and since it got me this far, I figure I may as well see where it leads.

I explore the large empty kitchen, the bare den, the dining room devoid of table and chairs, and the bathroom with only a small bar of soap and a single black towel, thinking how Riley was right—this place is vacant in a way that seems abandoned and creepy, with no personal mementos, no photos, no books. Nothing but dark wood floors, off-white walls, bare cupboards, a fridge stuffed with countless bottles of that weird red liquid, and nothing more. And when I get to the media room, I see the flat-screen TV Riley mentioned, a recliner she didn't mention, and a large pile of foreign-language DVDs whose titles I can't translate. Then I pause at the bottom of the stairs knowing I should leave, that I've seen more than enough, but something I can't quite define urges me on.

I grip the banister, cringing as the stairs groan beneath me, their high-pitched protest alarmingly loud in this vast vacant space. And when I make my way to the landing, I come face to face with the door Riley found locked. Only this time it's left open, pushed slightly ajar.

I creep toward it, summoning the voice in my head, desperate for some kind of guidance. But the only answer I get is the sound of my own beating heart as I press my palm flat against it, then gasp as it opens to a room so ornate, so formal, so grand, it seems straight out of Versailles.

I pause in the doorway, struggling to take it all in. The finely woven tapestries, the antique rugs, the crystal chandeliers, the golden candelabras, the heavy silk draperies, the velvet settee, the marble-topped table piled with tomes. Even the walls, the entire area between the wainscoting and crown molding is covered by large gilt-framed paintings—all of them capturing Damen in costumes that span several centuries, including one of him astride a white stallion, silver sword by his side, wearing the exact same jacket he wore Halloween night.

I move toward it, my eyes seeking the hole on the shoulder, the frayed spot he jokingly blamed on artillery fire. Startled to find it right there in the picture, as I run my finger along it, spellbound, mesmerized, wondering what kind of freaky elaborate ruse he's concocted as my fingertips graze all the way down to the small brass plaque at the bottom that reads:

DAMEN AUGUSTE ESPOSITO, MAY 1775

I turn to the one beside it, my heart racing as I gaze at a portrait of an unsmiling Damen, cloaked in a severe dark suit, surrounded by blue, its plaque bearing the words:

DAMEN AUGUSTE AS PAINTED BY PABLO PICASSO IN 1902

And the one next to that, its heavily textured swirls forming the likeness of

DAMEN ESPOSITO AS PAINTED BY VINCENT VAN GOGH

And on it goes, all four walls displaying Damen's likeness as painted by all the great masters.

I sink onto the velvet settee, eyes bleary, knees weak, my mind racing with a thousand possibilities, each of them equally ridiculous. Then I grasp the book nearest to me, flip to the title page, and read:

For Damen Auguste Esposito.

Signed by William Shakespeare.

I drop it to the floor and reach for the next, *Wuthering Heights, for Damen Auguste,* signed by Emily Brontë.

Every book made out to *Damen Auguste Esposito,* or *Damen Auguste,* or just *Damen*. All of them signed by an author who's been dead for more than a century.

I close my eyes, trying to concentrate on slowing my breath as my heart races, my hands shake, telling myself it's all some kind of joke, that Damen's some freaky history buff, antique collector, an art counterfeiter who's gone too far. Perhaps these are prized family heirlooms, left from a long line of great, great, great, grandfathers, all bearing the same name and uncanny resemblance.

But when I look around again, the chill down my spine tells the undeniable truth—these aren't merely antiques, nor are they heirlooms. These are Damen's personal possessions, the favored treasures he's collected through the years.

I stagger to my feet and stumble into the hall, feeling shaky, unstable, desperate to escape this creepy room, this hideous, gaudy, overstuffed mausoleum, this crypt-like house. Wanting to put as much distance between us as I possibly can, and to never, ever, under any circumstances, come back here again.

I've just reached the bottom stair when I hear a loud piercing scream followed by a long muffled moan, and without even thinking, I turn and race toward it, following the sound to the end of the hall and rushing through the door, finding Damen on the floor, his clothes torn, his face dripping with blood, while Haven thrashes and moans underneath him.

"Ever!" he shouts, springing to his feet and holding me back as I lunge, fight, and kick, desperate to get to her.

"What have you done to her?" I shout, glancing between them, seeing her pale skin, her eyes rolling back in her head, and knowing there's no time to waste.

"Ever, please, stop," he says, his voice sounding too sure, too measured for the incriminating circumstances he's in.

"WHAT HAVE YOU DONE TO HER?" I scream, kicking, hitting, biting, screaming, scratching, using every ounce of my strength, but it's no match for him. He just stands there, holding me with one hand, while absorbing my blows with barely a grimace.

"Ever, please, let me explain," he says, dodging my furiously kicking feet that are aiming right for him.

As I stare at my friend who's bleeding profusely, grimacing in pain, a terrible realization sweeps right through me—*this is why he tried to keep me away!*

"No! That's not it at all. You've got it all wrong. Yes, I didn't want you to see this, though it's not what you think."

He holds me up high, my legs dangling like a rag doll, and despite all my punching and fighting, he hasn't even broken a sweat.

But I don't care about Damen. I don't even care about me. All I care about is Haven, whose lips are turning blue, as her breath grows alarmingly weak.

"What have you done to her?" I glare at him with all the hate I can muster. *"What have you done to her, you freak?"*

"Ever, please, I need you to listen," he pleads, his eyes begging mine.

And despite all my anger, despite my adrenaline, I can still feel that warm languid tingle of his hands on my skin, and I fight like hell to ignore it. Yelling and screaming and kicking my feet, aiming for his most vulnerable parts, but always missing since he's so much quicker than me.

"You can't help her, trust me, I'm the only one who can."

"You're not helping her, you're killing her!" I shout.

He shakes his head and looks at me, his face appearing tired when he whispers, "Hardly."

I try to pull away again, but it's no use, I can't beat him. So I stop, allowing myself to go limp as I close my eyes in surrender.

Thinking: *So this is how it happens. This is how I disappear.*

And the moment he relaxes his grip, I kick my foot as hard as I can, my boot hitting its target as he loosens his grip and I drop to the floor.

I spring toward Haven, my fingers slipping to her blood-covered wrist as I search for a pulse, my eyes fixed on the two small holes in the center of her creepy tattoo, as I beg her to keep breathing, to hang on.

And just as I reach for my cell, intending to call 911, Damen comes up behind me, grabs the phone out of my hand, and says, "I was hoping I wouldn't have to do this."

twenty-four

When I wake, I'm lying in bed with Sabine looming over me, her face a mask of relief, her thoughts a maze of concern.

"Hey," she says, smiling and shaking her head. "You must've had *some* weekend."

I squint first at her and then at the clock. Then I spring out of bed when I realize the time.

"Are you feeling okay?" she asks, trailing behind me. "You were already asleep when I got home last night. You're not sick are you?"

I head for the shower, not sure how to answer. Because even though I don't feel sick, I can't imagine how I slept so long and so late.

"Anything I should know about? Anything you need to tell me?" she asks, standing outside the door.

I close my eyes and rewind the weekend, remembering the beach, Evangeline, Damen staying over and making me dinner, followed by breakfast—"No, nothing happened," I finally say.

"Well, you better hurry if you want to make it to school on time. You sure you're all right?"

"Yes," I say, trying to sound clear-cut, unambiguous, sure as sure can be, as I turn on the taps and step into the spray, not sure if I'm lying or if it's true.

The whole way to school Miles talks about Eric. Giving me the lowdown, the entire step-by-step of their Sunday night text-message breakup, trying to convince me that he couldn't care less, that he is completely and totally over him, which pretty much proves that he's not.

"Are you even listening to me?" He scowls.

"Of course," I mumble, stopping at a light, just a block from school, my mind running through my own weekend events, and always ending at breakfast. No matter how hard I try, I can't remember anything after that.

"Could've fooled me." He smirks and looks out the window. "I mean, if I'm boring you, just say so. Because believe me, I am *so* over Eric. Did I ever tell you about that time when he—"

"Miles, have you talked to Haven?" I ask, glancing at him briefly before the light turns green.

He shakes his head. "You?"

"I don't think so." I press down on the gas, wondering why just saying her name fills me with dread.

"You don't *think* so?" His eyes go wide as he shifts in his seat.

"Not since Friday."

I pull into the parking lot, my heart beating triple time when I see Damen in his usual spot, leaning against his car, waiting for me.

"Well, at least one of us has a shot at happily ever after," Miles says, nodding at Damen who comes around to my side, a single red tulip in hand.

"Good morning." He smiles, handing me the flower and kissing my cheek, as I mumble an incoherent reply and head for the gate. The bell rings as Miles sprints toward class and Damen takes my hand and leads me into English. "Mr. Robins is on his way," he whispers, squeezing my fingers as he leads me past Stacia, who scowls at me and sticks out her foot, before moving it out of my way at the very last second. "He's off the sauce, trying to get his wife back." His lips curve against my ear as I pick up the pace and move away.

I slide onto my seat and unload my books, wondering why my boyfriend's presence is making me feel so edgy and weird, then reach inside my iPod pocket and panic when I realize I left it at home.

"You don't need that," Damen says, reaching for my hand and smoothing my fingers with his. "You have me now."

I close my eyes, knowing Mr. Robins will be here in just three, two, one—

"Ever," Damen whispers, his fingers tracing over the veins on my wrist. "You feeling okay?"

I press my lips together and nod.

"Good." He pauses. "I had a great weekend, I hope you did too."

I open my eyes just as Mr. Robins walks in, noticing how his eyes aren't as puffy, his face not as red, though his hands are still a little shaky.

"Yesterday was fun, don't you think?"

I turn to Damen, gazing into his eyes, my skin infused with warmth and tingle merely because his hand is on mine. Then I nod in agreement, knowing it's the response he wants, even though I'm not sure that it's true.

The next couple of hours are a blur of classes and confusion, and it's not until I get to the lunch table that I learn the truth about yesterday.

"I can't believe you guys went in the water," Miles says, stirring his yoghurt and looking at me. "Do you have any idea how cold it is?"

"She wore a wet suit." Damen shrugs. "In fact, you left it at my house."

I unwrap my sandwich, not remembering any of it. I don't even own a wet suit. *Do I?* "Um, wasn't that Friday?" I ask, blushing when *all* the events of that day come rushing back to me.

Damen shakes his head. "You didn't surf on Friday, I did. Sunday was when I gave you a lesson."

I peel the crust off my sandwich, and try to remember, but it keeps coming up blank.

"So, was she any good?" Miles asks, licking his spoon and gazing from Damen to me.

"Well, it was pretty flat so there wasn't much to surf. Mostly we just lay on the beach, under some blankets. And yeah, she's pretty good at that." He laughs.

I gaze at Damen wondering if my wet suit was on or off under those blankets, and what, if anything happened under there. *Is it possible that I tried to make up for Friday, then blocked it out so I can't even remember it?*

Miles looks at me, brows raised, but I just shrug and take a bite of my sandwich.

"Which beach?" he asks.

But since I can't remember, I turn to Damen.

"Crystal Cove," he says, sipping his drink.

Miles shakes his head and rolls his eyes. "Please tell me you're not turning into one of those couples where the guy does all the talking. I mean, does he order for you in restaurants too?"

I look at Damen, but before he can answer Miles goes, "No, I'm asking *you*, Ever."

I think back to our two restaurant meals, one that wonderful day at Disneyland that ended so strangely, and the other at the racetrack when we won all that money. "I order my own meals," I say. And then I look at him and go, "Can I borrow your Sidekick?"

He pulls it from his pocket and slides it toward me. "Why? You forget your phone?"

"Yeah and I want to text Haven and see where she is. I have the weirdest feeling about her." I shake my head, not knowing how to explain it to myself, much less to them. "I can't stop thinking about her," I say, fingers tapping the tiny keyboard.

"She's at home, sick," Miles says. "Some kind of flu. Plus she's sad about Evangeline, though she swears she no longer hates us."

"I thought you said you hadn't talked to her." I pause and gaze up at him, sure that's what he said in the car.

"I sent her a text in history."

"So she's okay?" I stare at Miles, my stomach a jumble of nerves though I can't begin to grasp why.

"Puking her guts out, mourning the loss of her friend, but yeah, basically fine."

I return the Sidekick to Miles, figuring there's no use in bothering her if she's not feeling well. Then Damen puts his hand on my leg, Miles goes on about Eric, and I pick at my lunch, going through the motions of nodding and smiling, but unable to shake my unease.

Wouldn't you know it, the one day Damen decides to spend the whole day at school just happens to be the day I wish he would've ditched. Because every time I get out of class, I find him standing right outside the door, anxiously waiting, and asking if I'm feeling okay. And it's really starting to get on my nerves.

So after art, when we're walking to the parking lot and he offers to follow me home, I just look at him and say, "Um, if it's okay with you, I need to be by myself for a while."

"Is everything okay?" he asks for the millionth time.

But I just nod and climb inside, anxious to close the door and put some distance between us. "I just need to catch up on a few things, but I'll see you tomorrow, okay?" And not giving him a chance to reply, I back out of my space and drive away.

When I get home, I'm so incredibly tired I head straight for my bed, planning to take a short nap before Sabine comes home and starts worrying about me again. But when I wake up in the middle of the night, with my heart pounding and my clothes soaked with sweat, I have this undeniable feeling I'm not alone in my room.

I reach for my pillow, grasping it tightly as though those soft downy feathers will serve as some sort of shield, then I peer into the dark space before me, and whisper, "Riley?" Even though I'm pretty sure it's not her.

I hold my breath, hearing a soft muffled sound, like slippers on carpet, over by the french doors, and I surprise myself by whispering, "Damen?" as I peer into the dark, unable to make out anything other than a soft swishing sound.

I fumble for the light switch, squinting against the sudden brightness, and searching for the intruder, so sure I had company, so positive I wasn't alone, that I'm almost disappointed when I find my room empty.

I climb out of bed, still clutching my pillow, as I lock the french doors. Then I peek into my closet and under my bed, like my dad used to do those long-ago nights he reported for boogeyman duty. But not finding anything, I crawl back in bed, wondering if it was possibly my dream that sparked all these fears.

It was similar to the one I had before, where I was running through a dark windswept canyon, my filmy white dress a poor defense against the cold, inviting the wind to lash at my skin, chilling me straight through to my bones. And yet I barely noticed, I was so focused on running, my bare feet carving into the damp, muddy earth, heading toward a hazy refuge I couldn't quite see.

All I know is that I was running toward a soft glowing light.

And away from Damen.

twenty-five

The next day at school, I park in my usual space, jump out of my car, and run right past Damen, heading for Haven who's waiting by the gate. And even though I normally do everything possible to avoid physical contact, I grab onto her shoulders and hug her right to me.

"Okay, okay, I love you too." She laughs, shaking her head and pushing me away. "I mean, jeez, it's not like I was going to stay mad at you guys forever."

Her dyed red hair is dry and limp, her black nail polish is chipped, the hollows under her eyes seem darker than usual, and her face is decidedly pale. But even though she assures me she's okay, I can't help but reach out and hug her again.

"How're you feeling?" I ask, eyeing her carefully, trying to get a read, but other than her aura appearing gray, weak, and translucent, I can't *see* much of anything.

"*What* is going on with you?" she says, shaking her head and pushing me away. "What's with all the love and affection? I mean *you* of all people, you of the eternal iPod-hoodie combo."

"I heard you were sick, and then when you weren't at school yesterday—" I stop, feeling ridiculous to be hovering like this.

But she just laughs. "I know what's going on here." She nods. "This is your fault, isn't it?" She points at Damen. "You just had to come along and thaw out my icy cold friend, turning her into a sentimental, warm, fuzzy sap."

And even though Damen laughs, it doesn't quite reach his eyes.

"It was just the flu," she says as Miles loops his arm through hers and we head past the gate. "And I guess being all depressed about Evangeline made it that much worse. I mean, I was so feverish, I actually blacked out a few times."

"Seriously?" I break away from Damen so I can walk alongside her.

"Yeah, it was the weirdest thing. Every night I would go to bed wearing one thing, and when I woke up I'd be wearing something entirely different. And when I'd go looking for what I had on before, I couldn't find it. It was like it'd vanished or something."

"Well, your room is pretty messy." Miles laughs. "Or maybe you were hallucinating; you know that can happen when you have a monster fever."

"Maybe." She shrugs. "But all my black scarves were gone, so I had to borrow this one from my brother." She lifts the end of her blue wool scarf and waves it around.

"Was anyone there to take care of you?" Damen asks, coming up beside me and taking my hand, his fingers intertwining with mine, sending a flood of warmth through my system.

Haven shakes her head and rolls her eyes. "Are you kidding? I may as well be emancipated like you. Besides, I had my door locked the whole time. I could've *died* in there and nobody would've known."

"What about Drina?" I ask, my stomach clenching at the mention of her name.

Haven gives me a strange look and says, "Drina's in New York. She left Friday night. Anyway, I hope you guys don't get it, because even though some of the dream-state stuff was pretty cool, I know you guys wouldn't be into it." She stops near her class and leans against the wall.

"Did you dream about a canyon?" I ask, dropping Damen's hand, and moving so close I'm right up in her face again.

But Haven just laughs and pushes me away. "Um, excuse me, boundaries!" She shakes her head. "And no, there were no canyons. Just some wild goth stuff, hard to explain, though plenty of blood and gore."

And the second she says that, the second I hear the word "blood," everything goes black as my body tilts toward the floor.

"Ever?" Damen cries, catching me just seconds before I crash to the ground. "Ever," he whispers, his voice tinged with worry.

And when I open my eyes to meet his, something about his expression, something about the intensity of his gaze seems so familiar. But just as the memory begins to form, it's erased by the sound of Haven's voice.

"That's exactly how it starts." She nods. "I mean, I didn't pass out until later, but still, it definitely started with a major dizzy spell."

"Maybe she's pregnant?" Miles says, loud enough for several passing students to hear.

"Not likely," I say, surprised by how much better I feel, now that I'm wrapped in Damen's warm, supportive arms. "I'm okay, really." I stagger to my feet and move away.

"You should take her home," Miles says, looking at Damen. "She looks awful."

"Yeah." Haven nods. "You should rest, seriously. You *so* don't want to catch it."

But even though I insist on going to class, nobody listens to me. And the next thing I know, Damen's arm is wrapped around my waist and he's leading me back to his car.

"This is ridiculous," I say, as he pulls out of the parking lot and heads away from school. "Seriously, I'm fine. Not to mention that we're totally gonna get busted for ditching again!"

"No one's getting busted." He glances at me briefly, before focusing back on the road. "May I remind you that you fainted back there? You're lucky I caught you in time."

"Yes, but that's the thing, you *did* catch me in time. And now I'm fine. Seriously. I mean, if you're really so worried about me, then you should've taken me to the school nurse. You didn't have to kidnap me."

"I'm not *kidnapping* you," he says, clearly annoyed. "I just want to look after you, make sure you're okay."

"Oh, so now you're a doctor?" I shake my head and roll my eyes.

But he doesn't say anything. He just cruises up Coast Highway, passing right by the street that leads to my house until eventually stopping before a big imposing gate.

"Where are you taking me?" I ask, watching as he nods at a familiar attendant, who smiles and waves us right through.

"My house," he mumbles, driving up a steep hill before making a series of turns that lead into a cul-de-sac and a big empty garage at the end.

Then he takes my hand and leads me through a well-appointed kitchen and into the den where I stand, hands on hips, taking in all of his beautiful furnishings, the exact opposite of the frat-house chic I expected.

"Is this really all yours?" I ask, running my hand over a plush chenille sofa as my eyes tour exquisite lamps, Persian rugs, a collection of abstract oil paintings, and the dark wood coffee table covered in art books, candles, and a framed photo of me. "When'd you take this?" I lift it off the table and study it closely, having absolutely no memory of the moment.

"You act like you've never been here before," he says, motioning for me to sit.

"I haven't." I shrug.

"You *have*," he insists. "Last Sunday? After the beach? I've even got your wet suit hanging upstairs. Now sit." He pats the sofa cushion. "I want to see you resting."

I sink down into the overstuffed cushions, still clutching the photo and wondering when it was taken. My hair is long and loose, my face is slightly flushed, and I'm wearing a peach-colored hoodie I'd forgotten I had. But even though I appear to be laughing, my eyes are sad and serious.

"I took that one day at school. When you weren't looking. I prefer candid shots, it's the only way to really capture the essence of a person," he says, removing it from my grip and retuning it to the table. "Now, close your eyes and rest, while I make you some tea."

When the tea is ready he places the cup in my hands, then busies himself with the thick wool throw, tucking it in all around me.

"This is really nice and all, but it's not necessary," I say, placing the cup on the table and glancing at my watch, thinking if we leave right now, I can still make it to second period in time. "Seriously. I'm fine. We should get back to school."

"Ever, you *fainted*," he says, sitting down beside me, his eyes searching my face as he touches my hair.

"Stuff happens." I shrug, embarrassed by all the fussing, especially when I know nothing's wrong.

"Not on my watch," he whispers, moving his hand from my hair to the scar on my face.

"Don't." I pull away just before he can touch it, watching as his hand falls back to his side.

"What's wrong?" he asks, peering at me.

"I don't want you to catch it," I lie, not wanting to admit to the truth—that the scar is for me, and me only. A constant reminder, ensuring I'll never forget. That's why I refused the plastic surgeon, refused to let him "fix" it. Knowing what happened could never be fixed. It's my fault, my private pain, which is why I hide it under my bangs.

But he just laughs when he says, "I don't get sick."

I close my eyes and shake my head, and when I open them I say, "Oh, so now you don't get sick?"

He shrugs and brings the cup to my lips, urging me to drink.

I take a small sip then turn my head and push it away, saying, "So let's see, you don't get sick, you don't get in trouble for truancy, you get straight A's despite said truancy, you pick up a paint brush and *voilà,* you make a Picasso better than Picasso. You can cook a meal as good as any five-star chef, you used to model in New York—which was right before you lived in Santa Fe, which came after you lived in London, Romania, Paris, and Egypt—you're unemployed and emancipated, yet you somehow manage to live in a luxuriously decorated multimillion-dollar dream home, you drive an expensive car, and—"

"Rome," he says, giving me a serious look.

"What?"

"You said I lived in Romania, when it was actually Rome."

I roll my eyes. "Whatever, the point is—" I stop, my words caught in my throat.

"Yes?" He leans toward me. "The point is . . ."

I swallow hard and avert my gaze, my mind grasping the edges of something, something that's been gnawing at me for some time. Something about Damen, something about that almost, *otherworldly*, quality of his—*is he a ghost like Riley? No, that's impossible, everyone can see him.*

"Ever," he says, his palm on my cheek, turning my head so I'm facing him again. "Ever, I—"

But before he can finish, I'm off the couch and out of his reach, tossing the throw from my shoulders and refusing to look at him when I say, "Take me home."

twenty-six

The second Damen pulls into my drive, I jump out of the car and hit the ground running, racing through the front door and taking the stairs two at a time, hoping and praying that Riley will be there. I need to see her, need to talk to her about all the crazy thoughts that are building inside me. She's the only one I can even begin to explain it to, the only one who just might understand.

I check my den, my bathroom, my balcony, I stand in my room and call out her name, feeling strange, hectic, shaky, panicked in a way that I can't quite explain.

But when she fails to appear, I crumble onto my bed, curl my body into a small tight ball, and relive her loss all over again.

"Ever, honey, are you okay?" Sabine drops her bags and kneels down beside me, her palm cool and sure against my hot clammy skin.

I close my eyes and shake my head, knowing that despite the fainting spell, despite my recent bout of exhaustion, I'm not sick. At least not in the way that she means. It's more complicated than that, and not so easily cured.

I roll onto my side, using the edge of my pillowcase to wipe at my tears, then I turn to her and say, "Sometimes—sometimes it just hits me, you know? And, it's not getting any easier," I choke, my eyes flooding all over again.

She gazes at me, her face softened by sorrow as she says, "I'm not sure that it will. I think you just get used to the feeling, the hollowness, the loss, and somehow learn to live around it." She smiles, removing my tears with her hand.

And when she lies down beside me, I don't pull away. I just close my eyes and allow myself to feel her pain, and my pain, until it's all mixed together, raw and deep with no beginning or end. And we stay like that, crying and talking and sharing in the way we should've done long ago. If only I'd let her in. If only I hadn't pushed her away.

And when she finally gets up to make us some dinner, she pilfers through her tote bag and says, "Look what I found in the trunk of my car. I borrowed it ages ago after you first moved here. I didn't realize I had it all this time."

Then she tosses me the peach hoodie.

The one I'd forgotten all about.

The one I haven't worn since the first week of school.

The one I was wearing in the picture on Damen's coffee table even though we hadn't yet met.

The next day at school, I drive right past Damen, and that stupid spot he always saves for me, and park in what seems like the other side of the world.

"What the *hell*?" Miles says, gaping incredulously. "You drove right past it! And now look how far we have to walk!"

I slam my door and storm across the lot, marching right past Damen who's leaning against his car, waiting for me.

"Um, hel-*lo*! Tall dark and handsome at three o'clock, you walked right by him! What is going on with you?" Miles says, grabbing my arm and looking at me. "Are you guys in a fight?"

But I just shake my head and pull away. "*Nothing's* going on," I say, striding toward the building.

Even though the last time I checked Damen was well behind me, when I walk into class and head for my seat, he's already there. So I raise my hood and switch on my iPod, making a point to ignore him, while I wait for Mr. Robins to call roll.

"Ever," Damen whispers, as I stare straight ahead, focusing on Mr. Robins's receding hairline, just waiting for my turn to say "here."

"Ever, I know you're upset. But I can explain."

I stare straight ahead, pretending not to hear.

"Ever, *please,*" Damen begs.

But I just act like he's not even there. And just when Mr. Robins gets to my name, Damen sighs, closes his eyes, and says, "Fine. Just remember, you asked for it."

And the next thing I know, a horrible *thwonk!* resonates throughout the room, as nineteen heads hit the tops of their desks.

Everyone's head but Damen's and mine.

I gaze all around, mouth gaping, eyes trying to comprehend, and when I finally turn back to Damen, staring accusingly, he just shrugs and says, "This is exactly what I'd hoped to avoid."

"What've you done?" I stare at all the limp bodies, a terrible understanding beginning to emerge. "Omigod, you killed them! You killed everyone!" I shout, my heart pounding so fast I'm sure he can hear it.

But he just shakes his head and says, "Come on, Ever. What do you take me for? Of course, I didn't kill them. They're just taking a little . . . siesta, that's all."

I scoot to the edge of my seat, my eyes fixed on the door, plotting my escape.

"You can try, but you won't get very far. You see how I beat you to class even though you had a head start?" He crosses his legs and gazes at me, his face calm, voice steady as can be.

"You can read my mind?" I whisper, recalling some of my more embarrassing thoughts, my cheeks growing hot as my fingers grip the edge of my desk.

"Usually." He shrugs. "Well, pretty much always, yes."

"For how long?" I stare at him, part of me wanting to take my chance on escape, while the other part wants to get a few questions answered before my most certain demise.

"Since the first day I saw you," he whispers, his gaze locked on mine, sending a flood of warmth through my body.

"And when was that?" I ask, voice trembling, remembering the photo on his table, and wondering just how long he's been stalking me.

"I'm not stalking you." He laughs. "At least not in the way that you think."

"Why should I believe you?" I glare, knowing better than to trust him, no matter how trivial.

"Because I've never lied to you."

"You're lying now!"

"I've never lied to you about anything important," he says, averting his gaze.

"Oh really? What about the fact that you took a photo of me long before you were even enrolled here? Where does that fall on your list of important things to share in a relationship?" I glare.

He sighs, his eyes appearing tired when he says, "And where does being a clairvoyant who hangs out with her dead little sister fall upon yours?"

"You don't know anything about me." I stand, hands sweaty and shaky, heart slam-dancing in my chest, as I stare at all of the slumped-over bodies, Stacia with her mouth hanging open, Craig snoring so loud he's vibrating, Mr. Robins looking more happy and peaceful than I've ever seen him. "Is it the whole school? Or just this room?"

"I can't be sure, but I'm guessing it's the whole school." He nods, smiling as he glances around, clearly pleased with his handiwork.

And without another word, I spring from my seat, race out the door, sprint down the hall, across the quad, and through the office. Fleeing past all the slumped-over secretaries and administrators sleeping at their desks, before bursting through the door and into the parking lot, running toward my little red Miata, where Damen is already waiting, my bag dangling from the very tips of his fingers.

"I told you." He shrugs, returning my backpack.

I stand before him, sweaty, frantic, completely freaked out. All of those long-forgotten moments flashing before me—his blood-covered face, Haven thrashing and moaning, that weird creepy room—and I know he did something to my mind, something to keep me from remembering. And even though I'm no match for someone like him, I refuse to go down without a fight.

"Ever!" he cries, reaching toward me, then letting his hand

fall to his side. "You think I did all of this so that I can kill you?" His eyes are full of anguish, frantically searching my face.

"Isn't that the plan?" I glare. "Haven thinks it's all some wild, goth, fever dream. I'm the only one who knows the truth. I'm the only one who knows just how big of a monster you really are. The only thing I don't get is why you didn't just kill us both while you had the chance? Why bother suppressing the memory and keeping me alive?"

"I would *never* hurt you," he says, his eyes pinched with pain. "You've got it all wrong, I was trying to *save* Haven, not harm her. You just wouldn't listen."

"Then why did she look like she was on the brink of death?" I press my lips together to stop them from quivering, my eyes fixed on his but refusing their heat.

"Because she *was* on the brink of death," he says, sounding annoyed. "That tattoo on her wrist was infected in the worst way—it was killing her. When you walked in on us I was sucking the infection right out of her, like you do with a snake bite."

I shake my head. "I know what I saw."

He closes his eyes, pinching the bridge of his nose with his fingers and taking a long deep breath before he looks at me and says, "I know how it looks. And I know you don't believe me. But I've been trying to explain and you just wouldn't let me, so I did all of this to get your attention. Because, Ever, trust me, you've got it all wrong."

He looks at me, his eyes dark and intense, his hands relaxed and open, but I'm not buying it. Not a single word. He's had hundreds, maybe thousands of years to perfect such an act, resulting in a really good show, but still only a show. And even though I can't believe I'm about to say it, even though I can't quite get my mind wrapped around it, there's only one explanation, no matter how crazy.

"All I know is that I want you to go back to your coffin, or your coven, or wherever it is that you lived before you came here and—" I gasp for breath, feeling like I'm trapped in some horrible nightmare, wishing I'd wake up soon. "Just leave me alone—just go away!"

He closes his eyes and shakes his head, stifling a laugh as he says. "I'm not a vampire, Ever."

"Oh, yeah? Prove it!" I say, my voice shaky, my eyes on his, fully convinced I'm just a rosary, garlic clove, and wooden stake short of ending all this.

But he just laughs. "Don't be ridiculous. There's no such thing."

"I know what I saw," I tell him, picturing the blood, Haven, that strange and creepy room, knowing that as soon as I *see* it, he'll see it too. Wondering how he'll possibly try to explain his friendship with Marie Antoinette, Picasso, Van Gogh, Emily Brontë, and William Shakespeare—when they lived centuries apart.

He shakes his head, then looks at me and says, "Well, for that matter, I was also a good friend of Leonardo da Vinci, Botticelli, Francis Bacon, Albert Einstein, and John, Paul, George, and Ringo." He pauses, seeing the blank look on my face and groaning when he says, "Christ, Ever, the *Beatles*!" He shakes his head and laughs. "God, you make me feel old."

I just stand there, barely breathing, not comprehending, but when he reaches for me, I still have the good sense to pull away.

"I'm not a vampire, Ever. I'm an immortal."

I roll my eyes. "Vampire, immortal, same difference," I say, shaking my head and fuming under my breath, thinking how ridiculous it is to argue over a label.

"Ah, but it happens to be a label worth arguing over, as there *is* a big difference. You see, a vampire is a *fictional*, *made-up* creature that exists only in books, and movies, and, in your case, overactive imaginations." He smiles. "Whereas *I* am an immortal. Which means I've roamed the earth for hundreds of years in one continuous life cycle. Though, contrary to the fantasy you've conjured in your head, my immortality is not reliant on bloodsucking, human sacrifice, or whatever unsavory acts you've imagined."

I squint, suddenly remembering his strange red brew and wondering if that has something to do with his longevity. Like it's some kind of immortal juice or something.

"Immortal juice." He laughs. "Good one. Imagine the marketing possibilities." But when he sees I'm not laughing, his face softens when he says, "Ever, please, you've no need to fear me. I'm not dangerous, or evil, and I would never do anything to hurt you. I'm simply a guy who's lived *a very long time*. Maybe too long, who knows? But that doesn't make me bad. Just immortal. And I'm afraid . . ."

He reaches for me, but I back away, my legs shaky, unstable, refusing to hear any more. "You're lying!" I whisper, my heart filled with rage. "This is crazy! *You're crazy!*"

He shakes his head and gazes at me, eyes filled with unfathomable regret. Then he takes a step toward me and says, "Remember the first moment you saw me? Right here in the parking lot? And how the second your eyes met mine you felt an immediate rush of recognition? And the other day, when you fainted? How you opened your eyes and looked right into mine, and you were so close to remembering, on the very verge of recollection, but then you lost the thread?"

I stare at him, immobile, transfixed, sensing exactly what he's about to say, but refusing to hear it. "No!" I mumble, taking another step back, my head dizzy, my body off balance as my knees begin to buckle.

"I'm the one who found you that day in the woods. I'm the one who *brought you back*!"

I shake my head, my eyes blurred with tears. *No!*

"The eyes you looked into, on your—*return*—were mine, Ever. I was there. I was right there beside you. I brought you back. I *saved* you. I know you remember. I can see it in your thoughts."

"No!" I scream, covering my ears and closing my eyes. "Stop it!" I yell, not wanting to hear any more.

"Ever." His voice invades my thoughts, my senses. "I'm sorry but it's true. Though you have no reason to fear me."

I crumble to the ground, face pressed against my knees, as I break into violent, gasping, shoulder-shaking sobs. "You had no right to come near me, no right to interfere! It's your fault I'm a freak! It's your fault I'm stuck with this horrible life! Why didn't you just leave me alone, why didn't you just let me die?"

"I couldn't stand to lose you again," he mumbles, kneeling down beside me. "Not this time. *Not again.*"

I lift my gaze to his, having no idea what he means, but hoping he won't try to explain it. I've heard about all I can take, and I just want it to stop. I just want it to end.

He shakes his head, a pained expression masking his face. "Ever, please don't think that way, please don't—"

"So—so you just randomly decide to bring me back while my whole family dies?" I say, gazing up at him, my sorrow consumed by a crushing rage. *"Why?* Why would you do such a thing? I mean, if what you say is true, if you're so powerful you can raise the dead, then why didn't you save them too? *Why only me?*"

He winces at the hostility in my gaze, tiny arrows of hate directed at him. Then he closes his eyes when he says, "I'm not that powerful. And it was too late, they'd already moved on. But you—you lingered. And I thought that meant you wanted to live."

I lean against my car, closing my eyes, gasping for breath, thinking: *So it really is my fault. Because I procrastinated, lingered, wandered through that stupid field, distracted by those pulsating trees and flowers that shivered. While they moved on, crossed over, and I fell for his bait . . .*

He looks at me briefly, then averts his gaze.

And wouldn't you know it, the one time I'm so angry I could actually kill someone, my anger's directed at the one person who claims to be, well, *un-killable*.

"Go away!" I finally say, ripping the crystal-encrusted horseshoe bracelet from my wrist and throwing it at him. Wanting to forget about that, about him, about *everything*. Having seen and heard more than I can take. "Just—go away. I never want to see you again."

"Ever, please don't say that if you don't really mean it," he says, his voice pleading, sorrowful, weak.

I place my head in my hands, too weary to cry, too shattered to speak. And knowing he can hear the thoughts in my head, I shut my eyes and think:

You say you'd never harm me, but look what you've done! You've ruined everything, wrecked my whole life, and for what? So I could be alone? So I could live the rest of my life as a freak? I hate you—I hate you for what you've done to me—I hate you for what you've made me—I hate you for being so selfish! And I never, ever want to see you again!

I stay like that, head in my hands, rocking back and forth against the wheel of my car, allowing the words to flow through me, over and over again.

Just let me be normal, please just let me be normal again. Just go away, leave me alone. Because I hate you—I hate you—I hate you—I hate you—

When I finally look up, I'm surrounded by tulips—hundreds of thousands of tulips, all of them red. Those soft waxy petals glinting in the bright morning sun, filling up the parking lot and covering all the cars. And as I struggle to my feet and brush myself off, I know without looking: their sender is gone.

twenty-seven

It's weird in English, not having Damen beside me, holding my hand, whispering in my ear, and acting as my *off* switch. I guess I'd grown so used to having him around I'd forgotten just how mean Stacia and Honor could be. But watching them smirk, as they text each other with messages like—*Stupid freak, no wonder he left*—I know I'm back to relying on my hoodie, sunglasses, and iPod again.

Though it's not like I don't see the irony. It's not like I don't get the joke. Because for someone who sobbed in a parking lot, begging her immortal boyfriend to disappear so that she could feel normal again, well, obviously, the punch line is *me*.

Because now, in my new life without Damen, all of the random thoughts, the profusion of colors and sounds, are so overwhelming, so tremendously crushing, my ears constantly ring, my eyes continuously water, and the migraines appear so quickly, invading my head, hijacking my body, and rendering me so nauseous and dizzy I can just barely function.

Though it is funny how I was so worried about mentioning our breakup to Miles and Haven that a full week passed by before his name was even mentioned. And even then, I'm the one who brought it up. I guess they'd gotten so used to his erratic attendance they didn't see anything unusual about his latest extended absence.

So one day, during lunch, I cleared my throat, glanced between them, and said, "Just so you know, Damen and I broke up." And when their mouths dropped open and they both started to speak, I held up my hand and said, "And, he's gone."

"*Gone*?" they said, four eyes bugging, two jaws dropping, both of them reluctant to believe it.

And even though I knew they were concerned, even though I knew I owed them a good explanation, I just shook my head, pressed my lips together, and refused to say anything further.

Though Ms. Machado wasn't so easy. A few days after Damen left, she walked right up to my easel, did her best to avoid direct eye contact with my Van Gogh disaster, and said, "I know you and Damen were close, and I know how hard this must be for you, so I thought you should have this. I think you'll find it extraordinary."

She pushed a canvas toward me, but I just leaned it against the leg of my easel and kept painting. I had no doubt about its being extraordinary; everything Damen did was extraordinary. But then again, when you've roamed the earth for hundreds of years, you've plenty of time to master a few skills.

"Aren't you going to look at it?" she asked, confused by my lack of interest in Damen's masterpiece replica of a masterpiece.

But I just turned to her, forcing my face into a smile when I said, "No. But thank you for giving it to me."

And when the bell finally rang, I dragged it out to my car, tossed it into my trunk, and slammed down the hood, without once even looking.

And when Miles asked, "Hey, what was that?" I just jammed the key in the ignition and said, "Nothing."

But the one thing I didn't expect was how lonely I felt. I guess I failed to realize just how much I relied on Damen and Riley to fill up the gaps, to seal all the cracks in my life. And even though Riley warned me she wouldn't be around all that much, when it hit the three-week mark, I couldn't help but panic.

Because saying good-bye to Damen, my gorgeous, creepy, quite possibly evil, immortal boyfriend, was harder than I'll ever admit. But not getting to say good-bye to Riley is more than I can possibly bear.

Saturday, when Miles and Haven invite me to tag along on their annual Winter Fantasy pilgrimage, I accept. Knowing it's time to get out of the house, out of my slump, and rejoin the living. And since it's my first time there, they're pretty excited about showing me around.

"It's not as good as the summer Sawdust Festival," Miles says, after we buy our tickets and head through the gates.

"That's because it's better," Haven says, skipping ahead and turning to smile at us.

Miles smirks. "Well, other than the weather it doesn't really matter since they both have glassblowers, and that's always my favorite part."

"Big surprise." Haven laughs, looping her arm through Miles's as I follow alongside them, my head spinning from the crowd-generated energy, all of the colors, sights, and sounds swirling around me, wishing I'd had the good sense to just stay home where it's quieter, safer.

I've just lifted my hood and am about to insert my earbuds

when Haven turns to me and says, "Really? You're seriously doing that here?"

And I stop, and slip them back into my pocket. Because even though I want to drown everyone out, I don't want my friends to think I'm trying to drown them out too.

"Come on, you've *got* to see the glassblower, he's amazing," Miles says, leading us past an authentic-looking Santa and several silversmiths before stopping in front of some guy crafting beautiful, multicolored vases using only his mouth, a long metal tube, and fire. "I have *got* to learn how to do that." He sighs, completely transfixed.

I stand beside him, watching the swirl of liquid colors mold and take shape, then I head over to the next booth, where some really cool purses are displayed.

I hoist a small brown bag off its shelf and stroke its soft buttery leather, thinking it might make a good Christmas gift for Sabine, since it's something she'd never buy for herself, but might secretly want.

"How much for this one?" I ask, wincing as my voice reverberates through my head in a never-ending percussion.

"One hundred and fifty."

I gaze at the woman, taking in her blue batik tunic, faded jeans, and silver peace-sign necklace, knowing she's prepared to go lower, much lower. But my eyes are stinging so bad, and the throbbing in my head's so severe I don't have the strength to barter. In fact, I just want to go home.

I put it back where I found it and start to turn away, when she says, "But for you, one thirty."

And even though I'm well aware that she's still at the top of her offer, that there's plenty more room to bargain, I just nod and move away.

Then someone behind me says, "Now you and I both know her absolute bottom line is ninety-five. So why'd you give up so easily?"

And when I turn, I see a petite auburn-haired woman surrounded by the most brilliant purple aura.

"Ava." She nods, extending her hand.

"I know," I say, making a point to ignore it.

"How've you been?" she asks, smiling as though I didn't just do something incredibly cold and rude, which makes me feel even worse for having done it.

I shrug, glancing over to the glassblower, searching for Miles and Haven, and feeling the first hint of panic when I don't see them.

"Your friends are standing in line at Laguna Taco. But don't worry, they're ordering for you too."

"I *know,*" I tell her, even though I didn't. My head hurts far too much to get a read on anyone.

And just as I start to move away again, she grabs hold of my arm and says, "Ever, I want you to know my offer still stands. I'd really like to help you." She smiles.

My first instinct is to pull away, to get as far from her as possible, but the moment she placed her hand on my arm, my head stopped pounding, my ears stopped ringing, and my eyes stopped manufacturing tears. But when I look in her eyes, I remember who she really is—the horrible woman who's stolen my sister. And I narrow my gaze and yank my arm free, glaring at her as I say, "Don't you think you've *helped* enough already?" I press my lips together and glare. "You've already stolen Riley, so what more could you possible want?" I swallow hard and try not to cry.

She looks at me, brows merging with concern, her aura a beautiful vibrant beacon of violet. "Riley was never anyone's to take. And she'll always be with you, even if you can't actually *see* her," she says, reaching for my arm.

But I refuse to listen. And I refuse to let her touch me again, no matter how calming. "Just—just stay out of my life," I say, moving away. "Just leave me alone. Riley and I were fine until you came along."

But she doesn't leave. She doesn't go anywhere. She just stays right there, gazing at me in that horribly annoying, soft, caring way. "I know about the headaches," she whispers, her voice light and soothing. "You don't have to live like this, Ever. Really, I can help."

And even though I'd love a break from the onslaught of noise and pain, I turn on my heel and storm away, hoping I never see her again.

"Who was that?" Haven asks, plunging a tortilla chip into a tiny cup of salsa as I sit down beside her and shrug.

"No one," I whisper, cringing as my words vibrate in my ears.

"Looks like that psychic lady from the party."

I reach for the plate Miles slides toward me and pick up a plastic fork.

"We didn't know what you wanted so we got a little of everything," he says. "Did you buy a purse?"

I shake my head, then immediately regret it since it only intensifies the pounding. "Too expensive," I say, covering my mouth as I chew, the crunch reverberating so badly my eyes fill with tears. "You get a vase?" But I already know that he didn't, and not just because I'm psychic, but because there's no bag.

"No, I just like to watch 'em blow." He laughs, taking a sip of his drink.

"Hey you guys, shh! Is that my phone?" Haven digs through her oversized, overstuffed bag that often stands in for her closet.

"Well, since you're the only one at this table with a Marilyn Manson ring tone . . ." Miles shrugs, ignoring his taco shell and eating only the insides.

"Off the carbs?" I ask, watching as he picks at his food.

He nods. "Just because Tracy Turnblad's fat doesn't mean I have to be."

I take a sip of my Sprite and gaze at Haven. And when I see the elated expression on her face, I *know*.

She turns away from us, covers her other ear, and says, "Omigod! I totally thought you'd vanished—I'm out with Miles—yeah, Ever's here too—yeah, they're right here—okay." She covers the mouthpiece and turns toward us, her eyes lighting up when she says, "Drina says hi!" Then she waits for us to say *hi* back. But when we don't, she rolls her eyes, gets up, and walks away, saying, "They say hi too."

Miles shakes his head and looks at me. "I didn't say *hi*. Did you say *hi*?"

I shrug and mix my beans into my rice.

"Trouble," he says, gazing after her and shaking his head.

And even though I sense that it's true, I'm wondering what exactly he means. Because the energy in this place is bubbling and swirling like a big cosmic soup, too lumpy to slog through or try to tune in. "What do you mean?" I ask, squinting against the glare.

"Isn't it obvious?"

I shrug, my head pounding so badly I can't get inside his.

"There's something just so—*creepy* about their friendship. I mean, a harmless girl crush is one thing. But this—this just doesn't make any sense. Major creep factor."

"Creepy how?" I tear a piece off my taco shell and look at him.

He ignores his rice and favors the beans. "I know this is going to sound horrible, and trust me, I don't mean it to be, but it's almost like she's turning Haven into an acolyte."

I raise my brows.

"A follower, a worshipper, a clone, a Mini-Me." He shrugs. "And, it's just so—"

"Creepy," I provide.

He sips his drink and glances between Haven and me. "Look at how she's started dressing like her, the contacts, the hair color, the makeup, the clothing, she acts like her too—or at least she tries to."

"Is it just that, or is there something else?" I ask, wondering if he knows anything specific, or if it's just a general sense of doom.

"You need more?" He gapes.

I shrug, dropping my taco onto my plate, no longer hungry.

"But between you and me, that whole tattoo thing takes it to a whole new level. I mean, *what the hell?*" he whispers, glancing at Haven, making sure she can't hear. "What's it even supposed to *mean*?" He shakes his head. "I mean, okay, I *know* what it means, but what does it mean to *them*? Is it the latest in vampire chic? Because Drina's not exactly goth. I'm not sure what she's trying to be with her fitted silk lady dresses and purses that match her shoes. Is it a cult? Some kind of secret society? And don't get me started on that infection. Na-*sty*. And, by the way, *so* not normal like she thinks. It's probably what made her so sick."

I press my lips and stare at him, not sure how to respond, how much to share. And yet, wondering why I'm so determined to keep Damen's secrets—secrets that bring *creepy* to a whole new level. Secrets that, when I think about it, have nothing to do with *me*. But I hesitate for too long, and Miles continues, ensuring the vault stays locked, at least for today.

"The whole thing is just so—*unhealthy*." He cringes.

"What's unhealthy?" Haven asks, plopping down beside me and tossing her phone back into her purse.

"Not washing your hands after you go to the bathroom," Miles quips.

"And *that's* what you guys were talking about?" She eyes us suspiciously. "Like I'm supposed to believe that?"

"I'm telling you, Ever refuses to suds up, and I was just trying to warn her of the dangers she's exposing herself to. Exposing *all of us* to." He shakes his head and looks at me.

I roll my eyes, my face turning crimson even thought it's *not* true. Watching as Haven digs through her bag, pushing past stray tubes of lipstick, a cordless curling iron, stray breath mints—their wrappers long gone—before coming across a small silver flask, unscrewing the top, and dumping a fair amount of clear, odorless liquid into each of our drinks.

"Well, that's all very amusing, but it's obvious you were talking about *me*. But you know what? I'm so freaking happy I don't even care." She smiles.

I reach for her hand, determined to stop her from pouring. Ever since the night I puked my guts out at cheerleading camp, after drinking more than my share of the contraband bottle Rachel smuggled into our cabin, I've sworn off the vodka. But the moment I touch her I'm overcome with dread, seeing a calendar flash before me with December 21 circled in red.

"Jeez, relax, already. Stop being so *clenched*. Live a little, will ya?" She shakes her head and rolls her eyes. "Aren't you going to ask me why I'm so happy?"

"No, because I know you'll tell us anyway," Miles says, discarding his plate, having eaten all of the protein and saving the rest for the pigeons.

"You're right, Miles, you're absolutely right. Though it's always nice to be asked. Anyway, that was Drina. She's still in New York, enjoying a major shopping spree. She even bought a bunch of stuff for me, if you can believe it." She looks at us, her eyes wide, but when we don't respond, she makes a face and continues. "Anyway, she said *hi* even though you couldn't be bothered to say *hi* back. And don't think she didn't know it," she says, scowling at us. "But, she's heading back soon, and she just invited me to this really cool party and I totally cannot wait!"

"When?" I ask, trying not to sound as panicked as I feel. Wondering if it could possibly be on the twenty-first of December.

But she just smiles and shakes her head. "Sorry, no say. I promised not to tell."

"Why?" Miles and I both say.

"Because it's super exclusive, invitation only, and they don't need a bunch of crashers showing up."

"And that's how you see us? As party crashers?"

Haven shrugs and takes a hearty sip of her drink.

"Now that's just wrong." Miles shakes his head. "We're your best friends, so by law, you have to tell us."

"Not this," Haven says. "I'm sworn to secrecy. Just know that I'm so excited I could burst!"

I gaze at her, sitting before me, face flushed with a happiness that sets me on edge, but my head hurts so badly, and my eyes are really tearing, and her aura's so merged with everyone else's, I can't get a read.

I take a sip of my drink, forgetting about the vodka until a trail of hot liquid slips down my throat, courses into my bloodstream, and makes my head sway.

"You still sick?" Haven asks, shooting me a worried look. "You should take it easy. Maybe you're not completely over it."

"Over what?" I squint, taking another sip, and then another, my senses blunted a little more with each taste.

"The fever-dream flu! Remember how you fainted that day at school? I told you the whole dizzy nausea thing is just the beginning. Just promise to tell me if you have the dreams, because they're *amazing*."

"What dreams?"

"Didn't I tell you?"

"Not in detail." I take another sip, noting how my head feels woozy yet clear, all the visions, random thoughts, colors, and sounds suddenly shrinking and fading away.

"They were wild! And don't get mad, but Damen was in some of them, though it's not like anything happened. It wasn't *that* kind of dream. It was more like he was saving me, like he was fighting these evil forces to save my life. So bizarre." She laughs. "Oh, speaking of, Drina saw Damen in New York."

I stare at Haven, my body growing cold, despite the alcohol blanketing my insides. But when I take another sip, the chill slips away, taking my pain and anxiety with it.

So I take another.

And then another.

Then I squint at her and say, "Why did you just tell me that?"

But Haven just shrugs. "Drina just wanted you to know."

twenty-eight

After the festival, we pile into Haven's car, make a quick stop at her house to refill her flask, then head into town where we park on the street, stuff the meter full of quarters, and storm the sidewalks, three across, arms linked, making all the other pedestrians move out of our way, as we sing "(You Never) Call Me When You're Sober," at the top of our lungs and wildly off-key. Staggering in fits of laughter every time someone snickers and shakes their head at us.

And when we pass one of those New Age bookstores advertising psychic readings, I just roll my eyes and avert my gaze, thrilled that I'm no longer part of that world, now that the alcohol's released me, now that I'm free.

We cross the street to Main Beach, and stumble past Hotel Laguna, until we fall onto the sand, legs overlapping, arms entwined, passing the flask back and forth, and mourning its loss the moment it's empty.

"Crap!" I mumble, tilting my head all the way back and tapping hard on the bottom and sides, straining for every last drop.

"Jeez, take it easy." Miles looks at me. "Just sit back and enjoy the buzz."

But I don't want to sit back. And I am enjoying the buzz. I just want to make sure it continues. Now that my psychic bonds have been broken, I want to ensure they stay broken. "Wanna go to my house?" I slur, hoping Sabine's not at home so we can get to the leftover Halloween vodka and keep the buzz rolling.

But Haven shakes her head. "Forget it," she says. "I'm wrecked. I'm thinking of ditching the car and crawling back home."

"Miles?" I gaze at him, my eyes pleading, not wanting the party to end. This is the first time I've felt so light, so free, so unencumbered, so normal, since—well, since Damen went away.

"Can't." He shakes his head. "Family dinner. Seven-thirty sharp. Tie optional. Straightjacket required." He laughs, falling onto the sand, as Haven topples over and joins him.

"Well, what about me? What am I supposed to do?" I cross my arms and glare at my friends, not wanting to be left on my own, watching as they laugh and roll around together, oblivious to me.

The next morning, even though I oversleep, the first thing I think when I open my eyes is: *My head's not pounding!*

At least not in the usual way.

Then I roll over, reach under my bed, and retrieve the bottle of vodka I stashed there last night, taking a long deep swig and closing my eyes as its warm wonderful numbness blankets my tongue and sinks down my throat.

And when Sabine peeks her head in my room to see if I'm up, I'm thrilled to see her aura has vanished from sight.

"I'm awake!" I say, shoving the bottle under a pillow and rushing over to hug her. Anxious to see what kind of energy exchange there will be, and elated when there is none. "Isn't it a beautiful day?" I smile, my lips feeling clumsy and loose as they unveil my teeth.

She gazes out the window and back at me. "If you say so." She shrugs.

I look past my french doors and into a day that's gray, overcast, and rainy. But then again, I wasn't referring to the weather. I was referring to me. The new me.

The new, improved, nonpsychic me!

"Reminds me of home." I shrug, slipping out of my nightgown and into the shower.

The second Miles gets in my car he takes one look at me, and goes, "What *the*—?"

I gaze down at my sweater, denim mini, and ballet flats, relics Sabine saved from my old life, and smile.

"I'm sorry, but I don't accept rides from strangers," he says, opening the door and pretending to climb back out.

"It's me, really. Cross my heart and hope to—well, just trust that it's me." I laugh. "And close your door already, I don't need you falling out and making us late."

"I don't get it," he says, gaping at me. "I mean, when did this happen? *How* did this happen? Just yesterday you were practically wearing a burka, and now it looks like you've raided Paris Hilton's closet!"

I look at him.

"Only classier, way classier."

I smile, pushing down on the gas, my wheels sliding and lifting off the soggy wet street and easing up only when I remember how my internal cop radar is gone and Miles starts screaming.

"Seriously, Ever, *what the hell?* Omigod, are you still drunk?"

"No!" I say, a little too quickly. "I'm just, you know, coming out of my shell, that's all. I can be kind of—shy, for the first—several—months." I laugh. "But trust me, this is the *real* me." I nod, hoping he buys it.

"Do you realize you've picked the wettest, most miserable day of the year to *come out of your shell?*"

I shake my head and pull into the parking lot as I say, "You have no idea how beautiful it is. Reminds me of home."

I park in the closest available space, then we race for the gate, backpacks held over our heads like makeshift umbrellas, as the soles of our shoes splash water onto our legs. And when I see Haven shivering under the eaves, I feel like jumping with glee when I see she's aura-free.

"What *the*—?" she says, eyes bugging as she looks me up and down.

"You guys really need to learn how to finish a sentence." I laugh.

"Seriously, who *are* you?" she says, still gawking at me.

Miles laughs, wraps his arms around both of us, and leads us past the gate, saying, "Don't mind Miss Oregon, she happens to think it's a beautiful day."

When I walk into English, I'm relieved that I can no longer see or hear anything I'm not meant to. And even though Stacia and Honor are whispering back and forth, scowling at my clothes, my shoes, my hair, even the makeup I wear on my face, I just shrug it off and mind my own business. Because while I'm sure they're not saying anything remotely kind, the fact that I no longer have access to the actual words makes a whole world of difference. And when I catch them both looking at me again, I just smile and wave until they're so freaked out they turn away.

But by third-period chemistry, the buzz is nearly gone. Giving way to a barrage of sights, colors, and sounds that threaten to overwhelm me.

And when I raise my hand and ask for the hall pass, I'm barely out the door before I'm taken over completely.

I stagger toward my locker, spinning the dial around and around, trying to remember the correct number sequence.

Is it 24-18-12-3? Or 12-18-3-24?

I glance around the hall, my head pounding, my eyes tearing, and then I hit it—*18-3-24-12.* And I dig through a pile of books and papers, knocking them all to the ground but paying no attention as they splay around my feet, just wanting to get to the water bottle I've hidden inside, longing for its sweet liquid release.

I unscrew the cap and tilt my head back, taking a long deep pull, soon followed by another, and then another, and another. And hoping to make it through lunch, I'm taking one last swig when I hear:

"Hold it—smile—no? That's okay, I still got it."

And I watch in horror as Stacia approaches, camera held high, an image of me, guzzling vodka, clearly displayed.

"Who would've thought you'd be so photogenic? But then again, it's so rare we get the chance to see you without your hood." She smiles, her eyes grazing over me, from my feet to my bangs.

I stare at her, and even though my senses are blunted from drink, her intentions are clear.

"Who would you prefer I send this to first? Your mom?" She lifts her brows and covers her mouth in mock horror, as she says, "Oh, so sorry, my apologies. What I meant to say was your *aunt*? Or perhaps one of your teachers? Or maybe *all* of your teachers? No? No, you're right, this should go straight to the principal, one bird, one stone, a quick and easy kill, as they say."

"It's a *water* bottle," I tell her, leaning down to pick up my books and shoving them back in my locker, striving for nonchalance, acting as though I don't even care, knowing she can sniff out fear better than any police-trained bloodhound. "All you have is a photo of me, drinking from a water bottle. Big effin' deal."

"A *water* bottle." She laughs. "Yes, and so it is. And so *very* original I might add. I'm sure you're the absolute very first person to ever think of pouring vodka into a water bottle." She rolls her eyes. "Please. You are *so* going down, Ever. One quick sobriety test, and it's good-bye Bay View, hello Academy for Losers and Abusers."

I gaze at her standing before me, so sure, so smug, so completely overconfident, and I know she has every right to be, she caught me red-handed. And even though the evidence may appear circumstantial, we both know that it isn't. We both know that she's right.

"What do you want?" I finally whisper, figuring everybody has a price, I just need to find hers. I've heard enough thoughts over the past year, seen enough visions, to confirm this is true.

"Well, for starters, I want you to quit bothering me," she says, folding her arms across her chest, anchoring the evidence snugly under her armpit.

"But I don't bother you," I say, the words slightly slurred. "*You* bother *me*."

"*Au contraire.*" She smiles, looking me over, eyes scathing. "Just having to look at you day after day is a bother. A huge horrible bother."

"You want me to transfer out of English?" I ask, still holding that stupid bottle, unsure what to do with it. If I leave it in my locker, she'll nark and have it confiscated—and if I stow it in my backpack, same thing.

"You know you still owe me for that dress you destroyed in your spastic rampage."

So that's it, blackmail. Good thing I won all that money at the track.

I dig through my backpack and locate my wallet, more than willing to reimburse her if it'll put an end to all this. "How much?" I say.

She looks me over, trying to calculate my immediate net worth. "Well, like I said, it was *designer*—and not so easily replaced—so—"

"A hundred?" I pick off a Ben Franklin and offer it to her.

She rolls her eyes. "While I totally get how you're completely clueless about fashion and all things worth having, you really need to up the offer. Aim a little higher, a tad bit steeper," she says, eyeballing my wad.

But since blackmailers have a way of returning and constantly upping the ante, I know it's better just to deal with it now, before it can go any further. So I look at her and say, "Since we both know you bought that dress at the outlet mall, on your way home from Palm Springs"—I smile, remembering what I *saw* that day in the hall—"I'll reimburse you for the cost of the dress, which, if memory serves, was eighty-five dollars. In which case, a hundred seems like a pretty generous deal, wouldn't you say?"

She looks me over, her face twisting into a grin, as she takes the bill and shoves it deep into her pocket. Then she glances between the water bottle and me, and smiles when she says, "So, aren't you going to offer me a drink?"

If someone had told me just yesterday that I'd be hanging in the bathroom, getting whacked with Stacia Miller, I never would've believed it. But sure enough, that's exactly what I did. Trailed her right inside so we could huddle in the corner and suck down a water bottle full of vodka.

Nothing like shared addictions and hidden secrets to bring people together.

And when Haven walked in and found us like that, her eyes bugged out when she said, "What the *fug*?"

And I fell over in fits of howling laughter, as Stacia squinted at her and slurred, "Welthome gosh girthl."

"Am I missing something?" Haven asked, gazing between us, eyes narrowed, suspicious. "Is this supposed to be funny?"

And the way she looked, the way she stood there so authoritative, so derisive, so serious, so *not* amused, made us laugh even more. Then as soon as the door slammed behind her, we got back to drinking.

But getting tanked in the bathroom with Stacia does not ensure access to the VIP table. And knowing better than to even try, I head for my usual spot, my head so polluted, my brain so fuzzy, it takes a moment before I realize I'm not welcome there either.

I plop myself down, squint at Haven and Miles, then start laughing for no apparent reason. Or at least not one that's apparent to them. But if they could only see the looks on their faces, I know they'd laugh too.

"What's up with her?" Miles asks, glancing up from his script.

Haven scowls. "She's bent, totally and completely bent. I caught her in the bathroom, getting twisted with, of all people, Stacia Miller."

Miles gapes, his forehead all scrunched in a way that makes me start laughing all over again. And when I won't quiet down, he leans toward me, pinches my arm, and says, "Shh!" He glances all around and then back at me. "Seriously, Ever. Are you crazy? Jeez, ever since Damen left you've been—"

"Ever since Damen left—*what?*" I pull away so fast I lose my balance and nearly fall off the bench, righting myself just in time to see Haven shake her head and smirk. "Come on, Miles, spit it out already." I glare at him. "You too, Haven, spit it out." Only it comes out more like, *schthpititowt,* and don't think they don't notice.

"You want us to *schthpititowt*?" Miles shakes his head as Haven rolls her eyes. "Well, I'm sure we'd be happy to if we only knew what it meant. Do you know what it means?" He looks at Haven.

"Sounds German," she says, glaring at me.

I roll my eyes, and get up to leave, only I don't coordinate it so well, and I end up banging my knee. *"Owww!"* I cry, slumping back onto the bench, gripping my leg as my eyes squinch in pain.

"Here, drink this," Miles urges, pushing his VitaminWater toward me. "And hand over your keys, because you are *so* not driving me home."

Miles was right. I *so* did not drive him home. That's because he drove himself home.

I got a ride from Sabine.

She gets me settled in the passenger seat, then goes around to her side, and when she starts the engine and pulls out of the lot, she shakes her head, clenches her jaw, glances at me, and says, "*Expelled?* How do you go from honor roll to expelled? Can you please explain that to me?"

I close my eyes and press my forehead against the side window, the smooth, clean glass cooling my skin. "Suspended," I mumble.

"Remember? You pleaded it down. And quite impressively, I might add. Now I know why you earn the big bucks." I peer at her from the corner of my eye just as the shock of my words transform her face from concern to outrage, rearranging her features in a way I've never seen. And even though I know I should feel bad, ashamed, guilty, and worse—the fact is, it's not like I asked her to litigate. It's not like I asked her to plead *extenuating circumstances*. Claiming that my drinking on school grounds was: *clearly mitigated by the gravity of my situation, the huge toll of losing my entire family.*

And even though she said it in good faith, even though she truly believes it to be true, that doesn't mean that it *is* true.

Because the truth is, I wish she hadn't said anything. I wish she'd just let them expel me.

The moment they caught me in front of my locker, the buzz faded and the day's events came rushing right back like a preview for a movie I'd rather not see. Pausing on the frame where I forgot to make Stacia delete that photo, and playing it over and over again. Then later, in the office, when I learned that it was actually Honor's phone that was used, that Stacia had gone home sick with an unfortunate bout of "food poisoning" (though not before arranging for Honor to share the photo, along with her "concerns" to Principal Buckley), well, I have to admit, that even though I was in big trouble, I mean, big, huge, *you can be sure this will go on your permanent record* kind of trouble, there was still this small part of me that admired her. This part that shook its tiny head and thought:

Bravo! Well done!

Because despite the trouble I'm facing, not only with the school, but Sabine too, Stacia not only made good on her promise to destroy me, but she managed to bag one hundred dollars and the afternoon off for her troubles. And that is seriously admirable.

At least in a calculating, sadistic, sinister kind of way.

And yet, thanks to Stacia, Honor, and Principal Buckley's coordinated efforts, I don't have to go to school tomorrow. Or the next day. Or the day after that. Which means I'll get the whole house to myself, all day, every day, allowing me plenty of privacy to continue my drinking and build up my tolerance, while Sabine's busy at work.

Because now that I've found my path to peace, nobody's gonna stand in my way.

"How long has this been going on?" Sabine asks, unsure how to approach me, how to handle me. "Do I have to hide all the alcohol? Do I need to ground you?" She shakes her head. "Ever, I'm speaking to you! What *happened* back there? What is going *on* with you? Would you like for me to arrange for you to speak with someone? Because I know this great counselor who specializes in grief therapy . . ."

I can feel her looking at me, can actually feel the concern emanating off her face, but I just close my eyes and pretend to sleep. There's no way I can explain, no way I can unload the whole sordid truth about auras and visions and spirits and immortal ex-boyfriends. Because even though she hired a psychic for the party, she did it as a joke, a lark, a spooky bit of good clean fun. Sabine is left-brained, organized, compartmentalized, operating on pure black-and-white logic and avoiding all gray. And if I was ever dumb enough to confide in her, to reveal the real secrets of my life, she'd do more than just arrange for me to *speak with someone*. She'd have me committed.

Just like she promised, Sabine hides all the alcohol before she heads back to work, but I just wait till she's gone, then slink downstairs and head for the pantry, retrieving all the bottles of vodka left over from the Halloween party, the ones she shoved in the back and forgot all about. And after I haul 'em up to my room, I plop down on my bed, thrilled by the prospect of three full weeks without any school. Twenty-one long glorious days all sprawled out before me like food before an overfed cat. One week for my pleaded-down suspension, and two for the conveniently scheduled winter break. And I plan to make the most of every single moment, spending each long lazy day in a vodka-fueled haze.

I lean back against the pillows and unscrew the cap, determined to pace myself by limiting each sip, allowing the alcohol to trail all the way down my throat and into my bloodstream before taking another. No guzzling, no gulping, no chugging allowed. Just a slow and steady stream until my head starts to clear and the whole world grows brighter. Sinking down into a much happier place. A world without memories. A home without loss.

A life where I only *see* what I'm supposed to.

twenty-nine

On the morning of December 21, I make my way downstairs. And despite being dizzy, bleary eyed, and completely hungover, I put on a pretty good show of brewing coffee and making breakfast, wanting Sabine to leave for work convinced all is well, so I can return to my room and sink back into my liquid haze.

And the second I hear her car leave the drive, I pour the Cheerios down the drain and head upstairs to my room, retrieving a bottle from under the bed and unscrewing the cap, anticipating the rush of that warm sweet liquid that will soothe my insides, erase all my pain, gnaw away my anxieties and fears until nothing remains.

Though for some reason, I can't stop staring at the calendar hanging over my desk, the date jumping out at me, shouting and waving and nudging like an annoying poke in the ribs. So I get up and move toward it, peering at its blank empty square, no obligations, no appointments, not a birthday reminder in sight, just the words *WINTER SOLSTICE* in tiny black type, a date the publisher deems important, though it means nothing to me.

I plop back down on my bed, my head propped on a mound of pillows as I take another long pull from the bottle. Closing my eyes as that warm wonderful heat courses right through me, flushing my veins and soothing my mind—like Damen used to do with merely a gaze.

I take another sip, and then another, too fast, too reckless, not at all like I've practiced. But now that I've resurrected his memory, I only want to erase it. So I continue like that, drinking, sipping, guzzling, gulping—until I can finally rest, until he's finally faded away.

When I wake, I'm filled with the warmest, most peaceful feeling of all-consuming love. Like I'm bundled in a ray of golden sunlight, so safe, so happy, so secure, I want to stay in that place and live there forever. I clench my eyes shut, grasping the moment, determined to hang on, until a tickle on my nose, an almost imperceptible flutter, makes me open them again and bolt from my bed.

I clutch at my chest, my heart pounding so hard I can feel it, as I gaze at the single black feather that was left on my pillow.

The same black feather I wore the night I dressed as Marie Antoinette.

The same black feather Damen took as a *souvenir*.

And I know he was here.

I glance at the clock, wondering how I could've possibly slept for so long. And when I gaze across the room, I see the painting I'd left in the trunk of my car is now propped against the far wall, left for me to see. But instead of Damen's version of *Woman with Yellow Hair* I expected, I'm confronted with an image of a pale blond girl running through a dark, foggy canyon.

A canyon just like the one in my dream.

And without knowing why, I grab my coat, shove my feet

into some flip-flops, then race into Sabine's room, retrieving the car keys she hid in her drawer, before sprinting downstairs and into the garage, no idea where I'm going, or why. I just know I have to get there, and that I'll know it when I see it.

I drive north on PCH, heading straight for downtown Laguna. Weaving my way through the usual Main Beach bottleneck, before turning on Broadway and dodging pedestrians. And the moment I'm free of those overcrowded streets, I punch the gas and drive on instinct, burying some miles between me and downtown, before cutting in front of an oncoming car, braking in the lot for the wilderness park, pocketing my keys and cell phone, and rushing toward the trail.

The fog is rolling in fast, making it hard to see, and even though there's this part of me telling me to turn back, go home, that being here in the dark, all by myself, is nothing but crazy, I can't stop, I'm compelled to move on, as though my feet are moving of their own accord, and all I can do is just follow.

I bury my hands in my pockets, shivering against the cold, as I stumble along, with no idea where I'm going, no destination in mind, it's the same as how I got here, I'll just know it when I see it.

And when I stub my toe on a rock, I fall to the ground, howling with pain. But by the time my cell phone rings, I've toned it down to barely a whimper.

"Yeah?" I say, struggling to stand, my breath coming shallow and quick.

"Is that how you answer your phone these days? Because that is so not working for me."

"What's up, Miles?" I brush myself off and continue down the trail, this time with a little more caution.

"I just wanted you to know that you're missing a pretty wild party. And since we all know how much you like to party these days, I thought I'd invite you. Though, to be honest, I shouldn't build it up so much because it's really more funny than fun. I mean, you should see it, there's like, hundreds of goths filling up the canyon, it looks like a Dracula convention or something."

"Is Haven there?" I ask, my stomach involuntarily clenching when I say her name.

"Yeah, she's searching for Drina. Remember the big secret event? Well, this is pretty much it. That girl cannot keep a secret, even her own."

"I thought they weren't into goth anymore?"

"So did Haven, and believe me, she's pretty pissed about getting the dress code all wrong."

I've just made it to the crest of a hill when I see the valley flooded with light. "Did you say you're in the canyon?"

"Yeah."

"Me too. In fact, I'm almost there," I say, starting down the other side.

"Wait—*you're here?*"

"Yeah, I'm heading toward the light as we speak."

"Did you go through a tunnel first? Ha-ha, get it?" And when I don't respond, he says, "How'd you even know about it?"

Well, I woke up in a drunken stupor with a black feather tickling my nose and an eerily prophetic painting propped against my wall, so I did what any insane person would do, I grabbed a coat, slipped on some flip-flops, and ran out of the house in my nightgown!

Knowing I can't exactly say that, I don't say anything. Which only makes him even more suspicious.

"Did Haven tell you?" he asks, a definite edge to his voice. "Because she swore I was the only one she told. I mean, no offense or anything. *But still.*"

"No, Miles, I swear she didn't tell me, I just found out. Anyway, I'm almost there, so I'll see you in a minute—if I don't get lost in the fog . . ."

"Fog? There's no fo—"

And before he can finish, the phone is yanked out of my hand, as Drina smiles and says, "Hello, Ever. I told you we'd meet again."

thirty

I know I should run, scream, do *something*. But instead I just freeze, my rubber flip-flops sticking to the ground as though they've grown roots. And I stare at Drina, wondering not only how I ended up here, but what she could possibly have in mind.

"Ain't love a bitch?" She smiles, head cocked to the side as she looks me over. "Just when you meet the man of your dreams, a guy who seems too good to be true, *just like that*, you find out he *is* too good to be true. At least too good for *you*. And the next thing you know you're miserable and alone, and well, let's face it, drunk a good deal of the time. Though I must say, I have enjoyed watching your descent into adolescent addiction. So predictable, so—*textbook*. You know what I mean? The lying, the sneaking, the stealing, all of your energy focused on securing your fix. Which only made my task that much easier. Because every drink you took just weakened your defenses, blunted all the stimuli, yes, but it also left your mind vulnerable, open, and easier for me to manipulate." She grabs hold of my arm, her sharp nails pressing into my wrist, as she pulls me right to her. And even though I try to yank free, it's no use. She's freakishly strong.

"You mortals." She purses her lips. "You're such fun to tease, such easy targets. You think I set up this whole elaborate ruse just to end it so soon? Sure, there are easier ways to do this. Hell, if I wanted, I could've done away with you in your bedroom, while I was setting the stage. It would've been so much quicker, less time consuming, though clearly, not nearly as fun. For either of us, don't you agree?"

I gape at her, taking in her flawless face, coiffed hair, perfectly tailored black silk dress, nipping and flowing in all the right places, all of it highlighting her breathtaking beauty, and when she runs her hand through her shiny copper-tinged hair, I see her ouroboros tattoo. But as soon as I blink, it's vanished again.

"So let's see, you thought Damen was leading you here, summoning you, against your will. Sorry to disappoint you, Ever, but it was me, the whole elaborate ruse, created by me. I just love December twenty-first, don't you? The winter solstice, or longest night, all of those ridiculous goths partying in some dopey canyon." She shrugs, her elegant shoulders rising and falling, the tattoo on her wrist coming in and out of view. "Pardon my flair for the dramatic. Though it does keep life interesting, don't you agree?"

I try to pull away again, but she grips me that much tighter, her nails digging in, eliciting a terrible sharp ache as they pierce right through my flesh.

"Now let's just say that I did let you go. What would you do? Run away? I'm faster. Look for your friend? Oops, my bad. Haven's not even here. It seems I've sent her to the *wrong* party, in the *wrong* canyon. She's wandering around as we speak, pushing and shoving through hundreds of ridiculous vampire wannabes, looking for me." She laughs. "I thought we'd enjoy a smaller, more intimate gathering." She smiles, her eyes sweeping over me. "And it looks like our guest of honor is here."

"What do you want?" I say, gritting my teeth as she tightens her hold, the bones in my wrist giving way, crushing against each other in unbearable pain.

"Don't rush me." She narrows her amazing green eyes on mine. "All in good time. Now where was I before you so rudely interrupted? Ah, yes, we were talking about *you,* how you ended up here, and how it's not turning out anything like you expected. But then, nothing in your life is what you expected, is it? And, truth be told, it never has, was, or I suspect, will be. You see, Damen and I go way back. I'm talking way, way, way, way, way—well, you get the picture. And yet, despite all of those years together, despite our *longevity,* you just keep showing up and getting in the way."

I gaze at the ground, wondering how I could've been so stupid, so naïve. None of this was ever about Haven—it was all about me.

"Aw, don't be so hard on yourself. This isn't the first time you've made this mistake. I've been responsible for your demise, for, let's see—how many lifetimes?" She shrugs. "Well, I guess I lost count."

And suddenly I remember what Damen said, in the parking lot, about not being able to lose me *again*. But when I look at her and see her face harden and change, I clear my mind of such thoughts, knowing she can read them.

She walks around me, swinging my arm as she goes, making me spin in circles before her as she clucks her tongue against the inside of her cheek. "Let's see, if memory serves, and it *always* does, then the last few times we played a little game called *Trick or Treat*. And I think it's only fair to inform you up front that it didn't really work out so well for you. Still, you never seem to tire of it, so I thought perhaps you'd like to try it again?"

I gaze at her, dizzy from the spinning, the residual alcohol clinging to my veins, her thinly veiled threat.

"Ever watch a cat kill a mouse?" She smiles, eyes glowing, as her tongue snakes around the outside of her lips. "How they toy with their poor pathetic prey for the longest time, until they finally get bored and finish the job?"

I close my eyes, not wanting to hear any more. Thinking that if she's so intent on killing me then why doesn't she just hurry up and do it already?

"Well that would be the *treat,* at least for me." She laughs. "And the *trick*? Aren't you curious about the trick?" And when I don't respond, she sighs. "Well, you're rather dull, aren't you? Though I suppose I'll tell you anyway. You see, the *trick* is—I pretend to let you go, then I stand back and watch as you run around in circles, trying to evade me, until you finally wear yourself out, and I proceed toward the *treat*. So what'll it be? Slow death? Or agonizingly slow death? Come on, hurry up, clock's ticking!"

"Why do you want to kill me?" I look at her. "Why can't you just let me be? Damen and I aren't even a couple, I haven't seen him for weeks!"

But she just laughs. "Nothing personal, Ever. But Damen and I always seem to get along so much better once you've been—*eliminated.*"

And even though I thought I wanted a quick demise, I've now changed my mind. I refuse to give up without a fight. Even if it's one I'm destined to lose.

She shakes her head and looks at me, disappointment marring her face. "And so it is. You choose trick, right?" She shakes her head. "Very well then, off you go!"

She lets go of my arm and I flee through the canyon, knowing there's probably nothing that can save me, but knowing I still have to try.

I push the hair from my eyes and race blindly through the fog, hoping to locate the trail, get back to where I started. My lungs threatening to explode in my chest, as my flip-flops break and abandon my feet, but still I run. Running as the sharp cold rocks slice into my soles. Running as a searing hot pain burns a hole through my ribs. Running past trees whose sharp, unadorned branches snatch at my jacket and rip it right off me. Running for my life—even though I'm not sure it's worth living.

And as I'm running, I remember another time I ran like this.

But also like my dream, I have no idea how it ends.

I've just reached the edge of the clearing that leads back to the trail, when Drina steps out of the mist and stands right before me.

And even though I dodge, and try to move past her, she lifts one languid leg and assists me in a face plant.

I lie on the ground, blinking into a pool of my own blood, listening to the derisive laughter she directs right at me. And when I tentatively touch my face, my nose flops to the side, and I know that it's broken.

I struggle to stand, spitting rocks from my mouth, cringing in dismay as a stream of blood and teeth tumble out too. And I watch as she shakes her head and says, "Wow, you look *awful*, Ever." She grimaces in disgust. "Seriously awful. One wonders what Damen ever saw in you."

My body's racked with pain, my breath's shallow, unsteady, as mouthfuls of blood coat my tongue with a taste that's metallic and bitter.

"Well, I suppose you'll want all the details, even though you won't remember them the next time around. Still, it's always fun to see the shock on your face when I explain it to you." She laughs. "I don't know why, but for some reason, I never bore of this particular episode, no matter how many times we re-run it. Plus, if I'm going to be perfectly honest, then I have to admit it allows for a deliciously prolonged pleasure. Kind of like foreplay, not that *you* would know anything about *that*. All these lifetimes and somehow you always die a virgin. Which would be so sad, if it wasn't so funny." She scoffs. "So, where to begin, where to begin?" She looks at me, lips pursed, red-manicured nails tapping the sides of her hips. "Okay, well, as you know, I'm the one who swapped the picture from the one in your trunk. I mean, *you* as the woman with the yellow hair? I. Don't. Think. So. And between you and me, Picasso would've been *furious*. Still, I do love him. Damen, that is. Not that old dead artist." She laughs. "Anywho, let's see, I planted the feather." She rolls her eyes. "Damen can be so—*maudlin*. Oh, I even planted that dream in your head. How's *that* for months of mysterious foreshadowing? And no, I'm not going to explain all the hows and whys because that would take too long, and, quite frankly, it's hardly important where you're going. Too bad you didn't just die in that accident, because you could've saved us both a lot of trouble. Do you have any idea how much damage you've caused? I mean, because of you Evangeline is dead and Haven—well, look how close she came. I mean, really Ever, how selfish of you."

She looks at me but I refuse to respond. Wondering if that qualifies as an admission of guilt.

She laughs. "Well, you're about to exit now, so yes, no harm in confessing." She lifts her right hand as though solemnly swearing. "I, Drina Magdalena Auguste"—she raises her brow at me when she says that last part—"effectively eliminated Evangeline a.k.a. June Porter, who, by the way, was contributing nothing and only taking up space so it's not nearly as sad as you think. I needed to get her out of the way so I'd have full access to Haven." She smiles, her eyes grazing over me. "Yes, just like you suspected, I purposely stole your friend Haven. Which is so easy to do with those lost and unloved ones who are so desperately craving attention they'll do just about anything for someone who gives them the time of day. And yes, I convinced her to get a tattoo that nearly killed her, but only because I couldn't decide if I should *kill her–kill her,* or kill her so that I could bring her back and make her immortal. It's been so long since I last had an acolyte, and I must say, I really did enjoy it. But, then again, indecisiveness has always been a weakness of mine. When you have so many options spread out before you and an eternity to see them played out, well, it's hard not to get greedy and want to choose them all!" She smiles, like a child who's simply been naughty, but nothing more. "Still, I waited too long, and then Damen stepped in—well-meaning, altruistic sap that he is—and, well, you know the rest. Oh, and I got Miles that part in *Hairspray.* Though, in all fairness, he probably could've nailed it himself, because the kid has *loads* of talent. Still, I couldn't take any chances, so I climbed inside the director's head and swung the vote in his favor. Oh, and Sabine and Jeff? My bad. But still, it worked out beautifully, don't you think? Imagine, your smart, successful, savvy aunt falling for that loser." She laughs. "Pathetic, and yet, quite funny, don't you think?"

But why? Why would you do this? I think, no longer able to speak since I'm missing most of my teeth and gagging on my own blood, but knowing it's not necessary, knowing she can hear the thoughts in my head. *Why involve everyone else, why not just go after me?*

"I wanted to show you how lonely your life can be. I wanted to demonstrate how easy it is for people to abandon you in favor of something better, more exciting. You're all alone, Ever. Isolated, unloved, alone. Your life is pathetic and hardly worth living. So, as you can see, I'm doing you a favor." She smiles. "Though I'm sure you won't thank me."

I gaze at her, wondering how someone so amazingly beautiful could be so ugly inside. Then I stare into her eyes and take a tiny step back, hoping she won't notice.

I'm not even with Damen anymore. We broke up a long time ago. So why don't you go find him, we can go our separate ways, and forget this ever happened! I think, hoping to distract her.

She laughs and rolls her eyes. "Trust me, you're the only one who will forget this ever happened. Besides, it's really not that simple. You have no idea how this works, do you?"

She's got me there.

"You see, Damen is mine. And he's *always* been mine. But unfortunately, you keep showing up, in your stupid, boring, repetitive soul recycle. And since you insist on doing that, it's become my job to track you down and kill you each time." She takes a step toward me as I take a step back, the bloody sole of my foot landing on a pointy sharp rock as I close my eyes and wince in unbearable pain.

"You think *that* hurt?" She laughs. "Just wait."

I glance around the canyon, eyes darting furiously, scanning for a way out, some kind of escape. Then I take another step back and stumble again. My hand brushing the ground as my fingers curl around a sharp rock that I hurl at her face, smacking her square in the jaw and tearing a chunk from her cheek.

She laughs, the hole in her face spurting blood and revealing two missing teeth. Then I watch in horror as it rights itself again, returning her back to her pure seamless beauty.

"This again." She sighs. "Come on, try something new, see if you can amuse me for a change."

She stands before me, hands on hips, brows raised, but I refuse to run. I refuse to make the next move. I refuse to give her the satisfaction of yet another fool's race. Besides, everything she said is true. My life really is a lonely horrible mess. And everyone I touch gets dragged down in it too.

I watch as she advances on me, smiling in anticipation, knowing my end is near. So I close my eyes and remember the moment right before the accident. Back when I was healthy and happy and surrounded by family. Imagining it so vividly I can *feel* the warm leather seat beneath my bare legs, I can *sense* Buttercup's tail thumping against my thigh, I can *hear* Riley singing at the top of her lungs, her voice inharmonious, horribly off-key. I can *see* my mom's smile as she turns in her seat, her hand reaching out to chuck Riley's knee. I can *see* my dad's eyes, both of us gazing into the rearview mirror, his smile knowing, kind, and amused—

I hold on to that moment, cradling it in my mind, experiencing the feel, the scents, the sounds, the emotions, as though I'm right there. Wanting this to be the last moment I see before I go, reliving the last time I was truly happy.

And just when I'm so far in, it's as though I'm right there, I hear Drina gasp. "What the *hell*?"

And I open my eyes to see the shock on her face, her eyes sweeping over me, her mouth hanging open. Then I gaze down at a gown that's no longer torn, feet that are no longer bloody, knees that are no longer scraped, and when I run my tongue around a full set of teeth and bring my hand to my nose, I know that my face is healed too. And even though I've no idea what it means, I know I need to act fast, before it's too late.

And as Drina steps back, her eyes wide, full of questions, I move toward her, not sure what the next step will bring, or the one after that. All I know is that I'm running out of time, as I rush forward and say, "Hey Drina, trick or treat?"

thirty-one

At first she just stares, green eyes wide and unbelieving, then she lifts her chin and bares her teeth. But before she can attack, I lunge toward her. Determined to get to her first, to take her down while I can. But just as I spring forward, I see this shimmering veil of soft golden light, a luminous circle just off to the side, glowing and beckoning, like the one in my dream. And even though Drina planted those dreams, even though it's probably a trap, I can't help but veer toward it.

I tumble through a brilliant haze, a shower of light so loving, so warm, so intense, it calms my nerves and soothes all my fears. And when I land in a field of vibrant green grass, the blades hold me, support me, and cushion my fall.

I gaze at the meadow around me, its flowers blooming with petals that seem lit from within, surrounded by trees that reach far into the sky, their branches sagging with ripe juicy fruit. And as I lie there quietly, taking it all in, I can't help but feel like I've been here before.

"Ever."

I spring to my feet, poised and ready to fight. And when I see that it's Damen, I take a step back, having no idea whose side he's really on.

"Ever, relax. It's okay." He nods, smiling as he offers his hand.

But I refuse to take it, refuse to fall for his bait. So I take another step back as my eyes search for Drina.

"She's not here." He nods, his eyes fixed on mine. "You're safe, it's just me."

I hesitate, debating whether or not to believe him, doubting he could ever be thought of as *safe*. Staring at him, while weighing my options (which are admittedly few), until I finally ask, "Where are we?" In place of my actual question: *Am I dead?*

"I assure you, you're not dead." He laughs, reading my thoughts. "You're in Summerland."

I look at him, without even a hint of understanding.

"It's a sort of—place between places. Like a waiting room. Or a rest stop. A dimension between the dimensions, if you will."

"Dimensions?" I squint, the word sounding foreign, unfamiliar, at least in the way that he uses it. And when he reaches for my hand, I quickly pull away, knowing it's impossible to see anything clearly whenever he touches me.

He gazes at me, then shrugs, motioning for me to follow him through a meadow where every flower, every tree, every single blade of grass bends and sways and twists and curves like partners in an infinite dance.

"Close your eyes," he whispers. And when I don't he adds, "Please?"

I close them. Halfway.

"Trust me." He sighs. "Just this once."

So I do. "Now what?"

"Now imagine something."

"What do you mean?" I ask, immediately picturing a giant elephant.

"Imagine something else," he says, "quickly."

I open my eyes, startled to see a ginormous elephant charging right at us, then I gasp in amazement when I transform him into a butterfly—a beautiful Monarch butterfly that lands right on the tip of my finger. "How—?" I glance between Damen and the butterfly, its black antennae twitching at me.

Damen laughs. "Want to try again?"

I press my lips and look at him, trying to think of something good, something better than an elephant or a butterfly.

"Go ahead," he urges. "It's so much fun. It never gets old."

I close my eyes and imagine the butterfly turning into a bird, and when I open them again a colorful majestic macaw is perched on my finger. But when a messy trail of bird poop drips down my arm, Damen hands me a towel and says, "How about something with a little less—cleanup?"

I set the bird down and watch it fly away, then I close my eyes, fervently wishing, and when I open them again, Orlando Bloom has taken his place.

Damen groans and shakes his head.

"Is he real?" I whisper, gaping in amazement as Orlando Bloom smiles and winks at me.

Damen shakes his head. "You can't manifest actual people, only their likeness. Luckily, it won't be long before he fades."

And when he does, I can't help but feel a little sad.

"What's going on?" I ask, looking at Damen. "Where are we? And how is this even possible?"

Damen smiles and makes a beautiful white stallion appear. After getting me mounted and settled, he makes a black one for him. "Let's go for a ride," he says, leading me down a trail.

We ride side by side, down a beautiful, manicured path, cutting right through the valley of flowers and trees and a sparkling stream the color of rainbows. And when I see my parrot perched next to a cat I veer from the trail, ready to shoo him away, but Damen grabs the reins and says, "No worries. There are no enemies. All is at peace here."

We ride in silence as I gape at the surrounding beauty, struggling to take it all in, though it's not long before my mind starts reeling with all sorts of questions and no clue where to begin.

"The veil you saw? The one you were drawn to?" He looks at me. "I put it there."

"In the canyon?"

He nods. "And in your dream."

"But Drina says she created the dream." I look at him, seeing how he rides with such confidence, so sure in the saddle. But then I remember the painting on his wall, the one of him mounted on the white stallion, sword by his side, and I figure he's been at it for a while.

"Drina showed you the location, I showed you the exit."

"Exit?" I say, my heart pounding again.

He shakes his head and smiles. "Not *that* kind of exit. I already told you, you're *not* dead. In fact, you're more alive than ever. Able to manipulate matter and manifest anything you want. The ultimate in instant gratification." He laughs. "But don't come here too often. Because I'm warning you, it's addictive."

"So you *both* created my dreams?" I ask, squinting at him, trying to get a handle on all these bizarre events. "Like—like a *collaboration*?"

He nods.

"So I don't even control my own dreams?" I say, my voice rising, not liking the sound of any of this.

"Not that particular dream, no."

I scowl at him, shaking my head when I say, "Well, excuse me, but don't you think that's just *a little* invasive? I mean, jeez! And why didn't you try to stop it, if you knew it was coming?"

He looks at me, his eyes tired and sad. "I didn't know it was Drina. I was just observing your dreams, you were frightened by something, so I showed you the way here. This is always a safe place to come to."

"So why didn't Drina follow me?" I say, looking around for her again.

He reaches for my hand and squeezes my fingers. "Because Drina can't see it, only you could see it."

I squint at him. Everything's so weird, so strange, and none of it makes any sense.

"Don't worry, you'll get it. But for now, why not just try to enjoy it?"

"Why does it seem so familiar?" I say, feeling the tug of recognition, but unable to place it.

"Because this is where I found you."

I look at him.

"I found your body outside the car, true. But your soul had already moved on and was lingering here." He stops both our horses, and helps me dismount, then he leads me to a warm patch of grass, so brilliant and sparkling in the warm golden light that doesn't seem to emanate from any one place, and the next thing I know he's manifested a big cushy couch and a matching ottoman for our feet.

"Care to add anything?" He smiles.

I close my eyes and imagine a coffee table, some lamps, a few knickknacks, and a nice Persian rug, and when I open them again we're in a fully furnished outdoor living room.

"What happens if it rains?" I ask.

"Don't—"

But it's too late, we're already soaked.

"Thoughts create," he says, making a giant umbrella, the rain sloping steadily off the sides and onto the rug. "It's the same on Earth, it just takes a lot longer. But here in Summerland, it's instant."

"That reminds me of what my mom used to say—*'Be careful what you wish for, you just might get it!!'*" I laugh.

He nods. "Now you know where that originates. Care to make this rain stop, so we can dry off?" He shakes his wet hair at me.

"How—"

"Just think of someplace warm and dry." He smiles.

And the next thing I know we're lying on a beautiful pink-sand beach.

"Let's leave it at this? Shall we?" He laughs as I make us a plushy blue towel and a turquoise ocean to match.

And when I lie back and close my eyes against the warmth, he confirms it. Not that I didn't already start to figure it out for myself, but still not having it stated in a complete sentence. One that begins with:

"I'm an immortal."

And ends with:

"And you are too."

Is not something you hear every day.

"So, we're both immortals?" I say, opening one eye to peer at him, wondering how I could have such a bizarre conversation in such a normal tone of voice. But then again, I'm in Summerland, and it doesn't get more bizarre than that.

He nods.

"And you *made* me an immortal when I died in the crash?"

He nods again.

"But how? Does it have something to do with that weird red drink?"

He takes a deep breath before answering. "Yes."

"But how come I don't have to drink it all the time, like you do?"

He averts his gaze and looks out toward the sea. "Eventually you will."

I sit up picking at a loose string on my towel, still unable to fully wrap my mind around this. Remembering a time in the not-so-distant past when I thought just being psychic was a curse, and *now* look.

"It's not as bad as you think," he says, placing his hand over mine. "Look around, it doesn't get any better than this."

"But *why*? I mean, did it ever occur to you that maybe I don't want to be an immortal? That maybe you should've just let me go?"

I watch as he cringes, averting his gaze, looking all around, focusing on everything but me. Then he turns to me and says, "First of all, you're right. I was selfish. Because the truth is, I saved you more for myself than for you. I couldn't bear to lose you again, not after . . ." He stops and shakes his head. "But still, I wasn't sure if it worked. Obviously I knew I'd brought you back, but I wasn't sure for how long. I wasn't sure I'd actually turned you until I saw you in the canyon just now—"

"You were watching me in the canyon?" I stare at him incredulously.

He nods.

"You mean you were *there*?"

"No, I was watching you *remotely.*" He rubs his jaw. "It's a lot to explain."

"So let me get this straight. You were watching me, *remotely,* but still, you could see everything going on, and yet *you didn't try to save me?*" And when I say it out loud I'm so mad I can barely breathe.

He shakes his head. "Not until you wanted to be saved. That's when I made the veil appear, and urged you to move toward it."

"You mean you were going to let me die?" I scoot away from him, not wanting to be anywhere near him.

He looks at me, his face completely serious when he says, "If that's what you wanted, then yes." He shakes his head. "Ever, the last time we spoke, in the parking lot, you said you hated me for what I had done, for being selfish, for separating you from your family, for bringing you back. And even though your words really stung, I knew you were right. I had no business interfering. But then, in the canyon, when you filled yourself with such love, well, that love is what saved you, restored you, and it's then that I knew."

But what about the hospital? Why couldn't I restore myself then? Why did I have to suffer through all of the casts, and cuts, and contusions? Why couldn't I just—regenerate, like I did in the canyon? I think, folding my arms across my chest, not fully buying it.

"Only love heals. Anger, guilt, and fear can only destroy and separate you from your true capabilities." He nods, his eyes grazing over me.

"And that's another thing." I glare at him. "Your ability to read my mind, when I can't read yours. It's not fair."

He laughs. "Do you really want to read my mind? I thought my air of mystery was one of the things you liked about me?"

I gaze down at my knees, my cheeks burning as I think of all the embarrassing thoughts he's been privy to.

"There are ways to shield yourself, you know. Maybe you should go see Ava."

"You know Ava?" I gape, feeling suddenly ganged up on.

He shakes his head. "My only connection to Ava is through you, your thoughts about Ava."

I look away, watching a family of bunnies hop by, then back at him. "So the racetrack?"

"Premonition, you did it too."

"What about the race you lost?"

He laughs. "I have to lose a few, otherwise people tend to get suspicious. But I certainly made up for it, don't you think?"

"And the tulips?"

He smiles. "Manifesting. Same way you made the elephant, and this beach. It's simple quantum physics. Consciousness brings matter into being where there was once merely energy. Not nearly as difficult as people choose to think."

I squint, not really getting it. No mater how *simple* he thinks it is.

"We create our own reality. And yes you can do it at home," he says, anticipating my next question, the one that just formed in my head. "In fact, you already do, you're just not aware of it because it takes so much longer."

"It doesn't take longer for you."

He laughs. "I've been around awhile, plenty of time to learn a few tricks."

"How long?" I ask, gazing at him, remembering that room in his house and wondering exactly what I'm dealing with.

He sighs and looks away. "Very long."

"And now I'll live forever too?"

"That's up to you." He shrugs. "You don't have to do any of this. You can simply put the whole thing out of your mind and go on with your life. Choosing to *let go* when the time is right. I only provided the ability, but the choice is still yours."

I stare out at the ocean, its sparkling waters so brilliant, so beautiful, I can hardly believe it exists because of me. And even though it's fun to play with such powerful magic, my thoughts soon turn to darker things. "I need to know what happened with Haven. That day I caught you . . ." I grimace at the memory. "And what about Drina? She's immortal too, right? Did you make her that way? And how did this even begin? How did you become immortal in the first place? How does such a thing even happen? Did you know she killed Evangeline, and almost killed Haven too? And what's up with your creepy room?"

"Can you repeat the question?" He laughs.

"Oh, and another thing, what the heck did Drina mean when she said she's killed me over and over again?"

"Drina said that?" His eyes go wide as his face drains of color.

"Yeah." I nod, remembering her smug and haughty face as she broke the news. "She was all, *'Here we go again, stupid mortal, you always fall for this game, blah blah blah.'* I thought you were watching, I thought you saw the whole thing?"

He shakes his head, mumbling. "I didn't see the *whole* thing, I tuned in late. Oh God, Ever, it's all my fault, all of it. I should've known, I should've never gotten you involved, I should've left you alone—"

"She also said she saw you in New York. Or at least she told Haven that."

"She lied," he mumbles. "I didn't go to New York." And when he looks at me his eyes are etched with such pain, I reach for his hand and hold it in mine. Shaken by how sad and vulnerable he looks and wanting only to erase it. I press my lips against his warm waiting mouth, hoping to convey that whatever it is, there's a pretty good chance I'll forgive him.

"The kiss gets sweeter with every incarnation." He sighs, pulling away and brushing my hair off my face. "Though we never seem to make it further than that. And now I know why." He presses his forehead to mine, infusing me with such joy, such all-consuming love, then sighing deeply before pulling away. "Aw, yes, your questions," he says, reading my mind. "Where to begin?"

"How about the beginning?"

He nods, his gaze drifting away, all the way back to the beginning, as I cross my legs and settle in. "My father was a dreamer, an artist, a dabbler in sciences and alchemy, a popular idea at the time—"

"Which time?" I ask, hungry for places, dates, things that can be nailed down and researched, not some philosophical litany of abstract ideas.

"A *long* time ago." He laughs. "I *am* a tad bit older than you."

"Yes, but how old exactly? I mean, what kind of age difference am I dealing with here?" I ask, watching incredulously as he shakes his head.

"All you need to know is that my father, along with his fellow alchemists, believed that everything could be reduced down to one single element, and that if you could isolate that one element, then you could create anything from it. He worked on that theory for years, creating formulas, abandoning formulas, and then when he and my mother both . . . died, I continued the search, until I finally perfected it."

"And how old were you?" I ask, trying again.

"Young." He shrugs. "Quite young."

"So you can still age?"

He laughs. "Yes, I got to a certain point, and then I just stopped. I know you prefer the *frozen in time* vampire theory, but this is real life, Ever, not fantasy."

"Okay, so . . ." I urge, anxious for more.

"*So,* my parents died, I was orphaned. You know, in Italy, where I'm from, last names often depicted a person's origins or profession. *Esposito* means *orphan,* or *exposed.* The name was given to me, though I dropped it a century or two ago, since it no longer fit."

"Why didn't you just use your real last name?"

"It's complicated. My father was . . . hunted. So I thought it better to distance myself."

"And Drina?" I ask, my throat constricting at the mere mention of her name.

He nods. "Poverina—or, *little poor one*. We were wards of the church; that's where we met. And when she grew ill, I couldn't bear to lose her, so I had her drink too."

"She said you were married." I press my lips together, my throat feeling hot and constricted, knowing she didn't actually *say* that, though it was definitely implied when she stated her name, *her full name*.

He squints and looks away, shaking his head and mumbling under his breath.

"Is it true?" I ask, my stomach in knots, my heart pressing hard against my chest.

He nods. "But it's hardly what you think, it happened so long ago it hardly matters anymore."

"So why didn't you get divorced? I mean, if it *hardly matters,*" I say, my cheeks hot, my eyes stinging.

"So you're proposing I show up in court with a wedding certificate dating back *several centuries,* and ask for a divorce?"

I press my lips and look away, knowing he's right, but *still.*

"Ever, please. You've got to cut me some slack. I'm not like you. You've only been around, well in this life anyway, seventeen years, while I've lived hundreds! More than enough time to make a few mistakes. And while there are certainly plenty of things to judge me on, I hardly think my relationship with Drina is one of them. Things were different back then. *I* was different. I was vain, superficial, and extremely materialistic. I was out for myself, taking all that I could. But the moment I met you everything changed, and when I lost you, well, I never knew such agonizing pain. But then later, when you reappeared—" He stops, his gaze far away. "Well, no sooner had I found you, than I lost you again. And so it went, over and over. An endless cycle of love and loss—until now."

"So, we . . . *reincarnate*?" I say, the word sounding strange on my tongue.

"You do—not me." He shrugs. "I'm always here, always the same."

"So, who was I?" I ask, not sure if I really believe it, yet fascinated with the concept. "And why can't I remember?"

He smiles, happy to change the subject. "The journey back involves a trip down the River of Forgetfulness. You're not meant to remember, you're here to learn, to evolve, to pay off your karmic debts. Each time starting fresh, forced to find your own way. Because, Ever, life is not meant to be an open book test."

"Then aren't you cheating, by staying here?" I say, smirking at *Mr. Let Me Tell You How the World Works.*

He cringes. "Some might say."

"And how can you possibly know all of this if you've never done it yourself?"

"I've had plenty of years to study life's greatest mysteries. And I've met some amazing teachers along the way. All you need to know about your other selves is that you were always female." He smiles, tucking my hair behind my ear. "Always very beautiful. And always important to me."

I stare at the sea, manifest a few waves just for the heck of it, then make it all go away. Everything. All of it. Returning us to our outdoor living room.

"Change of scenery?" He smiles.

"Yes, but only the scenery, not the subject."

He sighs. "So after years of searching I found you again—and you know the rest."

I take a deep breath and stare at the lamp, clicking it off and on, on and off with my mind, trying to get a grip on all this.

"I broke off with Drina a long time ago, but she has this awful habit of *reappearing*. And the night at the St. Regis? When you saw us together? I was trying to convince her to move on, once and for all. Though obviously, it didn't quite work. And yes, I know she killed Evangeline, because that day at the beach, when you woke up alone?"

I narrow my eyes, thinking: *I knew it! I knew he wasn't surfing!*

"I'd just found her body, but it was too late to save her. And yes, I know about Haven too, though luckily, I was able to save her."

"So that's where you were that night—when you said you were getting a drink of water . . ."

He nods.

"So what else have you lied about?" I ask, folding my arms across my chest. "And where'd you go Halloween night, after you left my party?"

"I went home," he says, gazing at me intently. "When I saw the way Drina looked at you, well, I though it better to distance myself. Only I couldn't. I tried. I've been trying all along. But I just couldn't do it. I can't stay away from you." He shakes his head. "And now you know everything. Though I think it's obvious why I couldn't be quite so forthcoming at the time."

I shrug and look away, not willing to give in so easily, even if it's true.

"Oh, and my 'creepy room' as you call it? Well, it just so happens to be *my* happy place. Not unlike the memory you hold of those last blissful moments in the car with your family." And when he looks at me, I avert my gaze, ashamed for having said it. "Though I have to admit, I had a good laugh when I realized you thought I was a bloodsucker." He smiles.

"Oh, well excuse me. I mean since there are immortals running around, I figure we may as well bring on the faeries, wizards, werewolves, and—" I shake my head. "I mean jeez, you talk about all this like it's normal!"

He closes his eyes and sighs. And when he opens them again he says, "For me it is normal. This is my life. And now it's your life too, if you choose it. It's not as bad as you think, Ever, really." He looks at me for a long time, and even though part of me still wants to hate him for making me this way, I just can't. And when I feel that overwhelmingly warm, tingly pull, I gaze down at the hand that he's holding and say, "Stop it."

"Stop what?" He looks at me, his eyes tired, the skin surrounding them tense and pale.

"Stop making that warm, tingly, *you know*. Just stop it!" I say, my mind torn between love and hate.

"I'm not making that, Ever." His eyes are on mine.

"Of course you are! You're making it happen with your . . .

whatever." I roll my eyes and fold my arms across my chest, wondering where we possibly go from here.

"I'm not manifesting that. I swear. I'd never use trickery to seduce you."

"Oh, yeah, like the tulips?"

He smiles. "You have no idea what they mean, do you?"

I press my lips and look away.

"Flowers have meaning. There's nothing random about it."

I take a deep breath and rearrange the table with my mind, wishing I could rearrange my mind instead.

"There's so much to teach you," he says. "Though it's not all fun and games. You need to take caution, proceed with care." He pauses and looks at me, making sure that I'm listening. "You have to guard against the misuse of power; Drina's a good example of that. And you must be discreet—which means you can't share this with *anyone,* and I mean *no one,* understand?"

I just shrug, thinking: *Whatever.* Knowing he's read my thoughts when he shakes his head and leans toward me.

"Ever, I'm serious, you cannot tell a soul. Promise me."

I look at him.

He raises his brow, his hand squeezing mine.

"Scout's honor," I mumble, looking away.

He lets go of my hand and relaxes, leaning back against the cushions when he says, "But in the interest of full disclosure you need to know that there's still a way out. You can still *cross over.* In fact, you could've died right there in the canyon, but instead, you chose to stay."

"But I was prepared to die, I wanted to die."

"You empowered yourself with your memories. You empowered yourself with love. It's like I said earlier—*thoughts create.* And in your case, they created healing and strength. If you really wanted to die you would've simply given up. On some deeper level you must've known this."

And just when I'm about to ask him why he was sneaking into my room while I slept, he says, "It's not what you think."

"Then what was it?" I ask, wondering if I really want to know.

"I was there to . . . observe. I was surprised you could see me, I was *transmuted,* so to speak."

I wrap my arms around my knees and bring them close to my chest. Everything he just said went right over my head, but I get just enough of the gist to be suitably creeped out.

He shrugs. "Ever, I feel responsible for you, and—"

"And you wanted to check out the goods?" I look at him, eyebrows raised.

But he just laughs. "May I remind you of your penchant for flannel pajamas?"

I roll my eyes. "So you feel responsible for me, like—*like a dad?*" I say, laughing as he cringes.

"No, not like a dad. But Ever, I was only in your room that one time, the night we saw each other at the St. Regis, if there were other times—"

"Drina." I cringe, picturing her creeping around my room, spying on me. "Are you sure she can't come here?" I ask, glancing around.

He takes my hand and squeezes, wanting to reassure me when he says, "She doesn't even know it exists. Doesn't know how to get here. As far as she's concerned, you simply vanished into thin air."

"But how'd *you* get here? Did you die once, like me?"

He shakes his head. "There are two types of alchemy—physical, which I stumbled upon because of my father, and spiritual, which I stumbled upon when I sensed something more, something bigger, something grander than me. I studied and practiced and worked hard to get here, even learned TM." He stops and looks at me. "Transcendental Meditation from Maharishi Mahesh Yogi." He smiles.

"Um, if you're trying to impress me, it's not really working, I have no idea what any of that means."

He shrugs. "Let's just say it took hundreds of years for me to translate it from the mental to the physical. But you—from the moment you wandered into the field, you were granted a sort of backstage pass, your visions and telepathy are by-products of that."

"God, no wonder you hate high school," I say, wanting to change the subject to something concrete, something I can actually understand. "I mean, you must've finished like, a gazillion, bazillion years ago, right?" And when he winces, I realize his age is a serious sore spot, which is actually pretty funny, considering how he *chose* to live forever. "I mean, why bother? Why even enroll?"

"That's where you come in." He smiles.

"Oh, so you see some chick in baggy jeans and a hoodie, and you just have to have her so bad, you decide to repeat high school, just to get to her?"

"Sounds about right." He laughs.

"Couldn't you have found another way to ingratiate yourself into my life? It just doesn't make any sense." I shake my head and roll my eyes, getting worked up all over again, until he trails his fingers down the side of cheek and gazes into my eyes.

"Love never does."

I swallow hard, feeling shy, euphoric, and unsure all at once. Then I clear my throat and say, "I thought you said you suck at love." I narrow my eyes on his, my stomach like a cold bitter marble, wondering why I can't just be happy when the most gorgeous guy on the planet professes his love. Why do I insist on going all negative?

"I was hoping this time would be different," he whispers.

I turn away, my breath coming in short, shallow gasps as I say, "I don't know if I'm up for all this. I don't know what to do."

He pulls me tight against his chest, his arms wrapped around me, as he says, "There's no rush to decide." And when I turn, he has this faraway look in his eyes.

"What's the matter?" I ask. "Why are you looking at me like that?"

"Because I suck at good-byes," he says, attempting a smile that never gets past his mouth. "See, now there's two things I suck at—love and good-byes."

"Maybe they're related." I press my lips together, warning myself not to cry. "So where you going?" I fight to keep my voice calm and neutral, even though my heart doesn't want to beat, and my breath doesn't want to come, and I feel like I'm dying inside.

He shrugs and looks away.

"Are you coming back?"

"Up to you." Then he looks at me and says, "Ever, do you still hate me?"

I shake my head, but hold his gaze.

"Do you love me?"

I turn my head and look away. Knowing I do, knowing I love him with every strand of hair, with every skin cell, with every drop of blood, that I'm bursting with love, boiling over, but I just can't bring myself to say it. But then again, if he can truly read my mind, then I shouldn't have to say it. He should just *know.*

"It's always nicer when it's spoken," he says, tucking my hair behind my ear, and pressing his lips to my cheek. "When you do decide, about me, about being immortal, just say the word and I'll be there. I have all of eternity laid out before me; you'll find I'm quite patient." He smiles, then reaches into his pocket, retrieving the silver, crystal-encrusted, horse-bit bracelet he bought me at the track. The one I *returned* when I threw it at him that day in the parking lot. "May I?" he gestures.

I nod, my throat too constricted to speak, as he closes the clasp, then cradles my face between the palms of his hands. Brushing my bangs to the side, and pressing his lips to my scar, infusing me with all of the love and forgiveness I know I don't deserve. But when I try to pull away, he holds me that much tighter and says, "You have to forgive yourself, Ever. You're not responsible for any of it."

"What do you know?" I bite down on my lip.

"I know you blame yourself for something that's not your fault. I know you love your little sister with all of your heart and you ask yourself every day if you're doing thc right thing by encouraging her visits. I know *you,* Ever. I know everything about you."

I turn away, my face wet with tears I don't want him to see. "None of that's true. You've got it all wrong. I'm a freak, and bad things happen to everyone I come near, even though I'm the one who deserves it." I shake my head, knowing I don't deserve to be happy, don't deserve this kind of love.

He pulls me into his arms, his touch calm and soothing, but unable to erase the truth. "I have to go," he finally whispers. "But Ever, if you want to love me, if you truly want to be with me, then you'll have to accept what we are. I'll understand if you can't."

And then I kiss him, pressing into him, needing the feel of his lips against mine, basking in the wonderful, warm glow of his love, the moment growing and swelling and expanding until it fills every space, every nook, every cranny.

And when I open my eyes and pull away, I'm back in my room, all alone.

thirty-two

"So what happened? We looked everywhere and never found you. I thought you were on your way?"

I roll over, turning my back to the window and chiding myself for failing to craft an excuse, which puts me in the awkward position of winging it. "I was, but then—well, I kind of got cramps, and—"

"Stop right there," Miles says. "Seriously, say no more."

"Did I miss anything?" I ask, closing my eyes against the thoughts in his head, the words scrolling before me like a late-breaking news ribbon on CNN: *Ew! Disgusting! Why do they insist on talking about that stuff?*

"Other than the fact that Drina never showed? Nope, not a thing. I spent the first part of the night helping Haven look for her, and the second part, trying to convince her she's better off without her. I swear, you'd think they were dating. Creepiest friendship ever, Ever! Ha! Get it?" He loves making pun of my name.

I clutch my head and crawl out of bed, realizing it's the first morning in over a week that I've woken without a hangover. And even though I know that qualifies as *a very good thing,* that doesn't change the fact that I feel worse than ever.

"So what's going on? Care to indulge in a little Fashion Island Christmas shopping?"

"Can't. I'm still grounded," I say, pilfering through a pile of sweatshirts and pausing when I get to the one Damen bought me on our Disneyland date, before everything changed, before my life went from very weird to extraordinarily weird.

"How much longer?"

"No say." I drop the phone on my dresser and pull a lime green hoodie over my head, knowing it doesn't really matter how long Sabine grounds me, if I want to go out, I'll go out, I'll just make sure to return before she gets home. I mean, it's hard to contain a psychic. Though it does provide the perfect excuse to stay home, lay low, and avoid all that random energy, which is the only reason I'm going along with it.

I pick up the phone just in time to hear Miles say, "Okay, well, call me when you're released."

I step into some jeans, then sit down at my desk. And even though my head's pounding, my eyes are burning, and my hands are shaking, I'm determined to get through the day without the aid of alcohol, Damen, or illicit trips to the astral planes. Wishing I'd been more insistent—demanded that Damen show me how to shield myself. I mean, why does the solution always seem to flow back to Ava?

Sabine tentatively knocks on my door and I turn as she steps into my room. Her face is pale and pinched, her eyes rimmed with red, and her aura has gone all spotty and gray. And I cringe when I realize it's all because of Jeff, and the fact that she finally uncovered his mountain of lies. Lies I could've unveiled from the very beginning, sparing her all of this heartache, if only I hadn't put my needs before hers.

"Ever," she says, pausing by my bed. "I've been thinking.

Since I'm not really comfortable with this whole grounding business, and since you're almost an adult, I figure I may as well treat you like one so—"

So you're no longer grounded, I think, finishing the sentence in my head. But when I realize she still thinks my troubles are due to my grief, my face burns with shame.

"—you're no longer grounded." She smiles, a gesture of peace I do not deserve. "Though I was wondering if you changed your mind about talking to someone, because I know this therapist who—"

I shake my head before she can finish, knowing she means well, though refusing any part of it. And when she turns to leave, I surprise myself by saying, "Hey, you want to go out for dinner tonight?"

She hesitates in the doorway, clearly surprised by the offer.

"My treat." I smile encouragingly, having no idea how I'll possiby get through a night in a big, crowded restaurant, but figuring I can use some of my racetrack money to cover the bill.

"That would be great," she says, tapping the wall with her knuckles before heading into the hall. "I'll be home by seven."

The second I hear the front door close and the dead bolt click into place, Riley taps on my shoulder and shouts, "Ever! Ever! Can you see me?"

And I nearly jump out of my skin.

"Jeez, Riley, you scared the *hell* out of me! And why are you yelling?" I say, wondering why I'm acting so crabby, when the truth is, I'm overjoyed just to see her again.

She shakes her head and plops onto my bed. "For your information, I've been trying to get through to you for *days.* I thought you lost your ability to see me and I was totally starting to freak!"

"I *did* lose my ability. But only because I started drinking—heavily. And then I got expelled." I shake my head. "It was a mess."

"I know." She nods, brows knit with concern. "I was watching the whole time, jumping up and down in front of you, yelling and screaming and clapping my hands, anything to try to get through to you, but you were too whacked to see me. Remember that one time, when the bottle flew out of your hand?" She smiles and curtsies before me. "That was me. And you're lucky I didn't conk you over the head with it instead. So, what the heck happened?"

I shrug and gaze down at the ground, knowing I owe her an answer, a valid explanation to ease her concern, but not sure where to begin. "Well, it's like, all that random energy just became so overwhelming, I couldn't take it anymore. And when I realized how alcohol shielded me from it, I guess I just wanted to keep that good feeling going, I didn't want to go back to the way I was before."

"And now?"

"And now—" I hesitate, looking at her. "And now I'm right back where I started. Sober and miserable." I laugh.

"Ever—" She pauses, averting her gaze before looking at me. "Please don't get mad, but I think you should go see Ava." And when I start to balk, she raises her hand and says, "Just hear me out, okay? I really think she can help you. In fact I *know* she can help you. She's been *trying* to help you but you won't let her. But now, well, it's pretty clear that you're running out of options. I mean, you can either start drinking again, hide in your room for the rest of your life, or go see Ava. Pretty much a no-brainer, don't you think?"

I shake my head despite all the pounding, then I look at her and say, "Listen, I know you're all enamored with her, and fine, whatever, that's your choice. But she's got nothing for me, so please just—just give it a rest already, would you?"

Riley shakes her head. "You're wrong. Ava can help you. Besides, what could it hurt for you to give her a call?"

I sit there, kicking my bed frame and staring at the ground, thinking the only thing Ava's ever done for me is make my life even worse than it is. And when I finally look at Riley again, I notice how she's ditched the Halloween costumes for the jeans, T-shirt, and Converse sneakers of a normal twelve-year-old kid, but she's also turned filmy, translucent, and practically see-through.

"What happened with Damen? That day you went to his house? Are you still together?" she asks.

But I don't want to talk about Damen, I wouldn't even know where to begin. Besides, I know she's just trying to shift the attention from herself and her lucent appearance. "What's going on?" I ask, my voice rising, frantic. "Why are you fading like that?"

But she just looks at me and shakes her head. "I don't have much time."

"What do you mean—*you don't have much time?* You're coming back, *right?*" I shout, panicking as she waves good-bye and disappears from sight, leaving Ava's crumpled-up card in her place.

thirty-three

Before I can even shift into *park,* she's at the front door, waiting.

Either she really is psychic, or she's been standing there since we hung up.

But when I see the concern on her face, I feel guilty for thinking it.

"Ever, welcome," she says, smiling as she ushers me up the front steps and into a nicely decorated living room.

I gaze all around, taking in the framed photos, the elaborate coffee table books, the matching sofa and chairs, amazed by how normal it is.

"You were expecting purple walls and crystal balls?" She laughs, motioning for me to follow her into a bright sunny kitchen with beige stone floors, stainless steel appliances, and a sunlit skylight overhead. "I'll make us some tea," she says, setting the water to boil and offering me a seat at the table.

I watch as she busies herself, placing cookies onto a plate, and steeping our tea, and when she takes the seat across from mine, I look at her and say. "Um, sorry for acting so—rude—and—everything." I shrug, cringing at how awkward and inadequate I sound.

But Ava just smiles, and places her hand over mine, and the moment she makes contact, I can't help but feel better. "I'm just glad you came, I've been so worried about you."

I gaze down at the table, my eyes fixed on the lime green placemat, not knowing where to begin.

But since she's in charge, she handles it for me. "Have you seen Riley?" she asks, her eyes on mine.

And I can't believe she chose to start there. "Yes," I finally say. "And for your information, she's not looking so good." I press my lips together and avert my gaze, convinced that she's somehow responsible.

But Ava just laughs—*laughs!* "Trust me, she's fine." She nods, taking a sip of her tea.

"Trust *you?*" I gape, shaking my head. Watching her sip her tea and nibble at her cookie in that serene calm way that really sets me on edge. "Why should I? You're the one who brainwashed her! You're the one who convinced her to stay away!" I shout, wishing I hadn't even come here. What a huge colossal mistake!

"Ever, I know you're upset, and I know how much you miss her, but do you have any idea what she's sacrificed in order to be with you?"

I gaze out her window, my eyes grazing over the fountain, the plants, the small statue of Buddha, bracing myself for a really stupid answer.

"Eternity."

I roll my eyes. "Please, all she's got is time."

"I'm referring to something *more.*"

"Yeah, like what?" I ask, thinking I should just set the cookie down and get the hell out of there. Ava's a nut bag, a phony, and she talks with such authority about the most outrageous things.

"Riley's being here with you means she can't be with them."

"*Them?*"

"Your parents and Buttercup." She nods, tracing her finger along the rim of her cup while looking at me.

"How'd you know about—"

"Please, I thought we were past this?" she says, her eyes right on mine.

"This is ridiculous," I mumble, averting my gaze, wondering what Riley could ever see in such a person.

"Is it?" She brushes her auburn hair from her face, revealing a forehead that's unlined and smooth, free of all worry.

"Fine. I'll bite. If you know so much, then tell me, just where do you think Riley is when she's not with me?" I ask, my eyes meeting hers. Thinking: *This ought to be good.*

"Wandering." She lifts her cup to her lips and takes another sip.

"Wandering? Oh, okay." I laugh. "Like you would know."

"She has no other choice now that she's chosen to be with you."

I gaze out the window, my breath feeling hot, abbreviated, telling myself there's no way this is true.

"Riley didn't cross the bridge."

"You're wrong. I saw her." I glare. "She waved good-bye and everything, they all waved good-bye. I should know. *I was there.*"

"Ever, I've no doubt what you saw, but what I meant to say was, Riley didn't make it to the *other side*. She stopped halfway and ran back to find you."

"Sorry, but you're wrong," I tell her. "That's not at all true." My heart pounding in my chest as I remember that very last moment, the smiles, the waves, and then—and then nothing—they disappeared, while I fought and begged and pleaded to stay.

They were taken, while I remained. And it's entirely my fault. It should've been me. Every bad thing can be traced back to me.

"Riley turned back at the very last second," she continues. "When no one was looking, and your parents and Buttercup had already crossed. She told me, Ever, we've been through it many times. Your parents moved on, you came back to life, and Riley got stuck, left behind. And now she spends her time wandering between visits to you, me, old neighbors and friends, and a few naughty celebrities." She smiles.

"You know about that?" I look at her, eyes wide.

She nods. "It's only natural, though most earthbound entities bore of it pretty quickly."

"Earthbound what?"

"Entities, spirits, ghosts, it's all the same. Though it's quite different from those who've crossed over."

"So you're saying Riley is stuck?"

She nods. "You have to convince her to go."

I shake my head, thinking: *It's hardly up to me*. "She's already gone. She barely comes around anymore," I mumble, glaring at her like she's responsible, but that's only because she is.

"You have to give her your blessing. You have to let her know it's okay."

"Listen," I say, tired of this discussion, of Ava butting into my business, telling me how to run my life. "I came here for help, not to listen to this. If Riley wants to stick around, then fine, that's her business. Just because she's twelve doesn't mean I can tell her what to do. She's pretty stubborn you know?"

"Hmmm, wonder where she gets it?" Ava says, sipping her tea and gazing at me.

But even though she smiles, tries to make like it's a joke, I just look at her and say, "If you've changed your mind about helping me, then just say so." I rise from my seat, my eyes teary, my body panicky, my head pounding, yet fully prepared to leave if I have to. Remembering what my dad taught me about the key to negotiating—that you have to be willing to walk away—no matter what.

She looks at me for a moment, then motions for me to sit. "As you wish." She sighs. "Here's how you do it."

By the time Ava walks me outside, I'm surprised to see that it's already dark. I guess I spent more time in there than I realized, going through a step-by-step meditation, learning how to ground myself and create my own psychic shield. But even though things didn't start off so well, especially all that stuff about Riley, I'm still glad I came. It's the first time I've felt completely normal, without the crutch of alcohol or Damen, in a very long time.

I thank her again, and head for my car, and just as I'm about to climb in, Ava looks at me and says, "Ever?"

I gaze at her, seeing her framed only by the soft yellow light of her porch now that her aura is no longer visible.

"I really wish you'd let me show you how to undo the shield. You might be surprised and find that you miss it," she coaxes.

But we've already been through this, more than once. Besides, I've made my decision and there's no going back. I'm saying hello to a normal life, and good-bye to immortality, Damen, Summerland, psychic phenomenon, and everything else that goes with it. Ever since the accident, all I wanted was to be normal again. And now that I am, I plan to embrace it.

I shake my head and stick my key in the ignition, looking up again when she says, "Ever, please think about what I said. You've got it all wrong. You've said good-bye to the wrong person."

"What're you talking about?" I ask, just wanting to get home, so I can start enjoying my life once again.

But she just smiles. "I think you know what I mean."

thirty-four

No longer grounded and released of all that psychic baggage, I spend the next few days hanging with Miles and Haven, meeting for coffee, going shopping, seeing movies, trolling around downtown, watching his rehearsals, thrilled to have my life back to normal again. And on Christmas morning, when Riley appears, I'm relieved I can still see her.

"Hey, wait up!" she says, blocking the door just as I'm about to head down the stairs. "No way are you opening your presents without me!" And when she smiles, she's so radiant and clear she appears almost solid, nothing flimsy, filmy, or translucent about her. "I know what you're getting!" She grins. "Want a hint?"

I shake my head and laugh. "Absolutely not! I love not knowing for a change," I say, smiling as she walks over to the middle of my room and executes a perfect series of cartwheels.

"Speaking of surprises." She giggles. "Jeff bought Sabine a ring! Can you believe it? He moved out of his mom's house, got his own place, and is begging her to come back and start over!"

"Serious?" I say, taking in her faded jeans and layered tees, glad to see she's done with the costumes and no longer copying me.

She nods. "But Sabine will send it right back. I mean, at least from what I can tell. It's not like she's actually received the ring yet, so I guess we'll wait and see. Still, people rarely surprise you, you know?"

"Still spying on celebrities?" I ask, wondering if she has any dish.

She makes a face and rolls her eyes. "God no. I was being seriously corrupted. Besides, it's always the same old thing, shopping binges, food binges, drug binges, followed by rehab. Wash, rinse, and repeat—yawn."

I laugh, wishing I could reach out and hug her instead. I was so afraid I'd lost her.

"What'rc you looking at?" she asks, peering at me.

"You." I smile.

"And?"

"*And*, I'm so glad you're here. And that I can still see you. I was afraid I'd lost that ability when Ava showed me how to make that shield."

She smiles. "To be honest, you did. I really had to ramp up my energy so you could see me. In fact, I'm using some of yours. Do you feel tired?"

I shrug. "A little, but then again, I just woke up."

She shakes her head. "Doesn't matter. It's still me."

"Hey Riley." I look at her. "Are you still . . . *visiting Ava*?" I ask, holding my breath as I wait for the answer.

She shakes her head. "Nah. I'm over that too. Now come on, I cannot wait to see your face when you unwrap your new iPhone! Oops!" She laughs, placing her hand over her mouth as she backs right through the closed bedroom door.

"You're really staying?" I whisper, making my exit the traditional way. "You don't have to leave, or be somewhere else?"

She climbs on top of the banister and slides her way down, looking back at me and smiling when she says, "Nope, not anymore."

Sabine returned the ring, I had a new iPhone, Riley was back to visiting every day, sometimes even accompanying me to school, Miles started dating one of the *Hairspray* backup dancers, Haven dyed her hair dark brown, swore off everything goth, began the painful process of lasering off her tattoo, burned all of her Drina-dresses, and replaced them with emo. New Year's came and went, marked by a small gathering at my house that included sparkling cider for me (I was officially off the sauce), contraband champagne for my friends, and a midnight dip in the Jacuzzi, which was pretty tame as far as New Year's parties go, but not at all boring. Stacia and Honor still glared at me, pretty much the same as before, even worse on the days when I wore something cute, Mr. Robins got a life (one without his daughter or his wife), Ms. Machado still cringed when she looked at my art, and between it all was Damen.

Like caulk around a tile, like binding in a book, he filled all of my blank empty spaces and held everything together, kept it all contained. Through every pop quiz, every shampoo, every meal, every movie, every song, every dip in the Jacuzzi, I held him in my mind, comforted just by knowing he was out there—somewhere—even though I'd decided against him.

By Valentine's Day, Miles and Haven are in love—though not with each other. And even though we sit together at lunch, I may as well have been on my own. They were too busy hovering over their Sidekicks to notice my existence, while my iPhone sat beside me, silent and ignored.

"Omigod, this is *hilarious*! You can't *believe* how brilliant he is!" Miles says, for the gazillionth time, gazing up from his text, his face flushed with laughter, as he thinks of the perfect reply.

"Omigod, Josh just gifted me like, *a ton of songs!* I am so not worthy," Haven mumbles, thumbs tapping a response.

And even though I'm happy for them, happy that they're happy and all that, my mind is on sixth-period art, and I'm wondering if I should ditch. Because here at Bay View High, today is not only Valentine's Day, it's also Secret Heart Day. Which means that those big, red, heart-shaped lollipops, the ones with the little pink love notes they've been pushing all week, are finally distributed. And while Miles and Haven are fully expecting to receive theirs even though their boyfriends don't go here, I'm just hoping to get through the day, somewhat sane, and mostly unscathed.

And even though I fully admit that ditching the iPod/hoodie/dark sunglasses combo has allowed for a considerable amount of renewed male interest, it's not like I'm interested in any of them. Because the truth is, there's not one guy in this school (on this planet!), who could ever compare to Damen. No one. Nada. Just not possible. And it's not like I'm in a hurry to lower my standards.

But by the time the sixth-period bell rings, I know I can't ditch. My ditching days, like my drinking days, are pretty much over. So I suck it up and head to class, immersed in my latest, ill-fated assignment—to mimic one of the *isms*. And I happened to choose cubism—making the mistake of thinking it would be easy. But it's not. In fact, it's far from it.

And when I sense someone standing behind me, I turn and

say, "Yeah?" Peering at the lollipop he holds in his hand, then focusing back on my work, assuming it's a case of mistaken identity. But when he taps me again, this time I don't bother looking, I just shake my head and say, "Sorry, wrong girl."

He mumbles something under his breath, then clears his throat and says, "You're that Ever chick, right?"

I nod.

"Then take it already." He shakes his head. "I gotta get through this entire box before the bell rings."

He tosses me the lollipop and makes for the door, and I set down my charcoal, flip the card open, and read:

Thinking of you
Always.
Damen

thirty-five

I race through the door, anxious to get upstairs so I can show Riley my lollipop valentine, the one that made the sun shine, the birds sing, and turned my whole day around, even though I refuse to have anything to do with the sender.

But when I see her sitting alone on the couch, seconds before she turns and sees me, something about the way she looks, so small and alone, reminds me of what Ava said—that I've said good-bye to the wrong person. And the air rushes right out of me.

"Hey," she says, grinning at me. "You can't *believe* what I just saw on *Oprah*. There's this dog who's missing his two front legs, and yet he can still—"

I drop my bag on the floor and sit down beside her, grabbing the remote and pushing *mute*.

"What's up?" she says, scowling at me for silencing *Oprah*.

"What are you doing here?" I ask.

"Um, hanging on the couch, waiting for you to come home . . ." She crosses her eyes and sticks out her tongue. "Duh."

"No, I mean, why are you *here*? Why aren't you—*someplace else*?"

She twists her mouth to the side and turns back to the TV, her body stiff, face immobile, preferring a silent *Oprah* to me.

"Why aren't you with Mom and Dad and Buttercup?" I ask, watching as her bottom lip starts to quiver, at first only slightly, but soon, a full-blown tremble, making me feel so awful, I have to force the words to continue. "Riley." I pause, swallowing hard. "Riley, I don't think you should come here anymore."

"You're *evicting* me?" She springs to her feet, eyes wide with outrage.

"No, It's nothing like that, I just—"

"You can't stop me from visiting, Ever! I can do anything I want! *Anything!* And there's *nothing* you can do about it!" she says, shaking her head and pacing the room.

"I'm aware of that." I nod. "But I don't think I should encourage you either."

She crosses her arms and mashes her lips together, then plops back down on the couch, kicking her leg back and forth like she does when she's mad, upset, frustrated, or all three.

"It's just, well, for a while there it seemed like you were busy with something else, somewhere else, and you seemed perfectly happy and okay with it. But now it's like you're here all the time again and I'm wondering if it's because of me. Because even though I can't bear the thought of not having you around, it's more important for you to be happy. And spying on neighbors and celebrities, watching *Oprah,* and waiting for me, well, I don't think it's the best way to go." I stop, taking a deep breath, wishing I didn't have to continue, but knowing I do. "Because even though seeing you is the undisputed best part of my day, I can't help but think there's another—better—place for you to be."

She stares at the TV as I stare at her, sitting in silence until she finally breaks it. "For your information, I *am* happy. I'm perfectly fine and happy, *so there.*" She shakes her head and rolls her eyes, then crosses her arms against her chest. "Sometimes I live here, and sometimes I live somewhere else. In this place called Summerland, which is pretty dang awesome, in case you don't remember it." She sneaks a peek at me.

I nod. Oh, I definitely remember it.

She leans back against the cushions and crosses her legs. "So, best of both worlds, right? What's the problem?"

I press my lips and look at her, refusing to be swayed by her arguments, trusting that I'm doing the right thing, the only thing. "The *problem* is, I think there's someplace *even better.* Someplace where Mom and Dad and Buttercup are waiting for you—"

"Listen, Ever." She cuts me off. "I know you think I'm here because I wanted to be thirteen and since that didn't happen I'm living vicariously through you. And yeah, maybe that's partly true, but did you ever stop and think that maybe I'm here because I can't bear to leave you either?" She looks at me, her eyes blinking rapidly, but when I start to speak, she holds up her hand and continues. "At first I was following them, because, well, they're the parents and I thought I was supposed to, but then I saw how you stayed back, and I went to find you, but by the time I got there, you were already gone, I couldn't find the bridge again, and then, well, I got stuck. But then I met some people who've been there for years, well, the earth version of years, and they showed me around and—"

"Riley—" I start, but she cuts me right off.

"And just so you know, I *have* seen Mom and Dad and Buttercup, and they're fine. Actually, they're more than fine, they're *happy.* They just wish you'd stop feeling so guilty all the time.

They can see you. You know that, right? You just can't see them. You can't see the ones who crossed the bridge, you can only see the ones like me."

But I don't care about the details of who I can and can't see. I'm still stuck on that part about them wanting me to stop feeling so guilty, even though I know they're just being all nice and parental, trying to ease my guilt. Because the truth is, the crash is my fault. If I hadn't made my dad turn back so I could go get that stupid Pinecone Lake Cheerleading Camp sweatshirt I'd forgotten, we never would've been in that spot, on that road, at the exact same time that some stupid confused deer ran right in front of our car, forcing my dad to swerve, fly down the ravine, crash into the tree, and kill everyone but me.

My fault.

All of it.

Entirely mine.

But Riley just shakes her head and says, "If it's anyone's fault, then it's Dad's fault, because everyone knows you're not supposed to swerve when an animal darts in front of your car. You're supposed to just hit it and keep going. But you and I both know he couldn't bear to do that, so he tried to save us all but ended up sparing the deer. But then again, maybe it's the deer's fault. I mean, he had no business being on the road when he has a perfectly good forest to live in. Or perhaps it's the guardrail's fault for not being stronger, firmer, made of tougher stuff. Or maybe it's the car company's fault for faulty steering and crappy brakes. Or maybe—" She stops and looks at me. "The point is, it's *nobody's* fault. That's just the way it happened. That's just the way it was supposed to *be*."

I choke back a sob, wishing I could believe that, but I can't. I know better. I know the truth.

"We all know it, and accept it. So now it's time for you to know it and accept it too. Apparently it just wasn't your time."

But it was my time. Damen cheated, and I went along for the ride!

I swallow hard and stare at the TV. *Oprah* is over and *Dr. Phil* has taken her place—one shiny baldhead and a very large mouth that never stops moving.

"Remember when I was looking so filmy? That's because I was getting ready to cross over. Every day I crept closer and closer to the other side of the bridge. But just when I decided to go all the way, well, that's when it seemed like you needed me most. And I just couldn't bear to leave you—I still can't bear to leave you," she says.

But even though I really want her to stay, I've already robbed her of one life. I won't rob her of the afterlife too. "Riley, it's time for you to go," I say, whispering so softly part of me is hoping she didn't actually hear it. But once it's out, I know it's the right thing to do, so I say it again, louder this time, the words ringing with resonance, conviction. "I think you should go," I repeat, hardly believing my own ears.

She gets up from the couch, her eyes wide and sad, her cheeks shining with crystalline tears.

And I swallow hard as I say, "You have no idea how much you've helped me. I don't know what I would've done without you. You're the only reason I got up each day and put one foot in front of the other. But I'm better now, and it's time for you—" I stop, choking on my own words, unable to continue.

"Mom said you'd send me back eventually." She smiles.

I look at her, wondering what that means.

"She said, *'someday your sister will finally grow up and do the right thing.'* "

And the moment she says it, we both burst out laughing.

Laughing at the absurdity of the situation. Laughing at our mom's penchant for saying, *"Someday you'll grow up and—fill in the blank."* Laughing to relieve some of the tension and pain of saying good-bye. Laughing because it feels so damn good to do so.

And when the laughter dies down, I look at her and say, "You'll still check in and say hi, right?"

She shakes her head and looks away. "I doubt you'll be able to see me, since you can't see Mom and Dad."

"What about Summerland? Can I see you there?" I ask, thinking I can go back to Ava, have her show me how to remove the shield, but only to visit Riley in Summerland, not for anything else.

She shrugs. "I'm not sure. But I'll do my best to send some kind of sign, something so you'll know I'm okay, something specifically from me."

"Like what?" I ask, panicked to see her already fading. I didn't expect it to happen so quickly. "And how will I know? How can I be sure it's from you?"

"Trust me, you'll know." She smiles, waving good-bye as she fades.

thirty-six

The moment Riley is gone, I break down and cry, knowing I did the right thing, but still wishing it didn't have to hurt so damn much. I stay like that for a while, curled up on the couch, my body folded into a small tight ball, remembering everything she said about the accident, and how it wasn't really my fault. But even though I wish I could believe it, I know it's not true. Four lives were ended that day, and it's all because of me.

All because of a stupid, powder blue, cheerleading camp sweatshirt.

"I'll get you another one," my dad said, gazing into the rearview mirror, his eyes meeting mine, two matching sets of identical blues. "If I turn around now, we'll hit traffic."

"But it's my favorite," I whined. "The one I got at cheer camp. You can't buy it in a store." I pouted, knowing I was mere seconds from getting my way.

"You really want it that bad?"

I nodded, smiling as he shook his head, took a deep breath, and turned the car around, meeting my gaze in the rearview mirror the same moment the deer ran onto the road.

I wanted to believe Riley, to retrain my brain to this new way of thinking. But knowing the truth pretty much guaranteed I never would.

And as I wipe the tears from my face, I remember Ava's words. Thinking if Riley was the right person to say good-bye to, then Damen must be the wrong one.

I reach for the lollipop I'd placed on the table and gasp when I see it's morphed into a tulip.

A big, huge, shiny, red tulip.

Then I race for my room, pull my laptop onto my bed, and run a search on flower meanings, skimming down the page until I read:

> In the eighteen hundreds, people often communicated their intentions through the flowers they sent, as specific flowers held specific meanings. Here are a few of the more traditional ones:

I scroll down the alphabetical list, my eyes scanning for *tulips* and holding my breath as I read:

> Red tulips—Undying love.

Then, just for fun, I look up white rosebuds and laugh out loud when I read:

> White rosebuds—The heart that knows no love; heart ignorant of love.

And I know he was testing me. The whole entire time. Holding this huge life-changing secret with absolutely no idea how to tell me, not knowing if I'd accept it, reject it, or turn him away.

Flirting with Stacia just to get a reaction, so he could eavesdrop on my thoughts and see if I cared. And I'd become so adept at lying to myself, denying my feelings about practically everything, I ended up confusing us both.

And while I certainly don't condone what he did, I have to admit that it worked. And now, all I have to do to see him again is just say the words out loud and he'll manifest right here before me. Because the truth is, I do love him. I've loved him without ceasing. I've loved him since that very first day. I loved him even when I swore that I didn't. I can't help it, I just do. And even though I'm not so sure about this whole *immortal* business, Summerland *was* pretty cool. Besides, if Riley is right, if there is such a thing as fate and destiny, then maybe it applies to this too?

I shut my eyes and imagine the feel of Damen's warm wonderful body curled around mine, the whisper of his soft sweet lips on my ear, my neck, my cheek, the way his mouth feels when it parts against mine—I hold onto that image, the feel of our perfect love, our perfect kiss, as I whisper the words I've held all this time, the ones I was too scared to speak, the ones that will bring him back to me.

I say them over and over again, my voice gaining strength as they fill up the room.

But when I open my eyes, I'm alone.

And I know I waited too long.

thirty-seven

I head downstairs, in search of some ice cream, knowing a rich and creamy Häagen-Dazs Band-Aid can't possibly heal my broken heart, though it just might help soothe it. And after retrieving a quart from the freezer, I cradle it in my arms and reach for a spoon, then the whole thing crashes to the ground when I hear a voice say:

"So touching, Ever. So very, very touching."

I bend over, squeezing the toes that got nailed by a quart of Vanilla Swiss Almond, as I gape at a perfectly turned-out Drina—legs crossed, hands folded, a prim and proper lady, seated right there at my breakfast bar.

"So cute how you called out for Damen after conjuring that chaste little love scene in your head." She laughs, her eyes grazing over me. "Ah, yes, I can still see inside your head. Your little psychic shield? Thinner than the Shroud of Turin, I'm afraid. Anyway, as far as you and Damen and your happily ever after, and after, and after?" She shakes her head. "Well, you know I can't let that happen. As it turns out, my life's work has been destroying you, and little do you know, I still can."

I gaze at her, concentrating on my breath, keeping it slow

and steady, while I try to clear my mind of all incriminating thought, knowing she'll only use it against me. But the thing is, *trying* to clear your mind is about as effective as telling someone to *not* think about elephants—from that moment on that's *all* they'll think about.

"Elephants? Really?" She groans, a low evil sound that vibrates the room. "My God, what *does* he see in you?" Her eyes rake over me, filled with disdain. "Certainly not your intellect or wit, since we've yet to see any evidence it exists. And your idea of a love scene? So Disney, so Family Channel, so *dreadfully boring*. Really, Ever, may I remind you that Damen's been around for *hundreds* of years, including the free-love sixties?" She shakes her head at me.

"If you're looking for Damen, he's not here," I finally say, my voice scratchy, hoarse, like it hasn't been used for days.

She lifts her brow. "Trust me, I *know* where Damen is. I *always* know where Damen is. It's what I do."

"So you're a stalker." I press my lips together, knowing I shouldn't antagonize her, but hey, I have nothing to lose. Either way, she's here to kill me.

She twists her lips and holds up her hand, inspecting her perfectly manicured nails. "Hardly," she mumbles.

"Well, if that's how you've chosen to spend the last three hundred years, then some might say—"

"More like six hundred, you dreadful little troll, six hundred years." She looks me over and scowls.

Six hundred years? Is she serious?

She rolls her eyes and stands. "You mortals, so dull, so stupid, so predictable, so *ordinary*. And yet, despite all your obvious defects, you always seem to inspire Damen to feed the hungry, serve mankind, fight poverty, save the whales, stop littering, recycle, meditate for peace, just say no to drugs, alcohol, big spending, and just about everything else that's worthwhile—one horribly boring altruistic pursuit after another. And for what? Do you ever learn? *Hello! Global warming!* Apparently not. And yet, *and yet,* somehow Damen and I always seem to get through it, though it can take far too long to deprogram him, return him to the lusty, hedonistic, greedy, indulgent Damen I know and love. Though believe me, this is just another little detour, and before you know it, we'll be back on top of the world again."

She moves toward me, her smile growing wider with each approaching step, slinking around the large granite counter like a Siamese cat. "Quite frankly, Ever, I can't imagine what it is that you see in him. And I don't mean what every other female, and let's face it, most males, see in him. No, I mean, it's because of Damen that you always seem to suffer. It's because of Damen that you're going through all of this now. If only you hadn't lived through that damn accident." She shakes her head. "I mean, just when I thought it was safe to leave, just when I was sure you were dead, the next thing I know Damen's moved to California because, *surprise,* he brought you back!" She shakes her head again. "You'd think after all of these hundreds of years, I'd have a little more patience. But then, you really do bore me, and clearly that's not *my* fault."

She looks at me but I refuse to respond, I'm still deciphering her words—*Drina caused the accident?*

She looks at me and rolls her eyes. "*Yes,* I caused the accident. Why must everything be so spelled out for you?" She shakes her head. "It was *I* who spooked the deer that ran in front of your car. It was *I* who knew your father was a sappy, kindhearted fool who'd gladly risk his family's life to save a deer. Mortals are always so predictable. Especially the earnest ones who try to do good." She laughs. "Though, in the end, it was almost too easy to be any fun. But make no mistake, Ever, this time Damen's not here to save you, and I *will* stick around to get the job done."

I scan the room, searching for some sort of protection, eyeing the knife rack on the other side of the room, but knowing I'll never get to it in time. I'm not fast like Damen and Drina. At least I don't think I am. And there's no time to find out.

She sighs. "By all means, please, get the knife, see if I care." She shakes her head and checks her diamond-encrusted watch. "I'd really like to get started though, if you don't mind. Normally I like to take my time, have a little fun, but, today being Valentine's Day and all, well, I have plans to dine with my sweetie, just as soon as I've eliminated you." Her eyes are dark and her mouth is twisted, and for the briefest moment, all the evil inside springs right to the surface. But then just as quickly it's gone again, replaced by a beauty so breathtaking, it's hard not to stare.

"You know, before you came along, in one of your . . . earlier incarnations, I was his one true love. But then you showed up and tried to steal him away, and it's been the same old cycle ever since." She slinks forward, each step silent, quick, until she's standing directly before me, and I've had no time to react. "But now I'm taking him back. And he always comes back, Ever, be clear about that."

I reach for the bamboo cutting board, thinking I can slam it over her head, but she lunges for me so fast she knocks me off balance and slams my body into the fridge, the blow to my back stealing my breath as I gasp and fumble and fall to the ground. Hearing the *thwonk* of my head cracking open when it slams against the floor as a trail of warm blood seeps from my skull to my mouth.

And before I can move or do anything to fight back, she's on top of me, slashing at my clothing, my hair, my face, whispering into my ear, "Just give up, Ever. Just relax and let go. Go join your happy family, they're all waiting to see you. You're not cut out for this life. You have nothing left to live for. And now's your chance to leave it."

thirty-eight

I must've blacked out, but only for a moment, because when I open my eyes, she's still right there on top of me, her face and hands stained with my blood as she croons and coaxes and whispers, trying to convince me to let go, to just let myself go, once and for all, to just slip away and be done with it all.

But even though that might've been tempting before, it's not anymore. This bitch killed my family, and now she's gonna pay.

I shut my eyes, determined to get back to that place—all of us in the car, laughing, happy, so full of love, seeing it clearer now than ever before, now that it's no longer clouded by guilt, now that I'm no longer to blame.

And when I feel my strength surging inside me I lift her right off me and throw her across the room, watching as she flies right into the wall, her arm jutting out at an unnatural angle as her body tilts to the floor.

She looks at me, eyes wide with shock, but soon she's up and laughing as she dusts herself off. And when she lunges at me, I throw her off again, watching as she soars across the kitchen and all the way into the den, crashing through the closed french doors and sending an explosion of broken shards through the room.

"Quite the crime scene you're creating," she says, plucking glass daggers from her arms, her legs, her face, the wounds closing up as soon as they're cleared. "Very impressive. Can't wait to read all about it in tomorrow's paper." She smiles, and just like that, she's on me again, fully restored, determined to win. "You're in over your head," she whispers. "And frankly, your pathetic show of strength is getting a little redundant. Seriously, Ever, you're one lousy hostess. No wonder you don't have any friends; is this how you treat all your guests?"

I push her off, ready to toss her through a thousand windows if I have to. But I've barely completed the thought when I'm sideswiped by a horrible, sharp, squeezing pain. Watching as Drina steps toward me, face pulled into a grin, paralyzing me so that I can't even stop her.

"That would be the old *head in a vise with serrated jaws* trick." She laughs. "Works every time. Though, in all fairness, I did try to warn you. You just wouldn't listen. But really, Ever, it's your choice. I can ratchet up the pain—" She narrows her eyes as my body folds in agony, slumping toward the floor as my stomach swirls with nausea. "Or, you can just—let—yourself—go. Nice and easy. Your choice."

I try to focus on her, watching as she moves toward me, but my vision is distorted, and my limbs so rubbery and weak, she's like a fast-moving blur I know I can't beat.

So I close my eyes and think: *I can't let her win. I can't let her win. Not this time. Not after what she did to my family.*

And when I swing my fist toward her, my body so feeble, clumsy, and defeated, I'm surprised when it lands square in her chest, grazing the front of her, before falling away. And I stagger back, devoid of all breath, knowing it wasn't nearly enough, didn't do any good.

I shut my eyes and cringe, waiting for the end, and now that it's inevitable, I hope it comes soon. But when my head clears and my stomach calms, I open them again to find Drina staggering back toward the wall, clutching her chest, and staring accusingly.

"Damen!" she wails, looking right past me. "Don't let her do this to me, *to us*—"

I turn, to see him standing beside me, gazing at Drina and shaking his head. "It's too late," he says, taking my hand, entwining his fingers with mine. "It's time for you to go, Poverina."

"Don't call me that!" she wails, her once amazing green eyes now blurred by red. "You know how I *hate* that!"

"I know," he says, squeezing my fingers as she shrivels and ages then fades from our sight, a black silk dress and designer shoes the only evidence she ever existed.

"How—" I turn to Damen, searching for answers.

But he just smiles and says, "It's over. Absolutely, completely, eternally over." He pulls me into his arms, covering my face in a trail of warm wonderful kisses, promising, "She'll never bother us again."

"Did I—*kill her*?" I ask, not quite sure how I feel about that, despite what she did to my family, and all the times she claimed to have killed me.

He nods.

"But—*how*? I mean, if she's immortal, then wasn't I supposed to cut off her head?"

He shakes his head and laughs. "What kind of books are you reading?" Then his face becomes very serious when he says, "It doesn't work like that. There's no beheading, no wooden stakes, no silver bullets, it all comes down to the simple fact that revenge weakens and love strengthens. Somehow you managed to hit Drina right in her most vulnerable spot."

I squint, not quite understanding. "I hardly touched her," I say, remembering how my fist met her chest, but just barely.

"The fourth chakra was your target. And you hit the bull's-eye."

Huh?

"The body has seven chakras. The fourth chakra, or heart chakra as it's sometimes called, is the center of unconditional love, compassion, the higher self, all of the things Drina was lacking. And that left her defenseless, weakened. Ever, her *lack of love* is what killed her."

"But if she was so vulnerable, why didn't she guard it, protect it?"

"She was unaware, deluded, led by her ego. Drina never realized how dark she'd become, how resentful, how hateful, how possessive—"

"And if you knew all that, why didn't you tell me before?"

He shrugs. "It was just a theory I had. I've never killed an immortal, so I wasn't sure if it would work. Until now."

"You mean there are others? Drina's not the only one?"

He opens his mouth as if to say something, but then closes it firmly. And when I look in his eyes I see a flash of—regret, remorse? But just as quickly, it's gone.

"She said some things about you, and your past—"

"Ever," he says. "Ever, look at me." He tilts my chin until I finally do. "I've been around a long time—"

"I'll say, *six hundred years!*"

He cringes. "Give or take. The point is, I've seen a few things, done a few things, and my life hasn't always been so good or so pure. In fact, most of it's been quite the opposite." I start to pull away, not sure if I'm ready to hear this, but he pulls me back to him and says, "Trust me, you're ready to hear this, because the truth is I'm not a murderer, I'm also not evil. I just—" He pauses.

"I just enjoyed a taste for the good life. And yet, every time I met you, I was willing to throw it all away, just to be near you."

I yank free, this time successfully. Thinking: *Oh jeez! Oh no! Classic case of boy losing girl, only this time it's over and over again, spanning the centuries, each time ending before they can do the deed. No wonder he's interested, I'm the one who keeps getting away! I'm like a living, breathing, forbidden fruit! Does this mean I have to remain a virgin for eternity? Disappear every few years just to keep his interest? I mean, now that we're stuck with each other for all of eternity, the moment the deed is done it's just a matter of time before this particular train arrives in Boring Town U.S.A. and he'll be looking to enjoy the "good life" again.*

"*Stuck with me*? That's how you see it? As though you'll be *stuck with me,* for all of eternity?" And the way he looks at me I can't tell if he's amused or offended.

My cheeks burn, having temporarily forgotten that my thoughts are not at all private where he's concerned. "No, I—I was afraid you'd feel that way about *me*. I mean, it's classic love story fodder—the one who got away—*again and again and again!* No wonder you've remained so entranced! It had nothing to do with me! You've spent six hundred years trying to get in my pants!"

"Petticoats, pantaloons, trust me, pants didn't come into fashion until much, much later." But when I don't laugh, he pulls me to him and says, "Ever, it has *everything* to do with you. And if you don't mind my saying, it's been my experience that the best way to deal with eternity is by living it one day at a time."

He kisses me, but only briefly, before he shifts his body and starts to pull away, but I grab hold of his hand, and pull him back to me. "Don't go," I say, gazing at him. "Please don't ever leave me again."

"Not even to get you some water?" He smiles.

"Not even for water," I tell him, my hands exploring his face, his incredibly beautiful face. "I—" The words halt in my throat.

"Yes?" He smiles.

"I missed you," I finally manage.

"And so you did." He leans in, pressing his lips to my forehead, then quickly pulling away.

"What?" I say, seeing the way he's looking at me, his grin spread wide and warming his face. Then I slide my fingers under my bangs, and gasp when I realize my scar's disappeared.

"Forgiveness is healing." He smiles. "Especially forgiving yourself."

I gaze at him, looking right into his eyes, knowing there's something more to say, but not sure I can go through with it. So I close my eyes instead, thinking that if he can read my mind then I shouldn't have to say the words out loud.

But he just laughs. "It's always better when it's spoken."

"But I've already said it, that's why you came back, right? I thought you would've come sooner. I mean it would've been nice to have had some help."

"I heard you. And I would've come even sooner, but I needed to know you were truly ready, and not just lonely after saying good-bye to Riley."

"You know about that?"

He nods. "You did the right thing."

"So, you almost let me die in there, because you wanted to be sure?"

He shakes his head. "I never would've let you die. Not this time."

"And Drina?"

"I underestimated her, I had no idea."

"You can't read each other's thoughts?"

He gazes at me, smoothing his thumb against my cheek. "We learned how to cloak them from each other long ago."

"Will you show me how to cloak mine?"

He smiles. "In time I'll teach you everything, I promise. But Ever, you need to know what all of this really means. You'll never be with your family again. You'll never cross that bridge. You need to know what you're getting yourself into." He holds my chin and looks in my eyes.

"But I can always, sort of, just—*drop out*—right? You know, give up? Like you said?"

He shakes his head. "It becomes much harder once you're ingrained."

I look at him, knowing it's a lot to give up, but figuring there's got to be some way around it. Riley promised me a sign, and I'll take it from there. But in the meantime, if eternity starts today, then that's the way I'm going to live it. For this day, and this day only. Knowing that Damen will always be by my side. *I mean, always, right?*

He looks at me, waiting.

"I love you," I whisper.

"And I love you." He smiles, his lips seeking mine. "*Always* have. *Always* will."

blue moon

Every man has his own destiny;
the only imperative
is to follow it, to accept it,
no matter where it leads him.

—Henry Miller

one

"Close your eyes and picture it. Can you see it?"

I nod, eyes closed.

"Imagine it right there before you. *See* its texture, shape, and color—got it?"

I smile, holding the image in my head.

"Good. Now reach out and touch it. *Feel* its contours with the tips of your fingers, *cradle* its weight in the palms of your hands, then combine all of your senses—sight, touch, smell, taste—can you taste it?"

I bite my lip and suppress a giggle.

"Perfect. Now combine that with feeling. *Believe* it exists right before you. Feel it, see it, touch it, taste it, accept it, *manifest* it!" he says.

So I do. I do all of those things. And when he groans, I open my eyes to see for myself.

"Ever." He shakes his head. "You were supposed to think of an *orange*. This isn't even close."

"Nope, nothing fruity about him." I laugh, smiling at each of my Damens—the replica I manifested before me, and the flesh and blood version beside me. Both of them equally tall, dark, and so devastatingly handsome they hardly seem real.

"What am I going to do with you?" the real Damen asks, attempting a disapproving gaze but failing miserably. His eyes always betray him, showing nothing but love.

"Hmmm . . ." I glance between my two boyfriends—one real, one conjured. "I guess you could just go ahead and kiss me. Or, if you're too busy, I'll ask him to stand in, I don't think he'd mind." I motion toward manifest Damen, laughing when he smiles and winks at me even though his edges are fading and soon he'll be gone.

But the real Damen doesn't laugh. He just shakes his head and says, "Ever, please. You need to be serious. There's so much to teach you."

"What's the rush?" I fluff my pillow and pat the space right beside me, hoping he'll move away from my desk and come join me. "I thought we had nothing *but* time?" I smile. And when he looks at me, my whole body grows warm and my breath halts in my throat, and I can't help but wonder if I'll ever get used to his amazing beauty—his smooth olive skin, brown shiny hair, perfect face, and lean sculpted body—the perfect dark yin to my pale blond yang. "I think you'll find me a very eager student," I say, my eyes meeting his—two dark wells of unfathomable depths.

"You're insatiable," he whispers, shaking his head and moving beside me, as drawn to me as I am to him.

"Just trying to make up for lost time," I murmur, always so eager for these moments, the times when it's just us, and I don't have to share him with anyone else. Even knowing we have all of eternity laid out before us doesn't make me any less greedy.

He leans in to kiss me, forgoing our lesson. All thoughts of manifesting, remote viewing, telepathy—all of that psychic business replaced by something far more immediate, as he pushes me back against a pile of pillows and covers my body with his, the two of us merging like crumbled vines seeking the sun.

His fingers snake under my top, sliding along my stomach to the edge of my bra as I close my eyes and whisper, "I love you." Words I once kept to myself. But after saying it the first time, I've barely said anything else.

Hearing his soft muffled groan as he releases the clasp on my bra, so effortlessly, so perfectly, nothing awkward or fumbling about it.

Every move he makes is so graceful, so perfect, so—

Maybe too perfect.

"What's wrong?" he asks, as I push him away. His breath coming in short shallow gasps as his eyes seek mine, their surrounding skin tense and constricted in the way I've grown used to.

"Nothing's wrong." I turn my back and adjust my top, glad I completed the lesson on shielding my thoughts since it's the only thing that allows me to lie.

He sighs and moves away, denying me the tingle of his touch and the heat of his gaze as he paces before me. And when he finally stops and faces me, I press my lips together, knowing what's next. We've been here before.

"Ever, I'm not trying to rush you or anything. Really, I'm not," he says, his face creased with concern. "But at some point you're going to have to get over this and accept who I am. I can manifest anything you desire, send telepathic thoughts and images whenever we're apart, whisk you away to Summerland at a moment's notice. But the one thing I can't ever do is change the past. It just *is*."

I stare at the floor, feeling small, needy, and completely ashamed. Hating that I'm so incapable of hiding my jealousies and insecurities, hating that they're so transparent and clearly displayed. Because no matter what sort of psychic shield I create, it's no use. He's had six hundred years to study human behavior (to study *my* behavior), versus my sixteen.

"Just—just give me a little more time to get used to all this," I say, picking at a frayed seam on my pillowcase. "It's only been a few weeks." I shrug, remembering how I killed his ex-wife, told him I loved him, and sealed my immortal fate, less than three weeks ago.

He looks at me, his lips pressed together, his eyes tinged with doubt. And even though we're merely a few feet apart, the space that divides us is so heavy and fraught—it feels like an ocean.

"I'm referring to *this* lifetime," I say, my voice quickening, rising, hoping to fill up the void and lighten the mood. "And since I can't recall any of the others, it's all I have. I just need a little more *time*, okay?" I smile nervously, my lips feeling clumsy and loose as I hold them in place, exhaling in relief when he sits down beside me, lifts his fingers to my forehead, and seeks the space where my scar used to be.

"Well, that's one thing we'll never run out of." He sighs, trailing his fingers along the curve of my jaw as he leans in to kiss me, his lips making a series of stops from my forehead, to my nose, to my mouth.

And just when I think he's about to kiss me again, he squeezes my hand and moves away. Heading straight for the door and leaving a beautiful red tulip behind in his place.

two

Even though Damen can sense the exact moment my aunt Sabine turns onto our street and approaches the drive, that's not why he left.

He left because of me.

Because of the simple fact that he's been after me for hundreds of years, seeking me out in all of my incarnations, just so we could be together.

Only we never got *together.*

Which means *it* never happened.

Apparently every time we were about to take the next step and consummate our love, his ex-wife Drina managed to show up and kill me.

But now that I've killed her, eliminated her with one well-placed though admittedly feeble swipe to her rather compromised heart chakra, there's absolutely nothing or no one blocking our way.

Except me.

Because even though I love Damen with all of my being, and definitely want to take the next step—I can't stop thinking about those last six hundred years.

And how he chose to live them. (Outlandishly, according to him.)

And *whom* he chose to live them with. (Besides his ex-wife Drina, many others have been alluded to.)

And, well, as much as I hate to admit it, knowing all of that makes me feel a little insecure.

Okay, maybe *a lot* insecure. I mean, it's not like my pathetically meager list of guys I've kissed could ever compare to his six centuries' worth of conquests.

And even though I know it's ridiculous, even though I know Damen has loved me for centuries, the fact is, the heart and mind aren't always friendly.

And in my case, they're barely speaking.

Yet still, every time Damen comes over for my lesson, I always manage to turn it into a prolonged make-out session, each time starting out thinking: *This is it! It's really going to happen this time!*

Only to push him away like the worst kind of tease.

And the truth is, it's exactly like he said. He can't change his past, *it just is.* Once something is done it can't be undone. There's no rewind. No going back.

The only thing a person can ever really do is keep moving forward.

And that's exactly what I need to do.

Take that big leap forward without hesitation, without once looking back.

Simply forget the past and forge toward the future.

I just wish it were really that easy.

"Ever?" Sabine makes her way up the stairs as I run frantically around my room, trying to straighten it up before plopping in front of my desk and scrambling to look like I'm busy. "You still up?" she asks, poking her head inside. And even though her suit is wrinkled, her hair limp, and her eyes a little red and tired, her aura's hanging in there, beaming a nice shade of green.

"I was just finishing up some homework," I say, pushing my laptop away as though I'd been using it.

"Did you eat?" She leans against the doorjamb, her eyes narrowed and suspicious, as her aura reaches right toward me—the portable lie detector she unknowingly carries wherever she goes.

"Of course," I tell her. Nodding and smiling and doing my best to appear sincere, but the truth is, it feels false on my face.

I hate having to lie. Especially to her. After all that she's done for me, taking me in after the accident when my whole family died. I mean, it's not like she had to do that. Just because she's my only living relative didn't mean she couldn't say no. And believe me, half the time she probably wishes she had. Her life was way less complicated before I arrived.

"I meant something besides that red drink." She nods, motioning toward the bottle on my desk, the opalescent red liquid with the strange bitter taste I don't hate nearly as much as I used to. Which is good since, according to Damen, I'll be sipping it for the rest of eternity. Though it's not like I *can't* eat real food, it's just that I no longer want to. My immortal juice provides all of the nutrients I could ever need. And no matter how much or how little I drink, I always feel sated.

But still, I know what she's thinking. And not only because I can read all of her thoughts, but because I used to think the same things about Damen. I used to get really annoyed watching him push his food around and only *pretend* to eat. Until I found out his secret, that is.

"I, um, I grabbed something earlier," I finally say, trying not to press my lips together, avert my gaze, or cringe—all of my usual dead giveaways. "With Miles and Haven," I add, hoping it will explain the lack of dirty dishes, even though I know that providing too many details is bad, like a flashing red light signaling LIAR STRAIGHT AHEAD! Not to mention that Sabine being a lawyer, one of her firm's top litigators, makes her incredibly good at spotting a phony. Though she pretty much saves that particular gift for her professional life. In her private life, she chooses to believe.

Except for today. Today she's not buying a word of it. Instead, she just looks at me and says, "I'm worried about you."

I swivel around so I'm facing her, hoping to appear as though I'm open, ready to address her concerns, even though I'm pretty much freaked. "I'm fine," I tell her, nodding and smiling so that she'll believe it. "Really. My grades are good, I'm getting along with my friends, Damen and I are—" I pause, realizing I've never really talked to her about my relationship before, haven't really defined it, and have pretty much kept it to myself. And the truth is, now that I've started, I'm not sure how to finish.

I mean, referring to ourselves as boyfriend and girlfriend sounds so mundane and inadequate once our pasts, presents, and futures are taken into account, because clearly all of our shared history makes us so much more than that. But still, it's not like I'm going to publicly proclaim us as eternal partners or soul mates either—the *ick* factor on that is just way too high. And the truth is, I'd really rather not define it at all. At the moment, I'm confused enough as it is. Besides, what would I even tell her? That we've loved each other for centuries but still haven't made it past second base?

"Well, Damen and I are—doing really good," I finally say, gulping when I realize I said *good* instead of *great*, which may be the first real truth I've spoken all day.

"So he *was* here." She sets her brown leather briefcase onto the floor and looks at me, both of us fully aware of how easily I fell into her professional litigator's trap.

I nod, mentally kicking myself for insisting we hang out here, as opposed to his place like he originally wanted.

"I thought I saw his car whiz past." She shifts her gaze to my rumpled bed with the haphazard pillows and disheveled duvet, and when she turns back to face me, I can't help but cringe, especially when I sense what's about to be said.

"Ever." She sighs. "I'm sorry I'm not around all that much and that we're unable to spend more time together. And even though it feels like we're still sort of finding our way with each other, I want you to know that I'm here for you. If you ever need to talk to someone—I'll listen."

I press my lips together and nod, knowing she's not finished, but hoping that by staying quiet and complacent, it'll be over with soon.

"Because even though you probably think I'm too old to understand what you're going through, I do remember what it was like at your age. How overwhelming it can be with the constant pressure to measure up to models and actresses and other impossible images you see on TV."

I swallow hard and avoid her gaze, cautioning myself to not overreact, to not go all overboard with defending myself since it's much better for her to believe this than to suspect the real truth.

Ever since I got expelled, Sabine's been watching me closer than ever, and when she recently loaded up on a stack of self-help books, everything from: *How to Raise a Sane Teen in Insane Times Like These,* to: *Your Teen and the Media (And What You Can Do About it!),* it's gotten a gazillion times worse. With her underlining and highlighting all of the most disturbing adolescent behaviors, and then scrutinizing me, checking for symptoms.

"But I want you to know that you're a beautiful girl, far more beautiful than I ever was at your age, and that starving yourself to compete with all of those skinny celebrities who spend half their lives checking in and out of rehab is not only a completely unreasonable and unattainable goal, but will only end up making you sick." She gives me a pointed look, desperately wanting to get through to me, hoping her words will penetrate. "I want you to know that you're perfect just as you are, and it pains me to see you going through this. And if this is about Damen, well then, all I have to say about that is—"

"I'm not anorexic."

She looks at me.

"I'm not bulimic, I'm not on some crazy fad diet, I'm not starving myself, I'm not striving to be a size zero, and I'm not trying to look like an Olsen twin. Seriously, Sabine, do I *look* like I'm wasting away?" I stand, allowing for an unobstructed view of me in all of my tight-jeaned glory, because if anything, I feel like the opposite of wasting away. I seem to be bulking up at a pretty good pace.

She looks me over. And I mean *really* looks me over. Starting from the top of my head and going all the way down to my toes, her eyes coming to rest on my pale exposed ankles I had no choice but to display when I discovered that my favorite jeans are too short and rolled them up to compensate.

"I just thought . . ." She shrugs, unsure of what to say now that the evidence presented before her so clearly points to a *not guilty* verdict. "Because I never see you eating anymore—and you're always sipping that red—"

"So you just assumed I'd gone from adolescent binge drinker to anorexic food avoider?" I laugh so she'll know I'm not mad—a little annoyed maybe, though more with myself than with her. I should've faked it better. I should've at least *pretended* to eat. "You have nothing to worry about." I smile. "Really. And just so we're clear, I have no intention of taking and/or dealing drugs, experimenting with body modification, cutting, branding, scarification, extreme piercing, or whatever else makes this week's *Top Ten Maladjusted Behaviors to Look for in Your Teen* list. And for the record, my sipping that red drink has nothing to do with trying to be celebrity skinny or trying to please Damen. I just happen to like it, that's all. Besides, I happen to know for a fact that Damen loves me and accepts me exactly as I—" I stop, knowing I've just started a whole other topic I'm unwilling to explore. And before she can even get to the words now formulating in her head, I just hold up my hand and say, "And *no*, that's *not* what I meant. Damen and I are—" *Hooking up, dating, boyfriend and girlfriend, friends with benefits, eternally bound.* "Well, we're together. You know, committed, like a couple. But we *aren't* sleeping together."

Yet.

She looks at me, her face as pinched and uncomfortable as I feel inside. Neither of us wanting to explore this topic, but, unlike me, she feels it's her duty.

"Ever, I wasn't insinuating—" she starts. But then she looks at me, and I look at her, and she shrugs, deciding to just let it go since we both know she most certainly was.

And I'm so relieved that it's over and that I got off relatively easy, that I'm completely taken by surprise when she says, "Well, since you really seem to care about this young man, I think I should get to know him. So let's schedule a time when we can all go to dinner. How does this weekend sound?"

This weekend?

I swallow hard and look at her, knowing exactly what she's after, hoping to kill two birds with one meal. Having found the perfect opportunity to watch me scarf down a full plate of food, while putting Damen on the stand so she can totally grill him.

"Well, that sounds great and all except that Miles's play is on Friday." I fight to keep my voice steady and sure. "And then there's supposed to be an after party—and that'll probably run pretty late—so . . ."

She nods, her eyes right on mine, her gaze so uncanny and knowing it's making me sweat.

"So it's probably not going to work," I finish, knowing I'll have to go through with it eventually, but hoping for later rather than sooner. I mean, I love Sabine, and I love Damen, I'm just not sure I'm going to love them together, especially once the interrogation begins.

She looks at me for a moment, then nods and turns away. And just when I'm able to exhale, she glances over her shoulder to say, "Well, Friday's clearly out, but that still leaves Saturday. Why don't you tell Damen to be here at eight?"

three

Even though I oversleep, I still manage to get out the door and over to Miles's on time. I guess because it doesn't take me nearly as long to get ready now that Riley's no longer around to distract me. And even though it used to bug me the way she'd perch on my dresser wearing one of her crazy Halloween costumes while grilling me about boyfriends and making fun of my clothes, ever since I convinced her to move on, to cross the bridge to where our parents and our dog Buttercup were waiting, I haven't been able to see her.

Which pretty much means she was right. I can only see the souls who've stayed behind, not the ones who've crossed over.

And like always when I think about Riley, my throat constricts and my eyes start to sting, and I wonder if I'll ever get used to the fact that she's gone. I mean, permanently and irreversibly gone. But I guess by now I should know enough about loss to realize that you never really stop missing someone—you just learn to live around the huge gaping hole of their absence.

I wipe my eyes and pull into Miles's drive, remembering Riley's promise, that she'd send me a sign, something to show she's okay. But even though I've been holding tight to her pledge, staying alert, and searching vigilantly for some indication of her presence—so far I've got nothing.

Miles opens the door and just as I start to say *hi,* he holds up his hand and says, "Don't speak. Just look at my face and tell me what you see. What's the very first thing you notice? And *don't* lie."

"Your beautiful brown eyes," I say, hearing the thoughts in his head and wishing, not for the first time, that I could show my friends how to shield their thoughts and keep all their private stuff private. But that would mean divulging my mind-reading, aura-seeing, psychic-sensing secrets, and that I can't do.

Miles shakes his head and climbs inside, yanking down on the mirrored visor and inspecting his chin. "You're such a liar. Look, it's right there! Like a shining red beacon you can't possibly miss, so don't even try to pretend you don't see it."

I glance at him as I back out of the drive, seeing the zit that dared sprout on his face, though it's his bright pink nail polish that steals my attention. "Nice nails." I laugh.

"It's for the play." He smirks, still zit gazing. "I can't even believe this! It's like I'm totally falling apart just when everything was going so perfect. Rehearsals have been great, I know all of my lines as well as everyone else's . . . I thought I was totally and completely ready, and now *this*!" He jabs at his face.

"It's just nerves," I say, glancing at him as the light turns green.

"Exactly!" He nods. "Which just proves what an amateur I am. Because professionals, *real* professionals, they don't get nervous. They just go into their creative zone and . . . *create*. Maybe I'm not cut out for this?" He looks at me, his face tense with worry. "Maybe it's just a fluke that I got the lead."

I glance at him, remembering how Drina claimed to climb inside the director's head and sway him toward Miles. But even if that's true, that doesn't mean he can't handle it, doesn't mean he wasn't the best.

"That's ridiculous." I shake my head. "Tons of actors get nervous, suffer from stage fright or whatever. Seriously. You wouldn't believe some of the stories Riley used to—" I stop, eyes wide, mouth open, knowing I can never finish that sentence. Can never divulge the stories gleaned from my dead little sister who used to enjoy spying on the Hollywood elite. "Anyway, don't you wear, like, a ton of heavy pancake makeup?"

He glances at me. "Yeah. So. What's your point? The play's Friday, which, for your information, happens to be *tomorrow.* This will *never* be gone by then."

"Maybe." I shrug. "But what I meant was, can't you use the makeup to cover it?"

Miles rolls his eyes and scowls. "Oh, so I can sport a huge flesh-colored beacon instead? Would you look at this thing? There's no disguising it. It's got its own DNA! It's casting shadows!"

I pull into the school parking lot, claiming my usual space, the one right next to Damen's shiny black BMW. And when I look at Miles again, for some reason I feel compelled to touch his face. As though my index finger is inexplicably drawn to the zit on his chin.

"What're you doing?" he asks, cringing and pulling away.

"Just—just be still," I whisper, having no idea what I'm doing, or why I'm even doing it. All I know is my finger has a definite destination in mind.

"Well don't—*touch it!*" he shouts, the exact moment I make contact. "Great, that's just great. Now it'll probably double in size." He shakes his head and climbs out of the car, and I can't help but feel disappointed to see the pimple still there.

I guess I was hoping I'd developed some kind of enhanced healing ability. Ever since Damen told me, right after I'd decided to accept my fate and start drinking the immortal juice, that I could expect to go through some changes, anything from super-enhanced psychic abilities (which I was not looking forward to), to super-enhanced physical abilities (which could certainly have its benefits in P.E.), or something else altogether (like the ability to heal others, which has my vote since it would be totally cool), I've been on the lookout for something extraordinary. But so far, all I got is an extra inch of leg, which really doesn't do much for me besides requiring a new pair of jeans. And that probably would've happened eventually anyway.

I grab my bag and climb out of my car, my lips meeting Damen's the instant he comes around to my side.

"Okay, seriously. How much longer can this possibly last?"

We both pull away and look at Miles.

"Yeah, I'm talking to you." He wags his finger. "All of the kissing, and hugging, and let us not forget the constant whispering of sweet little nothings." He shakes his head and narrows his eyes. "Seriously. I was hoping you guys would be over it by now. I mean, don't get me wrong, we're all very happy that Damen's back in school, that you've found each other again, and will most likely live happily ever after. But really, don't you think it's time to maybe try and tone it down a little? Because *some* of us aren't quite as happy as you. *Some* of us are a little bit love deprived."

"*You're* love deprived?" I laugh, not at all offended by anything he just said, knowing it has far more to do with his anxiety about the play than anything to do with Damen and me. "What happened to Holt?"

"Holt?" He balks. "Don't even talk about Holt! Do not even go there, Ever!" He shakes his head and turns on his heel, heading toward Haven who's waiting by the gate.

"What's his problem?" Damen asks, reaching for my hand and entwining my fingers with his, gazing at me with eyes that still love me, despite yesterday.

"Tomorrow's opening night." I shrug. "So he's freaking out, has a zit on his chin, and naturally he's decided to hold us responsible," I say, watching as Miles links arms with Haven as he leads her toward class.

"We're not talking to them," he says, glancing over his shoulder and frowning at us. "We're on strike until they stop acting so love struck or this zit goes away, whichever comes first." He nods, only half joking.

Haven laughs and skips alongside him, as Damen and I head into English. Going right past Stacia Miller who smiles sweetly at him and then tries to trip me.

But just as she drops her small bag in my path, hoping to incite a nice, humiliating face plant, I *see* it lifting, and I *feel* it smacking—right into her knee. And even though I feel the pain too, I'm still glad I did it.

"Owww!" she wails, rubbing her knee and glaring at me, even though she has no tangible proof that I'm in any way responsible.

But I just ignore her and take my seat. I've gotten better at ignoring her. Ever since she got me suspended for drinking on campus, I've done my best to stay out of her way. But sometimes—sometimes I just can't help myself.

"You shouldn't have done that," Damen whispers, attempting a stern look as he leans toward me.

"Please. You're the one who wants me to practice manifesting." I shrug. "Looks like those lessons are finally starting to pay off."

He looks at me, shaking his head as he says, "You see, it's even worse than I thought, because for your information that was psychokinesis you just did, *not* manifesting. See how much there is to learn?"

"Psycho-what?" I squint, unfamiliar with the term, though the act itself was sure fun.

He takes my hand, a smile playing at the corner of his lips as he says, "I've been thinking . . ."

I glance at the clock, seeing it's already five minutes past nine and knowing Mr. Robins is just now leaving the teachers' lounge.

"Friday night. What do you say we go somewhere . . . special?" He smiles.

"Like Summerland?" I look at Damen, my eyes growing wide as my pulse quickens. I've been dying to get back to that magical, mystical place. The dimension between the dimensions, where I can manifest oceans and elephants, and move things far greater than projectile Prada bags—only I need Damen to get there.

But he just laughs and shakes his head. "No, not Summerland. Though we will return there, I promise. But I was thinking more like, I don't know, maybe the Montage, or the Ritz, perhaps?" He raises his brows.

"But Miles's play is Friday and I promised we'd be there!" I say, realizing just after I've said it that I'd conveniently forgotten all about Miles's *Hairspray* debut when I thought I was going to Summerland. But now that Damen wants to check into one of the area's most swanky hotels—my memory is somehow restored.

"Okay, then, how about after the play?" he offers. But when he looks at me, when he sees how I hesitate, how I press my lips together and search for a polite way to decline, he adds, "Or not. It was just a thought."

I gaze at him, knowing I need to accept, that I *want* to accept. Hearing the voice in my head shouting: *Say yes! Say yes! You promised yourself you'd leap forward, without once looking back, and now's your chance—so just go ahead and do it! JUST! SAY! YES!*

But even though I'm convinced that it's time to move on, even though I love Damen with all of my heart and am determined to get over his past and take the next step, what comes out of my mouth is entirely different.

"We'll see," I say, averting my gaze and focusing on the door, just as Mr. Robins walks in.

four

When the fourth-period bell finally rings, I get up from my desk and approach Mr. Munoz.

"Are you sure you're finished?" he asks, looking up from a pile of papers. "If you need another minute, that's perfectly okay."

I glance over my test sheet, then shake my head. Wondering what he'd do if he ever found out that I'd finished approximately forty-five seconds after he first handed it to me, then spent the next fifty minutes only pretending to struggle.

"I'm good," I tell him, knowing it's true. One of the perks of being psychic is that I no longer have to study, instead I just sort of *know* all the answers. And even though it's sometimes tempting to show off and ace all of my tests in a long steady stream of perfect scores, I usually try to hold back and get a few wrong since it's important to not overdo it.

Or at least that's what Damen says. Always reminding me how imperative it is to keep a low profile, to at least give the *appearance* of being normal—even though we're anything but. Though the first time he said it, I couldn't help but remind him of how there seemed to be an awful lot of tulip manifesting going on back when we first met. But he just said that certain allowances had to be made in his efforts to woo me, and that it took longer than necessary since

I didn't bother to look up their true meaning of *undying love,* until it was almost too late.

I hand the paper to Mr. Munoz, cringing when the tips of our fingers make contact. And even though our skin just barely brushed, it was still enough to *show* me far more than I ever needed to know, allowing for a pretty clear visual of his entire morning so far. Everything from his incredibly messy apartment with the kitchen table that's littered with takeout containers and multiple versions of the manuscript he's been working on for the past seven years, to him singing "Born to Run" at the top of his lungs as he tried to find a clean shirt before heading over to Starbucks where he bumped into a petite blonde who spilled her iced venti chai latte all down the front of it—resulting in a cold, wet, annoying stain that one flash of her beautiful smile seemed to erase. A glorious smile he can't seem to forget—a glorious smile that—*belongs to my aunt!*

"Want to wait while I grade it?"

I nod, practically hyperventilating as I focus on his red pen. Replaying the scene I just saw in my head, each time coming to the same horrific conclusion—*my history teacher is hot for Sabine!*

I can't let this happen. Can't allow her to *ever* go back there. I mean, just because they're smart, cute, and single, doesn't mean they need to date.

I stand there, frozen, unable to breathe, struggling to block out the thoughts in his head by focusing on the tip of his pen. Watching as he leaves a trail of tiny red dots that turn into checkmarks at numbers seventeen and twenty-five—just as I'd planned.

"Only two wrong. Very good!" He smiles, brushing his fingers against the stain on his shirt, wondering if he'll ever see *her* again. "Would you like to see the correct answers?"

Uh, not really, I think, eager to be out of there as soon as I can, and not just so I can get to the lunch table and see Damen, but in case his fantasy decides to pick up where I forced it to leave off.

But knowing that the normal thing would be to appear at least somewhat interested, I take a deep breath and smile and nod as though I'd like nothing more. And when he hands me the answer key, I just go through the motions, saying, "Oh, look at that, I got the wrong date." And, "Of course! How could I not know that? *Duh!*"

But he just nods, mostly because his thoughts are already back on the blonde—aka: *The only woman in the entire universe who he is absolutely forbidden to date!* Wondering if she'll be there tomorrow—same time and place.

And even though the idea of teachers in lust pretty much grosses me out in a general sense, this particular teacher's being in lust over someone who's practically *like a parent to me*—just will not do.

But then I remember how just a few months ago I had a vision of Sabine dating some cute guy in her building. And since Munoz works *here,* and Sabine works *there,* I figure there's really no threat of my two worlds colliding. But just in case I'm wrong, I still manage to say, "Um, it was a fluke."

He looks at me, brows merged, trying to make sense of my words.

And even though I know I've gone too far, even though I know I'm about to say something as far from normal as you can get, I really don't feel I have much of a choice. I cannot have my history teacher dating my aunt. I can't tolerate it. I just can't.

So I motion toward the stain on his shirt when I add, "You know, *her,* Miss Iced Venti Chai Latte?" I nod, seeing the alarmed look on his face. "I doubt she'll be back. She doesn't really go all that often."

Then before I can say anything else that will not only dash his dreams but confirm the full extent of my freakdom, I sling my bag over my shoulder and run for the door, shrugging off the last of Mr. Munoz's lingering energy as I make my way toward the lunch table where Damen is waiting—eager to be with him again after three very long hours apart.

But when I get there, it's not quite the homecoming I expected. There's a new guy sitting beside him, right in my usual place, and he's soaking up so much attention, Damen barely notices me.

I lean against the edge of the table, watching as they all break into laughter at something the new guy said. And not wanting to interrupt or come off as rude, I take the seat across from Damen rather than right beside him in my usual place.

"Omigod, you are *so* funny!" Haven says, leaning forward and briefly touching the new guy's hand. Smiling in a way that makes it clear her new boyfriend, Josh, her self-proclaimed soul mate, has been temporarily forgotten. "Too bad you missed it, Ever, he's *so* hysterical Miles even forgot to obsess on his zit!"

"Thanks for the reminder." Miles scowls, his finger seeking the spot on his chin—only it's no longer there.

His eyes go wide, looking to each of us for confirmation that his mammoth-sized zit, the bane of this morning's existence, really is gone. And I can't help but wonder if its sudden disappearance is because of me, because of when I touched it this morning, back in the parking lot. Which would mean I really do have magical healing abilities.

But just after I think it, the new guy says, "Told you it'd work. Stuff's brilliant. Keep the rest in case it returns."

And I narrow my gaze, wondering how he could've had enough time to intervene on Miles's complexion issues when it's the first I've yet to see of him.

"I gave him some salve," he says, turning toward me. "Miles and I are in homeroom together. I'm Roman, by the way."

I look at him, taking in the bright yellow aura that swirls all around him, its edges extended, beckoning, like a friendly group hug. But when I take in his deep navy blue eyes, tanned skin, blond tousled hair, and casual clothes with just the right amount of hipster chic—despite his good looks, my first reaction is to run away. Even when he flashes me one of those languid, easy, make-your-heart-swoon kind of smiles, I'm so on edge, I can't seem to return it.

"And you must be Ever," he says, retracting his hand, the one I hadn't even noticed was extended and waiting to be shaken until he pulled it away.

I glance at Haven who's clearly horrified by my rudeness, then over at Miles who is too busy mirror gazing to notice my faux pas. But when Damen reaches under the table and squeezes my knee, I clear my throat, look at Roman, and say, "Um, yeah, I'm Ever." And even though he shoots me that smile again, it still doesn't work. It just makes my stomach go all jumpy and queasy.

"Seems we have a lot in common," he says, though I can't imagine what that could possibly be. "I sat two rows behind you in history. And the way you were struggling, I couldn't help but think, well there's a girl who hates history almost as much as I do."

"I don't hate history," I say, only it comes out too quickly, too defensively, my voice containing a sharp abrasive edge that makes everyone stare. So I glance at Damen, looking for confirmation, sure I can't be the only one who feels the unsettled stream of energy that starts with Roman and flows right to me.

But he just shrugs and sips his red drink as though everything's perfectly normal and he hasn't noticed a thing. So I turn back to Roman and delve into his mind, eavesdropping on a steady stream of harmless thoughts that while slightly juvenile for sure, are basically benign. Which pretty much means the problem is mine.

"Really?" Roman raises his brows and leans toward me. "All that delving into the past, exploring all those long-ago places and dates, examining the lives of people who lived centuries before and bear absolutely no relevance now—that doesn't bother you? Or bore you to death?"

Only when those people, places, and dates involve my boyfriend and his six hundred years of carousing!

But I only think it. I don't say it. Instead, I just shrug and say, "I did fine. In fact, it was easy. I aced it."

He nods, his eyes grazing over me, not missing an inch. "Good to know." He smiles. "Munoz is giving me the weekend to catch up, perhaps you can tutor me?"

I glance at Haven, watching as her eyes grow dark and her aura turns a jealous puke green, then at Miles who's moved on from his zit and is now texting Holt, and then I look at Damen who's oblivious to us both, his gaze far away, focused on something I can't see. And even though I know I'm being ridiculous, that everyone else seems to like him and I should do what I can to help, I just shrug when I say, "Oh, I'm sure that's not necessary. You don't need me."

Unable to ignore the prick of my skin and the ping in my stomach when his eyes meet mine—revealing a set of flawless white teeth when he says, "Nice of you to give me the benefit of the doubt, Ever. Though I'm not sure you should."

five

"What's up with you and the new kid?" Haven asks, lagging behind as everyone else heads for class.

"Nothing." I shake off her hand and forge straight ahead, her energy streaming right through me as I watch Roman, Miles, and Damen laugh and carry on as though they're old friends.

"Please." She rolls her eyes. "It's so obvious you don't like him."

"That's ridiculous," I say, my eyes focused on Damen, my gorgeous and glorious boyfriend/soul mate/eternal partner/cohort (I really need to find the right word) who's barely spoken to me since this morning in English. And I'm hoping it's not because of the reason I think—because of my behavior yesterday and my refusal to commit to this weekend.

"I'm totally serious." She looks at me. "It's like—it's like you hate new people or something." Which happened to come out much kinder than the actual words in her head.

I press my lips together and stare straight ahead, resisting the urge to roll my eyes.

But she just peers at me, hand on one hip, heavily made-up eyes squinting from under the flaming red stripe in her bangs. "Because if I remember right, and we both know I do, you hated Damen when he first came to this school."

"I didn't *hate* Damen," I say, rolling my eyes despite my recent vow not to. Thinking: *Correction, I only gave the* appearance *of hating Damen. When the truth is, I loved him that whole entire time. Well, except for that short period of time when I truly did hate him. But still, even then, I loved him. I just didn't want to admit it. . . .*

"Um, excuse me, but I beg to differ," she says, artfully messy black hair falling into her face. "Remember how you didn't even invite him to your Halloween party?"

I sigh, completely annoyed by all this. All I want to do is get to class so I can pretend to pay attention while I telepathically IM Damen.

"Yes, and if you'll remember that's also the night we hooked up," I finally say, though the second it's out, I regret it. Haven's the one who found us making out by the pool, and it pretty much broke her heart.

But she just ignores it, more determined to make her case than revisit that particular past. "Or maybe you're jealous because Damen has a new friend. You know, someone other than you."

"That's ridiculous," I say, though it comes out too quickly to ever be believed. "Damen has plenty of friends," I add, even though we both know it's not true.

She looks at me, lips pursed, completely unmoved.

But now that I'm this far in, I've no choice but to continue, so I say, "He has you, and Miles, and—" *And me,* I think, but I don't want to say it because it's a sad little list, which is exactly her point. And the truth is, Damen never hangs with Haven and Miles unless I'm there too. He spends every free moment with me. And the times we're not together he sends a steady stream of thoughts and images to make up for the distance. It's like we're always connected. And I have to admit that I like it that way. Because only with Damen can I be my true self—my thought-hearing, energy-sensing, spirit-seeing self. Only with Damen can I let my guard down and be the real me.

But when I look at Haven, I can't help but wonder if maybe she's right. Maybe I am jealous. Maybe Roman really is just some nice normal guy who moved to a new school and wants to make some new friends—as opposed to the creepy threat I assume him to be. Maybe I really have become so paranoid, jealous, and possessive I automatically assume that just because Damen wasn't as focused on me as he usually is, I'm about to be replaced. And if that's the case, well, it's way too pathetic to admit. So I just shake my head and fake a laugh when I say, "Again, ridiculous. All of this is seriously ridiculous." Then I try to look as though I really do mean it.

"Yeah? Well, what about Drina, then? How do you explain *that*?" She smirks and says, "You hated her from the moment you saw her, and don't even try to deny it. And then, once you found out she knew Damen, you hated her even more."

I cringe when she says it. And not only because it's true, but because hearing the name of Damen's ex-wife always makes me cringe. I can't help it, it just does. But I have no idea how to explain it to Haven. All she knows is that Drina pretended to be her friend, ditched her at a party, and then disappeared forever. She has no memory of Drina trying to kill her with the poisonous salve she used for that creepy tattoo she recently had removed from her wrist, no memory of—

Oh my God! The salve! Roman gave Miles a salve for his zit! I knew *there was something strange about him. I knew* I *wasn't making it up!*

"Haven, what class does Miles have now?" I ask, my eyes scanning the campus, unable to find him and in too big of a hurry to use remote sensing, which I still haven't mastered.

"I think English, why?" She gives me a strange look.

"Nothing, I just—I gotta run."

"Fine. Whatever. But just so you know, I still think you hate new people!" she shouts.

But it lingers behind me. I'm already gone.

I sprint across campus, focusing on Miles's energy and trying to sense which classroom he's in. And as I round a corner and see a door on my right, without even thinking, I burst in.

"Can I help you?" the teacher asks, turning away from the board, holding a broken piece of white chalk in his hand.

I stand before the class, cringing as a few of Stacia's minions mock me as I fight to catch my breath.

"Miles," I pant, pointing at him. "I need to speak to Miles. It'll only take a sec," I promise, as his teacher crosses his arms and gives me a dubious look. "It's important," I add, glancing at Miles who's now closed his eyes and is shaking his head.

"I assume you have a hall pass?" his teacher asks, a stickler for the rules.

And even though I know it might very well alienate him and end up working against me, I don't have time to get bogged down in all this red tape, the high school bureaucracy designed to keep us all safe—but that is actually, at this very moment, keeping me from handling a matter that is clearly life and death!

Or at least it might be.

I'm not sure. Though I'd like a chance to find out.

And I'm so frustrated, I just shake my head and say, "Listen, you and I both know I don't have a hall pass, but if you'll just do me the favor of letting me speak with Miles outside for a sec, I promise to send him right back."

He looks at me, his mind sifting through all the alternatives, all the different ways this could play out: kicking me out, escorting me to class, escorting me to Principal Buckley's office—before glancing at Miles and sighing when he says, "Fine. Make it quick."

The second we head into the hall and the door closes behind us, I look at Miles and say, "Give me the salve."

"What?" He gapes.

"The salve. The one Roman gave you. Give it to me. I need to see it," I tell him, extending my hand and wiggling my fingers.

"Are you crazy?" he whispers, looking around even though it's just wall-to-wall carpet, taupe colored walls, and us.

"You have no idea how serious this is," I say, my eyes on his, not wanting to scare him, though I will if I have to. "Now come on, we don't have all day."

"It's in my backpack." He shrugs.

"Then go get it."

"Ever, seriously. What the—?"

I just fold my arms and nod. "Go on. I'll wait."

Miles shakes his head and disappears inside the room. Emerging a moment later with a sour expression and a small white tube in the palm of his hand. "Here. Happy now?" He tosses it to me.

I take the tube and examine it, twirling it between my thumb and index finger. It's a brand that I recognize, from a store that I frequent. And I don't understand how that could be.

"You know, in case you've forgotten, my play is tomorrow, and I really don't need all of this extra drama and stress right now, so if you don't mind . . ." He extends his hand, waiting for me to return the salve so he can get back to class.

Only I'm not willing to hand it over just yet. I'm looking for some kind of needle hole or puncture mark, something to prove it's been tampered with, that it's not what it seems.

"I mean, today at lunch when I saw how you and Damen toned down the whole smoochy business, I was ready to high-five you, but now it's like you've replaced it with something way worse. I mean, seriously, Ever. Either unscrew the cap and use it, or give it back already."

But I don't give it back. Instead, I close my fingers around it and try to read its energy. But it's just some stupid zit cream. The kind that actually works.

"Are we done here?" He frowns at me.

I shrug and give the tube back. To say I'm embarrassed would be putting it mildly. But when Miles shoves it into his pocket and heads for the door, I can't help but say, "So you noticed?" The words feel hot and sticky in my throat.

"Noticed what?" He stops, clearly annoyed.

"The, um, the absence of the whole *smoochy business*?"

Miles turns, performing an exaggerated eye roll before leveling his gaze right on mine. "Yeah, I noticed. I figured you guys were just taking my threat seriously."

I look at him.

"This morning—when I said Haven and I were on strike until you guys stopped with all of your—" He shakes his head. "Whatever. Can I please get to class?"

"Sorry." I nod. "Sorry about all the—"

But before I can finish, he's already gone, the door closed firmly between us.

six

When I get to sixth period art, I'm relieved to see Damen's already there. Since Mr. Robins kept us so busy in English and we barely spoke at lunch, I'm looking forward to a little alone time with him. Or at least as alone as you can be in a classroom with thirty other students.

But after slipping on my smock and gathering my supplies from the closet, my heart sinks when I see that, once again, Roman has taken my place.

"Oh, hey, Ever." He nods, placing his brand-new blank canvas on *my* easel while I stand there, cradling my stuff in my arms and staring at Damen who's so immersed in his painting he's completely oblivious to me.

And I'm just about to tell Roman to scram when I remember Haven's words, how she said I hate new people. And fearing she might be right, I force a smile onto my face and place my canvas on the easel on Damen's other side, promising myself to get here much earlier tomorrow so I can reclaim my space.

"So tell me. Wot are we doin' 'ere, mate?" Roman asks, lodging a paintbrush between his front teeth and glancing between Damen and me.

And that's another thing. Normally, I find British accents really appealing, but with this guy, it just grates. But that's probably because it's totally bogus. I mean, it's so obvious with the way he only slips it in when he wants to seem cool.

But as soon as I think it, I feel guilty again. Everyone knows that trying too hard to look cool is just another sign of insecurity. And who wouldn't feel a little insecure on their first day at this school?

"We're studying the *isms*," I say, determined to play nice despite the nagging ping in my gut. "Last month we got to pick our own, but this month, we're all doing photorealism since nobody picked that last time."

Roman looks at me, starting with my growing-out bangs and working his way all the way down to my gold Haviana flip-flops—a slow leisurely cruise along my body that makes my stomach go all jumpy and twisted—and not in a good way.

"Right. So you make it look real then, like a photograph," he says, his eyes on mine.

I meet his gaze, a gaze he insists on holding for several seconds too long. But I refuse to squirm or look away first. I'm determined to stay in the game for as long as it takes. And even though it may seem totally benign on the surface, something about it feels dark, threatening, like some kind of dare.

Or maybe not.

Because right after I think that, he says, "These American schools are amazing! Back home, in soggy old London—" he winks, "it was always theory over practice."

And I'm instantly ashamed for all of my judgmental thoughts. Because apparently, not only is he from London, which means his accent is real, but Damen, whose psychic powers are *way* more refined than mine, doesn't seem the least bit alarmed.

If anything, he seems to like him. Which is even worse for me, because it pretty much proves that Haven is right.

I really am jealous.

And possessive.

And paranoid.

And apparently I hate new people too.

I take a deep breath and try again, talking past the lump in my throat and the knot in my stomach, determined to come off as friendly, even if it means I have to fake it at first. "You can paint anything you want," I say, using my upbeat friendly voice, which in my old life, before my whole family died in the accident and Damen saved me by making me immortal, was pretty much the only voice I ever used. "You just have to make it look real, like a photograph. Actually, we're supposed to use an actual photograph to show our inspiration, and, of course, for grading purposes too. You know, so we can prove that we accomplished what we set out to."

I glance at Damen, wondering if he's heard any of this and feeling annoyed that he's chosen his painting over communicating with me.

"And what's he painting?" Roman asks, nodding at Damen's canvas, a perfect depiction of the blooming fields of Summerland. Every blade of grass, every drop of water, every flower petal, so luminous, so textured, so tangible—it's like being there. "Looks like paradise." He nods.

"It is," I whisper, so awed by the painting I answered too quickly, without time to think about what I just said. Summerland is not just a sacred place—it's our secret place. One of the many secrets I've promised to keep.

Roman looks at me, brows raised. "So it's a real place then?"

But before I can answer, Damen shakes his head and says, "She wishes. But I made it up, it only exists in my head." Then he shoots me a look, tacking on a telepathic message of—*careful.*

"So how do you ace the assignment, then? If you don't have a photo to prove it exists?" Roman asks, but Damen just shrugs and gets back to painting.

But with Roman still glancing between us, his eyes all squinty and questioning, I know I can't leave it like that. So I look at him and say, "Damen's not so big on following the rules. He prefers to make his own." Remembering all the times he convinced me to ditch school, bet at the track, and worse.

And when Roman nods and turns toward his canvas, and Damen sends me a telepathic bouquet of red tulips, I know that it worked—our secret is safe and all is okay. So I dip my brush in some paint and get back to work. Eager for the bell to ring so we can head back to my house, and let the real lesson begin.

After class, we pack up our stuff and head for the parking lot. And despite my bid to be nice to the new guy, I can't help but smile when I see he's parked clear on the other side.

"See you tomorrow," I call, relieved to put some distance between us, because despite everyone's instant infatuation with him, I'm just not feeling it, no matter how hard I try.

I unlock my car and toss my bag on the floor, starting to slide onto my seat as I say to Damen, "Miles has rehearsal and I'm heading straight home. Want to follow?"

I turn, surprised to find him standing before me, swaying ever so slightly from side to side with a strained look on his face. "You okay?" I lift my palm to his cheek, feeling for heat or clamminess, some sign of unease, even though I really don't expect to find any. And when Damen shakes his head and looks at me, for a split second all the color drains right away. But then it's over as soon as I blink.

"Sorry, I just—my head feels a bit strange," he says, pinching the bridge of his nose and closing his eyes.

"But I thought you never get sick, that *we* don't get sick?" I say, unable to hide my alarm as I reach for my backpack. Thinking a sip of immortal juice might make him feel better since he requires so much more than I. And even though we're not exactly sure why, Damen figures that six centuries of chugging it have resulted in some kind of dependency, requiring him to consume more and more with each passing year. Which probably means I'll eventually require more too. And even though it seems like a long way off, I just hope he shows me how to make it by then so I won't have to bug him for refills all the time.

But before I can get to it, he retrieves his own bottle and takes a long hearty swig, pulling me to him and pressing his lips to my cheek when he says, "I'm okay. Really. Race you home?"

seven

Damen drives fast. Insanely fast. I mean, just because we both have advanced psychic radar, which comes in handy for zoning in on cops, opposing traffic, pedestrians, stray animals, and anything else that might get in our way, that doesn't mean we should abuse it.

But Damen thinks otherwise. Which is why he's already waiting on my front porch before I can even pull in and park.

"I thought you'd never make it." He laughs, following me up to my room, where he plops onto my bed, pulls me down with him, and leans in for a nice lingering kiss—a kiss that, if it were up to me, would never end. I'd happily spend the rest of eternity wrapped in his arms. Just knowing we have an infinite number of days to spend side by side provides more happiness than I can bear.

Though I didn't always feel that way. I was pretty upset when I first learned the truth. So upset that I spent some time away from him until I could get it all straight in my head. I mean, it's not everyday you hear someone say: *Oh, by the way, I'm an immortal, and I made you one too.*

And while I was pretty reluctant to believe him at first, after he walked me through it, reminding me of how I died in the accident, how I looked right into his eyes the moment he returned me to life, and how I recognized those eyes the first time I met him at school—well, there was no denying it was true.

Though that doesn't mean I was willing to accept it. It was bad enough dealing with the barrage of psychic abilities brought on by my NDE (near death experience—they insist on calling it *near,* even though I really did *die*), and how I started hearing other people's thoughts, getting their life stories by touch, talking to the dead, and more. Not to mention that being immortal, as cool as it may sound, also means I'll never get to cross the bridge. I'll never make it to the *other side* to see my family again. And when you think about it, that's a pretty big trade.

I pull away, my lips reluctantly leaving his as I gaze into his eyes—the same eyes I've gazed into for four hundred years. Though no matter how hard I try, I can't summon our past. Only Damen, who's stayed the same for the last six hundred years—neither dying nor reincarnating—holds the key.

"What're you thinking?" he asks, his fingers smoothing the curve of my cheek, leaving a trail of warmth in their path.

I take a deep breath, knowing how committed he is to staying in the present, but determined to know more of my history—*our* history. "I was thinking about when we first met," I say, watching his brow lift as he shakes his head.

"Were you? And what exactly do you remember from that time?"

"Nothing." I shrug. "Absolutely nothing. Which is why I'm hoping you'll fill me in. You don't have to tell me everything—I mean, I know how you hate looking back. I'm just really curious about how it all started—how we first met."

He pulls away and rolls onto his back, his body still, his lips unmoving, and I fear this is the only response that I'll get.

"Please?" I murmur, inching toward him and curling my body around his. "It's not fair that you get all the details while I'm left out here in the dark. Just give me something to go on. Where did we live? What did I look like? How did we meet? Was it love at first sight?"

He shifts ever so slightly, then rolls onto his side, burying his hand in my hair as he says, "It was France, 1608."

I gulp, taking a quick intake of breath as I wait to hear more.

"Paris, actually."

Paris! I immediately picture elaborate gowns, stolen kisses on the Pont Neuf, gossiping with Marie Antoinette . . .

"I attended a dinner at a friend's house—" He pauses, his gaze moving past mine, centuries away now. "And you were working as a servant."

A servant?

"One of their servants. They were very wealthy. They had many."

I lie there, stunned. This is *not* what I expected.

"You weren't like the others," he says, his voice lowered to almost a whisper. "You were beautiful. Extraordinarily beautiful. You looked a lot like you do now." He smiles, gathering a chunk of my hair and rubbing it between his two fingers. "And also like now, you were orphaned, having lost your family in a fire. And so, left penniless, with no one to support you, you were employed by my friends."

I swallow hard, not sure how I feel about this. I mean, what's the point of reincarnating if you're forced to relive the same kind of painful moments all over again?

"And yes, just so you know, it *was* love at first sight. I fell completely and irreversibly in love with you. The very moment I saw you I knew that my life would never be the same."

He looks at me, his fingers on my temples, his gaze luring me in, presenting the moment in all its intensity, unfolding the scene as though I'm right there.

My blond hair is hidden under a cap, my blue eyes are shy and afraid to make contact, and with clothes so drab and fingers so calloused, my beauty is wasted, easily missed.

But Damen sees it. The moment I enter the room his eyes find mine. Looking past my scruffy exterior to the soul that refuses to hide. And he's so dark, so striking, so refined, so handsome—I turn away. Knowing the buttons on his coat alone are worth more than I'll make in a year. Knowing without looking twice that he's out of my league . . .

"Still, I had to move cautiously because—"

"Because you were already married to Drina!" I whisper, watching the scene in my head and overhearing one of the dinner guests inquire about her, our eyes meeting briefly as Damen says:

"Drina is in Hungary. We have gone our separate ways." Knowing he'll be the source of scandal, but wanting me to hear it more than caring what they'll think . . .

"She and I were already living apart, so it wasn't an issue. The reason I had to tread cautiously is because fraternizing outside of one's class was severely frowned upon back then. And because you were so innocent, so vulnerable in so many ways, I didn't want to cause you any trouble, especially if you didn't feel the same way."

"But I did feel the same way!" I say, watching as we move past that night, and how every time I went into town, I'd manage to run into him.

"I'm afraid I resorted to following you." He looks at me, his face chagrined. "Until we finally bumped into each other so often, you began to trust me. And then . . ."

And then we met in secret—stolen kisses just outside the servant's entrance, a passionate embrace in a dark alleyway or inside his carriage . . .

"Only now I know that it wasn't nearly as *secret* as I'd thought . . ." He sighs. "Drina was never in Hungary, she was there all along. Watching, planning, determined to win me back—no matter the cost." He takes a deep breath, the regret of four centuries displayed on his face. "I wanted to take care of you, Ever. I wanted to give you anything and everything your heart desired. I wanted to treat you like the princess you were born to be. And when I finally convinced you to come away with me, I'd never felt so happy and alive. We were to meet at midnight—"

"But I never showed," I say, *seeing* him pacing, worried, distressed, convinced I'd changed my mind . . .

"It wasn't until the next day that I learned you'd been killed in an accident, run over by a coach on your way to meet me." And when he looks at me, he shows me his grief—his unbearable, all-consuming, soul-crushing grief. "At the time, it never occurred to me that Drina was responsible, I had no idea until she confessed it to you. It seemed like an accident, a horrible, unfortunate accident. And I guess I was too numb with grief to suspect anything else—"

"How old was I?" I ask, barely able to breathe, knowing I was young, but wanting the details.

He pulls me closer, his fingers tracing the planes of my face when he says, "You were sixteen, and your name was Evaline." His lips play at my ear.

"Evaline," I whisper, feeling an instant connection to my tragic former self who, orphaned young, loved by Damen, and dead at sixteen—is not so different from my current self.

"It wasn't until many years later when I saw you again in New England, having incarnated as a Puritan's daughter—that I began to believe in happiness again."

"A Puritan's daughter?" I gaze into his eyes, watching as he shows me a dark-haired, pale-skinned girl in a severe blue dress. "Were all of my lives so boring?" I shake my head. "And what kind of horrible accident took me that time?"

"Drowning." He sighs, and the moment he says it, I'm overcome by his grief all over again. "I was so devastated I sailed right back to London, where I lived off and on for many years. And I was just about to head off to Tunisia when you resurfaced as a beautiful, wealthy, and rather spoiled I might say—landowner's daughter in London."

"Show me!" I nuzzle against him, eager to view a more glamorous life—his finger tracing my brow as a pretty brunette in a gorgeous green dress with a complicated updo and a smattering of jewels appears in my mind.

A rich, spoiled, conniving flirt—her life a series of parties and shopping trips—whose sights are set firmly on someone else—until she meets Damen . . .

"And that time?" I ask, sad to see her go, but needing to know how she went.

"A terrible fall." He closes his eyes. "By that point, I was sure I was being punished—granted eternal life, but one without love."

He cradles my face in his hands, his fingers emitting such tenderness, such reverence, such delicious warm tingle—I close my eyes and snuggle closer. Focusing on the feel of his skin as our bodies press tightly together, everything around us slipping away until there's nothing but us—no past, no future, nothing but this moment in time.

I mean, I'm with him, and he's with me, and that's the way it's meant to eternally be. And while all those prior lives may be interesting, their only real purpose was to get us to this one. And now that Drina is gone, there's nothing that can stand in our way, nothing that can keep us from moving forward—except me. And even though I want to know *everything* that happened before, for now it can wait. It's time for me to move past my petty jealousies and insecurities, to stop finding excuses and finally commit to taking that big leap forward after all of these years.

But just as I'm about to tell him, he moves away so abruptly, it's a moment before I can get to his side.

"What is it?" I cry, seeing his thumbs pressed to his temples as he struggles to breathe. And when he turns to me, there's no recognition. His gaze goes right through me.

But just as soon as I perceive it, it's already passed. Replaced with the loving warmth I've grown used to, as he rubs his eyes and shakes his head, looking at me when he says, "I haven't felt like this since before—" He stops and stares into space. "Well, maybe never." But when he sees the concern on my face, he adds, "But I'm fine, really." And when I refuse to loosen my grip, he smiles and says, "Hey, how about a trip to Summerland?"

"Seriously?" I say, my eyes lighting up.

The first time I visited that wonderful place, that magical dimension between the dimensions—I was dead. And I was so entranced by its beauty I was reluctant to leave. The second time I visited was with Damen. And after he showed me all of its glorious possibilities, I've longed to return. But as Summerland can only be accessed by the spiritually advanced (or those already dead), I can't get there alone.

"Why not?" He shrugs.

"Well, what about my lessons," I say, trying to appear interested in studying and learning new tricks, when the truth is, I'd much rather go to Summerland where everything is effortless and instant. "Not to mention how you're not feeling so well." I squeeze his arm again, noticing how the usual warmth and tingle still hasn't fully returned.

"There are lessons to be learned in Summerland too." He smiles. "And if you'll hand me my juice, I'll feel well enough to make us the portal."

But even after I hand it over and he takes several long hearty gulps, he can't make it appear.

"Maybe I can help?" I say, staring at the sweat on his brow.

"No—I just—I almost had it. Just give me another second," he mumbles, clenching his jaw, determined to get there.

So I do. In fact, I let the seconds turn into minutes, and still nothing.

"I don't understand." He squints. "This hasn't happened since—since I first learned how to do it."

"Maybe it's because you're not feeling well." I watch as he takes another drink, followed by another, and then another. And when he closes his eyes and tries again, he gets the exact same results as before. "Can I try?"

"Forget it. You don't know how," he says, his voice containing an edge I try not to take personally, knowing it's due more to his frustration with himself than with me.

"I *know* I don't know how, but I thought maybe you could teach me and then I—"

But before I can finish, he's up from the bed, pacing before me. "It's a *process,* Ever. It took me years to learn how to get there. You can't just skip to the end of the book without reading the middle." He shakes his head and leans against my desk, his body rigid and tense, his gaze refusing mine.

"And when was the last time you *read* a book without already knowing the beginning, middle, and end?" I smile.

He looks at me, his face a series of hard edges and angles, but only for a moment before he sighs and moves toward me, taking my hand as he says, "You want to try?"

I nod.

He looks me over, clearly doubting it'll work, but wanting to please me more than anything else. "Okay then, make yourself comfortable, but don't cross your legs like that. It cuts off the chi."

"Chi?"

"A fancy word for energy." He smiles. "Unless you want to sit in the lotus position, then that's perfectly fine."

I kick off my flip-flops and press my soles against the carpeted floor, getting as comfortable and relaxed as my excitement will allow.

"Usually it requires a long series of meditations, but in the interest of time, and since you're already pretty advanced, we're just going to cut to the chase, okay?"

I nod, eager to get started.

"I want you to close your eyes and imagine a shimmering veil of soft golden light hovering before you," he says, entwining his fingers with mine.

So I do, picturing an exact replica of the one that got me there before, the one Damen placed in my path to save me from Drina. And it's so beautiful, so brilliant, and so luminous, my heart swells with joy as I raise my hand toward it, eager to immerse it in that radiant shower of glistening light, longing to return to that mystical place. And just as my fingers make contact and are about to submerge, it shrinks from my sight and I'm back in my room.

"I can't believe it! I was *so* close!" I turn toward Damen. "It was right there before me! Did you see it?"

"You came remarkably close," he says. And even though his gaze is tender, his smile is forced.

"What if I try it again? What if we do it together this time?" I say, my hope plummeting the instant he shakes his head and turns away.

"Ever, we *were* doing it together," he mutters, wiping his brow and averting his gaze. "I'm afraid I'm not turning out to be a very good teacher."

"That's ridiculous! You're a great teacher, you're just having an off day, that's all." But when I look at him, it's clear he's not swayed. So I switch tactics, placing the blame back on me when I say, "It's my fault. I'm a bad student. I'm lazy, sloppy, and spend most of my time trying to distract you from my lessons so we can make out." I squeeze his hand. "But I'm past all that now. And I'm about to get very serious. So just give me another chance, you'll see."

He looks at me, doubting it'll work, but not wanting to disappoint me, he takes my hand and we both try again, the two of us closing our eyes, envisioning that glorious portal of light. And just as it starts to take shape, Sabine walks through the front door and starts up the stairs, catching us so off guard, we scramble to opposite sides of the room.

"Damen, I thought that was your car in the drive." She slips off her jacket and covers the space from the door to my desk in a handful of steps. The amped-up energy of her office still clinging to her as she shakes his hand and focuses on the bottle balanced on his knee. "So *you're* the one who got Ever hooked." She glances between us, her eyes narrowed, her lips pursed, like she's got all the evidence she needs.

I peek at Damen, panic rising in my throat, wondering how he'll explain. But he just laughs it off when he says, "Guilty! Most people don't have the taste for it, but for whatever reason, Ever seems to like it." Then he smiles in a way that's meant to be persuasive, if not charming, and if you ask me, it nails both.

But Sabine just continues to gaze at him, completely unmoved. "That's all she seems to be interested in anymore. I buy bags and bags of groceries, but she refuses to eat."

"That's not true!" I say, annoyed that she's starting this all over again, especially in front of Damen. But when I see the chai latte stain on her blouse, my annoyance turns to outrage. "How'd you get that?" I motion toward the spot like it's a scarlet letter, a mark of disgrace, knowing I have to do whatever it takes to dissuade her from returning anytime soon.

She gazes down at her blouse, her fingers rubbing against it as she pauses to think, then she shakes her head and shrugs when she says, "I bumped into someone." And the way she says it, so casual, so offhand, so blasé, it's obvious she's not nearly as impressed with the encounter as Munoz seemed to be.

"So, are we still on for dinner Saturday night?" she asks.

I swallow hard, telepathically urging Damen to just nod and smile and answer in the affirmative even though he has no idea what she's talking about, since I failed to mention it before.

"I made reservations for eight."

I hold my breath, watching as he nods and smiles just like I asked him to. Even choosing to take it a step further by adding, "Wouldn't miss it."

He shakes Sabine's hand and heads out the door, his fingers entwined around mine, sending a warm wonderful thrum through my body. "Sorry about the whole dinner thing," I say, gazing up at him. "I guess I was hoping she'd get really busy and forget all about it."

He presses his lips to my cheek, then slides into his car. "She cares about you. Wants to make sure I'm good enough, sincere, and not out to hurt you. Believe me, we've been through this before. And though I may have come close once or twice, I don't remember ever failing inspection." He smiles.

"Aw yes, the strict Puritan father," I say, figuring he's the perfect description of an overbearing parental type.

"You'd be surprised." Damen laughs. "The wealthy landowner was much more of a gatekeeper. And yet still, I managed to sneak by."

"Maybe someday you'll show me *your* past," I say. "You know, how your life was before we met. Your home, your parents, how you became this way . . ." My voice trails off, seeing the flash of pain in his eyes and knowing he's still unwilling to discuss it. He always shuts down, refuses to share, which only makes me even more curious.

"None of that matters," he says, releasing my hand and fiddling with his mirrors, anything to avoid looking at me. "All that matters is *now.*"

"Yeah, but Damen—" I start, wanting to explain that it's not just curiosity I'm after, but a closeness, a bond, wishing he'd trust me with those long-ago secrets. But when I look at him again, I know better than to press. Besides, maybe it's time I extend a little trust too.

"I was thinking . . ." I say, my fingers fiddling with the hem on my shirt.

He looks at me, his hand on the clutch, ready to shift into reverse.

"Why don't you go ahead and make that reservation." I nod, my lips pressed together, my gaze focused on his. "You know, for the Montage or the Ritz?" I add, holding my breath as his beautiful dark eyes graze over my face.

"You sure?"

I nod. Knowing I am. We've been waiting for this moment for hundreds of years, so why delay any longer? "More than sure," I say, my eyes meeting his.

He smiles, his face lighting up for the first time all day. And I'm so relieved to see him looking normal again after that strange behavior from before—his remoteness at school, his inability to make the portal appear, his not feeling well—all of it so unlike the Damen I know. He's always so strong, sexy, beautiful, and invincible—immune to weak moments and bad days. And seeing him vulnerable like that has left me far more shaken than I care to admit.

"Consider it done," he says, filling my arms with dozens of manifested red tulips before speeding away.

eight

The next morning when I meet Damen in the parking lot, all my worries disappear. Because the moment he opens my door and helps me out of my car, I notice how healthy he looks, how devastatingly handsome he is, and when I look in his eyes, it's clear that all of yesterday's weirdness is over. We are more in love than ever.

Seriously. All through English he can barely keep his hands off of me. Constantly leaning toward my desk and whispering into my ear, much to Mr. Robins's annoyance, and Stacia and Honor's disgust. And now that we're at lunch, he hasn't let up a bit, stroking my cheek and gazing into my eyes, pausing only to take the occasional sip of his drink before picking up right where he left off, murmuring sweet nothings into my ear.

Usually when he acts like that, it's partly out of love, and partly to tone down all of the noise and energy—all of the random sights, sounds, and colors that constantly bombard me. Ever since I broke the psychic shield I'd made a few months back, a shield that shut everything out and made me as clueless as I was before I died and came back psychic, I've yet to find a way to replace it that will allow me to channel the energies I want while blocking the energies I don't want. And since Damen's never struggled with this, he's not sure how to teach me.

But now that he's back in my life, it no longer seems all that urgent, because the mere sound of his voice can silence the world, while the touch of his skin makes my whole body tingle. And when I look in his eyes, well, let's just say that I'm instantly overcome by this warm, wonderful, magnetic *pull*—like it's just him and I and everything else has ceased to exist. Damen's like my perfect psychic shield. My ultimate other half. And even when we can't be together, the telepathic thoughts and images he sends provide that same calming effect.

But today, all of those sweet murmurings aren't just to shield me—they're mostly about our upcoming plans. The suite he booked at the Montage Resort. And how he's yearned so long for this night.

"Do you have any idea what it's like to wait for something for four hundred years?" he whispers, his lips nipping at the curve of my ear.

"Four hundred? I thought you've been around for six hundred?" I say, pulling away to get a better view of his face.

"Unfortunately a couple of centuries had to pass before I found you," he whispers, his mouth making its way from my neck to my ear. "Two very lonely centuries, I might add."

I swallow hard. Knowing thc *loneliness* he refers to does *not* necessarily mean he was *alone*. In fact, quite the contrary. But still, I don't call him on it. In fact, I don't say a word. I'm committed to moving past all of that, getting over my insecurities and moving forward. Just like I promised I would.

I refuse to think about how he spent those first two hundred years without me.

Or how he spent the next four hundred getting over the fact that he'd lost me.

Nor will I even begin to consider the six-hundred-year head start he has on studying and *practicing* the—um—sensual arts.

And I will absolutely, positively, *not* dwell on all of the beautiful, worldly, experienced women he *knew* over the span of those years.

Nope.

Not me.

I refuse to even go there.

"Shall I pick you up at six?" he asks, gathering my hair at my nape and twisting it into a long blond rope. "We can go to dinner first."

"Except we don't really eat," I remind him.

"Ah, yes. Good point." He smiles, releasing my hair so that it flows back around my shoulders and drops down to my waist. "Though I'm sure we can find something else to occupy our time?"

I smile, having already told Sabine that I'm staying at Haven's and hoping she doesn't try to follow up. She used to be so good about taking me at my word, but ever since I was caught drinking, got suspended, and basically stopped eating, she's been prone to following through.

"Are you sure you're okay with all this?" Damen asks, misreading the look on my face as indecision, when it's really just nerves.

I smile and lean in to kiss him, eager to erase any lingering doubts (mine more than his), just as Miles tosses his bag on the table and says, "Oh, Haven, look! They're back. The lovebirds have returned!"

I pull away, my face flushing with embarrassment as Haven laughs and sits down beside him, her eyes scanning the tables as she says, "Where's Roman? Anyone seen him?"

"He was in homeroom." Miles shrugs, removing the top from his yogurt and hunching over his script.

And he was in history, I think, remembering how I ignored him all through class, despite his numerous attempts to get my attention, and how after the bell rang, I hung back, pretending to look for something in my bag. Preferring the weight of Mr. Munoz's penetrating stare and his conflicted thoughts about me (my good grades versus my undeniable weirdness) to dealing with Roman.

Haven shrugs and opens her cupcake box, sighing when she says, "Well, it was nice while it lasted."

"What're you talking about?" Miles looks up as she points straight ahead, her lips twisted to the side, her eyes completely dejected, as we all follow her finger, all the way to where Roman is talking and laughing with Stacia, Honor, Craig, and the rest of the A-list crew. "Big deal." He shrugs. "You just wait, he'll be back."

"You don't know that," Haven says, shedding the skirt from her red velvet cupcake, her gaze still focused on Roman.

"Please. We've seen it a million times before. Every new kid with the slightest potential for cool has ended up at that table at some point. Only the truly cool never last long—because the truly cool end up here." He laughs, tapping the yellow fiberglass table with the tips of his bright pink nails.

"Not me," I say, eager to steer the conversation away from Roman, knowing I'm the only one who's happy to see he's abandoned us for a much cooler crowd. "I started out here from the very first day," I remind them.

"Yeah, go figure." Miles laughs. "Though I was referring to Damen. Remember how he got sucked over to the other side for a while? But eventually he came to his senses and found his way back, just like Roman will."

I gaze down at my drink, twisting the bottle around in my hand. Because even though I know Damen was never sincere about his brief flirtation with Stacia, that he only did it to get to me, to see if I cared, the images of the two of them standing so close together are forever burned into my brain.

"Yes, I did," Damen says, squeezing my hand and kissing my cheek, sensing my thoughts even if he can't always read them. "I certainly came to my senses."

"You see? So, we can only have faith that Roman will too." Miles nods. "And if he doesn't, then he was never truly cool to begin with, *right?*"

Haven shrugs and rolls her eyes, licking a glob of frosting from her thumb and mumbling, "Whatever."

"Why do you care so much anyway?" Miles peers at her. "I thought you were all about Josh?"

"I *am* all about Josh," she says, avoiding his gaze as she wipes some nonexistent crumbs from her lap.

But when I look at her and *see* the way her aura wavers and flares a deceitful shade of green, I can tell it's not true. She's smitten and that's all there is to it. And if Roman becomes smitten too, then it's *adios Josh, hello creepy new guy.*

I unzip my lunch pack, going through the motions of pretending I'm still interested in food when I hear: "Ay, mate, what time's the premiere?"

"Curtain's at eight. Why? You coming?" Miles asks, his eyes lighting up, his aura glowing in a way that makes it pretty obvious he hopes that he will.

"Wouldn't miss it," Roman says, sliding onto the space beside Haven and bumping her shoulder in the smarmiest, most insincere way. Clearly aware of the effect it elicits and not afraid to exploit it.

"So how was life among the A-list? Everything you dreamed it would be?" she asks in a voice that, if you couldn't see her aura, you'd think she was flirting. But I know she's serious, because auras don't lie.

Roman reaches toward her, gently pushing her bangs away from her face. A gesture so intimate her cheeks flush bright pink. "*Wot's* that now?" he says, his gaze fixed on hers.

"You know, table A? Where you were sitting?" She mumbles, struggling to keep her composure while under his spell.

"The lunchtime caste system," Miles says, breaking their enchantment and pushing his half-eaten yogurt aside. "It's the same at every school. Everyone divides into cliques designed to keep others out. They can't help themselves, they just do. And those people you were just with? They're the top clique, which, in the high school caste system, makes them The Rulers. As opposed to the people you're sitting with now—" He points at himself. "Who are otherwise known as The Untouchables."

"Bullocks!" Roman says, pulling away from Haven and popping the top on his soda. "Complete rubbish. I don't buy it."

"Doesn't matter if you do. It's still a fact." Miles shrugs, gazing longingly at table A. Because despite how he goes on and on about our table being the truly cool table, the truth is, he's painfully aware that in the eyes of the Bay View student body, there's nothing cool about it.

"It may be your fact, but it's not mine. I don't do with segregation, mate. I like a free and open society, room to roam around and explore all my options." Then, looking at Damen, he says, "What about you? You believe in all this?"

But Damen just shrugs and continues gazing at me. He couldn't care less about A-lists and B-lists, who's cool and who's not. I'm the only reason he enrolled in this school, and I'm the only reason he stays.

"Well, it's nice to have a dream." Haven sighs, inspecting her short black nails. "But it's even nicer when there's a remote possibility of it coming true."

"Aw, but that's where you're wrong, luv. It's not a dream at all." Roman smiles in a way that makes her aura beam a bright shimmery pink. "I'll make it happen. You'll see."

"So what? You fancy yourself the Che Guevara of Bay View High?" My voice contains a sting I don't bother to hide. Though to be honest, I'm more surprised by my use of the word *fancy* than the tone of my voice. I mean, since when do I talk like that? But when I glance at Roman and see his expansive, overwhelming, yellow-orange aura, I know he's affecting me too.

"I rather *fancy* that, yes." He smiles his languid grin, his eyes gazing into mine so deeply, I feel like I'm naked—like he sees everything, *knows* everything, and there's nowhere to hide. "Just think of me as a revolutionary, because by the end of next week, this lunchtime caste system will come to an end. We're going to break these self-imposed barriers, push all the tables together, and have ourselves a party!"

"Is that your prediction?" I narrow my gaze, trying to deflect all of his intrusive energy away.

But he just laughs, not the least bit offended. A laugh that, on the surface, is so warm, engaging, and all-encompassing—no one would guess at the subtext beneath—the creepy edge, the hint of malice, the barely concealed threat meant solely for me.

"I'll believe it when I see it," Haven says, wiping red crumbs from her lips.

"Seeing *is* believing," Roman says, his eyes right on mine.

"So what's your take on all that?" I ask, just after the bell rings and Roman, Haven, and Miles head off to class as Damen and I lag behind.

"Of all what?" he asks, pulling me to a stop.

"Of Roman. And all of his lunch-table revolution nonsense?" I say, desperate for some validation that I'm not jealous, possessive, or crazy—that Roman really is a creep—and that it has nothing to do with me.

But Damen just shrugs. "If you don't mind, I'd rather not focus on Roman right now. I'm far more interested in *you*."

He pulls me toward him, bestowing me with a long, deep, breath-stealing kiss. And even though we're standing right in the middle of the quad, it's as though everything around us no longer exists. Like the entire world has shrunk down to this one single point. And by the time I break away, I'm so charged, so heated, and so breathless, I can barely speak.

"We're going to be late," I finally manage, taking his hand and pulling him toward class.

But he's stronger than I am, so he simply stays put. "I was thinking—what do you say we skip it?" he whispers, his lips on my temple, my cheek, then my ear. "You know, just blow off the rest of the day—since there are so many other, *better* places we could be."

I gaze at him, nearly swayed by his magnetism, but I shake my head and pull away. I mean, I get that he finished school hundreds of years ago and now finds it all rather tedious. And even though I mostly find it tedious too, since having instant knowledge of all the stuff they're trying to teach really does make it seem pretty pointless, it's still one of the few things in my life that feels somewhat normal. And ever since the accident, when I realized I'd never be normal again, well, it made me prize it that much more.

"I thought you said we were supposed to maintain a normal façade at all costs," I say, pulling him along as he grudgingly lags behind. "Isn't attending class and feigning interest part of that façade?"

"But what could be more normal than two hormonal teens, ditching school and getting an early start on the weekend?" He smiles, the warmth of his beautiful dark eyes nearly luring me in.

But I shake my head again and hold firm, gripping his arm even tighter as I drag him toward class.

nine

Since we're spending the night together, Damen doesn't follow me home after school. Instead, we share a brief kiss in the parking lot before I climb into my car and head for the mall.

I want to buy something special for tonight—something pretty for Miles's play and my big date—both of us starring in our own kind of debut. But after checking my watch and seeing I don't have as much time as I thought, I wonder if I should've taken Damen up on his offer to ditch school.

I cruise through the parking lot, wondering if I should try to find Haven. We haven't really hung out that much since that whole weird thing with Drina, and then when she met Josh, well, even though he doesn't go to our school, they've been pretty much joined at the hip ever since. He even managed to wean her from her support group addiction. Her after-school ritual of scoping out random church basements and loading up on punch and cookies, while making up some sob story about that particular day's addiction.

And up until now, I haven't really minded seeing less of her since she seems so happy. Like she's finally found someone who not only likes her but who's good for her too. But lately I'm starting to miss her, and I'm thinking a little time together might do me some good.

I spot her and Roman leaning against his vintage red sports car, watching as Haven grabs hold of his arm and laughs at something he said. The severity of her black skinny jeans, black shrunken cardigan, Fall Out Boy tank, and purposely messy dyed black hair with shocking red stripe, all softened by her rosy pink aura, its edges expanding, reaching, until it swallows them both. Leaving no room for doubt that if Roman feels the same way, Josh will soon be replaced. And even though I'm determined to stop it before it's too late, I've just started to cruise by when Roman glances over his shoulder and peers at me with a gaze so insistent, so intimate, so loaded with unknown intent—I punch the pedal and zoom past.

Because despite the fact that my friends all think he's so cool, despite the fact that the A-list agrees, despite the fact that Damen isn't the least bit alarmed—I don't like him.

Even though my feelings are based on nothing more substantial than a constant ping in my gut whenever he's near—the fact is: That new guy really gives me the creeps.

Since it's hot, I head over to the indoor mall of South Coast Plaza as opposed to the outdoor mall of Fashion Island, even though the locals would probably do the opposite.

But I'm not a local. I'm an Oregonian. Which means I'm used to my pre-spring weather being much more, well, pre-springlike. You know, gobs of rain, overcast skies, and plenty of mud. Like a *real* spring. Not this hot, weird, unnatural, summer hybrid that tries to pass as spring. And from what I hear, it's only going to get worse. Which makes me miss home even more.

Normally, I go out of my way to avoid places like this—a place so overrun with light and noise and all of that crowd-generated energy that always overwhelms me and sets me on edge. And without Damen by my side, standing in as my psychic shield, I'm back to relying on my iPod again.

Though I refuse to wear my hoodie and sunglasses to block out the noise like I used to. I'm done with looking like a freak. Instead, I narrow my focus to what's right before me, and block out all the peripherals like Damen taught me to do.

I insert my earbuds and crank up the volume, allowing the noise to bar everything but the swirling rainbow of auras and the few disembodied spirits floating about (which, despite my narrowed focus, really are right in front of me). And when I head into Victoria's Secret, aiming straight for the naughty nighties section, I'm so focused, so intent on my mission, I fail to see Stacia and Honor just off to the side.

"O. Migawd!" Stacia sings, approaching me with such purpose you'd think I was a bin labeled: GUCCI—HALF OFF! "You *cannot* be serious." She points at the negligee I hold in my hand, her perfectly manicured nail motioning toward the slit that starts from both the top and bottom and meets at a crystal-encrusted circle somewhere in the middle.

And even though I was merely curious, and not even thinking about buying it, seeing her face all scrunched up like that and hearing the mocking thoughts in her head makes me feel totally foolish.

I drop it back on the rack and fidget with my earbud, pretending as though I didn't hear a thing as I move toward the matching cotton sets, which are way more my style and speed.

But just as I begin browsing through several hot-pink-and-orange-striped camis, I realize they're probably nowhere near Damen's speed. He'd probably prefer something a little more racy. Something with a lot more lace and a lot less cotton. Something that could actually be considered *sexy*. And without even looking, I know Stacia and her faithful lapdog have followed.

"Aw, look, Honor. Freak can't decide between skanky or sweet." Stacia shakes her head and smirks at me. "Trust me, when in doubt, always go with skanky. It's pretty much a sure thing. Besides, from what I recall about Damen, he's not so big on sweet."

I freeze, my stomach clenching with unreasonable jealousy as my throat squeezes tight. But only for a moment before I force myself to resume breathing and browsing, refusing to let her think, even for a second, that her words might've gotten to me.

Besides, I know all about what happened between them, and I'm happy to report that it was neither skanky nor sweet. Mostly because it wasn't anything at all. Damen merely *pretended* to like her so he could get to me. And yet, just the thought of him even pretending still makes me queasy.

"Come on, let's go. She can't hear you," Honor says, scratching her arm and glancing between Stacia and me, then checking her phone for the hundredth time to see if Craig answered her text.

But Stacia remains rooted, enjoying herself far too much to give up so easily. "Oh, she can hear me just fine," she says, a smile playing at the corner of her lips. "Don't let the iPod and earbuds fool you. She can hear everything we say and everything we think. Because Ever's not just a freak, she's also a witch."

I turn away and head for the other side of the store, browsing a rack of push-up bras and corsets, telling myself: *Ignore her, ignore her, just focus on shopping and she'll go away.*

But Stacia's not going anywhere. Instead, she grabs hold of my arm and pulls me right to her, saying, "Come on, don't be shy. *Show* her. Show Honor what a freak you are!"

Her eyes stare into mine, sending a flood of disturbing dark energy coursing right through me as she squeezes my arm so tight her thumb and index finger practically meet. And I know she's trying to bait me, incite me, aware of exactly what I'm capable of after that time when I lost control in the hallway at school. Only that time she didn't do it on purpose—she had no idea what I could do.

Honor starts to fidget, standing beside her and whining, "Come on, Stacia. Let's go. This is *bor*-ing."

But Stacia ignores her and grips my arm harder, her nails pressing into my flesh as she whispers, "Go on, tell her. Tell her what you see!"

I close my eyes, my stomach swirling as my head fills with images similar to the ones I saw before: Stacia scratching and clawing her way to the top of the popularity pyramid, stomping much harder than necessary on all those beneath her. Including Honor, *especially* Honor, who's so afraid of being unpopular she does nothing to stop it . . .

I could tell her what a horrible friend Stacia really is, expose her for the awful person I know her to be. . . . I could pry Stacia's hand from my arm and fling her across the room so hard she'd fly straight through the plate glass window before crashing into the mall directory. . . .

Only I can't. The last time I let loose at school, when I told Stacia all the awful things I know about her, it was a colossal mistake—one I don't have the luxury of making again. There's so much more to hide now, much bigger secrets at stake—secrets that belong not only to me but to Damen as well.

Stacia laughs as I fight to stay calm and not overreact. Reminding myself that while appearing weak is okay, giving in to weakness is definitely *not*. It's absolutely imperative to appear normal, clueless, and allow her the illusion that she's so much stronger than me.

Honor checks her watch, rolling her eyes, wanting to leave. And just as I'm about to pull away, and maybe even *accidentally* backhand Stacia while I'm at it, I *see* something so awful, so repulsive, I knock an entire rack of lingerie to the floor in an attempt to break free.

Bras, thongs, hangers, and fixtures—all of it crashing to the ground in one big heap.

With me as the cherry on top.

"O. Migawd!" Stacia shrieks, grabbing hold of Honor as they fall all over themselves laughing at me. "You are such a freakin' *spaz*!" she says, going straight for her cell so she can capture it all on video. Zooming in to get close-up footage of me attempting to break free of a red lace garter belt that's wrapped around my neck. "Better get crackin' and get this cleaned up!" She squints, adjusting her angle as I struggle to stand. "You know what they say, you break it, you buy it!"

I get to my feet, watching as Stacia and Honor bolt for the door the moment a salesperson arrives. Stacia pausing long enough to glance over her shoulder and say, "I'm watching you, Ever. Believe me, I'm not through with you yet." Before running away.

ten

The moment I sense Damen turning onto my street, I run to the mirror (again) and fidget with my clothes, making sure everything is right where it should be—the dress, the bra, the new lingerie—and hoping it all stays in place (well, at least until it's time to come off).

After the Victoria's Secret salesgirl and I cleaned up the mess, she helped me choose this really pretty matching bra and panty set that isn't made of cotton, isn't embarrassingly sexy, and doesn't actually support or cover much of anything, but then I guess that's the point. Then I moved on to Nordstrom where I bought this pretty green dress and some cute strappy wedges to go with it. And on the way home I stopped for a quick manicure/pedicure, which is something I haven't done since, well, since before the accident that robbed me of my old life forever—when I used to be popular and girly like Stacia.

Only I was never *really* like Stacia.

I mean, I may have been popular and a cheerleader, but I was never a bitch.

"What are you thinking?" Damen asks, having let himself in and coming straight up to my room since Sabine's not at home.

I gaze at him, watching as he leans against the doorjamb and smiles. Taking in his dark jeans, dark shirt, dark jacket, and the black motorcycle boots he always wears and feeling my heart skip two beats.

"I was thinking about the last four hundred years," I say, cringing when his eyes grow dark and worried. "But not in the way that you think," I add, eager to assure him I wasn't obsessing over his past yet again. "I was thinking about all of our lifetimes together, and how we never . . . um . . ."

He lifts his brow as a smile plays at his lips.

"I guess I'm just glad those four hundred years are over," I mumble, watching as he moves toward me, slips his arms around my waist, and pulls me tight to his chest. My eyes grazing over the planes of his face, his dark eyes, smooth skin, his irresistible lips, drinking all of him in.

"I'm glad too," he says, his eyes teasing mine. "Nope, on second thought, scratch that, because the truth is, I'm more than glad. In fact—I'm ecstatic." He smiles, but a moment later he's merging his brows, saying, "No, that still doesn't explain it. I think we need a new word." He laughs, lowering his mouth to my ear as he whispers, "You are more beautiful tonight than you've *ever* been. And I want everything to be perfect. I want it to be everything you dreamed it would be. I just hope I don't disappoint you."

I balk, pulling away to gaze at his face, wondering how he could even think such a thing, when all of this time it's been *me* who's been worried about disappointing *him*.

He places his finger under my chin, lifting my face until my lips meet his. And I kiss him back with such fervor, he pulls away and says, "Maybe we should head straight for the Montage instead?"

"Okay," I murmur, my lips seeking his. Regretting the joke when he pulls away and I see how hopeful he is. "Except that we can't. Miles will *kill* me if I miss his debut." I smile, waiting for him to smile too.

Only he doesn't. And when he looks at me with his face so drawn and serious, I know I strayed too close to the truth. All of my lives have always ended on this night—the night we'd planned to be together. And even though I don't remember the details, he clearly does.

But then just as quickly his color's returned and he takes my hand when he says, "Well, lucky for us you're quite *unkillable* now, so there's nothing that can keep us apart."

The first thing I notice as we head for our seats is that Haven's sitting beside Roman. Taking full advantage of Josh's absence by pressing her shoulder against his and cocking her head in a way that allows her to gaze up at him adoringly and smile at everything he says. The second thing I notice is that my seat is also beside Roman's. Only unlike Haven, I'm not at all thrilled. But since Damen's already claimed the outside seat, and I don't want to make a big show of moving, I reluctantly sink down onto mine. Feeling the invasive push of Roman's energy as his eyes peer into mine—his attention so focused on me, I can't help but squirm.

I gaze around the mostly full theater, trying to get my mind off of Roman and am relieved when I see Josh heading down the aisle, clad in his usual tight black jeans, studded belt, crisp white shirt, and skinny checkered tie, his arms loaded down with candy and bottles of water as his black swoop of hair flops into his eyes. And I can't help but breathe a sigh of relief, seeing how perfect he and Haven are for each other, and I'm thrilled that he's not been replaced.

"Water?" he asks, plopping onto the seat on Haven's other side and passing two bottles my way.

I take one for myself and try to pass the other to Damen, but he just shakes his head and sips his red drink.

"*Wot* is that?" Roman asks, leaning across me and motioning toward the bottle, his unwelcome touch sending a chill through my skin. "You suck that stuff down like it's spiked. In which case, share the wealth, mate. Don't leave us out here in the cold." He laughs, extending his hand and wiggling his fingers, glancing between us with a dare in his eye.

And just as I'm about to butt in, fearing that Damen's so nice he might agree to give Roman a taste, the curtain unfolds and the music begins. And even though Roman gives up and leans back in his seat, his gaze never once wavers from me.

Miles was amazing. So amazing that every now and then I find myself actually focusing on the lines that he speaks and the lyrics he sings, while the rest of the time my mind is preoccupied with the fact that I'm about to lose my virginity—for the very first time—in four hundred years.

I mean, it's so amazing to think that out of all of those incarnations, out of all the times we met and fell in love, we never once managed to seal the deal.

But tonight, all of that changes.

Everything changes.

Tonight we bury the past and move toward the future of our eternal love.

When the curtain finally closes, we all get up and head for backstage. But just as we reach the back door, I turn to Damen and say, "Damn! We forgot to stop by the store and pick up some flowers for Miles."

But Damen just smiles. Shaking his head as he says, "What're you talking about? We've got all the flowers we need right here."

I squint, wondering what he's up to, because according to my eyes, he's as empty-handed as I. "What're *you* taking about?" I whisper, feeling that warm wonderful charge course through me as he places his hand on my arm.

"Ever," he says, an amused look on his face. "Those flowers already exist on the quantum level. If you want to access them on a physical level, all you have to do is manifest them like I taught you to do."

I glance all around, making sure no one's eavesdropping on our strange conversation and feeling embarrassed when I admit that I can't. "I don't know how," I say, wishing he'd just make the flowers and get it over with already. This is really no time for a lesson.

But Damen's not buying it. "Of course you can. Have I taught you nothing?"

I press my lips together and stare at the floor, because the truth is, he's tried to teach me plenty. But I'm a horrible student and I've slacked off so much it'll be better for both of us if I leave the manifesting of flowers to him.

"You do it," I say, wincing at the disappointment that transforms his face. "You're so much quicker than I am. If I try to do it, it'll turn into a big scene, people will notice, and then we'll be forced to explain. . . ."

He shakes his head, refusing to be swayed by my words. "How will you ever learn if you always rely on me?"

I sigh, knowing he's right but still not wanting to waste precious time trying to manifest a bouquet of roses that may or may not ever appear. All I want is to get the flowers in hand, tell Miles *Bravo,* and move on to the Montage and the rest of our plans. And a moment ago it seemed like he only wanted that too. But now he's gone all serious and professorlike on me, and to be honest, it's kind of wrecking the mood.

I take a deep breath and smile sweetly, my fingers crawling along the edge of his lapel when I say, "You're absolutely right. And I will get better, I promise. But I was thinking that maybe just this once, you could do it since you're so much quicker than I am—" I stroke the spot just under his ear, knowing he's *this* close to caving. "I mean, the sooner we get the bouquet, the sooner we can leave, and then . . ."

And I'm not even finished before he's closing his eyes, his hand held before him as though gripping a spray of spring blooms, as I glance all around, making sure no one is watching, hoping to get this over with soon.

But when I look at Damen again, I start to panic. Because not only is his hand still empty, but a trail of sweat is coursing its way down his cheek for the second time in two days.

Which wouldn't seem all that strange except for the fact that Damen doesn't sweat.

Just like he never gets sick and never has *off* days, he also never sweats. No matter what the temperature outside, no matter what the task at hand, he always remains cool, calm, and perfectly able to handle whatever's before him.

Until yesterday, when he failed to access the portal.

And now, as he fails to manifest a simple bouquet for Miles.

And when I touch his arm and ask if he's okay, I get only the slightest trickle of the usual tingle and heat.

"Of course I'm okay." He squints, raising his lids just enough to peer at me, before closing them tightly again. And even though our gaze was brief, what I glimpsed in his eyes made me grow cold and weak.

Those were not the warm loving eyes I've grown used to. Those eyes were cold, distant, remote—just like I glimpsed earlier this week. And I watch as he focuses, his brow furrowed, his upper lip beaded with sweat, determined to get this over and done with so we can both move on to our perfect night. And not wanting this to drag on any further or repeat the other day when he failed to make the portal appear, I stand right beside him and close my eyes too. *Seeing* a beautiful bouquet of two dozen red roses clutched in his hand, *inhaling* their heady sweet scent while *feeling* the soft plush of petals that just happen to be mounted above long thorny stems—

"Ouch!" Damen shakes his head and brings his finger to his

mouth, even though the wound is already healed long before it can get there. "I forgot to make a vase," he says, clearly convinced he made the flowers himself, and I have every intention of keeping it that way.

"Let me do it," I say, in an effort to please him. "You're absolutely right, I need the practice," I add, closing my eyes and envisioning the one in the dining room at home, the one with the complicated pattern of swirls and etches and luminous facets.

"Waterford crystal?" He laughs. "How much do you want him to think we spent on this thing?"

I laugh too, relieved that all the weirdness is over and he's back to joking again. Taking the vase he thrusts into my hands as he says, "Here. You give these to Miles while I get the car and pull it around."

"You sure?" I ask, noting how the skin around his eyes appears tense and pale, and his forehead is the slightest bit clammy. "Because we can just run in, say *congrats,* and run out. It doesn't have to be a big deal."

"This way we can avoid the long line of cars and make an even quicker getaway." He smiles. "I thought you were anxious to get there."

I am. I'm as anxious as he. But I'm also concerned. Concerned about his inability to manifest, concerned about the fleeting cold look in his eyes—holding my breath as he takes a swig from his bottle, reminding myself of how quickly his wound healed, convincing myself it's a good sign.

And knowing my concern will only make him feel worse, I clear my throat and say, "Fine. You go get the car. And I'll meet you inside."

Unable to ignore the startling coolness of his cheek when I lean in to kiss it.

eleven

By the time I get backstage, Miles is surrounded by family and friends and still dressed in the white go-go boots and minidress of his very last scene as *Hairspray*'s Tracy Turnblad.

"Bravo! You were amazing!" I say, handing over the flowers in place of a hug since I can't risk taking on any additional energy when I'm so nervous inside I can barely handle my own. "Seriously, I had no idea you could sing like that."

"Yes you did." He sweeps his long wig to the side and buries his nose in the petals. "You've heard me perform car karaoke plenty of times."

"Not like that." I smile, and I'm serious. In fact, he was so good I plan to catch a repeat performance on another, less nervous-making night. "So where's Holt?" I ask, already knowing the answer but just trying to make conversation until Damen arrives. "Surely you've made up by now?"

Miles frowns and motions toward his dad, while I cringe and mouth *sorry*. Having forgotten he's out of the closet with his friends, but not yet his parents.

"Don't you worry, all is well," he whispers, batting his false eyelashes and running his hands through his blond-streaked locks. "I had a temporary meltdown, but it's over with now, and all is forgiven. And speaking of Prince Charming . . ."

I turn toward the door, eager to see Damen walk through it. My heart going into overdrive at just the mere thought of him—the whole, wonderful, glorious thought of him—and not doing much to mask my disappointment when I realize he's referring to Haven and Josh.

"What do you think?" he asks, nodding at them. "They gonna make it?"

I watch as Josh slides his arm around Haven's waist, cupping his fingers and pulling her closer. But no matter how hard he tries, it's no use. Despite the fact that they're perfect together, she's focused on Roman—mirroring the way he stands, the way he tilts his head back when he laughs, the way he holds his hands—all of her energy flowing straight toward him as though Josh doesn't exist. But even though it seems mostly one-sided, unfortunately Roman's the type who'd be more than willing to take her out for a test drive.

I turn back to Miles and force a casual shrug.

"There's a cast party at Heather's," Miles says. "We're all headed there soon. You guys coming?"

I give him a blank look. I don't even know who that is.

"She played Penny Pingleton?"

I don't know who that is either, but I know better than to admit it, so I nod like I do.

"Don't tell me you guys were macking so much you missed the whole show!" He shakes his head in a way that makes it clear he's only partly joking.

"Don't be ridiculous, I saw the whole thing!" I say, my face flushing a thousand shades of red and knowing he'll never believe me even though it's more or less true. Because even though we were behaving ourselves and not at all *macking,* it was almost like our hands we're *macking*—with the way Damen entwined his fingers with mine—and like our thoughts were *macking*—with the telepathic messages we sent back and forth. Because even though my eyes were watching the whole entire time—my mind was elsewhere, already occupying our room at the Montage.

"So you coming or not?" Miles asks, his mind correctly guessing *not,* and not nearly as upset as I thought he might be. "So, where you two headed, anyway? What could be more exciting than partying with the cast and crew?"

And when I look at him, I'm so tempted to tell him, to share my big secret with someone I know I can trust. But just as I've convinced myself to spill it, Roman walks up with Josh and Haven in tow.

"We're heading over, anybody need a ride? It's only a two-seater, but there's room for one more." Roman nods at me, his gaze pushing, probing, even after I turn away.

Miles shakes his head. "I'm grabbing a ride with Holt, and Ever better-dealed me. Some top-secret plan she refuses to spill."

Roman smiles, his lips lifting at the corners as his eyes graze over my body. And even though, technically speaking, his thoughts could probably be considered more flattering than crude, the fact that they're coming from him is enough to give me the creeps.

I avert my gaze, glancing toward the door, knowing Damen should've been here by now. And I'm just about to send him a telepathic message, telling him to step it up and meet me inside, when I'm interrupted by the sound of Roman's voice saying, "Must've kept it secret from Damen too, then. He already left."

I turn, my eyes meeting his, feeling that undeniable ping in my gut as a chill blankets my skin. "He didn't *leave,*" I say, not even trying to clear the edge from my voice. "He just went to pull the car around back."

But Roman just shrugs, his gaze filled with pity when he says, "Whatever you say. I just thought you should know that just now, when I stepped out for a smoke, I saw Damen pulling out of the parking lot and speeding away."

twelve

I burst through the door and into the alley, gazing around the narrow empty space as my eyes adjust to the darkness, making out a row of overflowing Dumpsters, a trail of broken glass, a hungry stray cat—but no Damen.

I stumble forward, my eyes searching relentlessly as my heart beats so fast I fear it might break free from my chest. Refusing to believe he's not here. Refusing to believe that he ditched me. Roman's awful! He's lying! Damen would never just up and leave me like this.

Trailing my fingers along the brick wall for guidance, I close my eyes and try to tune in to his energy, calling him to me in a telepathic message of love, need, and worry, but getting only a solid black void in response. Then I slalom through cars all heading for the exit, cell phone pressed to my ear while I peer into windows, leaving a series of messages on his voice mail.

Even when my right heel breaks off my sandal, I just toss them aside and keep going. I don't care about my shoes. I can make a hundred more pairs.

But I can't make another Damen.

And as the lot slowly empties, with still no sign of him, I crumble to the curb, feeling sweaty, exhausted, deflated. Watching the cuts and blisters on my feet simultaneously mend, and wishing I could close my eyes and access his mind—get a read on his thoughts, if not his whereabouts.

But the truth is, I've never been able to get inside his head. It's one of the things I liked best about him. His being so psychically off limits made me feel normal. And wouldn't you know, the one thing that once seemed so appealing is now the very thing that's working against me.

"Need a lift?"

I look up to find Roman standing over me, jangling a set of keys in one hand, my broken sandals in the other.

I shake my head and look away, knowing I'm in no position to refuse a ride, though I'd rather crawl through a trail of hot coals and broken glass than climb inside a two-seater with him.

"C'mon," he says. "I promise not to bite."

I gather my things, tossing my cell into my bag and smoothing my dress as I stand up and say, "I'm good."

"Really?" He smiles, moving so close our toes nearly touch. "'Cause, to be honest, you're not looking so good."

I turn, making my way toward the exit, not bothering to stop when he says, "What I meant was the *situation* isn't looking so good. I mean, look at you, Ever. You're disheveled, shoeless, and though I can't be too sure, it appears that your boyfriend has ditched you."

I take a deep breath and keep going, hoping he'll soon tire of this game, tire of *me,* and move on.

"And yet, even in that frenetic, slightly desperate state, I have to admit, you're still smokin'—if you don't mind my saying."

I stop, suddenly turning to face him despite my vow to keep moving. Cringing as his eyes slowly rake over my body, lingering on my legs, my waist, and my chest—with an unmistakable gleam.

"Makes one wonder what Damen's thinking, 'cause if you ask me—"

"No one asked you," I say, feeling my hands starting to shake and reminding myself that I'm completely in charge here, that I've no reason to feel threatened. That even though I may look like your average defenseless girl on the outside, I'm anything but. I'm stronger than I used to be, so strong that if I really wanted, I could take him down with one swing. I could pick him up off his feet and toss him clear across the parking lot to the other side of the street. And don't think I'm not tempted to prove it.

He smiles, that lazy grin that works on just about everyone but me, his steely blue eyes peering straight into mine with a gaze so knowing, so personal, so amused—my first instinct is to flee.

But I don't.

Because everything about him feels like a challenge, and no way am I letting him win.

"I don't need a ride," I finally say. Turning to pick up the pace and feeling his chill as he trails right behind me. His icy cold breath on the back of my neck when he says, "Ever, please, slow down a minute, would ya? I didn't mean to upset you."

But I don't slow down. I keep going. Determined to put as much distance between us as I possibly can.

"Come on now." He laughs. "I'm only trying to help. Your friends have all left, Damen's buggered off, the cleaning crew went home, which makes me your only hope left."

"I've plenty of options," I mumble, wishing he'd just go away so I can try to manifest a car, some shoes, and be on my way.

"None that I can see."

I shake my head and keep walking. This conversation is over.

"So what you're saying is, you'd rather foot it all the way home than get in a car with me?"

I reach the end of the street and punch the signal again and again, willing the light to turn green so I can get to the other side and be rid of him.

"I don't know how we got off to such a bad start, but it's pretty clear that you hate me and I've no idea why." His voice is smooth, inviting, as though he really wants to start over, let bygones be bygones, make amends, and all that.

But I don't want to start over. Nor do I want to make amends. I just want him to turn around, go somewhere else, and leave me alone so I can find Damen.

And yet, I can't let it go, can't let him get the last word. So I glance over my shoulder and say, "Don't flatter yourself, Roman. Hating requires caring. In which case, I couldn't possibly hate you."

Then I storm across the street even though the light has yet to turn green. Dancing around a couple of speeders intent on beating the yellow, and feeling the insistent chill of his gaze.

"What about your shoes?" he shouts. "Shame to just leave 'em like this. I'm sure the heel can be fixed."

But I just keep moving. *Seeing* him bow deeply behind me, his arm sweeping upward in an exaggerated arc, my sandals dangling from the tips of his fingers. His all-encompassing laugh chasing behind me, following me across the boulevard and onto the street.

thirteen

The moment I cross the street I duck behind a building, peer around the corner, and wait until Roman's cherry red Aston Martin Roadster pulls onto the road and drives away. Then I wait a few minutes more until I'm fully convinced he really is gone and won't be returning anytime soon.

I need to find Damen. I need to find out what happened to him, why he disappeared without saying a word. I mean, he's (we've) been looking forward to this night for four hundred years, so the fact that he's not here beside me proves something's gone terribly wrong.

But first I need a car. You can't get anywhere in Orange County without one. So I close my eyes and picture the first thing that comes to mind—a sky blue VW Bug—just like the one Shayla Sparks, the coolest senior to ever walk the halls of Hillcrest High, used to drive. Remembering its cartoonish round shape and the black cloth top that seemed so glamorous and yet took such a beating in the relentless Oregon rain. Picturing it so clearly it's as though it's right there before me—all shiny and curvy and adorably cute. *Feeling* my fingers bend around the door handle, and the soft stroke of leather as I slide onto the seat, and when I place a single red tulip in the flower holder before me, I open my eyes and see that my ride is complete.

Only I don't know how to start the engine.

I forgot to manifest a key.

But since that's never stopped Damen, I just close my eyes again and *will* the engine to life, remembering the exact sound Shayla's car used to make as my ex–best friend Rachel and I stood on the curb after school, watching in envy as her super cool friends piled into the front and back seats.

And the moment the engine turns, I head toward Coast Highway. Figuring I'll start at the Montage, the place we were supposed to end up, and take it from there.

The traffic is thick this time of night, but it doesn't slow me. I just focus on all of the surrounding cars, *seeing* what everyone's next move is going to be, then adjusting my journey around it. Moving quickly and smoothly into each open space, until I arrive at the entrance, jump out of the Bug, and sprint for the lobby.

Stopping only when the valet calls out from behind me, "Hey, wait up! What about the key?"

I pause, my breath coming in short shallow gasps, not realizing until I catch him staring at my feet that I'm not only keyless but shoeless as well. Yet knowing I can't afford to waste any more time than I already have, and reluctant to go through the whole manifesting process in front of him, I run through the door, yelling, "Just leave it running, I'll only be a sec!"

I make a beeline for the front desk, bypassing a long line of disgruntled people, all of them weighed down with golf bags and monogrammed luggage, all of them complaining about checking in late due to a four-hour delay. And when I cut in front of the middle-aged couple that was supposed to be next, the griping and grumbling hits the next level.

"Has Damen Auguste checked in?" I ask, ignoring the protests behind me, as my fingers curl around the edge of the counter and I fight to steady my nerves.

"I'm sorry, *who?*" The clerk's gaze darts to the couple behind me, shooting them a look meant to say—*don't worry, I'll be done with this psycho chick soon!*

"Damen. Auguste." I enunciate slowly, succinctly, with far more patience than I have.

She squints at me, her thin lips barely moving as she says, "I'm sorry, that information is confidential." Flicking her long dark ponytail over her shoulder in a move so final, so dismissive, it's like a period at the end of a sentence.

I narrow my eyes, focusing on her deep orange aura and knowing it means strict organization and self-control are the virtues she prizes the most—something I showed a glaring lack of when I jumped the turnstile a moment ago. And knowing I need to get on her good side if I've any hope of obtaining the info I need, I resist the urge to act all huffy and indignant, and calmly explain how I'm the *other* guest who's sharing the room.

She looks at me, looks at the couple behind me, then says, "I'm sorry, but you'll have to wait your turn. Just. Like. Everyone. Else."

And I know I have less than ten seconds between now and when she calls for security.

"I *know.*" I lower my voice and lean toward her. "And I really am sorry. It's just that—"

She looks at me, her fingers inching toward the phone as I take in her long straight nose, thin unadorned lips, and the hint of puffiness just under her eyes, and just like *that,* I *see* my way in.

She's been dumped. She's been dumped so recently she still cries herself to sleep every night. Reliving the horrible event every day, *all day*—the scene following her wherever she goes, from her waking state to her dreams.

"It's just that, well—" I pause, trying to make it seem as though it hurts too much to say the actual words, when the truth is I'm not sure which words I'll actually use. Then I shake my head and start over, knowing it's always better to stick with some semblance of the truth when you need the lie to seem real. "He didn't show up when he was supposed to, and because of that . . . well . . . I'm not sure if he's even still coming." I swallow hard, cringing when I realize the tears in my eyes are for real.

But when I look at her again, seeing her face soften—the grim judging mouth, the squinty narrowed eyes, the superior tilt of her chin—all of it suddenly transformed by compassion, solidarity, and unity—I know that it worked. We're like sisters now, loyal members of an all-female tribe, recently jilted by men.

I watch as she taps some commands on her keyboard, tuning in to her energy so I can see what she sees—the letters on the screen flashing before me, showing that our room, suite 309, is still empty.

"I'm sure he's just running late," she says, though she doesn't believe it. In her mind, all men are scum, of this she's convinced. "But if you can show me some ID and prove that you're you, I can—"

But before she can finish, I'm already gone, turning away from the desk and running outside. I don't need a key. I could never check into that sad empty room, waiting for a boyfriend who clearly won't show. I need to keep moving, keep searching. I need to hit the only other two places where he might be. And as I jump in my car and head for the beach—I pray that I'll find him.

fourteen

I park near the Shake Shack and head toward the ocean, feeling my way down the dark winding path, determined to locate Damen's secret cave even though I've only been there one other time, which happens to be the one *other* time we came really close to doing the deed. And we would have too—if it weren't for me. I guess I have a long history of slamming the brakes at the most crucial moment. Either that, or I end up dying. So obviously, I was hoping tonight would be different.

But the moment my feet hit the sand and I make my way down to his hideout, I'm sorry to see that it's pretty much the same as we left it: blankets and towels folded and stacked in the corner, surfboards lined up against the walls, a wet suit draped over a chair—but no Damen.

And with only one place left on my list, I cross my fingers and run for my car. Amazed by the way my limbs move with such speed and grace, the way my feet merely glance over the sand, covering the distance so quickly, I've barely started and I'm already back in my car pulling out of my space. Wondering just how long I've been able to do this, and what other immortal gifts I might have.

• • •

When I arrive at the gate, Sheila, the gate guard who's used to seeing me by now and knows I'm on Damen's permanent list of welcome guests, just smiles and waves me right in. And as I head up the hill toward his house and pull into his drive, the first thing I notice is that the lights are all off.

And I mean *all* of them. Including the one over the door that he always leaves on.

I sit in the Bug, its engine idling as I gaze up at those cold dark windows. Part of me wanting to break down the door, tear up the stairs, and burst into his "special" room—the one where he stores his most precious mementos—the portraits of himself as painted by Picasso, Van Gogh, and Velázquez, along with the piles of rare, first-editions tomes—the priceless relics of his long and storied past, all hoarded into one overstuffed, gilt-laden room. While the other part prefers to stay put, knowing I don't need to enter to prove he's not there. The cold, foreboding exterior, with its stone-covered walls, tiled roof, and vacant windows, is completely devoid of his warm loving presence.

I close my eyes, struggling to recall the last words he said—something about getting the car so that *we* could make an even quicker getaway. Sure that he really meant *we*—that *we* were supposed to make the quick getaway so that *we* could finally be together—our four-hundred-year quest culminating on this one perfect night.

I mean, he couldn't have been looking for a quicker getaway from *me*—

Could he?

I take a deep breath and climb out of my car, knowing the only way to get answers is to keep moving. The soles of my cold wet feet slipping along the dew-covered walkway as I fumble for the key, remembering too late that I left it at home, never dreaming I'd need it tonight of all nights.

I stand before the front door, memorizing its curving arch, mahogany finish, and bold, detailed carvings, before I close my eyes and picture another just like it. *Seeing* my imaginary door unlock and swing open, never having tried this before, but knowing it's possible after seeing Damen unlock a gate at our school—a gate that'd been decidedly locked just a few moments before.

But when I open my eyes again, all I've managed to manifest is another giant wood door. And having no idea how to dispose of it (since up until now I've only manifested things I wanted to keep), I lean it against the wall and head toward the back.

There's a window in his kitchen, the one just behind the sink that he always leaves cracked. And after sliding my fingers under the rim and pushing the window all the way up, I crawl over a sink overflowing with empty glass bottles before jumping to the ground, my feet landing with a muffled *thud* as I wonder if breaking and entering applies to concerned girlfriends too.

I gaze around the room, taking in the wooden table and chairs, the rack of stainless steel pots, the high-tech coffeemaker, blender, and juicer—all part of the collection of the most modern kitchen gadgets money can buy (or Damen can manifest). Carefully selected to give the appearance of a normal, well-to-do life, like accessories in a beautifully decorated model home, perfectly staged and completely unused.

I peer into his fridge, expecting to see the usual abundant supply of red juice, only to find just a few bottles instead. And when I peek inside his pantry, the place where he allows the newer batches to ferment or marinate or whatever they do in the dark for three days—I'm shocked to find that it's barely stocked too.

I stand there, staring at the handful of bottles, my stomach thrumming, my heart racing, knowing something's terribly wrong with this picture. Damen's always so obsessive about keeping plenty of juice on hand—even more so now that he's responsible for supplying me—that he would never allow things to get to this point.

But then again, he's also been going through an awful lot of it lately, chugging it to the point where his consumption has nearly doubled. So it's entirely possible he hasn't had time to make a new batch.

Which sounds good in theory, sure, but it's not at all plausible.

I mean, who am I fooling? Damen's extremely organized with these things, even bordering on obsessive. He would never let his brewing duties slide—not for one day.

Not unless something was terribly wrong.

And even though I don't have any proof, I just know in my gut that the way he's been acting so *off* lately—with the sudden blank looks that are impossible to miss no matter how quickly they fade, not to mention the sweating, the headaches, the inability to manifest everyday objects, or access the Summerland portal—well, when I add it all up, it's clear that he's sick.

Only Damen doesn't get sick.

And when he pricked his finger on that thorny rose just a little while ago, I watched as it healed right before me.

But still, maybe I should start calling the hospitals—just to be sure.

Except Damen would *never* go to the hospital. He'd see it as a sign of weakness, defeat. He's far more likely to crawl off like a wounded animal, hiding out somewhere where he could be alone.

Only he doesn't have any wounds because they instantly heal. Besides, he'd never crawl off without telling me first.

Then again, I was also convinced he'd never drive off without me, and look how that turned out.

I riffle through his drawers, searching for the Yellow Pages—yet another accessory in his quest to seem normal. Because while it's true that Damen would never take himself to the hospital, if there were an accident, or some other event beyond his control, then it's possible that someone else might've taken him without his consent.

And while that completely contradicts Roman's (most likely bogus) story of watching Damen speed away, that doesn't stop me from calling every hospital in Orange County, asking if a Damen Auguste has been admitted, and coming up empty each time.

When the last hospital is called, I consider calling the police but quickly decide against it. I mean, what would I say? That my six-hundred-year-old immortal boyfriend went missing?

I'd have just as much luck cruising Coast Highway, searching for a black BMW with dark tinted windows and a good-looking driver inside—the proverbial needle in the haystack of Laguna Beach.

Or—I can always just settle in here, knowing he's got to turn up eventually.

And as I climb the stairs to his room, I comfort myself with the thought that if I can't be with him, then at least I can be with his things. And as I settle myself upon his velvet settee, I gaze among the things he prizes the most, hoping I'm still one of them too.

fifteen

My neck hurts. And my back feels weird. And when I open my eyes and glimpse my surroundings—I know why. I spent the night in this room. Right here on this ancient velvet settee, which was originally intended for light banter, coquettish flirting, but definitely not sleeping.

I struggle to stand, my muscles tightening in protest as I stretch toward the sky then down toward my toes. And after bending my torso from side to side and swiveling my neck to and fro, I head over to his thick velvet drapes and yank them aside. Flooding the room with a light so bright my eyes water and sting, barely having enough time to adjust before I've closed them again. Ensuring the edges overlap and no amount of sunlight is allowed to creep in, returning the space to its usual state of permanent midnight, having been warned by Damen that those harsh Southern California rays can wreak havoc on the contents of this room.

Damen.

Just thinking about him makes my heart swell with such longing, such all-consuming ache—my head grows dizzy and my whole body sways. And as I grab hold of an elaborate wood cabinet, grasping its fine detailed edge, my eyes search the room, reminding me that I'm not nearly as alone as I think.

Everywhere I look his image surrounds me. His likeness perfectly captured by the world's greatest masters, matted in museum-quality frames, and mounted on these walls. The Picasso in the dark somber suit, the Velázquez on the rearing white stallion—each of them depicting the face I thought I knew so well—only now the eyes seem distant and mocking, the chin raised and defiant, and those lips, those warm wonderful lips that I crave so bad I can taste them, appear so remote, so aloof, so maddeningly distant, as though warning me not to come near.

I close my eyes, determined to block it all out, sure that my panicked state of mind is influencing me for the worst. Forcing myself to take several deep breaths, before trying his cell phone again. His voice mail prompting yet another round of: *Call me . . . where are you . . . what happened . . . are you okay . . . call me*—messages I've left countless times already.

I slip my phone back into my bag and gaze around the room one last time, my eyes carefully avoiding his portraits while assuring myself there's nothing I missed. No blatant clue to his disappearance that I might've overlooked, no small, seemingly insignificant hint that might make the *how* and *why* a little easier to grasp.

And when I'm satisfied I've done all I can, I grab my purse and head to the kitchen, stopping just long enough to leave a short note, repeating all the same words I said on the phone. Knowing the moment I walk out the door my connection to Damen will feel even more tenuous than it already does.

I take a deep breath and close my eyes, picturing the future that just yesterday seemed so sure—the one of Damen and me, both of us happy, together, complete. Wishing it was possible to manifest such a thing, yet knowing deep down it's no use.

You can't manifest another person. Or at least not for very long.

So I shift my attention to something I *can* create. Picturing the most perfect red tulip—its soft waxy petals and long fluid stem the ideal symbol for our undying love. And when I feel it take shape in my hand, I head back to the kitchen, tear up the note, and leave the tulip on the counter instead.

sixteen

I miss Riley.

I miss her so much it's like a physical ache.

Because the second I realized I had no choice but to inform Sabine that Damen wouldn't be making it to dinner (which I waited to do until ten minutes past eight when it was clear he wouldn't show), the questions began. And they pretty much kept coming for the remainder of the weekend, with her asking stuff like: *What's wrong? I know something's wrong. I wish you would talk to me. Why won't you tell me? Is it something with Damen? Are you two in a fight?*

And even though I did talk to her (over dinner when I somehow managed to eat enough to convince her that I really and truly do *not* have an eating disorder), trying to assure her that everything was A-OK, that Damen was just busy, and that I was overtired after spending such a long, fun-filled night at Haven's—it was clear she didn't believe me. Or at least not the part about me being fine. She totally believed the part about me staying at Haven's.

Instead, she kept insisting that there had to be a better explanation for my constant sighing and mood swings, the way I went from morose to manic to mopey and back again. But even though I felt bad for lying to her—I stuck with my story. I guess it seemed easier since lying to Sabine made it easier to lie to myself. Fearing that *retelling* the story, explaining how even though my heart refuses to believe it, my head can't help but wonder if he might've purposely ditched me—might somehow *make* it come true.

If Riley were here, things would be different. I could talk to her. I could tell her the whole sordid tale from beginning to end. Knowing she'd not only understand, but that she'd get answers too.

Her being dead is like an all-access pass. Allowing her to go anywhere she wants merely by thinking about it. Making no place off-limits—the entire planet is fair game. And I've no doubt she'd be far more effective than all of my frantic phone calls and drive-bys combined.

Because in the end, all my disjointed, clumsy, ineffective investigating really amounts to is: ___________ (nothing).

Leaving me just as clueless this Monday morning as I was on Friday night when it occurred. And no matter how many times I call Miles or Haven, their answer is always the same—*nothing to report, but we'll call you if anything changes.*

But if Riley were here, she'd close this case in no time. Getting quick results and in-depth answers—she'd be able to tell me just exactly what I'm dealing with, and how to proceed.

But the fact is, Riley's not here. And despite her promising me a sign, seconds before she left, I'm starting to doubt it'll happen. And maybe, just maybe, it's time I stop looking and get on with my life.

I slip on some jeans, slide my feet into some flip-flops, pull on a tank top, and chase it with a long-sleeved T—and just as I'm about to walk out the door and head for school, I turn right around and grab my iPod, hoodie, and sunglasses, knowing I'd better prepare for the worst since I've no idea what I'll find.

• • •

"Did you find him?"

I shake my head, watching as Miles climbs into my car, throws his bag on the floor, and shoots me a look filled with pity.

"I tried calling," he says, brushing his hair off his face, his nails still sporting a bright flashy pink. "Even tried to swing by his house but didn't get past the front gate. And trust me, you do *not* want to mess with Big Sheila. She takes her job *very* seriously." He laughs, hoping to lighten the mood.

But I just shrug, wishing I could laugh along with him, but knowing I can't. I've been a wreck since Friday and the only cure is to see Damen again.

"You shouldn't worry so much," Miles says, turning toward me. "I'm sure he's fine. I mean, it's not like it's the first time he's disappeared."

I glance at him, sensing his thoughts before the words leave his lips. Knowing he's referring to the last time Damen disappeared, the time I sent him away. "But that was different," I tell him. "Trust me, that was nothing like this."

"How can you be so sure?" His voice is careful, measured, his eyes still on me.

I take a deep breath and stare at the road, wondering whether or not I should tell him. I mean, I haven't *really* talked to anyone in so long, haven't confided in a friend since well before the accident—before everything changed. And sometimes, having to hoard all of these secrets can really feel lonely. I long to get out from under their weight and gossip like a normal girl again.

I look at Miles, sure that I can trust him, but not all that sure if I can trust me. I'm like a soda can that's been dropped and shaken, and now all of my secrets are rushing to the top.

"You okay?" he asks, eyeing me carefully.

I swallow hard. "Friday night? After your play?" I pause, knowing

I've got his full attention. "Well . . . we, um . . . we sort of made plans."

"Plans?" He leans toward me.

"*Big* plans." I nod, a smile hinting at the corner of my lips, then instantly fading when I remember how it all went so tragically wrong.

"How big?" he asks, eyes on mine.

I shake my head, gazing at the road ahead when I say, "Oh, just your usual Friday night. You know, room at the Montage, new lingerie, chocolate dipped strawberries, and two flutes of champagne . . ."

"Omigod, you *didn't*!" he squeals.

I glance at him, watching as his face falls when he realizes the truth.

"Oh God, I mean, you *really* didn't. You didn't get a chance to, since he . . ." He looks at me. "Oh Ever, I'm *so* sorry."

I shrug, seeing the devastation I feel so clearly displayed on his face.

"Listen," he says, reaching for my arm as I stop at a light, then pulling away when he remembers how I don't like to be touched by anyone other than Damen, not knowing that it's only because I go out of my way to avoid any and all unsolicited energy exchange. "Ever, you're gorgeous, seriously. I mean, especially now that you stopped wearing those dumpy hoodies and baggy—" He shakes his head. "Anyway, I think it's safe to say that there's no way Damen would have *willingly* walked out on you. I mean, let's face it, the guy's totally in love, anyone can see it. And believe me, with the way you two are constantly going at it, everyone *has* seen it. There's just no possible way he could've bailed!"

I glance at him, wanting to remind him of what Roman said about Damen speeding away, and how I have this terrible feeling he's somehow connected, maybe even responsible—but just as I'm about to, I realize I can't. I've no evidence to go on, nothing to prove it.

"You call the police?" he asks, his expression suddenly serious.

I press my lips together and squint at the light straight ahead, hating the fact that I did indeed call the cops. Knowing that if everything turns out to be fine, and Damen shows up unscathed, he's going to be pretty unhappy about my drawing that kind of attention his way.

But what was I supposed to do? I mean, if there *was* an accident or something, I figured they'd be the first to know. So Sunday morning, I went down to the station and filed a report, answering all of the usual questions like: *male, Caucasian, brown eyes, brown hair . . .* Until we got to his age and I nearly choked when I almost said: *um . . . he's approximately six hundred and seventeen years old . . .*

"Yeah, I filed a report," I finally say, pressing hard on the gas the second the light turns green and watching the speedometer rise. "They took down the info and said they'd look into it."

"That's it? Are you kidding? He's underage, he's not even an adult!"

"Yeah, but he's also emancipated. Which is like a whole other set of circumstances, making him legally responsible for himself, and other things I don't quite understand. Anyway, it's not like I'm privy to their investigation techniques, it's not like they filled me in on the big plan," I say, slowing to a more normal speed, now that we've entered the school zone.

"Do you think we should pass out flyers? Or hold a candlelight vigil like you see on the news?"

My stomach curls when he says it, even though I know he's just being his usual overly dramatic, though well-meaning self. But up until now, I hadn't imagined it ever coming to that. I mean, surely Damen will show up soon. He's *got* to. He's *immortal*! What could possibly happen to him?

But no sooner do I think it than I pull into the parking lot and see him climbing out of his car. Looking so sleek, so sexy, so gorgeous—you'd think everything was perfectly normal. That the last few days had never occurred.

I slam on the brakes, my car lurching forward then back, causing the driver behind me to slam on their brakes too. My heart racing, my hands shaking, as I watch my completely gorgeous, up until now MIA boyfriend, run a hand through his hair so deliberately, so insistently, and with such focused concentration you'd think it was his most pressing concern.

This is not what I expected.

"What the *hell*?" Miles shrieks, gaping at Damen as a whole slew of cars honk behind us. "And what's he doing parked all the way over *there*? Why isn't he in the second-best spot, saving the *best* one for us?"

And since I don't know the answers to any of those questions, I pull up beside Damen, thinking he might.

I lower my window, feeling inexplicably shy and awkward when he merely glances at me before looking away. "Um, is everything okay?" I ask, wincing when he just barely nods, which is pretty much the most imperceptible acknowledgment of my presence he could possibly give.

He reaches into his car and grabs his bag, taking the opportunity to admire himself in the driver's side window as I swallow hard and say, "Because you sort of took off Friday night . . . and I couldn't find you or reach you all weekend . . . and I got kinda worried . . . I even left you some messages . . . did you get them?" I press my lips together and cringe at my pathetic, ineffective, wuss-laden inquiry.

You *sort* of took off? I got *kinda* worried?

When what I really want to scream is:

HEY YOU—IN THE SUPER-SLICK ALL-BLACK ENSEMBLE—WHAT THE HELL HAPPENED?

Watching as he slips his bag onto his shoulder and gazes at me, his quick powerful stride closing the distance between us in a handful of seconds. But only the physical distance, not the emotional one, because when I look into his eyes they seem miles away.

And just when I realize I've been holding my breath, he leans into the window, his face close to mine when he says, "Yeah. I got your messages. All fifty-nine of them."

I can feel his warm breath on my cheek as my mouth drops open and my eyes search his, seeking the heat his gaze always provides, and shivering when I come away cold, dark, and empty. Though it's nothing like the lack of recognition I glimpsed the other day. No, this is far worse.

Because now when I look in his eyes—it's clear that he knows me—he just wishes he didn't.

"Damen, I—" My voice cracks as a car honks behind me and Miles mutters something unintelligible under his breath.

And before I've had a chance to clear my throat and start over, Damen's shaking his head and walking away.

seventeen

"Are you *all right*?" Miles asks, his face displaying all of the heartbreak and pain I'm too numb to feel.

I shrug, knowing I'm not. I mean, how can I be all *right* when I'm not even sure what's all *wrong*?

"Damen's an asshole," he says, a hard edge to his voice.

But I just sigh. Even though I can't explain it, and even though I don't understand it, I just know in my gut that things are far more complicated than they might seem.

"No he's not," I mumble, climbing out of the car and closing the door much harder than necessary.

"Ever, please . . . I mean, I'm sorry to be the one to point it out, but you *did* just see what I saw, right?"

I head toward Haven who's waiting by the gate. "Trust me, I saw *everything*," I say. Replaying the scene in my mind, each time pausing on his distant eyes, his tepid energy, his complete lack of interest in me—

"So you agree? That he's an asshole?" Miles watches me carefully, assuring himself I'm not the kind of girl who would ever allow a guy to treat her like that.

"Who's an asshole?" Haven asks, glancing between us.

Miles looks at me, his eyes asking permission, and after seeing me shrug, he looks at Haven and says, "Damen."

Haven squints, her mind swimming with questions. But I've got my own set of questions, questions with no probable answer. Such as:

What the hell just happened back there?

And:

Since when does Damen have an aura?

"Miles can fill you in," I say, glancing between them before walking away. Wishing more than ever that I could be normal, that I could lean on them and cry on their shoulders like a regular girl. But there just happens to be more to this situation than meets their mortal eyes. And even though I can't yet prove it—if I want answers, I'll have to go straight to the source.

When I get to class, instead of hesitating at the door, like I thought I would, I surprise myself by bursting right in. And when I see Damen leaning against the edge of Stacia's desk, smiling and joking and flirting with her—I feel like I've stepped into a major case of déjà vu.

You can handle this, I think. *You've been here before.*

Remembering the time, not so long ago, when Damen pretended to be interested in Stacia, but only to get to me.

But the closer I get, the more I realize that this is nothing at all like the last time. Back then all I had to do was look into his eyes to find the smallest glimmer of compassion, a sliver of regret he just couldn't hide.

But now, watching as Stacia outdoes herself with her hair-tossing, cleavage-flaunting, eyelash-batting routine—it's like I'm invisible.

"Um, excuse me," I say, causing them to look up, clearly annoyed by the interruption. "Damen, could I, um, could I talk to you for a sec?" I shove my hands in my pockets so he can't see them shake, forcing myself to breathe like a normal, relaxed person would—in and out, slow and steady, with no gasping or wheezing.

Watching as he and Stacia glance at each other, then burst out laughing at the exact same time. And just as Damen's about to speak, Mr. Robins walks in and says, "Seats, everyone! I want to see you all in your seats!"

So I motion to our desks, and say, "Please, after you."

I follow behind, resisting the urge to grab him by the shoulder, spin him around, and force him to look me in the eye as I scream:

Why did you leave me? What on earth happened to you? How could you do that—on that *night—of all nights?*

Knowing that sort of direct, confrontational approach will only work against me. That if I want to get anywhere at all, then I'll have to act cool, calm, and easy.

I toss my bag to the floor, stacking my book, notebook, and pen on my desk. Smiling as though I'm no more than a casual friend interested in a little Monday morning chat when I say, "So, what'd you do this weekend?"

He shrugs, his eyes grazing over me before resting on mine. And it's a moment before I realize the horrible thoughts that I hear are coming straight from his head.

Well, if I'm gonna have a stalker, at least she's hot, he thinks, his brows merging together as I instinctively reach for my iPod, wanting to tune him out, yet knowing I can't risk missing something important, no matter how much it might hurt. Besides, I've never had access to Damen's mind before, never been able to hear what he's thinking. But now that I can, I'm not sure that I want to.

And when he twists his lips to the side and narrows his eyes, thinking: *Too bad she's totally psycho—definitely not worth risking a tap.*

The bite of his words is like a stake in my chest. And I'm so taken aback by his casual cruelty, I forget they weren't spoken out loud when I shriek, "Excuse me? What did you just say?"

Causing all of my classmates to turn and stare, their sympathies lying with Damen for having to sit next to me.

"Is something wrong?" Mr. Robins asks, glancing between us.

I sit there, totally speechless. My heart caving when Damen looks at Mr. Robins and says, "I'm fine. She's the freak."

eighteen

I followed him. I'm not ashamed to admit it. I had to. He left me no choice. I mean, if Damen's going to insist on avoiding me, then surveillance is my only option.

So I followed him out of English, waited for him after second period—third and fourth too. Staying in the background and observing from afar, wishing I'd agreed to let him transfer to all of my classes like he originally wanted, but thinking it was too creepy, too codependent, I wouldn't let him. So now I'm forced to linger outside his door, eavesdropping on his conversations along with the thoughts in his head—thoughts that, I'm horrified to report, are depressingly vain, narcissistic, and shallow.

But that's not the real Damen. Of this I'm convinced. Not that I think he's a manifest Damen because those never last more than a few minutes. What I mean is, something's happened to him. Something serious that's making him act and think like—well, like most of the guys in this school. Because even though I never had access to his mind until now, I *know* he didn't think like that before. He didn't act like that either. No, this new Damen is like an entirely new creature, where only the outside is familiar—while the inside is something else altogether.

I head toward the lunch table, steeling myself for what I might find, though it's not until I've unzipped my lunch pack and shined my apple on my sleeve, that I realize that the real reason I'm alone isn't because I'm early.

It's because everyone else has abandoned me too.

I look up, hearing Damen's familiar laugh, only to find him surrounded by Stacia, Honor, and Craig, along with the rest of the A-list crew. Which wouldn't be all that surprising with the way things are going, except for the fact that Miles and Haven are there too. And as my eyes sweep the length of the table, I drop my apple and my mouth runs dry when I see that *all* of the tables are now pushed together.

The lions are now lunching with lambs.

Which means Roman's prediction came true.

Bay View High School's lunchtime caste system has come to an end.

"So, what do you think?" Roman says, sliding onto the bench opposite me, hooking his thumb over his shoulder as a smile widens his cheeks. "Sorry for just dropping in on you like this, but I saw you admiring my work, so I thought I'd stop by for a chat. Are you *all right*?" He leans toward me, his face appearing genuinely concerned, though luckily I'm not stupid enough to fall for it.

I meet his gaze, determined to hold it for as long as I can. Sensing he's responsible for Damen's behavior, Miles's and Haven's defection, and the entire school living in harmony and peace—but lacking the evidence needed to prove it.

I mean, to everyone else he's a hero, a true Che Guevara, a lunchtime revolutionary.

But to me he's a threat.

"So I assume you made it home safely?" he asks, chugging his soda though his eyes are on me.

I glance at Miles, watching as he says something to Craig that makes them both laugh, then I move on to Haven, seeing her lean toward Honor, whispering into her ear.

But I don't look at Damen.

I refuse to watch him gaze into Stacia's eyes, place his hand on her knee, and tease her with his very best smile as his fingers creep along her thigh . . .

I saw plenty of that already in English. Besides, I'm pretty sure that whatever they're up to is just foreplay—the first tentative step toward the kind of horrible things I saw in Stacia's head. The vision that freaked me so bad I took down a whole rack of bras in my panic. And yet, by the time I got myself upright and settled again, I was sure she'd done it on purpose, never considered it to be some kind of prophecy. And even though I still think she created it just out of spite, and that their being together now is merely a coincidence, I have to admit it's pretty disturbing to see it played out.

But even though I refuse to watch it, I still try to listen—hoping to hear something pertinent, some vital information exchange. But just as I focus my attention and try to tune in, I'm met by a big wall of sound—all of those voices and thoughts merging together, making it impossible to distinguish any particular one.

"You know, Friday night?" Roman continues, his long fingers tapping the sides of his soda can, refusing to budge from this line of questioning, even though I refuse to participate. "When I found you alone? I have to tell you, Ever, I felt awful leaving you like that, but then again, you insisted."

I glance at him, uninterested in playing this game but thinking that if I just answer his question, then maybe he'll leave. "I made it home just fine. Thanks for your concern."

He smiles, the grin that probably makes a million hearts swoon—but only chills mine. Then he leans in and says, "Aw, now look at that, you're being sarcastic, aren't you?"

I shrug and gaze down at my apple, rolling it back and forth across the table.

"I just wish you'd tell me what I've done to make you hate me so much. I'm sure there's got to be some kind of peaceful solution, some way to remedy this."

I press my lips together and stare at my apple, rolling it along on its side as I push it hard against the table, feeling its flesh soften and give as the skin starts to break.

"Let me take you to dinner," he says, his blue eyes focused on mine. "What do you say? A right and proper date. Just the two of us. I'll get the car detailed, buy some new clothes, make a reservation somewhere swank—a good time guaranteed!"

I shake my head and roll my eyes, the only response I plan to give.

But Roman's undaunted, refusing to fold. "Aw, come on, Ever. Give a bloke a chance to change your mind. You can opt out at anytime, scout's honor. Hell, we'll even make up a safe word. You know, if at any time you decide things have strayed too far from your comfort level, you just shout out the safe word, all activity will cease, and neither of us will ever speak of it again." He pushes his soda aside and slides his hands toward mine, the tips of his fingers creeping so close, I yank mine away. "Come on, give a little, will ya? How can you say no to an offer like that?"

His voice is deep and persuasive, his gaze right on mine, but I just continue rolling my apple, watching the flesh burst free of the skin.

"I promise it'll be nothing like those rubbish dates that wanker Damen probably takes you on. For one thing, I'd never leave a girl as gorgeous as you to fend for herself in a parking lot." He looks at me, a smile playing at his lips when he says, "Well, I suppose I did leave a gorgeous girl like you to fend for herself, but only because I was honoring your request. See? I've already proven I'm at your service, willing to jump at your every command."

"What's with you?" I finally say, peering into those blue eyes without flinching or looking away. Wishing he'd just give it a rest and rejoin the only other lunch table in this school, the one where everybody's welcome but me. "I mean, does *everyone* have to like you? Is that it? And if so, don't you think that's just a *tad* insecure?"

He laughs. And I mean, a genuine, thigh-slapping laugh. And when he finally calms down, he shakes his head and says, "Well no, not *everyone.* Though I do have to admit, it *is* usually the case." He leans toward me, his face mere inches from mine. "What can I say? I'm a likable guy. Most people find me quite charming."

I shake my head and look away, tired of being toyed with and eager to put an end to this game. "Well, I'm sorry to break it to you, but I'm afraid you're going to have to count me among the rare few who aren't the least bit charmed by you. But please, do us both a favor and try not to view it as a challenge and set out to change my mind. Why don't you just go rejoin your table and leave me alone. I mean, why bring everyone together if you don't plan to enjoy all the fun?"

He looks at me, smiling and shaking his head as he slides off the bench, his eyes right on mine when he says, "Ever, you are mad hot. Seriously. And if I didn't know better, I'd think you were purposely trying to drive me insane."

I roll my eyes and look away.

"But, not wanting to wear out my welcome and recognizing the signs of a bloke being told to *sod off,* I think I'll just—" He jabs his thumb toward the table where the whole school is sitting. "Though, of course, if you change your mind and want to come join me, I'm sure I can convince them to make room."

I shake my head and motion for him to go, my throat hot and tight, unable to speak, knowing that despite all appearances, I haven't won this one—in fact, I'm not even close.

"Oh, and I thought you might want these," he says, placing my shoes on the table, as though my strappy, faux snakeskin wedges are some kind of peace offering. "But don't worry, no need to thank me." He laughs, glancing over his shoulder to say, "You might want to take it easy on that apple though, you're giving it quite the beating."

I squeeze tighter, watching as he heads straight for Haven, trails a finger down the length of her neck and presses his lips to her ear. Causing me to grip the apple so hard it explodes in my hand—its sticky wet juice slipping down the length of my fingers and onto my wrist—as Roman looks over and laughs.

nineteen

When I get to art, I head straight for the supply closet, slip into my smock, gather my supplies, and am just heading back into the room when I see Damen standing in the doorway, wearing a strange look on his face. A look that, while it may be strange, also fills me with hope, as his eyes are sort of vacant, his jaw slack, and he seems lost and unsure, like he might need my help.

Knowing I need to seize the moment while it's standing there slack jawed before me, I lean toward him, gently touching his arm as I say, "Damen?" My voice shaky, scratchy, as though it's the first time I've used it all day. "Damen, honey, are you okay?" My eyes graze over him, fighting the urge to press my lips hard against his.

He looks at me with a flash of recognition that's soon joined by kindness, longing, and love. And as my fingers strain toward his cheek, my eyes fill with tears, seeing his reddish brown aura fade and knowing he's mine once again—

And then:

"Ay mate, move along, move along, you're holdin' up the flow of traffic 'ere."

And just like *that,* the old Damen's gone, and the new Damen's back.

He pushes past me, his aura flaring, his thoughts repulsed by my touch. Then I press against the wall, cringing as Roman follows behind, *accidentally* brushing his body against mine.

"Sorry 'bout that, luv." He smiles, his face leering.

I close my eyes and grasp the wall for support. My head swaying as the euphoric swirl of his bright sunshiny aura—his intense, expansive, optimistic energy—washes right through me. Infusing my mind with images so hopeful, so friendly, so innocuous, they fill me with shame—shame for all my suspicions—shame for being so unkind—

And yet—there's something not quite right about it. Something off in the rhythm. Most minds are a jumble of beats, a rush of words, a swirl of pictures, a cacophony of sounds all tumbling together like the most disjointed jazz. But Roman's mind is orderly, organized, with one thought flowing cleanly into the next. Making it sound forced, unnatural, like a prerecorded script—

"By the looks of you, darlin', it seems that was almost as good for you as it was for me. You sure you won't change your mind about that date?"

His chilled breath presses my cheek, his lips so close I fear he might try to kiss me. And just as I'm about to push him away, Damen walks past us and says, "Dude, seriously, what're you doing? That spaz is not worth your time."

That spaz is not worth your time that spaz is not worth your time that spaz is not worth your time that spaz is not worth your time that spaz is not worth your time that spaz is not—

"Ever? Have you grown?"

I look up to find Sabine standing next to me, handing me a freshly rinsed bowl that's meant for the dishwasher. And it's only after I blink a few times that I remember it's my job to put it there.

"Sorry, what?" I ask, my fingers gripping the soapy wet porcelain as I ease it onto the rack. Unable to think about anything but Damen, and the hurtful words I use to torture myself with, by replaying them again and again.

"You look like you've grown. In fact, I'm sure of it. Aren't those the jeans I just bought you?"

I gaze down at my feet, startled to find several inches of ankle exposed. Which is even more bizarre when I remember how just this morning the hems dragged on the floor. "Um—maybe," I lie, knowing that we both know they are.

She squints, shaking her head when she says, "I thought for sure they'd be the right size. Looks like you're going through a growth spurt." She shrugs. "But then, you're only sixteen, so I suppose it's not too late."

Only sixteen, but damn close to seventeen, I think, longing for the day when I turn eighteen, graduate, and head off on my own so I can be alone with my weird creepy secrets and Sabine can get back to her regularly scheduled life. Having no idea how I'll ever repay her for her kindness, and now adding a pair of overpriced jeans to the tab.

"I was done growing by fifteen, but it looks like you're going to end up a lot taller than me." She smiles, handing me a fistful of spoons.

I smile weakly, wondering just how tall I'll get and hoping I don't turn into some kind of giantess freak, some Ripley's *Believe it or Not!* cover girl. Knowing that growing three inches in the course of one day is no ordinary growth spurt—not by a long shot.

But now that she mentions it, I've also noticed that my nails are starting to grow so fast I have to clip them nearly every day, and that my bangs are now past my chin even though I've only been growing them for the past few weeks. Not to mention how the blue of my eyes seems to be deepening, while my slightly crooked front teeth have righted themselves. And no matter how much I abuse it, how irregularly I cleanse it, my complexion remains clear, poreless, and completely blemish-free.

And now I've grown three inches since breakfast?

Obviously, it can only be due to one thing—the immortal juice I've been drinking. I mean, even though I've been immortal for the better half of a year, nothing really changed (well, other than my instantaneous healing abilities) until I started drinking it. But now that I have, it's like all my better physical traits are suddenly magnified and enhanced, while the more mediocre ones are fully improved.

And while part of me feels excited by the prospect and curious to see what else is in store, the other part can't help but notice how I'm developing toward full immortal capacity just in time to spend the rest of eternity alone.

"Must be that juice you're always guzzling." Sabine laughs. "Maybe I should try it. I wouldn't mind breaking the five-foot-four barrier without the aid of high heels!"

"No!" I say, the words spilling from my lips before I can stop them, knowing that answering like that will only pique her interest.

She looks at me, brows merged, damp sponge in hand.

"I mean, I'm sure you won't like it. In fact, you'll most likely hate it. Seriously, it's got kind of a weird taste." I nod, attempting a light breezy expression, not wanting her to know how her statement has left me totally freaked.

"Well, I won't know until I try, right?" she says, her eyes still on mine. "Where do you get it anyway? I don't remember ever seeing it in stores. And I've never seen a label on it either. What's it even called?"

"I get it from Damen," I say, enjoying the feel of his name on my lips, even though it does nothing to fill up the void his absence has left.

"Well, ask him to get me some too, will you?"

And the moment she says it, I know this is no longer just about the juice. She's trying to get me to open up, to explain his absence at our Saturday night dinner, and every day since.

I close the dishwasher and turn away. Pretending to wipe down a counter that's already clean and avoiding her eyes when I say, "Well, I can't actually do that. Mostly because . . . we're um . . . we're sort of taking a break," I say, my voice cracking in the most embarrassing way.

She reaches for me, wanting to hug me, comfort me, tell me it will all be okay. And even though my back is turned so that I can't see her in the physical sense, I can still *see* it in my head, so I step to the side and move out of her way.

"Oh Ever—I'm so sorry—I didn't know—" she says, her hands hanging awkwardly at her sides, unsure what to do with them now that I've moved.

I nod, feeling guilty for being my usual cold distant self. Wishing I could somehow explain that I can't risk the physical contact because I can't risk knowing her secrets. That it will only distract me and provide images I don't need to see. I mean, I'm barely handling my own secrets, so it's not like I'm eager to add hers to the mix.

"It—it was kind of sudden," I say, knowing she's not willing to let the case rest until she's gotten a little more out of me. "I mean, it just sort of happened—and—well, I don't really know what to say . . ."

"I'm here if you need to talk."

"I'm not ready to talk about it yet. It's—it's too new still and I'm trying to sort it all out. Maybe later . . ." I shrug, hoping that by the time *later* arrives, Damen and I will be back together again, and the whole issue resolved.

twenty

When I get to Miles's, I'm a little nervous, having no idea what to expect. But when I see him outside, waiting on his front stoop, I heave a small sigh of relief, knowing things aren't nearly as bad as I thought.

I pull up to his drive, lower my window, and call, "Hey Miles, hop in!"

Then I watch as he glances up from his phone, shaking his head as he says, "Sorry, I thought I told you, I'm getting a ride from Craig."

I gape, my smile frozen in place as I replay his words in my head.

Craig? As in Honor's boyfriend Craig? The sexually confused Cro-Magnon jock whose true preferences I learned by eavesdropping on his thoughts? The one who practically lives to make fun of Miles because it makes him feel "safe"—like he's not one of "them."

That Craig?

"Since when are you friends with Craig?" I ask, shaking my head and squinting at him.

Miles reluctantly rises and comes around to my side. Pausing from his texting pursuits long enough to say, "Since I decided to get a life, branch out, and expand my horizons. Maybe you should try it too. He's pretty cool once you get to know him."

I watch as his thumbs get back to work, as I struggle to get a grip on his words. Feeling like I've landed in some crazy, implausible, alternate universe where cheerleaders gossip with goths, and jocks hang with drama freaks. A place so unnatural it could never truly exist.

Except that it does exist. In a place called Bay View High.

"This is the same Craig that called you a fag and gave you a swirly on your first day of school?"

Miles shrugs. "People change."

I'll say.

Except that they don't.

Or at least not that much in one day unless they have a very good reason for doing so—unless someone else, someone behind the scenes, is *prompting* them, *engineering* it so to speak. Manipulating them against their will and causing them to say and do things that are totally against their true nature—all without their permission, without their even realizing it.

"Sorry, I thought I told you, but I guess I got busy. But you don't need to come by anymore, I've got it all covered," he says, dismissing our friendship with a shrug, as though it bore no more importance than a ride to school.

I swallow hard, resisting the urge to grab him by the shoulders and demand to know what happened—why he's acting like this—why *everyone* is acting like this—and why they've all unanimously decided against me.

But I don't. Somehow, I manage to restrain myself. Mostly because I have a terrible suspicion I might already know. And if it turns out that I'm right, then it's not like Miles is responsible anyway.

"Okay, well, good to know." I nod, forcing a smile I definitely don't feel. "I guess I'll just see you around then," I say, my fingers drumming against the gearshift, waiting for a response that's not coming anytime soon, and backing out of his drive only when Craig pulls up behind me, honks his horn twice, and motions for me to move.

In English, it's even worse than I anticipated. And I'm not even halfway down the aisle before I notice that Damen is now sitting by Stacia.

And I'm talking hand-holding, note-passing, whispering distance from Stacia.

While I remain alone in the back like a complete and total reject.

I press my lips together as I make my way toward my desk, listening to *all* of my classmates hiss:

"Spaz! Watch out, Spaz! Don't fall, Spaz!"

The same words I've been hearing since the moment I got out of my car.

And even though I've no idea what it means, I can't say I'm all that bothered by it—until Damen joins in. Because the moment he starts laughing and sneering along with the rest, all I want to do is go back. Back to my car, back home where it's safe—

But I don't. I can't. I need to stay put. Assuring myself that it's temporary—that I'll soon get to the bottom of it—that there's no possible way I've lost Damen for good.

And somehow, this helps me get through it. Well, that, and Mr. Robins telling everyone to *shush*. So when the bell finally rings, and everyone's filed out, I'm almost out the door when I hear:

"Ever? Can I speak to you for a moment?"

I grip the door handle, my fingers closed and ready to twist.

"I won't keep you long."

And I take a deep breath and surrender, my fingers cranking the sound on my iPod the second I see his face.

Mr. Robins never keeps me after class. He's just not the stop and chat type. And all of this time I was sure that completing my homework and acing my tests insured me against this exact kind of thing.

"I'm not sure how to say this, and I don't want to overstep my bounds here—but I really feel I must say something. It's about—"

Damen.

It's about my one true soul mate. My eternal love. My biggest fan for the last four hundred years, who is now completely repulsed by me.

And how just this morning he asked to change seats.

Because he thinks I'm a stalker.

And now, Mr. Robins, my recently separated, well-meaning English teacher who hasn't a clue, about me, about Damen, about much of anything outside of musty old novels written by long-dead authors, wants to explain how relationships work.

How young love is intense. How it all feels so urgent, like it's the most important thing in the world while it's happening—only it's not. There will be plenty of other loves, if I just allow myself to move on. And I have to move on. It's imperative. Mostly because:

"Because stalking is not the answer," he says. "It's a crime. A very serious crime, with serious consequences." He frowns, hoping to relay the seriousness of all this.

"I'm not stalking him," I say, realizing too late that defending myself against the *S* word before going through all the usual steps of: *He said what? Why would he do that? What could he mean?* like a normal, more clueless person would, makes me appear suspiciously guilty. So I swallow hard when I add, "Listen, Mr. Robins, with all due respect, I know you mean well, and I don't know what Damen told you, but—"

I look in his eyes, *seeing* exactly what Damen told him: *that I'm obsessed with him, that I'm crazy, that I drive by his house day and night, that I call him over and over again, leaving creepy, obsessive, pathetic messages*—which may be partially true, *but still.*

But Mr. Robins isn't about to let me finish, he just shakes his head and says, "Ever, the last thing I want to do is choose sides or get between you and Damen, because frankly, it's just none of my business and it's something you're ultimately going to have to work out on your own. And despite your recent expulsion, despite the fact that you rarely pay attention in class, and leave your iPod on long after I've asked you to turn it off—you're still one of my best and brightest students. And I'd hate to see you jeopardize what could turn out to be a very bright future—*over a boy.*"

I close my eyes and swallow hard. Feeling so humiliated I wish I could just vanish into thin air—disappear.

No, actually it's much worse than that—I feel mortified, disgraced, horrified, dishonored, and everything else that defines wanting to slink off in shame.

"It's not what you think," I say, meeting his gaze and silently urging him to believe it. "Despite whatever stories Damen might've told you, it's not at all what it appears to be," I add, hearing Mr. Robins sigh along with the thoughts in his head. How he wishes he could share how lost he felt when his wife and daughter walked out, how he never thought he'd make it through another day—but fearing it's inappropriate, which it *is.*

"If you just give yourself some time, focus your attention on something else," he says, sincerely wanting to help me, and yet afraid of overstepping his bounds. "You'll soon find that—"

The bell rings.

I shift my backpack onto my shoulder, press my lips together, and look at him.

Watching as he shakes his head and says, "Fine. I'll write you a tardy pass. You're free to go."

twenty-one

I'm a YouTube star. Apparently the footage of me untangling myself from a seemingly never-ending string of Victoria's Secret bras, thongs, and garter belts has not only earned me the oh so clever nickname of *Spaz* but has also been viewed 2323 times. Which just happens to be the number of students enrolled here at Bay View. Well, with a few of the faculty members tossed in.

It's Haven who tells me. Finding her at her locker after barely making it through a gauntlet of people shouting, "Hey, Spaz! Don't fall, Spaz!" she's kind enough not only to fill me in on the origin of my newfound celebrity but to lead me to the video so I can watch the spectacle of myself *spazzing* out right there on my iPhone.

"Oh, that's just great," I say, shaking my head, knowing it's the least of my problems, but still.

"It's pretty fuggin' bad," she agrees, closing her locker and looking at me with an expression that could only be read as pity—well, pity on a time crunch with only a few seconds to spare for a spaz like me. "So—anything else? 'Cause I need to get going, I promised Honor I'd—"

I look at her, I mean, really look at her. Seeing how the flame-red stripe in her hair is now pink, and how her usual pale-skinned, darkly clad, Emo look has been swapped for the spray-tanned, sparkle-dress, fluffy-haired ensemble of those same cliquey clones she always made fun of. But despite her new dress code, despite her new A-list membership, despite all the evidence presented before me, I still don't believe she's responsible for anything she wears, says, or does at this point. Because even though Haven has a tendency to latch on to others and mimic their ways—she still has her standards. And I know for a fact that the Stacia and Honor brigade is one group she never aspired to join.

But still, knowing all that doesn't make it any easier to accept. And even though I know it's useless, even though it clearly won't change a thing, I still look at her and say, "I can't believe you're friends with them. I mean, after everything they've done to me." I shake my head, wanting her to know just how much that hurts.

And even though I hear her response a few seconds earlier, it does little to soften the blow when she says, "Did they push you? Did they shove you or trip you or make you fall on top of that rack? Or did you do that all on your own?" She looks at me, brows raised, lips pursed, narrowed eyes focused on mine. As I stand there stunned, mute, my throat searing so hot I couldn't speak if I tried.

"It's like—lighten up already, would you?" She rolls her eyes and shakes her head. "They meant for it to be funny. And you'd be a helluva lot happier if you could just unclench, stop taking yourself and everything around you so damn seriously, and fuggin' learn to live a little! I mean, seriously, Ever. Think about it, okay?"

She turns, merging seamlessly into the crowd of students, all of them heading for the extra long table in their new lunchtime exodus, while I make a run for the gate.

I mean, why torture myself? Why hang around just so I can watch Damen flirt with Stacia, and get called *spaz* by my friends? Why have all of these advanced psychic abilities if I'm not going to exploit them and put them to good use—like ditching school?

"Leaving so soon?"

I ignore the voice behind me and keep going. Roman's pretty much the last person I'm willing to talk to at this point.

"Ever, hey, hold up! Seriously." He laughs, picking up his pace until he's right alongside me. "Where's the fire?"

I unlock my car and slide in, yanking the door and almost getting it closed, until he stops it with the palm of his hand. And even though I know I'm stronger, that if I really wanted I could just slam the door closed and be on my way, the fact that I'm still not used to my new immortal strength is the one thing that stops me. Because as much as I dislike him, I'm a little reluctant to slam it so hard I sever his hand.

I'd much rather save that kind of thing for when I might need it.

"If you don't mind, I really need to get going." I pull the door again, but he just grips it tighter. And when I combine the amused look on his face with the surprising strength in his fingers, I feel the strangest ping in my gut when I realize those two seemingly random things support my deepest suspicions.

But when I look at him again, watching as he lifts his hand to sip from his soda, exposing a wrist that's free of all markings, bearing no tattoos of a snake eating its own tail—the mythical Ouroboros symbol which happens to be the sign of an immortal turned rogue—it just doesn't add up.

Because the fact is, not only does he eat and drink, not only are his aura and thoughts accessible (well, to me anyway), but as much as I hate to admit it, from what I can see, he bears no outward signs of evil. And when you put that together, it's obvious my suspicions are not only paranoid but unfounded as well.

Which means he's not the malevolent immortal rogue I supposed him to be.

Which also means he's not responsible for Damen dumping me, or Miles's and Haven's defection. Nope, that would point right back to me.

And even though all the evidence supports that—I refuse to accept it.

Because when I look at him again, my pulse quickens, my stomach pings, and I'm overcome by a feeling of unease and dread. Making it impossible for me to believe he's just some jolly young chap from England who wound up at our school and found himself all smitten with me.

Because the one thing I know for sure is: Everything was fine until he arrived.

And nothing's been the same since.

"Skipping out on lunch, are you?"

I roll my eyes. I mean, it's pretty obvious what I'm up to, so I won't waste my time with an answer.

"And I see you have room for one more. Mind if I join you?"

"As a matter of fact, I do. So if you'd kindly remove your—" I motion toward his hand, flicking my fingers in the international sign for *scram*.

He holds up his hands in surrender, shaking his head when he says, "I don't know if you've noticed, Ever, but the more you evade me, the faster I chase. It'll be a lot easier for both of us if you just stop running."

I narrow my gaze, trying to *see* past the sunshiny aura and well-ordered thoughts, but I'm blocked by a barrier so impenetrable it's either the end of the road, or he's way worse than I thought.

"If you insist on the chase," I say, my voice much surer than I feel. "Then you better start training. 'Cause, dude, you're in for a marathon."

He winces, body flinching, eyes widening as though he's been stung. And if I didn't know better, I'd think it was real. But the fact is, I do know better. He's just hamming it up, practicing a few facial expressions for dramatic effect. And I don't have time to be the butt of his joke.

I shift into reverse and back out of my space, hoping to leave it at that.

But he just smiles, slapping the hood of my car when he says, "As you wish, Ever. Game on."

twenty-two

I don't go home.

I started to. In fact, I had every intention of driving home, hauling upstairs, and flinging myself on my bed, burying my face in a fat pile of pillows and crying my eyes out like a big pathetic baby.

But then, just as I was turning onto my street, I thought better. I mean, I can't allow myself that kind of luxury. I can't waste the time. So instead, I make a U-turn and head toward downtown Laguna. Making my way through those steep narrow streets, driving past well-tended cottages with beautiful gardens and the double-lot McMansions that sit right beside them. Heading for the address of the only person I know who can help me.

"Ever." She smiles, pushing her wavy auburn hair off her face as her large brown eyes settle on mine. And even though I arrived unannounced, she doesn't seem the least bit surprised. But then her being psychic makes her pretty hard to startle.

"I'm sorry for just showing up and not calling first, I guess I—"

But she doesn't let me finish. She just opens the door and waves me right in, ushering me toward the kitchen table where I sat once before—the last time I was in trouble and had nowhere to turn.

I used to loathe her, *really* loathed her. And when she started convincing Riley to move on—to cross the bridge to where our parents and Buttercup were waiting—it got even worse. But even though I used to count her as my worst enemy besides Stacia, all of that seems like so long ago now. And as she fusses around the kitchen, setting out cookies and brewing green tea, I watch, feeling guilty for not keeping in touch, for only coming around when I'm desperately in need.

We exchange the usual pleasantries, then she takes the seat across from me and cradles her teacup as she says, "You've grown! I know I'm short, but you positively tower over me now!"

I shrug, unsure how to deal with this but knowing I better get used to it. When you grow several inches in a matter of days, people tend to notice. "I guess I'm a late bloomer. You know, going through a growth spurt—or—something," I say, my smile feeling clumsy on my lips, realizing I need to come up with a much more convincing reply, or at least learn how to reply with conviction.

She looks me over and nods. Not buying a word of it but deciding to just let it go. "So, how's the shield holding up?"

I swallow hard, blinking once, twice. I was so focused on my mission I'd forgotten about the shield she helped me create. The one that blocked out all the noise and sound the last time Damen went away. The one I dismantled the moment he returned.

"Oh, um, I kind of got rid of it," I say, cringing as the words spill from my lips, remembering how it took the better part of an afternoon just to put it in place.

She smiles, gazing at me from over the top of her cup. "I'm not surprised. Being normal's not all it's cracked up to be, once you've experienced something *more*."

I break off a piece of oatmeal cookie and shrug. Knowing that if it were up to me, I'd choose *normal* over *this* any day.

"So, if this isn't about the shield—then what is it?"

"You mean you don't know? What kind of psychic are you?" I laugh, far too loud for such a dumb, feeble joke.

But Ava just shrugs, tracing a heavily ringed finger along the rim of her cup as she says, "Well, I'm no advanced mind reader like you. Though I do sense something rather serious in the works."

"It's about Damen," I start, pausing to press down on my lips. "He's—he's changed. He's become cold, distant, cruel even, and I—" I drop my gaze, the truth behind the words making them so much harder to say. "He won't return my calls, won't talk to me at school, he even moved his seat in English, and now he—he's dating this girl who—well, she's just *awful*. I mean, really, truly awful. And now he's awful too—"

"Ever—" she starts, her voice warm and gentle, her eyes kind.

"It's not what you think," I tell her. "It's not that at all. Damen and I didn't break up, we weren't having problems, it was nothing like that. It's like, one day everything was great—and the next—*not*."

"And did something happen to precipitate this change?" Her face is thoughtful, her eyes on mine.

Yeah, Roman happened. But since I can't explain my suspicions, that he's an immortal rogue (despite all evidence to the contrary), employing some sort of mass mind control or hypnosis or spell casting (which I'm not even sure is possible) over the entire Bay View student body, I just tell her about Damen's recent bout of odd behavior—the headaches, the sweating, and a few other safe-to-talk-about nonsecret things.

Then I sit there, holding my breath as she sips her tea and looks out the window at the beautiful garden beyond, her gaze returning to me when she says, "Tell me everything you know about Summerland."

I stare at the two halves of my uneaten cookie and clamp my lips shut, never having heard the word mentioned so openly and casually like that. I'd always thought of it as Damen's and my sacred space, never realizing that mere mortals might know of it too.

"Certainly you've visited?" She sets down her cup and raises her brow. "During your near-death experience perhaps?"

I nod, remembering both of my visits, the first time when I was dead, the second with Damen. And I was so taken with that magical, mystical dimension with its vast fragrant fields and pulsating trees—I was reluctant to leave.

"And did you visit its temples while you were there?"

Temples? I didn't see any temples. Elephants, beaches, and horses—things we both manifested, but certainly no buildings or dwellings of any kind.

"Summerland is legendary for its temples, or Great Halls of Learning as they're called. I'm thinking your answer lies there."

"But—but I'm not even sure how to get there without Damen. I mean, short of dying and all . . ." I look at her. "How do you even know about it? Have you been there?"

She shakes her head. "I've been trying to access it for years. And though I've come close a few times, I've never been able to get through the portal. But maybe if we merge our energy together, pool our resources so to speak, we just might get through."

"It's impossible," I say, remembering the last time I tried to access it that way. And even though Damen was already showing signs of distress, he's still way more advanced than Ava on her very best day. "It's not that easy. Even if we do pool our energy, it's still a lot more difficult than you think."

But she just shakes her head and smiles, rising from her seat as she says, "But we'll never know until we try, right?"

twenty-three

I follow her down a short hallway. My flip-flops snapping against a red woven rug as I think: *This'll never work.*

I mean, if I couldn't access the portal with Damen, how can I possibly access it with Ava? Because even though she seems to be a pretty gifted psychic, her skills are mostly saved for the party circuit, telling fortunes over a fold-up card table, embellishing them in hopes of a generous tip.

"It'll never work if you don't believe," she says, pausing before an indigo door. "You need to have faith in the process. And so, before we enter, I need you to clear your mind of all negativity. I need you to rid yourself of any sad or unhappy thoughts, or anything else that's dragging you down and serves the word *can't.*"

I take a deep breath and stare at the door, fighting the urge to roll my eyes as I think: *Great. I should've known.* This is just the sort of hokey stuff you're forced to tolerate when you're dealing with Ava.

But all I say is, "Don't worry about me, I'm good." Nodding in a way I hope is convincing, wanting to avoid her usual twenty-step meditation, or whatever woo-woo practice she might have in mind.

But Ava just stands there, hands on hips, eyes on mine. Refusing to let me in until I agree to lighten my emotional load.

So when she says, "Close your eyes," I do. But only to speed things along.

"Now I want you to imagine long spindly roots sprouting from the soles of your feet and delving deep into the earth, carving into the soil and stretching their limits. Digging deeper and deeper into the ground until they've reached the earth's core and can't go any farther. Got it?"

I nod, picturing what she asks, but only so we can get this show on the road and not because I believe in it.

"Now take a deep breath, take several deep breaths, and let your whole body relax. Feel your muscles loosening, while your tension fades away. Allowing any lingering negative thoughts or emotions to disappear. Just banish them from your energy field and tell them good riddance. Can you do that?"

Um, whatever, I think. Just going through the motions and feeling pretty surprised when my muscles really do start to relax. And I mean, *really* relax. Like I'm at peace after a long hard battle.

I guess I wasn't aware of just how tense I've been or how much negativity I was lugging around until Ava made me release it. And even though I'm willing to do just about anything to get into that room and closer to Summerland, I have to admit that some of this mumbo-jumbo stuff might really work.

"Now draw your attention up until you're focused on the crown of your head, the area right at the top. And imagine a solid beam of the purest golden white light penetrating that very spot and easing its way all down your neck, your limbs, your torso, all the way down to your feet. Feel that warm, wonderful light healing every part of you, coating every last cell both inside and out, allowing any lingering sadness or anger to be transformed into loving energy by this powerful healing force. Feel the light surging inside you like a steady beam of lightness, love, and forgiveness with no beginning or end. And when you start to feel lighter, when you start to feel yourself purified and cleansed, open your eyes and look at me, but only when you're ready."

So I do, I go through the whole white light ritual, determined to participate and at least pretend to take these steps seriously since it's important to Ava. And just as I imagine a golden beam coursing through my body, coating my cells and all that, I also try to calculate just how long I should delay opening my eyes so it won't look too fake.

But then, something odd happens. I find myself feeling lighter, happier, stronger, and despite the desperate state I arrived in—fulfilled.

And when I do open my eyes, I see that she's smiling at me, her entire body surrounded by the most beautiful violet aura I've ever seen.

She opens the door and I follow her inside, blinking and squinting as I adjust to the deep purple walls of this small spare room that, from the looks of it, seems to double as a shrine.

"Is this where you give your readings?" I ask, taking in the large collection of crystals and candles and iconic symbols that cover the walls. Watching as she shakes her head and settles onto an elaborate embroidered floor cushion, patting the one right beside her and motioning for me to sit too.

"Most of the people who show up here are occupying a dark emotional space, and I can't risk letting them in. I've worked very hard to keep the energy in this room pure, clean, and free of all darkness, and I don't allow anyone to enter until their energy is cleared, including me. That cleansing exercise I just put you through, I do it first thing every morning, just after I wake, and then again before entering this room. And I recommend you do it too. Because even though I know you thought it was nonsense, I also know you're surprised by how much better you feel."

I press my lips together and avert my gaze. Knowing she doesn't have to read my mind to know what I'm thinking. My face always betrays me—it's incapable of lying.

"I get the whole healing light thing," I say, gazing at the bamboo blinds covering the window and the shelf lined with stone statues of deities from all over the globe. "And I have to admit that it did make me feel better. But what was that root thing all about? It seemed kind of weird."

"That's called *grounding*." She smiles. "When you came to my door, your energy felt very scattered and this helps to contain it. I suggest you perform that exercise daily as well."

"But won't it keep us from reaching Summerland? You know, by *grounding* us here?"

She laughs. "No, if anything, it'll help you stay focused on where you really want to go."

I gaze around the room, noticing how it's so crammed with stuff, it's hard to take it all in. "So is this like your sacred space?" I finally say.

She smiles, her fingers picking at a loose thread on her cushion. "It's the place where I come to worship and meditate and try to reach the dimensions beyond. And I have a very strong hunch that this time, I'll get there."

She folds her legs into the lotus position and motions for me to do so as well. And at first I can't help but think that my new long and gangly legs will never bend and entwine like hers. But a moment later I'm shocked by the way they just slip right into place, folding around each other in a way that's so natural and comfortable without the least bit of resistance.

"Ready?" she asks, her brown eyes on mine.

I shrug, gazing at the soles of my feet, amazed to see them so visible as they rest on top of my knees, wondering what kind of ritual she'll put us through next.

"Good. Because now it's your turn to lead." She laughs. "I've never been there before. So I'm counting on you to show us the way."

twenty-four

I had no idea it would be so easy. Didn't believe we'd be able to get there. But just after I lead us through the ritual of closing our eyes and imagining a brilliant portal of shimmering light, we joined hands and toppled right through, landing side by side on that strange buoyant grass.

Ava looks at me, her eyes wide, her mouth open, but unable to form any words.

I just nod and gaze all around, knowing just how she feels. Because even though I've been here before, that doesn't make it any less surreal.

"Hey, Ava," I say, rising to my feet and brushing the seat of my jeans, eager to play tour guide and show her just how magical this place can be. "Imagine something. Anything. Like an object, an animal, or even a person. Just close your eyes and see it as clear as you can and then . . ."

I watch as she closes her eyes, my excitement building as her brows merge together and she focuses on her object of choice.

And when she opens her eyes again, she clasps her hands to her chest and stares straight ahead, crying, "Oh! Oh, it can't be—but look—it looks just like him and he's *so* real!"

She kneels on the grass, clapping her hands together and laughing with glee as a beautiful golden retriever leaps into her arms and smothers her cheeks with wet sloppy licks. Hugging him tightly to her chest, murmuring his name again and again, and I know it's my duty to warn her he's not the real deal.

"Ava, um, I'm sorry but I'm afraid he won't—" but before I can finish, the dog slips from her grasp, fading like a pattern of vibrating pixels that soon vanish completely. And when I see the devastation on her face, my stomach sinks, feeling guilty for initiating this game. "I should've explained," I say, wishing I hadn't been so impulsive. "I'm so sorry."

But she just nods, blinking back tears as she brushes the grass from her knees. "It's okay. Really. I knew it was too good to be true, but just to see him like that again, just to have that moment—" She shrugs. "Well, even if it wasn't real, I don't regret it for a second. So don't you regret it either, okay?" She grasps my hand and squeezes it tight. "I've missed him so much, and just to have him for those few brief seconds was like a rare and precious gift. A gift I got to experience thanks to you."

I nod, swallowing hard, hoping she means it. And even though we could spend the next several hours manifesting everything our hearts desire, the truth is, my heart desires only one thing. Besides, after witnessing Ava's reunion with her beloved pet, the pleasure of material goods no longer seems worth it.

"So this is Summerland," she says, gazing all around.

"This is it." I nod. "But all I've ever seen of it is this field, that stream, and a few other things that didn't exist until I manifested them here. Oh, and see that bridge? Way over there, off in the distance, where the fog settles in?"

She turns, nodding when she sees it.

"Don't go near it. It leads to the *other side.* That's the bridge Riley told you about, the one I finally convinced her to cross—after a little coaxing from you."

Ava stares at it, her eyes narrowed as she says, "I wonder what happens if you try to go across? You know, without dying, without that kind of invite?"

But I just shrug, not having nearly enough curiosity to ever try and find out. "I wouldn't recommend it," I say, seeing the look in her eyes and realizing she's actually weighing her options, wondering if she should try to cross it, out of sheer curiosity if nothing else. "You might not come back," I add, trying to relay the potential seriousness since she doesn't seem to get it. But I guess Summerland has that effect—it's so beautiful and magical it tempts you to take chances you normally wouldn't.

She looks at me, still not fully convinced but too eager to see more than to just sit around here. So she links her arm through mine, and says, "Where do we begin?"

Since neither of us has any idea just where to begin—we begin by walking. Heading through the meadow of dancing flowers, making our way through the forest of pulsating trees, crossing the rainbow-colored stream filled with all manner of fish, until finding a trail that, after curving and winding and meandering forever, leads us to a long empty road.

But not a yellow brick road or one paved with gold. This is just a regular street, made of everyday asphalt, like the kind you see at home.

Though I have to admit that it's better than the streets at home because this one is clean and pristine, with no potholes or skid marks. In fact, everything around here appears so shiny and new you'd think it'd never been used, when the truth is—or at least the truth according to Ava—Summerland is older than time.

"So what exactly do you know about these temples, or Great Halls of Learning as you call them?" I ask, gazing up at an impressive white marble building with all sorts of angels and mythical creatures carved into its columns and wondering if it could be the place that we seek. I mean, it looks fancy yet serious, impressive but not exactly formidable, everything I imagine a hall of higher learning to be.

But Ava just shrugs as though she's no longer interested. Which is a tad more noncommittal than I'd like.

She was so sure the answer lay here, was so insistent on binding our energy and traveling together, but now that we've made it, she's a little too enamored with the power of instant manifestation to concentrate on anything else.

"I just know they exist," she says, her hands held out before her, turning them this way and that. "I've come across their mention many times in my studies."

And yet, all you seem to be studying now are those large jewel-encrusted rings you've manifested onto your fingers! I think, not stating the actual words but knowing that if she's interested enough to look, she'll see the annoyance stamped on my face.

But she just smiles as she manifests an armful of bangles to match her new rings. And when she starts gazing down at her feet, in pursuit of new shoes, I know it's time to rein her back in.

"So what should we do when we get there?" I ask, determined to get her to focus on the true reason we're here. I mean, I did my part, so the least she could do is reciprocate and help me find the way. "And what do we research once we find it? Sudden headaches? Extreme bouts of uncontrollable sweatiness? Not to mention, will they even let us in?"

I turn, fully expecting a lecture on my persistent negativity, my rampant pessimism that vanishes for a while but never fully subsides—only to find that she's no longer there.

And I mean, she's completely, unmistakably, one hundred percent *not* present!

"Ava!" I call, turning around and around, squinting into the shimmering mist, the eternal radiance that emanates from nowhere specific but manages to permeate everything here. "Ava, where are you?" I shout, running down the middle of the long, empty road, stopping to peer into windows and doorways, and wondering why there are so many stores and restaurants and art galleries and salons when there's no one around to use them.

"You won't find her."

I turn, seeing a petite dark-haired girl standing behind me. Her stick-straight hair hanging to her shoulders, and her nearly black eyes framed by bangs so severe they seem slashed with a razor.

"People get lost here. Happens all the time."

"Who—who are you?" I say, taking in her starched white blouse, plaid skirt, blue blazer, and kneesocks, the outfit of your typical private school girl, but knowing this is no ordinary student—not if she's here.

"I'm Romy," she says. Except that her lips didn't move. And the voice that I heard came from behind me.

And when I spin around, I find the same exact girl laughing as she says, "And she's Rayne."

I turn again, seeing Rayne still behind me as Romy comes around to join her. Two identical girls standing before me, everything about them—their hair, their clothes, their faces, their eyes—exactly the same.

Except for the kneesocks. Romy's have fallen, while Rayne's are pulled tight.

"Welcome to Summerland." Romy smiles, as Rayne looks me over with suspicious narrowed eyes. "We're sorry about your friend." She nudges her twin, and when she doesn't respond, she says, "Yes, even Rayne is sorry. She just won't admit it."

"Do you know where I can find her?" I ask, gazing between them and wondering where they could've come from.

Romy shrugs. "She doesn't want to be found. So we found you instead."

"What're you talking about? And where did you even come from?" I ask, never having seen another person on my previous visits here.

"That's only because you didn't *want* to see another person," Romy says, answering the thought in my head. "You didn't *desire* it until now."

I look at her, my face blank, my mind spinning with the realization—*she can read my thoughts?*

"Thoughts are energy." She shrugs. "And Summerland consists of rapid, intense, magnified energy. So intense you can read it."

And the moment she says it, I remember my visit with Damen, and how we were able to communicate telepathically. But at the time, I thought it was just us.

"But if that's true, then why wasn't I able to read Ava's mind? And how was she able to just disappear like that?"

Rayne rolls her eyes, while Romy leans forward, her voice soft and low as though speaking to a small child even though they appear younger than I. "Because you have to *desire* it in order for it to be." Then, seeing the blank look on my face, she explains, "Within Summerland exists the possibility for everything. *For all things*. But you must first desire it to bring it into existence. Otherwise it remains only a possibility—one of many possibilities—unmanifested and incomplete."

I gaze at her, trying to make sense of her words.

"The reason you didn't see people before is because you didn't want to. But now, look around and tell me what you see."

And when I look around, I see that she's right. The shops and restaurants are now filled with people, a new art installation is being hung in the gallery, and a crowd gathers on the museum steps. And as I focus on their energy and thoughts, I realize just how diverse this place really is, every nationality and religion is present and accounted for, with everyone coexisting in peace.

Wow, I think, my eyes darting everywhere, trying to take it all in.

Romy nods. "And so the moment you desired to find your way to the temples, we showed up to help you. While Ava faded away."

"So I *made* her disappear?" I ask, beginning to grasp the truth of all this.

Romy laughs, while Rayne shakes her head and rolls her eyes, looking at me like I'm the densest person she's ever met. "Hardly."

"So all of these people—" I motion toward the crowd. "Are all of them—*dead*?" I direct my question at Romy, having given up on Rayne.

Watching as she leans in and whispers into her sister's ear, causing Romy to pull away and say, "My sister says you ask too many questions."

Rayne scowls, popping her hard on the arm with her fist, but Romy just laughs.

And as I gaze at the two of them, taking in Rayne's steady glare and Romy's insistence on speaking in riddles, I realize that as entertaining as it's been, they're starting to get on my nerves. I've got things to do, temples to find, and engaging in this kind of confusing banter is turning into a big waste of time.

Remembering too late that they both can read my thoughts when Romy nods and says, "As you wish. We'll show you the way."

twenty-five

They lead me down a series of streets, the two of them marching side by side, their stride so measured and quick I struggle to follow. We pass vendors peddling all types of wares—everything from hand-dipped candles to small wooden toys—their patrons lining up for those carefully wrapped goods and offering only a kind word or smile in exchange. We walk alongside fruit stands, candy stores, and a few trendy boutiques, before pausing on a corner as a horse-drawn carriage crosses our path followed by a chauffeur-driven Rolls-Royce.

And just as I'm about to ask how all of these things can exist in one place, how seemingly ancient buildings can sit beside the sleekest, most modern designs, Romy looks at me and says, "I already told you. Summerland contains the possibility of *all things*. And since different people desire different things, most everything you can think of has been brought into existence."

"So all of this was *manifested*?" I say, gazing around in awe, as Romy nods and Rayne storms straight ahead. "But who's manifesting these things? Are they day-trippers like me? Are they living or dead?" I glance between Romy and Rayne, knowing my question applies to them too, because even though they *appear* to be normal on the outside, there's something very strange about them, something almost—eerie—and *timeless* as well.

And just as my gaze settles on Romy, Rayne decides to address me for the first time today, saying, "You desired to find the temples and so we are helping you. But make no mistake, we are under no obligation to answer your questions. Some things in Summerland are just none of your business."

I swallow hard, looking at Romy and wondering if she'll step in and apologize for her sister, but she just leads us down another well-populated street, into an empty alleyway, and onto a quiet boulevard where she stops before a magnificent building.

"Tell me what you see," she says, as both she and her sister peer closely at me.

I gawk at the glorious building before me, my eyes wide as my mouth drops in awe, taking in its beautiful elaborate carvings, its grand sloping roof, its imposing columns, its impressive front doors—all of its vast and varied parts rapidly changing and shifting, conjuring images of the Parthenon, the Taj Mahal, the great pyramids of Giza, the Lotus Temple, my mind reeling with imagery as the building reshapes and reforms, until all of the world's greatest temples and wonders are clearly represented in its ever-changing façade.

I see—I see everything! I think, unable to utter the words. The awesome beauty before me has rendered me speechless.

I turn to Romy, wondering if she sees what I see, and watching as she pops Rayne hard on the arm when she says, "I *told* you!"

"The temple is constructed from the energy, love, and knowledge of *all good things.*" She smiles. "Those who can see that are permitted to enter."

The second I hear that, I sprint up the grand marble steps, eager to get past this glorious façade and see what's inside. But just as I reach the huge double doors, I turn back to say, "Are you coming?"

Rayne just stares, her eyes narrowed, suspicious, wishing they'd never bothered with me. While Romy shakes her head and says, "Your answers lie inside. You're no longer in need of us now."

"But where do I start?"

Romy peers at her sister, a private exchange passing between them. Then she turns to me and says, "You must seek the akashic records. They are a permanent record of everything that has ever been said, thought, or done—or ever will be said, thought, or done. But you will only find them if you are meant to. If not—" She shrugs, wishing to leave it right there, but the look of sheer panic in my eyes drives her to continue. "If you are not meant to know, then you will not know. It's as simple as that."

I stand there, thinking how that wasn't the least bit reassuring, and feeling almost relieved when they both turn to leave.

"And now we must go, Miss Ever Bloom," she says, using my full name even though I'm sure I never revealed it. "Though I'm sure we'll meet again."

I watch as they move away, remembering one last question when I call, "But how do I get back? You know, once I'm done here?"

Watching as Rayne's back stiffens and Romy turns, a patient smile spread across her face as she says, "The same way you arrived. Through the portal, of course."

twenty-six

The moment I turn toward the door it opens before me. And since it's not one of those automatic doors like the kind they have in supermarkets, I'm guessing it means I'm worthy of entering.

I step into a large spacious entry filled with the most brilliant warm light—a luminous showering radiance that, like the rest of Summerland, permeates every nook and cranny, every corner, every space, allowing no shadows or dark spots, and doesn't seem to emanate from any one place. Then I move along a hall flanked on either side by a row of white marble columns carved in the style of ancient Greece, where robe-wearing monks sit at long carved wooden tables, alongside priests, rabbis, shamans, and all manner of seekers. All of them peering at large crystal globes and levitating tablets—each of them studying the images that unfold.

I pause, wondering if it would be rude to interrupt and ask if they can point me in the direction of the akashic records. But the room is so quiet and they're all so engrossed, I'm reluctant to disturb them, so I keep going instead. Passing a series of magnificent statues carved from the purest white marble, until entering a large ornate room that reminds me of the great cathedrals of Italy (or at least the pictures I've seen). Bearing the same sort of domed ceilings, stained-glass windows, and elaborate frescoes containing the kind of glorious images that would make Michelangelo weep.

I stand in the center, my head thrown back in awe as I struggle to take it all in. Twirling around and around until I grow tired and dizzy, realizing it's impossible to glimpse it all in one sitting. And knowing I've wasted enough time already, I shut my eyes tightly and follow Romy's advice—that I must first *desire* something in order for it to be. And just after asking to be led to the answers I seek, I open my eyes and a long hallway appears.

Its light is dimmer than what I've grown used to seeing—it's sort of glowy, incandescent. And even though I've no idea where it leads, I start walking. Following the beautiful Persian runner that seems to go on forever, running my hands along a wall covered in hieroglyphs, my fingertips grazing the images as their likeness appears in my head—the entire story unfolding merely by touch, like some sort of telepathic Braille.

Then suddenly, with no sign or warning, I'm standing at the entrance to yet another elaborate room. Only this one is elaborate in a different way—not by carvings or murals—but by its pure unadulterated simplicity.

Its circular walls are shiny and slick, and even though they first appear to be merely white, on closer inspection I realize there's nothing *mere* about it. It's a *true* white, a white in the purest sense. One that can only result from the blending of *all* colors—an entire spectrum of pigments all merging together to create the ultimate color of light—just like I learned in art class. And other than the massive cluster of prisms hanging from the ceiling, containing what must amount to thousands of fine-cut crystals, all of them shimmering and reflecting and resulting in a kaleidoscope of color that now swirls around the room, the only other object in this space is a lone marble bench that's strangely warm and comfortable, especially for a substance known to be anything but.

And after taking a seat and folding my hands in my lap, I watch as the walls seamlessly seal up behind me as though the hallway that led me here never existed.

But I'm not afraid. Even though there's no visible exit and it appears that I'm trapped in this strange circular room, I feel safe, peaceful, cared for. As though the room is cocooning me, comforting me, its round walls like big strong arms in a welcoming hug.

I take a deep breath, wishing for answers to all of my questions, and watching as a large crystal sheet appears right before me, hovering in what was once empty space, waiting for me to make the next move.

But now that I'm so close to the answer, my question has suddenly changed.

So instead of concentrating on: *What's happened to Damen and how do I fix it?* I think: *Show me everything I need to know about Damen.*

Thinking this may be my only chance to learn everything I can about the elusive past he refuses to discuss. Convincing myself that I'm not at all prying, that I'm looking for solutions and that any information I can get will only help my cause. Besides, if I'm truly not worthy of knowing, then nothing will be revealed. So what harm is there in asking? And no sooner is the thought complete, than the crystal starts buzzing. Vibrating with energy as a flood of images fills up its face, the picture so clear it's like HDTV.

There's a small cluttered workshop, its windows covered by a swath of heavy dark cotton, its walls lit up by a profusion of candles. And Damen is there, no older than three, wearing a plain brown tunic that hangs well past his knees, and sitting at a table littered with small bubbling flasks, a pile of rocks, tins filled with colorful powders, mortars and pestles, mounds of herbs, and vials of dye. Watching as his father dips his quill into a small pot of ink and records the day's work in a series of complicated symbols, pausing every so often to read from a book titled: *Ficino's Corpus Hermeticism,* as Damen copies him, scribbling onto his own scrap of paper.

And he looks so adorable, so round-cheeked and cherubic, with the way his brown hair flops over those unmistakable dark eyes and curls down the nape of his soft baby neck, I can't help but reach toward him. It all looks so real, so accessible, and so *close,* I'm fully convinced that if I can only make contact, I can experience his world right beside him.

But just as my finger draws near, the crystal heats up to an unbearable degree and I yank my hand back, watching my skin briefly bubble and burn before healing again. Knowing the boundaries are now set, that I'm allowed to observe but not interfere.

The image fast-forwards to Damen's tenth birthday, a day deemed so special it's marked by treats and sweets and a late-afternoon visit to his father's workshop. The two of them sharing more than wavy dark hair, smooth olive skin, and a nicely squared jaw, but also a passion for perfecting the alchemical brew that promises not only to turn lead into gold but also to prolong life for an indefinite time—the perfect philosopher's stone.

They settle into their work, their established routine, with Damen grinding individual herbs with the mortar and pestle, before carefully measuring the salts, oils, colored liquids, and ores, which his father then adds to the bubbling flasks. Pausing before each step to announce what he's doing, and lecturing his son on their task:

"Transmutation is what we are after. Changing from sickness to health, from old age to youth, from lead to gold, and quite possibly, immortality too. Everything is born of one fundamental element, and if we can reduce it to its core, then we can create anything from there!"

Damen listens, rapt, hanging on to his father's every word even though he's heard the exact same speech many times before. And though they speak in Italian, a language I've never studied, somehow I understand every word.

He names each ingredient before adding it in, then deciding, just for today, to withhold the last one. Convinced that this final component, this odd-looking herb, will create even more magic if added to an elixir that's sat for three days.

After pouring the opalescent red brew into a smaller glass flask, Damen covers it carefully, then places it into a well-hidden cupboard. And they've just finished cleaning the last of their mess, when his mother—a creamy-skinned beauty in a plain watered-silk dress, her golden hair crimped at the sides and confined by a small cap at the back—stops by to call them to lunch. And her love is so apparent, so tremendously clear, illustrated in the smile she reserves for her husband, and the look she gives Damen, their dark soulful eyes a perfect mirror of each other.

And just as they're preparing to head home for lunch, three swarthy men storm through the door. Overpowering Damen's father and demanding the elixir, as his mother thrusts her son into the cupboard where it's stored—warning him to stay put, to not make a sound, until it's safe to come out.

He cowers in that dark, dank space, peering through a small knot in the wood. Watching as his father's workshop—his life's work—is destroyed by the men in their search. But even though his father turns over his notes, it's not enough to save them. And Damen trembles, watching helplessly, as both of his parents are murdered.

I sit on the white marble bench, my mind reeling, my stomach churning, feeling everything Damen feels, his swirling emotions, his deepest despair—my vision blurred by his tears, my breath hot, jagged, indistinguishable from his. We are one now. The two of us joined in unimaginable grief.

Both of us knowing the same kind of loss.

Both of us believing we were somehow at fault.

He washes their wounds and cares for their bodies, convinced that when three days have passed, he can add the final ingredient, that odd-looking herb, and bring them both back. Only to be awakened on that third and final day by a group of neighbors alerted by the smell, finding him curled up beside the bodies, the bottle of elixir clutched in his hand.

He struggles against them, retrieving the herb and desperately shoving it in. Determined to get it to his parents, to make them both drink, but overpowered by his neighbors long before he can.

Because they're convinced that he's practicing some sort of sorcery, he's declared a ward of the church, where devastated by loss and pulled from everything he knows and loves, he's abused by priests determined to rid him of the devil inside.

He suffers in silence, suffers for years—until Drina arrives. And Damen, now a strong and handsome man of fourteen, is transfixed by the sight of her flaming red hair, her emerald green eyes, her alabaster skin—her beauty so startling it's hard not to stare.

I watch them together, barely able to breathe as they form a bond so caring, so protective, I regret ever asking to see this. I was brash, impulsive, and reckless—I didn't take the time to think it all through. Because even though she's now dead and is no threat to me, watching him fall under her spell is more than I can bear.

He tends to the wounds she suffered at the hands of the priests, handling her with great reverence and care, denying his undeniable attraction, determined only to protect her, save her, to aid her escape—the day arriving much sooner than expected when the plague sweeps through Florence—the dreaded Black Death that killed millions of people, rendering them all into a bloated, pus-ridden, suffering mess.

He watches helplessly as many of his fellow orphans grow ill and die, but it's not until Drina is stricken that he returns to his father's life's work. Re-creating the elixir he'd sworn off all these years—associating it with the loss of everything he held dear. But now, left with no other choice, and unwilling to lose her, he makes Drina drink. Sparing enough for himself and the remaining orphans, hoping only to shield them from disease, having no idea it would grant immortality too.

Infused with a power they can't understand and immune to the agonized cries of the sick and dying priests, the orphans disband. Heading back to the streets of Florence where they loot from the dead, while Damen, with Drina by his side, is intent on only one thing: seeking revenge on the trio of men who murdered his parents, ultimately tracking them down only to find that without the aid of the final ingredient, they've succumbed to the plague.

He waits for their death, taunting them with the promise of a cure he never intends to fulfill. Surprised by the hollowness of the victory when their bodies finally do yield, he turns to Drina, looking for comfort in her loving embrace . . .

I shut my eyes, determined to block it all out but knowing it's burned there forever, no matter how hard I try. Because while knowing they were lovers off and on for nearly six hundred years is one thing.

Having to watch it unfold—is another.

And even though I hate to admit it, I can't help but notice how the old Damen with his cruelty, greed, and abundance of vanity—has an awful lot in common with the new Damen—the one who ditched me for Stacia.

And after watching over a century of the two of them bonded by a never-ending supply of lust and greed, I'm no longer interested in getting to the part where we meet. No longer interested in seeing the previous versions of me. If it means having to view another hundred years of this, then it just isn't worth it.

And just as I close my eyes and plead—*Just get me to the end! Please! I can't stand to see another moment of this!*—the crystal flickers and flares as a blur of images race past, fast-forwarding with such speed and intensity I can barely distinguish one image from the next. Getting only the briefest flash of Damen, Drina, and me in my many incarnations—a brunette, a redhead, a blonde—all of it whirling right past me—the face and body unrecognizable, though the eyes are always familiar.

Even when I change my mind and ask for it to slow down, the images continue to whir. Culminating in a picture of Roman—his lips curled back, his eyes filled with glee—as he gazes upon a very *aged*, very *dead* Damen.

And then—

And then—nothing.

The crystal goes blank.

"No!" I shout, my voice bouncing off the walls of the tall empty room and echoing right back at me. *"Please!"* I beg. "Come back! I'll do better. Really! I promise not to get jealous or upset. I'll watch *the whole entire thing* if you'll only just rewind!"

But no matter how much I beg, no matter how much I plead to view it again, the crystal is gone, vanished from sight.

I gaze all around, searching for someone to help, some sort of akashic record reference librarian, even though I'm the only one here. Dropping my head in my hands, wondering how I could've been so stupid as to allow my petty jealousies and insecurities to take over again.

I mean, it's not like I didn't know about Drina and Damen. It's not like I didn't know what I was going to see. And now, since I was too big of a wuss to just suck it up and deal with the info before me, I've no idea how to save him. No idea of how we possibly could've gone from such a wonderful A to such a horrible Z.

All I know is that Roman's responsible. A pathetic confirmation of what I already guessed. Somehow he's weakening Damen, reversing his immortality. And if I've any hope of saving him, I need to learn *how* if not *why*.

Because one thing I know for sure is that Damen does *not* age. He's been around for over six hundred years and still looks like a teen.

I drop my head in my hands, hating myself for being so petty, so small, so foolish—so heinously pathetic, that I robbed myself of the answers I came here to know. Wishing I could rewind this whole session and start over—wishing I could go back—

"You can't go back."

I turn, hearing Romy's voice sneak up from behind me, and wondering how she found her way into this room. But when I look around, I realize I'm no longer in that beautiful circular space, I'm back in the hall. A few tables away from where the monks, priests, shamans, and rabbis once were.

"And you should never fast-forward into the future. Because every time you do, you rob yourself of the journey, the present moment, which, in the end, is all there really is."

I turn, wondering if she's referring to my crystal tablet debacle or life in general.

But she just smiles. "You okay?"

I shrug and look away. I mean, why bother explaining? She probably already knows anyway.

"Nope." She leans against the table and shakes her head. "I don't know a thing. Whatever happens in here is yours and yours to keep. I just heard your cry of distress so I thought I'd check in. That's all. Nothing more, nothing less."

"And where's your evil twin?" I ask, gazing around, wondering if she's hiding somewhere.

But Romy just smiles and motions for me to follow. "She's outside, keeping an eye on your friend."

"Ava's here?" I ask, surprised by how relieved that makes me feel. Especially considering how I'm still annoyed with her for ditching me like that.

But Romy just waves again, leading me through the front door and out to the steps where Ava is waiting.

"Where've you been?" I ask, my question sounding more like an accusation.

"I got a little sidetracked." She shrugs. "This place is so amazing, I—" She looks at me, hoping I'll lighten up and cut her a break, and averting her gaze when it's clear that I won't.

"How'd you end up here? Did Romy and Rayne—" But when I turn, I realize they're gone.

Ava squints, her fingers playing with the newly manifested gold hoops at her ear. "I desired to find you, so I ended up here. But I can't seem to get inside." She frowns at the door. "So is this it? Is this the hall you were looking for?"

I nod, taking in her expensive shoes and designer handbag, and growing more annoyed by the second. Here I take her to Summerland so she can help me save someone's life, and all she wants to do is go shopping.

"I *know,*" she says, responding to the thoughts in my head. "I got carried away, and I'm sorry. But I'm ready to help if you still need it. Or did you get all the answers you sought?"

I press my lips together and gaze down at the ground, shaking my head when I say, "I um—I ran into some trouble." A flood of shame washes right over me, especially when I remember how the *trouble* was pretty much of my making. "And I'm afraid I'm right back where I started," I add, feeling like the world's biggest loser.

"Maybe I can help?" She smiles, squeezing my arm so I'll know she's sincere.

But I just shrug, doubting she can do much of anything at this point.

"Don't give up so easily," she says. "After all, this is Summerland, anything is possible here!"

I glance at her, knowing it's true but also knowing I've got some serious work to do back home on the earth plane. Work that's going to require all of my attention and focus, no distractions allowed.

So as I lead her down the stairs, I look at her and say, "Well, there's one thing you can do."

twenty-seven

Even though Ava wanted to stay, I pretty much grabbed hold of her hand and forced her to leave, knowing we'd both wasted plenty of time in Summerland already and I had other places to be.

"Damn!" She squints at her fingers just after we land on the floor cushions in her small purple room. "I was hoping they'd keep."

I nod, noticing how the jewel-encrusted gold rings she'd manifested have returned to her usual silver, while the designer shoes and handbag didn't survive the trip either.

"I was wondering about that," I say, rising to my feet. "But you know you can do that here, right? You can manifest anything you want, you just have to be patient." I smile, wishing to leave things on a positive note by repeating the exact same pep talk Damen gave me back when my lessons first began. Lessons I wished I'd paid a lot more attention to now, having assumed that being immortal meant we had nothing but time. Besides, I'm starting to feel guilty for being so hard on her. I mean, who wouldn't get a little carried away on their first visit to that place?

"So what now?" she calls, following me to the front door. "When do we go back? I mean, you won't return without me—will you?"

I turn, my eyes meeting hers, seeing how consumed she is with her visit and wondering if I'd made a mistake by taking her there.

Avoiding her eyes as I head for my car, calling over my shoulder to say, "I'll give you a call."

The next morning I pull into the parking lot and head for class. Merging into the usual swarm of students just like any other day, except this time I don't strive to keep my distance and maintain my personal space. Instead, I just go with the flow. Not reacting in the slightest when random people brush up against me, despite the fact that I left my iPod, hoodie, and sunglasses at home.

But that's because I'm no longer reliant on those old accessories that never worked all that well anyway. Now I carry my quantum remote wherever I go.

Yesterday, just as Ava and I were about to leave Summerland, I asked her to help me build a better shield. Knowing I could just go back into the hall while she waited outside and receive the answer on my own, but since she wanted to help, and figuring she might learn something too, we lingered at the bottom of the steps, both of us focusing our energy on *desiring* a shield that would allow us (well, me mostly, since Ava doesn't hear thoughts and get life stories by touch) to tune in and out at will. And the next thing you know, we both looked at each other and at the exact same second said, *"A quantum remote!"*

So now, whenever I want to hear someone's thoughts I just surf over to their energy field and hit *select*. And if I don't want to be bothered, I hit *mute*. Just like the remote I have at home. Only this one is invisible so I can pretty much take it everywhere I go.

I head into English, arriving early so I can observe all the action from start to finish. Not wanting to miss a single second of my planned surveillance. Because even though I have visual proof that Roman's responsible for what's happening to Damen—it gets me only so far. And now that the *who* part of the equation is solved, it's time to move on to the *how* and *why*.

I just hope it doesn't take too long. I mean, for one thing, I miss Damen. And for another, I'm so low on immortal juice I'm already forced to ration it. And since Damen never got around to giving me the recipe, I've no idea how to replace it, much less what will happen without it. Though I'm sure it's not good.

Originally, Damen thought he could just drink the elixir once and be cured of all ills. And while that worked for the first one hundred and fifty years, when he started to see subtle signs of aging he decided to drink it again. And then again. Until he ultimately became totally dependent.

He also didn't realize that an immortal could be killed until after I took down his ex-wife, Drina. And while both of us were sure that targeting the weakest chakra was the only method (the heart chakra in Drina's case), and while I'm still sure that we're the only ones who know that—according to what I saw yesterday in the akashic records, Roman's discovered another way. Which means if I have any hope of saving Damen, I need to learn what Roman knows, before it's too late.

When the door finally opens, I lift my gaze as a horde of students burst in. And even though it's not the first time I've seen it, it's still hard to watch them all laughing and joking and getting along, when just last week they barely acknowledged each other. And even though it's pretty much the kind of scene anyone would dream of seeing in their school, under the circumstances, it's not giving me the thrill that it should.

And not just because I'm stuck on the outside looking in, but because it's creepy, unnatural, and weird. I mean, high schools don't operate like this. Heck, *people* don't operate like this. Like will always seek like and that's just the way it is. It's just one of those unspoken rules. Besides, this isn't something they've *chosen* to do. Because little do they realize that all of that hugging, laughing, and ridiculous high-fiving is not because of their newfound love for each other—it's because of Roman.

Like a master puppeteer controlling his subjects for his own amusement—Roman is responsible. And while I don't know *how* or *why* he's doing it, and while I can't prove that he actually *is* doing it, I just know in my heart that it's true. It's as clear as the ping in my gut or the chill that blankets my skin whenever he's near.

I watch as Damen slides onto his seat as Stacia leans on his desk, her heavily padded pushed-up chest looming close to his face as she swings her hair over her shoulder and laughs at her own stupid wit. And even though I can't *hear* the joke since I purposely tuned her out in order to better hear Damen, the fact that he thinks it's stupid, is good enough for me.

It also gives me a small burst of hope.

A burst of hope that soon ends the second his attention returns to her cleavage.

I mean, he's so banal, so juvenile, and to be honest—completely embarrassing. And if I thought my feelings were hurt yesterday, when I was forced to watch him make out with Drina, well, in retrospect, that was nothing compared to *this*.

Because Drina was *then*, nothing more than a beautiful, empty, shallow image on a rock.

But Stacia is *now*.

And even though she's beautiful, empty, and shallow too—she happens to be standing right before me in all of her three-dimensional glory.

I listen to Damen's diluted brain wax all rhapsodic over the virtues and abundance of Stacia's heavily padded chest, and I can't help but wonder if this is his *real* taste in women.

If these bratty, greedy, vain girls are the kind of females he *truly* prefers.

And if I'm just some weird anomaly, some quirky odd fluke, that kept getting in the way the last four hundred years.

I keep my eye on him all through class, watching from my lone seat in the back. Automatically answering Mr. Robins's questions without even thinking, just repeating the answer I *see* in his head. My mind never straying from Damen, reminding myself, again and again, of who he *really* is: That despite all appearances, he's good, kind, caring, and loyal—the undisputed love of my numerous lives. And that this version sitting before me is *not* the real deal—no matter how much it may mirror some of the behaviors revealed yesterday—it's not who he is.

And when the bell finally rings, I follow him. Keeping tabs on him all through second period P.E. (mostly because I don't go), choosing to linger outside his classroom when I'm supposed to be running track. Slipping out of sight the moment I sense the hall monitors about to stroll by, then returning as soon as they've passed. Peering at him through the window and eavesdropping on all of his thoughts, just like the stalker he's accused me of being. Not knowing whether to feel disturbed or relieved when I discover that his attentions aren't strictly relegated to Stacia—that they're pretty much available for whoever's semi–good-looking and sitting nearby—unless, of course, that someone is *me*.

And while third period is also spent spying on Damen, by fourth, I switch my focus to Roman. Looking him right in the eye as I head for my desk, swiveling around and acknowledging him whenever I sense that he's focused on me. And even though his thoughts about me are as banal and embarrassing as Damen's thoughts about Stacia, I refuse to blush or react. I just keep smiling and nodding, determined to grin and bear it, because if I'm going to find out who this guy *really is*, then avoiding him like the Black Plague will no longer do.

So when the bell rings, I decide to break free from this outcast pariah *spaz* role I'm unwillingly cast in, and head straight for the long line of tables. Ignoring the ping in my gut that gets worse with each step, determined to land myself a spot and sit with the rest of my class.

And when Roman nods as I make my approach, I can't help but feel disappointed that he's not nearly as surprised as I'd assumed he would be.

"Ever!" He smiles, patting the narrow space right next to him. "So it wasn't just my imagination. We really did share a moment in class."

I smile tightly and squeeze in beside him, my gaze instinctively switching to Damen, but only for a moment before I force myself to look away. Reminding myself that I need to stay focused on Roman, that it's imperative not to get sidetracked.

"I knew you'd come around eventually. I just wish it 'adn't taken so long. We've so much lost time to make up for." He leans in, his face looming so close I can see the individual flecks of color in his eyes, brilliant points of violet that would be so easy to get lost in—

"This is *nice*. Isn't this *nice*? Everyone together like this—all joined as one. And all this time you were the missing link. But now that you're 'ere, my mission's complete. And you thought it couldn't be done." He tilts his head back and laughs—eyes closed, teeth exposed, as his tousled golden hair catches the glint of the sun. And even though I hate to admit it, the truth is, he's mesmerizing.

Not in the same way as Damen, in fact, not even close. Roman's good looking in a way that reminds me of my old life, having just the right amount of superficial charm and well-calculated hotness that I would've fallen for before. Back when I accepted things at face value and rarely, if ever, looked past the surface.

I watch as he takes a bite of his Mars bar, then I switch my gaze back to Damen. Taking in his gorgeous dark profile as my heart fills with such overwhelming longing I can hardly bear it. Watching his hands flail about as he amuses Stacia with some stupid story, though

I'm far less interested in the anecdote than the hands themselves, remembering how wonderful they once felt on my skin—

". . . so, as nice as it is to have you join us, I can't help but wonder what this is *really* about," Roman says, his eyes still on me.

But I'm still looking at Damen. Watching as he presses his lips against Stacia's cheek, before working their way around her ear and down the length of her neck . . .

"Because as much as I'd like to pretend you were overcome by my undeniable good looks and charm, I know better. So tell me, Ever, what gives?"

I can hear Roman talking, his voice droning on and on in the background like a vague incessant hum that's easy to ignore, but my gaze stays on Damen—the love of my life, my eternal soul mate who's completely unaware of the fact that I even exist. My stomach twisting as his lips brush over her collarbone before heading back to her ear, his mouth moving softly as he whispers to her, trying to coax her into ditching the rest of their classes so they can head back to his house . . .

Wait—coax her? He's trying to convince *her? Does that mean she's not ready and willing?*

Am I the only one around here who just assumed they'd already jumped each other's bones?

But just as I'm about to tune in to Stacia and see what she could possibly be up to by playing hard to get, Roman taps me on the arm and says, "Aw, come on, Ever. Don't be shy. Tell me what you're doing here. Tell me just exactly what it is that put you over the edge."

And before I can even reply, Stacia looks at me and says, "Jeez, Spaz, *stare much*?"

I don't respond. I just pretend I didn't hear while I focus on Damen. Refusing to acknowledge her presence, even though they're so entwined they're practically fused. Wishing he'd just turn around and *see* me—really *see* me—in the way that he used to.

But when he does finally look, his gaze goes right through me, as though I'm not worth the bother, as though I'm invisible now.

And seeing him glance through me like that leaves me numb, breathless, frozen, unable to move—

"Um, hel-*lo*?" Stacia shouts, loud enough for everyone to hear. "I mean, seriously. Can we *help* you? Can *anyone* help you?"

I glance at Miles and Haven sitting just a few feet away, watching as they shake their heads, both of them wishing they'd never had anything to do with me. Then I swallow hard and remind myself that they're not in control—that Roman's the writer, producer, director, and creator of this God-awful show.

I meet Roman's gaze, my stomach twisting, pinging, as I peer into the thoughts in his head. Determined to dig past the superficial layer of the usual inane stuff, curious to see if there's anything more than the horny, annoying, sugar-addicted teen he portrays himself to be. Because the fact is, I'm not buying it. The image I saw on that crystal, with the evil grin of victory spread wide across his face, hints at a much darker side. And as his smile grows wider and his gaze narrows on mine—everything dims.

Everything except Roman and me.

I'm hurtling through a tunnel, pulled faster and faster by a force beyond my control. Slipping uncontrollably into the dark abyss of his mind, as Roman carefully selects the scenes he wants me to see—Damen throwing a party in our suite at the Montage, a party that includes Stacia, Honor, Craig, and all the other kids who never talked to us before, a party that lasts several days, until he's finally kicked out for trashing the place. Forcing me to view all manner of unsavory acts, stuff I'd rather not see—culminating on the final image I saw on the crystal that day—the very last scene.

I fall back from my seat, landing on the ground in a tangle of limbs, still caught in his grip. Finally coming around just as the entire school breaks into a shrill mocking chorus of "*Spaz!*" And watching in horror as my spilled red elixir races across the tabletop and drips down the sides.

"You *all right*?" Roman asks, gazing at me as I struggle to stand. "I know it's tough to watch. Believe me, Ever, I've been there. But it's all for the best, really it is. And I'm afraid you'll just have to trust me on that."

"I *knew* it was you," I whisper, standing before him, shaking with rage. "I knew it all along."

"So you did." He smiles. "So you did. Score one for you. Though I should warn you, I'm still a good ten points ahead."

"You won't get away with this," I say, watching in horror as he dips his middle finger into the puddle of my spilled red drink, allowing the drops to fall onto his tongue in such a deliberate, measured way, it's like he's trying to tell me something, give me a nudge.

But just as an idea begins to form in my head, he licks his lips and says, "But see, that's where you're wrong." Turning his head in a way that displays the mark on his neck, the finely detailed Ouroboros tattoo now flashing in and out of view. "I've already gotten away with it, Ever." He smiles. "I've already won."

twenty-eight

I didn't go to art. I left right after lunch.

No, scratch that. Because the truth is I left in the *middle* of lunch. Seconds after my horrible encounter with Roman, I sprinted for the parking lot (chased by a never-ending chorus of *Spaz!*), where I jumped in my car and sped away long before the bell was scheduled to ring.

I needed to get away from Roman. To put some distance between me and his creepy tattoo—the intricate Ouroboros design that flashed in and out of view just like the one on Drina's wrist used to do.

The undeniable symbol marking Roman as a rogue immortal—just as I'd thought all along.

And even though Damen failed to warn me of them, didn't even know they existed until Drina went bad, I still can't believe it took me so long to get it. I mean, even though he eats and drinks, even though his aura is visible and his thoughts are available to read (well, for me anyway), I realize now it was all a façade. Like those buildings on Hollywood back lots that are carefully crafted to look like something they're not. And that's what Roman did—he purposely projected this happy-go-lucky, jolly young lad from England veneer, with his bright shiny aura, and happy, horny thoughts, when all the while, deep down inside, he's anything but.

The real Roman is dark.

And sinister.

And evil.

And everything else that adds up to *bad*. But even worse is the fact that he's out to kill my boyfriend, and I still don't know why.

Because motive was the one thing in my brief but disturbing visit to the inner recesses of his mind that I failed to see.

And motive will prove very important if I'm ever forced to kill him, since it's imperative to hit just the right chakra to be rid of him for good. And not knowing the motive means I could fail.

I mean, would I go for the first chakra—or root chakra, as it's sometimes called—the center for anger, violence, and greed? Or maybe the navel chakra, or sacral center, which is where envy and jealousy live. But with no idea of what's driving him, it'd be far too easy to hit the wrong one. Which would not only serve in *not* killing him but would probably make him incredibly angry as well. Leaving me with six more chakras to choose from, and at that point, I'm afraid he'd catch on.

Besides, killing Roman too soon will only hurt me—ensuring he takes his secret of whatever he's done to Damen and the rest of the school along with him. And that's one risk I just can't afford. Not to mention that I'm really not all that big on killing people anyway. The only times I've ever gotten physical in the past are when I was left with no choice but to fight or die. And as soon as I realized what I'd done to Drina, I hoped I'd never have to do it again. Because even though she killed me many times before, even though she admitted to killing my entire family—including my dog—that doesn't do much to alleviate the guilt. I mean, knowing I'm solely responsible for her ultimate exit makes me feel awful.

And since I'm pretty much right back where I started, I decide to head back to the beginning. Turning right on Coast Highway and heading for Damen's, figuring I'll use the next couple hours while they're all still at school to break into his house and take a good look around.

I pull up to the guard post, wave at Sheila, and continue toward the gate. Naturally assuming it would open before me, and having to slam on my brakes to avoid major front-end damage when it stays put.

"Excuse me. *Excuse me!*" Sheila shouts, storming toward my car as though I'm some kind of intruder, as though she's never seen me before. When the truth is, up until last week, I was pretty much here every day.

"Hey, Sheila." I smile in a nice, friendly, nonthreatening way. "I'm just heading up to Damen's, so if you could just open the gate, I'll be on my way and—"

She looks at me, her eyes narrowed, her lips pressed together in a thin grim line. "I'm going to have to ask you to leave."

"What? But *why*?"

"You're off the list," she says, hands planted firmly on hips, her face betraying not even the slightest trace of remorse after all those months of smiling and waving.

I sit there, lips pressed together, allowing the words to sink in.

I'm off the list. I'm off the permanent list. Blackballed or blacklisted or whatever it's called when you're denied access to a glorious gated community for an indefinite time.

Which would be bad enough on its own, but having to hear the official breakup message delivered by Big Sheila instead of my boyfriend—makes it even worse.

I gaze down at my lap, gripping the gearshift so hard it threatens to pop off in my hand. Then I swallow hard and look at her when I say, "Well, as you've obviously been made aware, Damen and I broke up. But I was just hoping to drop in real quick and retrieve a few of my things, because as you can see—" I unzip my bag and quickly shove my hand inside. "I still have the key."

I raise it up high, watching as the noonday sun catches and reflects the gold shiny metal, too caught up in my own mortification to foresee that she'd reach out and snatch it.

"Now, I'm asking you nicely to vacate the premises," she says, shoving the key deep into her pocket, its shape visible as the fabric strains over her mammoth-sized breasts. Barely giving me enough time to switch my foot from the brake to the gas before adding, "Go on now. Back up. Don't you make me ask twice."

twenty-nine

This time when I arrive in Summerland, I skip the usual landing in that vast fragrant field, choosing instead to touch down smack in the middle of what I now like to think of as the main drag. Then I pick myself up and brush myself off, amazed to see everyone around me just carrying on with their normal business, as though seeing someone drop right out of the sky and onto the street is a normal, everyday occurrence. Though I guess in these parts it is.

I make my way past karaoke bars and hair salons, retracing the steps Romy and Rayne showed me, knowing I can probably just *desire* to be there instead, but still anxious to learn my own way around. And after a quick pass through the alley and a sudden turn onto the boulevard, I run up those steep marble steps and stand before those massive front doors, watching as they swing open for me.

I step into the great marble hall, noticing how it's much more crowded than the last time I was here. Reviewing the questions in my head, unsure if I need the akashic records or if I can just get my answers right here. Wondering if questions like *Exactly who is Roman and what has he done to Damen?* and: *How can I stop him and spare Damen's life?* require that kind of secured access.

But then, feeling like I need to simplify and sum it all up in one tidy sentence, I close my eyes and think: *Basically, what I want to know is: How can I return everything back to the way it was before?*

And as soon as the thought is complete, a doorway opens before me, its warm inviting light beckoning me in as I enter a solid white room, that same sort of rainbow white as before, only this time, rather than a white marble bench, there's a worn leather recliner instead.

I move toward it, plopping onto the seat, extending the leg rest, and settling in. Unaware that I'm lounging on an exact replica of my dad's favorite chair until I see the initials *R.B.* and *E.B.* scratched onto its arm. Gasping when I recognize it as the exact same markings I convinced Riley to make with her Girl Scout camping knife. The exact same markings that not only proved we were the culprits but also earned us a week's worth of restriction.

Or at least until mine got extended to ten days when my parents realized I'd coached her into doing it—a fact that, in their eyes, made me the pre-calculating perpetrator who clearly deserved extra time.

I run my fingers over the gouged leather, my nails digging into the stuffing where the curve of her *R* went too deep. Choking back a sob as I remember that day. *All* of those days. Every single one of those deliciously wonderful days that I once took for granted but now find myself missing so much I can barely stand it.

I'd do *anything* to go back. *Anything* if it meant I could return and put it all back to the way it once was—

And no sooner is the thought complete, when the formerly empty space begins to transform. Rearranging itself from a nearly empty room with a lone recliner to an exact replica of our old den in Oregon.

The air infused with the scent of my mom's famous brownies, as the walls morph from pearlescent white to the soft beige-like hue she referred to as *driftwood pearl*. And when the three-colors-of-blue afghan my grandma knit suddenly covers my knees, I gaze toward the door, seeing Buttercup's leash hanging on the knob, and Riley's old sneakers lying next to my dad's. Watching as all the pieces fill in, until every photo, book, and knickknack are present and accounted for. And I can't help but wonder if this is because of my question, because I asked for everything to return to the way it was before.

Because the truth is, I was actually referring to Damen and me.

Wasn't I?

I mean, is it really possible to *go back in time*?

Or is this lifelike replica, this Bloom family diorama, the closest I'll ever get?

But just as I'm questioning my surroundings and the true meaning of what I actually meant, the TV turns on, and a flash of colors race across the screen—a screen made of crystal, just like the crystal I viewed the other day.

I pull the afghan tighter around me, tucking it snugly under my knees, as the words L'HEURE BLEUE fill up the screen. And just as I'm wondering what it could possibly mean, a definition scripted in the most beautiful calligraphy appears, stating:

> ***A French expression,* l'heure bleue, *or "blue hour" refers to the hour experienced between daylight and darkness. A time revered for its quality of light, and also when the scent of flowers is at its strongest.***

I squint at the screen, watching as the words fade and a picture of the moon takes its place—a full and glorious moon—shimmering the most beautiful shade of blue—a hue that nearly matches the sky . . .

And then—and then I see *me*—up on that very same screen. Dressed in jeans and a black sweater, my hair hanging loose, gazing out a window at that same blue moon—glancing at my watch as though I'm waiting for something—something that's soon to arrive. And despite the fuzzy, dreamlike state of watching a me that's not *really* me, I can still feel what she's feeling, hear what she's thinking. She's going somewhere, somewhere she once thought was off limits. Anxiously waiting for the moment when the sky turns the same shade as the moon, a wonderful deep dark blue with no trace of the sun—knowing it heralds her only chance to find her way back to this room and return to a place she once thought was lost.

I watch, my gaze glued to the screen, gasping as she raises her hand, presses her finger to the crystal, and is pulled back in time.

thirty

I tear out of the hall and sprint down the steps. My vision so blurred, my heart pounding so fast, I'm completely unaware of Romy and Rayne until it's too late, and Rayne is crumpled beneath me.

"Omigod, I'm so sorry, I—"

I bend down, my hand outstretched, waiting for her to grab hold of it so I can help her to her feet, asking repeatedly if she's all right, and wincing with embarrassment when she ignores my gesture and struggles to stand. Straightening her skirt and pulling up her kneesocks as I watch in amazement as her skinned knees instantly heal—never having considered the possibility that they might be like me.

"Are—are you—"

But before I can even get to the word, Rayne shakes her head and says, "We are most certainly *not.*" Making sure her kneesocks are of exact equal height. "We are *nothing* like *you,*" she mumbles, straightening her blue blazer and plaid skirt, then glancing at her much nicer sister who's shaking her head.

"Rayne, please. Remember your manners." Romy frowns.

But even though Rayne continues to glare, her voice loses some of its steam when she says, "Well, we're *not.*"

"So—so you know about me?" I ask, hearing Rayne think: *Well, duh!* As Romy nods her head solemnly. "And you think that I'm *bad*?"

Rayne rolls her eyes, while Romy smiles gently, saying, "Please, ignore my sister. We think nothing of the sort. We are in no position to judge."

I glance between them, taking in their pale skin, huge dark eyes, razor-slashed bangs, and thin lips, their features so exaggerated they're like Manga characters come to life. And I can't help but think how strange it is for two people to be so identical on the outside and yet so opposite inside.

"So, tell us what you've learned," Romy says, smiling as she heads down the street, assuming we'll all just follow along—which we do. "Did you find all the answers you seek?"

And more.

I've been wide-eyed and speechless ever since that crystal went blank. Having no idea what to make of the knowledge I've been given, but well aware of the fact that it holds the potential to change not only my life but quite possibly the world. And while I have to admit that it's pretty amazing to have access to such powerful wisdom, the responsibility that goes with it is undeniably huge.

I mean, what am I expected to *do* with it now that I know? Was I shown the information for a reason? Some kind of big global reason? Is there some new expectation of me of which I'm not even aware? And if not, then what's the point?

Seriously—*why me?*

Surely I'm not the first person to ask that sort of question.

Am I?

And the only plausible answer I can seem to come up with is: Maybe I'm meant to go back. Maybe I'm meant to return.

Not to halt assassinations, stop wars, and basically change the course of history—I just don't think I'm the right girl for that job.

Though I do think I've been shown this information for a reason—one that leads right back to what I've been thinking all along: That this whole scenario of the accident, my psychic powers, and Damen making me an immortal has all been a terrible mistake. And that if I can just pop back in time and stop the accident from ever happening—then I can put it all back to the way it was before. I can go back to Oregon and re-enter my old life like my new life never even occurred. Which is what I've wished for all along.

But where does that leave Damen? Does he go back too?

And if so, will he still be with Drina until she manages to kill me, and everything happens all over again?

Will I just be delaying the inevitable?

Or does everything stay the same except me? Does he die at Roman's hands while I'm back in Oregon, completely unaware he exists?

And if that's the case, then how can I let that happen?

How can I turn my back on the one and only person I've ever truly loved?

I shake my head, noticing Romy and Rayne still looking at me, waiting for an answer, though I've no idea what to say. So, instead, I just stand there, my mouth hanging open like a ginormous dork. Thinking how even in Summerland, a place of absolute love and perfection, I'm still a total dweeb.

Romy smiles, closing her eyes as her arms fill with red tulips—beautiful red tulips she promptly offers to me.

But I refuse to take them. I just narrow my eyes and start backing away. "What are you doing?" I glance between them, my voice tenuous, fragile, noticing how they look just as confused as I am.

"I'm sorry," Romy says, trying to ease my alarm. "I'm not sure why I did it. The thought just popped into my head, and so—"

I watch as the tulips dissolve from her fingers, going back to wherever they came from. But having them gone doesn't make the least bit of difference, and all I want now is for them to go too.

"Isn't *anything* private around here?" I shout, knowing I'm overreacting but unable to stop. Because if those tulips were some kind of message, if she was listening in on my thoughts and trying to persuade me to give up the past and stay put, well, it's just none of her business. They may know all about Summerland, but they know *nothing* about me, and they've no right to butt in. They've never had to make a decision like this. They've no idea how it feels to lose every single person you've ever loved.

I take another step back, seeing Rayne furrow her brow as Romy shakes her head, saying, "We didn't hear a thing. Honest. We can't read *all* of your thoughts, Ever. Only the ones we're permitted to see. Whatever you see in the akashic records is yours and yours to keep. We are merely concerned by your distress. That is all. Nothing more, nothing less."

I narrow my eyes, not trusting her for a second. They've probably been snooping in my thoughts all along. I mean, why else give me the tulips? Why else manifest such a thing?

"I wasn't even visiting the akashic records," I say. "This room was—" I pause, swallowing hard as I remember the smell of my mom's brownies, the feel of my grandma's blanket, and knowing I can have it all again. All I have to do is wait for the right day and time and I can return to my family and friends. I shake my head and shrug. "This room was *different*."

"The Akashic Hall has many faces." Romy nods. "It becomes whatever you need it to be." She looks at me, her eyes roaming over my face as she says, "We only showed up to help, not to upset or confuse you."

"So, what? You're like my guardian angels or spirit guides? Two private-school-uniform-wearing fairy godmothers?"

"Not quite." Romy laughs.

"Then who are you? And what're you doing here? And how come you always manage to find me?"

Rayne glares and pulls on her sister's sleeve, urging her to leave. But Romy stays put, looking me in the eye when she says, "We are only here to aid and assist. That is all you need to know."

I look at her for a moment, glance at her sister, then shake my head and walk away. They're deliberately mysterious and way beyond weird, and I've a pretty good hunch their intentions aren't good.

Even as Romy calls out from behind me, I keep going. Eager to put some distance between us as I head for an auburn-haired woman waiting just outside the theater, the one who, from behind anyway, looks exactly like Ava.

thirty-one

The huge disappointment I felt when I tapped that auburn-haired woman on the shoulder only to discover she wasn't Ava, made me realize just how badly I need to talk to her. So I exit Summerland and land back in my car, plopping onto the driver's seat right in front of the Trader Joe's in the Crystal Cove Promenade parking lot, and startling an unsuspecting shopper so badly she drops both her bags, scattering numerous cans of coffee and soup under a whole row of cars. And I promise myself that from now on, I'll make sure my exits and entries are a bit more discreet.

When I get to Ava's, she's in the middle of a reading, so I wait in her bright sunny kitchen while she finishes up. And even though I know it's none of my business, even though I know I shouldn't be snooping, I go right for my quantum remote and access their session, amazed by the amount of accuracy and detail Ava provides.

"Impressive," I say, after her client is gone and she comes into the kitchen to join me. "*Very* impressive. Seriously, I had no idea." I smile, watching as she goes through her usual ritual of filling the teapot to boil, then placing some cookies onto a plate and pushing it my way.

"That's quite a compliment coming from you." She smiles, taking the seat just across from me. "Though if I remember right, I gave you a pretty accurate reading once too."

I reach for a cookie, knowing it's expected. And when I lick the little bits of sugar from the top, I can't help but feel sad that it no longer holds the allure that it used to.

"You remember that reading? On Halloween night?" She watches me closely.

I nod. I remember it well. That's the night I discovered she could see Riley. Up until then I'd been sure I was the only one who could communicate with my dead little sister, and I wasn't too happy to learn that was no longer the case.

"Did you tell your client she's dating a loser?" I break the cookie in half. "That he's cheating on her with someone she thinks is a friend and that she should dump them both ASAP?" I ask, removing some crumbs that fell onto my lap.

"In so many words," she says, getting up to fetch our tea the moment the pot starts to whistle. "Though I can only hope you'll learn to soften the message if you ever decide to give readings."

I pause, overcome by a sudden pang of sadness when I realize just how long it's been since I last thought about my future, about what I might want to be when I grow up. I went through so many phases—wanting to be a park ranger, a teacher, an astronaut, a supermodel, a pop star—the list was endless. But now that I'm immortal, now that I'm in a position to try out *all* of those things over the course of the next thousand-plus years—I no longer feel that ambitious.

Lately, all I've been thinking about is how to get Damen back.

And now, after this last trip to Summerland, all I can think about is getting the old me back.

I mean, having the entire world at my feet is not so enticing when there's no one to share it with.

"I—I'm still not sure what I want to do. I haven't really thought about it," I lie, wondering if it will be easy for me to slip back into my old life—if I decide to return to it, that is. And if I'll still want to be a pop star like I used to, or if the changes I've experienced here will follow me there.

But when I look at Ava, watching as she lifts her cup to her lips and blows twice before sipping, I remember that I didn't come here to discuss my future. I came to discuss my past. Deciding to bring her into my confidence and share some of my biggest secrets. Convinced not only that I can trust her but that she'll be able to help me as well.

Because the truth is, I need someone I can count on. There's just no way I can go it alone. And it's not about helping me decide whether I should stay or go, because I'm beginning to realize I really don't have much of a choice. I mean, the thought of leaving Damen—the thought of never seeing him again—is almost more painful than I can bear. But when I think about my family, and how they unwittingly sacrificed their lives for me—either because of a stupid blue sweatshirt I insisted my dad return for, which ultimately caused the accident that killed everyone—or because Drina intentionally made the deer run in front of our car so she could be rid of me and have Damen to herself—I feel I have to do something to make it all right.

Because either way you look at it, it leads back to *me*. It's my fault they're no longer living their lives, it's my fault their bright shiny futures were cut so tragically short. If I hadn't gotten in the way, none of this ever would've happened. And even though Riley insisted it all turned out the way it was meant to, the fact that I'm being given the choice just proves that I need to sacrifice my future with Damen so they can have theirs.

It's the right thing to do.

It's the *only* thing to do.

And with the way things are going, with my social exile from school, Ava's pretty much my only friend left. Which means I'll need her to pick up any stray pieces I might leave behind.

I bring my teacup to my lips, then set it back down without drinking. Tracing my fingers around the curve of the handle as I take a deep breath and say, "I think someone's poisoning Damen." Seeing her eyes bug out as she gapes. "I—I think someone's tampering with his—" *Elixir* "—favorite drink. And it's making him act—" *Mortal* "—normal, but not in a good way." I press my lips together and rise from my seat, barely giving her a chance to catch her breath when I say, "And since I'm banned from the gate, I'm gonna need you to help me break in."

thirty-two

"Okay, we're here. Just act cool," I say, crouching down in the back as Ava approaches the gate. "Just nod and smile and give her the name I told you."

I pull my legs in, trying to make myself smaller, less obtrusive, a task that would've been a heck of a lot easier just two weeks ago, before I was faced with this ridiculous growth spurt. Crouching down even farther and pulling the blanket tighter around me as Ava lowers her window and smiles at Sheila, giving her the name of Stacia Miller (my replacement on Damen's list of welcomed guests), who I hope hasn't come around quite enough yet for Sheila to recognize her.

And the moment the gate swings open and we're headed for Damen's, I toss the blanket aside and climb onto the seat, seeing Ava gaze around the neighborhood with obvious envy, shaking her head and muttering, "Swanky."

I shrug and glance around too, never having given it much notice before. Always viewing this place as a blur of phony Tuscan farmhouses and upscale Spanish haciendas with well-landscaped yards and subterranean garages one has to pass in order to reach Damen's faux French chateau.

"I have no idea how he affords it, but it sure is nice," she says, glancing at me.

"He plays the ponies," I mumble, concentrating on the garage door as she pulls into his drive, taking note of its most minute details before closing my eyes and *willing* for it to open.

Seeing it rise and lift in my mind, then opening my eyes just in time to watch it sputter and spurt before dropping back down with a very loud *thud.* An unmistakable sign that I'm still a long way from mastering psychokinesis—or the art of moving anything heavier than a Prada bag.

"Um, I think we should just go around back like I usually do," I say, feeling embarrassed for failing so miserably.

But Ava won't hear of it, grabbing my bag and heading for the front door. And even when I scramble behind, telling her it's no use, that it's locked and we can't possibly enter that way, she just keeps going, claiming we'll just have to unlock it then.

"It's not as easy as you think," I tell her. "Believe me, I've tried it before and it didn't work." Glancing at the extra door I accidentally manifested the last time I was here—the one that's still leaning against the far wall, which is exactly where I left it since apparently Damen's too busy acting cool and chasing Stacia to take the time to get rid of it.

But the moment I think that, I wish I could erase it. The thought leaves me sad, empty, and feeling far more desperate than I care to admit.

"Well, this time you have *me* to help." She smiles. "And I think we've already proved just how well we work together."

And the way she looks at me, with such anticipation, such optimism, I can't see the point in refusing to try. So I close my eyes as we both join hands, envisioning the door springing open before us. And just seconds after hearing the dead bolt slide back, the door opens wide, allowing us in.

"After you." Ava nods, glancing at her watch and scrunching her brow as she says, "Tell me again, exactly how much time do we have here?"

I gaze at my wrist, seeing the crystal horseshoe bracelet Damen gave me that day at the track, the one that makes my heart swell with longing every time I see it. Yet I refuse to remove it. I mean, I just can't. It's my only physical reminder of what we once had.

"Hey? You okay?" she asks, her face creased with concern.

I swallow hard and nod. "We should be okay on time. Though I should warn you, Damen has a bad habit of cutting class and coming home early."

"Then we best get started." Ava smiles, slipping into the foyer and looking all around, her eyes moving from the huge chandelier in the entry to the elaborate wrought-iron banister that leads up the stairs. Turning to me with a gleam in her eye when she says, "This guy is seventeen?"

I move toward the kitchen, not bothering to answer since she already knows that he is. Besides, I've got much bigger things at stake than square footage and the seeming implausibility of a seventeen-year-old who's neither a pop star nor a member of a hit TV show owning such a place.

"Hey—hold up," she says, reaching for my arm and stopping me in my tracks. "What's upstairs?"

"Nothing." And the second it's out I know I totally blew it, answering far too quickly to ever be believed. Still, the last thing I need is for Ava to go snooping around and barging into his "special" room.

"Come on," she says, smiling like a rebellious teen whose parents are gone for the weekend. "School gets out at what? Two fifty?"

I nod, just barely, but it's still enough to encourage her.

"And then it takes, what? Ten minutes to drive home from there?"

"More like two." I shake my head. "No, scratch that. More like thirty seconds. You have no idea how fast Damen drives."

She checks her watch again, then looks at me. A smile playing at the corner of her lips when she says, "Well, that still leaves us plenty of time to take a quick look around, switch out the drinks, and be on our way."

And when I look at her, all I can hear is the voice in my head shouting: *Say no! Say no! Just. Say. No!* A voice I should heed.

A voice that's immediately canceled by hers when she says, "Come on, Ever. It's not every day I get to tour a house like this. Besides, we might find something useful, did you ever consider that?"

I press my lips together and nod like it pains me. Reluctantly following behind as she races ahead like an excited schoolgirl about to see her crush's cool room, when the fact is she's got over a decade on me. Heading straight for the first open door she sees, which just happens to be his bedroom. And as I follow her inside I'm not sure if I'm more surprised or relieved to find it just like I left it.

Only messier.

Way messier.

And I refuse to even think about how *that* might've happened.

Still, the sheets, the furniture, even the paint on the walls—none of it—I'm happy to report—have been changed. It's all the same stuff I helped him pick out a few weeks ago when I refused to spend another minute hanging out in that creepy mausoleum of his, where, believe it or not, he used to sleep. I mean, making out among all those dusty old memories really started to skeeve me out.

Never mind the fact that, technically speaking, I'm one of those dusty old memories too.

But even after all the new furniture was put into place, I still preferred to hang out at my house. I guess it just felt—I don't know—*safer*? Like the threat of Sabine coming home any minute would keep me from doing something I wasn't sure I was ready to do. Which now, after all that's happened, seems more than a little ridiculous.

"Wow, check out this master bath," Ava says, eyeing the Roman shower with the mosaic design and enough showerheads to bathe twenty. "I could get used to living like this!" She perches on the edge of the Jacuzzi tub and plays with the taps. "I've always wanted one of these! Have you used this?"

I look away, but not before she catches a glimpse of the color that flushes my cheeks. I mean, just because I spilled a few secrets and allowed her to come up here doesn't mean she gets an all-access pass to my private life too.

"I have one at home," I finally say, hoping that'll suffice so we can end this tour and be on our way. I need to get back downstairs so I can switch Damen's elixir with mine. And if she stays up here alone, I'm afraid she'll never leave.

I tap my watch, reminding her of just who's in charge around here.

"All right," she says, practically dragging her feet as I lead her out of the bedroom and into the hall. Only to stop just a few doors down and say, "But real quick, what's in here?"

And before I can stop her, she's entered *the room*—Damen's sacred space. His private sanctuary. His creepy mausoleum.

Only it's changed.

And I mean, drastically and dramatically changed.

Every last trace of Damen's personal time warp completely vanished—with not a Picasso, Van Gogh, or velvet settee in sight.

All of it replaced by a red felt pool table, a well-stocked black marble bar with shiny chrome stools, and a long row of recliners facing a wall covered with a ginormous flat screen TV. And I can't help but wonder what became of his old stuff—those priceless artifacts that used to get on my nerves, but now that they've been replaced with such slick modern designs, seem like lost symbols of much better times.

I miss the old Damen. I miss my bright, handsome, chivalrous boyfriend who clung so tightly to his Renaissance past.

This sleek, new-millennium Damen is a stranger to me. And as I look around this room once more, I wonder if it's too late to save him.

"What's wrong?" Ava squints. "Your face has gone white."

I grab hold of her arm and pull her down the stairs. "We need to hurry," I tell her. "Before it's too late!"

thirty-three

I flee down the stairs and into the kitchen, yelling, "Grab the bag by the door and bring it to me!"

I race for the fridge, eager to empty its contents and exchange them with mine, needing to wrap it all up before Damen can come home and catch us.

But when I open his oversized Sub-Zero fridge, just like the room upstairs, it's not at all what I expected. For one thing, it's filled with food.

And I mean lots and lots of food—like he's planning a really huge party—one that will last for three days.

I'm talking sides of beef, slabs of steak, huge wedges of cheese, half a chicken, two large pizzas, ketchup, mayonnaise, assorted takeout containers—the works! Not to mention several six packs of beer all lined up along the bottom shelf.

And even though it appears to be totally normal, here's the thing:

Damen's *not* normal. He hasn't really eaten in six hundred *years.*

He also doesn't drink *beer.*

Immortal juice, water, the occasional glass of champagne—yes.

Heineken and Corona—not so much.

"What is it?" Ava asks, dropping the bag on the floor and peering over my shoulder, trying to figure out what I'm so worked up about, and opening the freezer only to find it fully stocked with vodka, frozen pizzas, and several tubs of Ben & Jerry's. "Okay . . . so he's been to the supermarket recently . . . is there some cause for alarm I don't get? Do you two normally just manifest all of your food whenever you're hungry?"

I shake my head, knowing I can't tell her that Damen and I never *get* hungry. Just because she knows we're psychic with the ability to manifest stuff both here and in Summerland, doesn't mean she needs to know the other part of the story, the—*Oh, yeah, did I mention we're both immortal*—part too.

All she knows is what I told her—that I've a very strong suspicion that Damen is being poisoned. What I didn't tell her is that he's being poisoned in a way that's breaking down all of his psychic abilities, his enhanced physical strength, his vast intelligence, his carefully honed talents and skills, even his long-term memories of what went before—all of it's being slowly erased, as he returns to mortal form.

But while he may appear to be just your average high school junior—well, one with screamin' good looks, fistfuls of money, and his own parent-free, multimillion-dollar pad—it's just a matter of time before he begins to age.

And then deteriorate.

And then—ultimately—*die,* like I saw on that screen.

And that's exactly why I need to switch out these drinks. I need to get him back on the good juice so he can start building up his strength and hopefully repair some of the damage that's already been done. While I try to figure out an antidote that'll hopefully save him and return him to the way he once was.

And if his messy house, remodeled room, and well-stocked fridge are any indication, Damen's progressing much more quickly than I assumed.

"I don't even see these bottles you're talking about," Ava says, peering over my shoulder and squinting into the refrigerator light. "Are you sure this is where he keeps them?"

"Trust me, they're there." I rummage through the world's largest condiment collection, before spotting the elixir. Sliding my fingers around the necks of several bottles, which I then hand to Ava. "Just as I thought." I nod, finally making some headway.

Ava looks at me, her brow raised as she says, "Don't you think it's weird he's still drinking it? Because if it really is poisoned, don't you think the flavor must've changed?"

And just like *that*, I begin to doubt.

I mean, what if I'm wrong?

What if this isn't it at all?

What if Damen just grew tired of me, if *everyone* just grew tired of me, and Roman has nothing to do with it?

I grab a bottle and bring it to my lips, stopping only when Ava cries, "You're not going to drink that, are you?"

But I just shrug and take a sip, figuring there's only one way to know for sure if it's poisoned, and hoping one tiny taste won't do any harm. Knowing the second I taste it why Damen didn't notice a difference—because there isn't one. At least not until the aftertaste makes itself known.

"Water!" I gasp, rushing toward the sink and sticking my head under the faucet, gulping all the tap water I can until that awful taste is diluted.

"That bad?"

I nod, wiping my mouth with my sleeve. "Worse. But if you've ever seen Damen drink it, you'd know why he didn't notice. He gulps that stuff like—" I start to say *like a dying man,* but it hits too close to home. So I swallow hard and say, "Like someone who's very thirsty."

Then I hand Ava the remaining bottles so she can set them beside the sink, positioning the poisoned ones along the edge, after pushing all the dirty dishes aside to make room. Both of us working in such smooth seamless tandem I've barely given the last bottle to her, when I'm already bending down to retrieve the "safe" bottles from my bag. Knowing they're safe since Damen last supplied me a few weeks ago, long before Roman appeared. Intending to place them right where the others once were, so Damen will never suspect I was here.

"So what should I do with these old ones?" Ava asks. "Throw them out? Or save them for evidence?"

And just as I look up to answer, Damen walks through the side door and says, "What the hell are you doing in my kitchen?"

thirty-four

I freeze. Two bottles of untainted brew dangling halfway between the fridge and me. Realizing I'd been so preoccupied with thinking *about* Damen that I forgot to tune in and sense if he was anywhere near.

Ava gapes, her face displaying the same wide-eyed, openmouthed mask of sheer panic I'm trying to hide. Then I look at Damen and clear my throat before saying, "It's not what you think!"

Which is pretty much the lamest, most ridiculous thing I could've said since it's *exactly* what he thinks. Ava and I broke into his house so we could tamper with his food supply. Pure and simple.

He drops his bag and moves toward me, his eyes focused on mine. "You have no idea what I'm thinking."

Oh, but I do. Wincing at the horrible thoughts scrolling through his head, his mental accusation of: *Stalker! Freak!* And things far worse than that.

"And how the hell did you even get in here?" he asks, glancing between us.

"Um, Sheila let me in," I say, not quite sure what to do with the bottle I still hold in my hand.

A vein throbs in his temple as he shakes his head and clenches his fists, and I realize I've never seen him this angry before, didn't even know he was capable of it, and feel pretty cruddy to know I inspired it.

"I'll deal with Sheila," he says, his temper barely in check. "What I meant was, what are you doing in *here*? In my *house*? Messing around in my fridge—" His eyes narrow. "What the hell do you think you're up to?"

I glance at Ava, embarrassed to have her witness my one true love talking to me in this way.

"And what's up with her?" He points at Ava. "You bring your party psychic along to cast some kind of spell?"

"You remember that?" I lower the bottle to my side. I'd been wondering what he might've retained from our past, and even though it's dumb, the fact that he remembers meeting Ava fills me with hope. "You remember Halloween night?" I whisper, recalling the first time we kissed, out by the pool, both of us dressed in perfectly matching costumes of Marie Antoinette and her lover, Count Fersen, without having planned it.

"Yeah, I remember." He shakes his head. "And I hate to break it to you, but it was a moment of weakness that'll *never* happen again. One you took far too seriously. And believe me, if I'd known what a freak you'd turn out to be, I wouldn't have bothered. It wasn't worth it."

I swallow hard and blink back the tears. Feeling empty, hollowed out, my insides excavated and tossed aside, as any chance of reclaiming our love—the only thing that makes this particular life worth living—slips out of reach. And even though I remind myself that those are Roman's words not his—that the real Damen isn't capable of treating *anyone* like this—it doesn't make it hurt any less.

"Damen, *please*," I finally manage. "I know it looks bad. Really, I do. But I can explain. You see, we're only trying to *help* you."

He looks at me, his gaze so derisive it fills me with shame. But I force myself to continue, knowing I at least have to try. "*Someone* is trying to poison you." I swallow, meeting his eyes. "Someone you know."

He shakes his head, not buying a word of it. Convinced that I'm stark raving mental and should be locked up immediately.

"And this *person* responsible for poisoning me, this *person* I happen to know, would that, by any chance, be *you*?" He takes another step toward me. "Because *you're* the one breaking into my home. *You're* the one getting all up in my fridge and messing with my drinks. I think the evidence speaks for itself."

I shake my head, talking past the searing heat in my throat when I say, "I know how it looks, but you've *got* to believe me! It's all true, I'm not making it up!"

He takes another step closer, advancing on me in a way so intentional, so slow and deliberate, it's like he's stalking his prey. So I decide to just go for it, to let it all out. I mean, I've got nothing to lose anyway.

"It's Roman, okay?" I suck in my breath, watching his expression change from accusatory to outraged. "Your new friend Roman is—" I glance at Ava, knowing I can't say what Roman *actually* is—an immortal rogue set on killing Damen for some reason I've yet to determine. But it's not like it matters anyway. Damen has no memory of Drina or being immortal, he's so far gone he'd never understand.

"Get out," he says, the look in his eyes so cold it chills me more than the air flowing from his fridge.

"Get the hell out before I call the police."

I peer at Ava, seeing her pour the tampered contents down the drain the second he makes the threat. Then I gaze at Damen, grasping his phone, his index finger already pressing the nine, followed by the one, and then—

I have to stop him. There's no way I can allow him to complete that call. No way I can risk getting the police involved. So I stare into his eyes, even though he refuses to look at me. I just focus all of my energy on him, my thoughts reaching out to him, attempting to meld and influence. Showering him with the most compassionate loving white light along with a bouquet of telepathic red tulips. All the while whispering, "No need for trouble." I slowly back away. "You don't need to call anyone, we're leaving right now." Holding my breath as he stares at the phone, not understanding why he can't seem to press the last *one*.

He lifts his gaze, and for the briefest moment, just a flicker really, the old Damen's returned. Looking at me in the way that he used to—sending a delicious warm tingle all over my skin. And even though it's gone just as soon as it appeared—I'll happily settle for whatever I get.

He tosses his phone onto the counter and shakes his head. And knowing we'd better move fast before my influence ends, I grab my bag and head for the door. Turning just as he empties his cupboards and fridge of every last bottle of juice. Removing their caps and pouring their contents right down the drain, convinced they're not safe for consumption, now that I've tampered with them.

thirty-five

"What will happen now that he no longer has the drink? Will he get better or worse?"

That's the question Ava asked as soon as we got in my car. And the truth is, I had no idea how to answer. I still don't. So I didn't say anything. I just shrugged.

"I'm so sorry," she said, clasping her hands in her lap, looking at me in a way that proved her sincerity. "I feel responsible."

But I just shook my head. Because even though it *was* kind of her fault for wasting so much time when she insisted on touring his house, I'm the one who came up with the brilliant idea of breaking in. I'm the one who got so caught up in the task at hand I forgot to keep my eye on the door. So if anyone's to blame, I am.

But even worse than getting caught is knowing that in Damen's eyes, I've gone from being some weird freaky stalker chick, to a pathetic, delusional loser. Fully convinced I tried to spike his red brew with some crazy, black magic, voodoo concoction in hopes that he'd like me again.

Because that's exactly what Stacia convinced him of just after he relayed the story.

And that's exactly what he's chosen to believe.

In fact, it's what the whole school believes. Including a few of my teachers.

Which makes going to school an even more miserable experience than it was before. Because now, not only must I suffer through endless taunts of *Spaz! Loo-ser!* and *Witch!* but I've also been asked to stay after class by not one but now two of my teachers.

Though I can't say Mr. Robins's request came as much of a surprise. I mean, since we'd already had a little talk about my supposed inability to move on and build a life for myself post-Damen, I can't say I was all that shocked when he kept me after class in order to discuss the *incident*.

What did surprise me was the way I reacted. How quickly I resorted to doing the one thing I thought I'd never do—I lawyered up.

"Excuse me," I said, cutting him off before he could finish. Not interested in any well-meaning though ultimately boundary-crossing "relationship advice" my newly divorced, semi-alcoholic English teacher was prepared to dish out. "But the last time I checked this was all just a *rumor.* An *alleged* event with no evidence to support it." I looked at him, meeting his eyes despite the fact I'd just lied. I mean, while Ava and I were pretty much caught red-handed, it's not like Damen took a picture. It's not like there's yet another video of me making the YouTube circuit. "So unless I'm officially charged and tried—" I paused to clear my throat, partly for dramatic effect and partly because I couldn't believe what I was about to say next. "I shall remain innocent until proven guilty." He balked, preparing to speak, but I wasn't finished. "So unless you need to discuss my behavior in this class, which you and I both know is exemplary, or my grades, which happen to be more than exemplary, unless you're interested in discussing either one of those things—I'm thinking we're pretty much done here."

Fortunately, Mr. Munoz is a little easier. Though that's probably because I'm the one who approaches *him*. Thinking my Renaissance-obsessed history teacher is just the man to help me track down the name of a particular herb I need to make the elixir.

Last night, when I tried to research it on Google, I realized I had no idea what to put in the search box. And with Sabine still watching me like a hawk even though I eat and drink and act as normal as I can, slipping off to Summerland, even for a few minutes, was out of the question.

Which makes Mr. Munoz my last hope—or at least my most immediate hope. Because yesterday, when Damen tossed all of those bottles down the drain, there went half of my already meager supply. Which means I need to make more. Lots more. Not only to keep up my strength between now and the time when I leave, but I also need plenty left over for Damen's recovery.

And since he never got around to giving me the recipe, all I have to go on is what I saw on that crystal when I watched his father prepare the brew, naming all of the ingredients out loud, before stopping to whisper the very last one in his son's ear, speaking so softly there was no way I could hear.

But Mr. Munoz turns out to be no help at all. And after futzing around with a bunch of old books and coming up with zilch, he looks at me and says, "Ever, I'm afraid I can't find the answer to this, but since you're already here—"

I raise my hand, blocking his words from going any further than they already have. And even though I'm not proud of the way I handled Mr. Robins, if Munoz doesn't back off, he'll get the same speech as well.

"Trust me, I know where you're going." I nod, my eyes right on his. "But you've got it all wrong. It's not what you think—" I stop, realizing that as far as denials go, this one is turning out to be incredibly lame. I mean, I just alluded to the fact that while it *might've* occurred—it didn't occur in the *way* that he thinks. Which basically amounts to me pleading guilty—but with extenuating circumstances.

I shake my head, inwardly rolling my eyes at myself, thinking: *Good one, Ever. Keep it up and you will need Sabine to represent you.*

And then he looks at me, and I look at him, and we both shake our heads, mutually agreeing to leave it at that.

But just as I grab my bag and start to leave, he reaches toward me, his hand touching my sleeve, when he says, "Hang in there. It'll all be okay."

And that's all it takes. That simple gesture is all I need to *see* that Sabine has been frequenting Starbucks, just about every single day. The two of them enjoying a tentative flirtation that, while it (thankfully) hasn't moved past a smile, Munoz is definitely anticipating the day when it will. And even though I know I have to do whatever I can to stop them from, God forbid, *dating,* at the moment, I don't have time to deal with it.

I shake off his energy and head out the door, barely making it into the hall before Roman approaches, adjusting his stride so it's timed right to mine. Leering at me when he says, "Was Munoz any help?"

I keep going, wincing when his cool breath hits my cheek.

"You're running out of time," he says, his voice as soft and soothing as a lover's embrace. "It's all moving rather quickly now, wouldn't you agree? And before you know it, it'll all be over. And then—well—then there's just you and me."

I shrug, knowing that's not exactly true. I viewed the past. I saw what happened in that Florentine church. And if I'm not mistaken, there are six immortal orphans quite possibly still roaming the earth. Six little urchins who could be just about anywhere by now—providing they made it. But if Roman's unaware of that fact, well, it's hardly my place to inform him.

So I gaze into his eyes, resisting the lure of those deep navy blues, when I say, "How lucky for me."

"And *me*." He smiles. "You're going to need someone to help mend your broken heart. Someone who understands you. Someone who knows just *what* you really are." He trails his finger down the length of my arm, his touch so shockingly cold, even through the cotton of my sleeve, I quickly pull away.

"You know *nothing* about me," I say, my eyes raking his face. "You've underestimated me. If I were you, I'd be a little more cautious about celebrating so soon. You're a long way from winning this one."

And even though I meant it as a threat, my voice is far too shaky to be taken seriously. So I pick up the pace, leaving his mocking laughter behind as I head for my lunch table where Miles and Haven are waiting.

I slide onto the bench, smiling as I glance between them. It feels like so long since we last hung out, the sight of them sitting here now makes me ridiculously happy.

"Hey you guys," I say, unable to keep the grin off my face, watching as they glance first at me, then at each other, nodding their heads in perfect unison as though this moment was rehearsed.

Miles sips his soda, a drink he never would've gone near before. His bright pink nails tapping the sides of the can as my stomach fills with dread. Debating whether or not to tune in to their thoughts, knowing it'll prepare me for whatever reason they're here, but deciding against it since I'd rather not hear it twice.

"We need to talk," Miles says. "It's about Damen."

"No," Haven cuts in, shooting Miles a look before retrieving her bag of carrot sticks from her purse, the zero-calorie signature lunch of the girls of the A-list. "It's about Damen and *you*."

"What's there to talk about? I mean, he's with Stacia, and I'm—dealing."

They glance at each other, exchanging a look that's loaded but brief. "But *are* you dealing?" Miles asks. "Because seriously, Ever, breaking into his house and messing with his food supply is pretty twisted. Not exactly the actions of someone who's moving on with their life—"

"So, what? You guys just believe every rumor you hear? All those months of friendship, all those times you hung at my house, and you think I'm capable of that—" I roll my eyes and shake my head, refusing to go any further. I mean, if all I managed to get out of Damen was the most fleeting moment of recognition before it was replaced with disdain, when we have a bond that dates back centuries—what can I hope to accomplish with Miles and Haven whom I've known for less than a year?

"Well, I really don't see why Damen would make all that up," Haven says, her eyes on mine, her gaze so harsh and judgmental I realize she didn't actually come here to help. Because while she may act as though she's got only my best interests at heart, the truth is, she's enjoying my fall. After losing Damen to me, after seeing how Roman continues to chase me even after she's made her interest clear, she's happy to see me knocked down. And the only reason she's deigning to sit by me now is so she can look me in the eye while she gloats.

I gaze down at the table, surprised by how much it hurts. But I try not to judge or hold it against her. I know all too well what it's like to feel jealous, and there's nothing rational about it.

"You need to let it go," Miles says, sipping his drink, though his eyes never leave mine. "You need to let go and move on."

"*Everyone* knows you're stalking him," Haven says, covering her mouth with nails painted the color of ballet slippers as opposed to her usual black. "*Everyone* knows you broke into his house—*twice*—that we know of. Seriously, you're out of control, you're acting insane."

I gaze down at the table, wondering how much longer the assault will continue.

"Anyway, as your friends, we just want to convince you that you need to let go. You need to back off and move on. Because the truth is, your behavior is creepy, not to mention . . ."

Haven drones on, hitting all the bullet points I'm sure they agreed upon before they approached me. But I stopped listening after she said *as your friends.* Wanting to hang on to that and reject all the rest, even though it's no longer true.

I shake my head and look up, seeing Roman sitting at the lunch table with his gaze fixed on mine. Tapping his watch, then pointing at Damen in a way so ominous, so threatening, I spring from my seat. Leaving Haven's voice fading behind me like a distant hum as I race for my car, chastising myself for wasting my time with this stuff when there are far more important things to be done.

thirty-six

I'm through with school. Done with subjecting myself to that unbearable gauntlet of torture each day. I mean, what's the point of going when I'm getting nowhere with Damen, taunted by Roman, and lectured by teachers and pseudo well-meaning ex-friends? Besides, if things work out in the way that I hope, then I'll soon be back at my old school in Oregon, living my life as though this never existed. So there's really no point in putting myself through that again.

I head down Broadway, weaving my way through pedestrian traffic before moving on to the canyon, hoping to go someplace quiet where I can make the portal appear without scaring any unsuspecting shoppers. Not remembering until I've already parked that this is the same place where my first showdown with Drina occurred—a showdown that resulted in my first visit to Summerland when Damen provided the way.

I hunker down in my seat, imagining that golden veil of light hovering before me and landing right in front of the Great Hall of Learning. Barely taking the time to notice its magnificent ever-changing façade before rushing into the grand marble hall with my thoughts focused on two things:

Is there an antidote to save Damen?

And how do I locate the secret herb, the final ingredient needed to prepare the elixir?

Repeating the questions again and again as I wait for the doorway to the akashic records to appear—

But getting nothing.

No globes. No crystal sheets. No white circular rooms or hybrid TVs.

Nothing. Nada. Nien.

Just a soft voice behind me saying, "It's too late."

I turn, expecting to see Romy but finding Rayne there instead. Following behind as I roll my eyes and make for the door, eager to put some distance between us as she echoes those same words again.

I don't have time for this. I don't have time to decipher a bunch of cryptic nonsense from the world's creepiest twin. Because even though there's no concept of time in Summerland where everything happens in a constant state of *now,* I know for a fact that the time I spend here will be duly noted back home. Which means I need to keep going, keep moving forward, heading down the street as fast as I can until her voice turns to a whisper. Knowing I need to save Damen before I turn back time and go home. And if the answers aren't here—then I'll look somewhere else.

I start running. Turning into the alleyway just as I'm overcome by such sudden excruciating pain, I crumple to the ground. My fingers clamped to my temples, my head aching as though it's being stabbed from all sides, as a swirl of images unfold in my mind. A series of sketches, one turning into the next like pages in a book, followed by a detailed description of what it includes. And I've just made it to the third page when I realize these are instructions for making the antidote to save Damen, including herbs planted during the new moon, rare crystals and minerals I've never heard of, silk pouches embroidered by Tibetan monks—all of it needing to be carefully assembled in a series of very precise steps before soaking up the energy of the next full moon.

And just after I'm shown the exact herb needed to complete the immortal elixir, my head clears as though it never happened. So I reach for my bag, fumbling for a scrap of paper and a pen, jotting down the final step when Ava appears.

"I made the portal!" she says, her face lighting up as her eyes meet mine. "I didn't think I could do it, but this morning when I sat down for my usual meditation, I thought: What could it hurt to give it a try? And the next thing I knew—"

"You've been here since *morning*?" I say, taking in her beautiful dress, designer shoes, heavy gold bracelets, and jewel-adorned fingers.

"There's no time in Summerland," she scolds.

"Maybe so, but back home it's past noon," I tell her, watching as she shakes her head and frowns, refusing to get bogged down in the tedious rules of the earth plane.

"Who cares? What could I possibly be missing? A long line of clients wanting me to tell them they're about to become extremely rich and famous despite all evidence to the contrary?" She closes her eyes and sighs. "I'm tired of it, Ever. Tired of the grind. But here, everything's so wonderful, I think I might stay!"

"You can't," I say, quickly, automatically, though I'm not sure it's true.

"Why not?" She shrugs, lifting her arms to the sky and twirling around and around. "Why can't I stay here? Give me one good reason."

"Because—" I start, wishing I could just leave it at that, but since she's not a child I'm forced to come up with something better. "Because it's not right," I finish, hoping she'll hear me. "You have work to do. We all have work to do. And hiding out here is like—*cheating*."

"Says who?" She squints. "You telling me *all* of these people are dead?"

I gaze around, taking in the crowded sidewalks, the long line for the movie theaters and karaoke bars, realizing I have no idea how to answer. I mean, just how many of them are like Ava—tired, fed-up, disillusioned souls who've found their way here and decided to drop out from the earth plane and never return? And how many of them have died and refused to cross over like Riley once did?

I look at Ava again, knowing I've no right to tell her what to do with her life, especially when I remember what I've chosen to do with mine.

Then I reach for her hand and smile when I say, "Well, at the moment, *I* need you. Tell me everything you know about astrology."

thirty-seven

"So?" I lean toward Ava, elbows pressed against the tabletop, trying to keep her focused on me as opposed to the sights and sounds of Saint-Germain.

"I know that I'm an Aries." She shrugs, her eyes preferring the River Seine, the Pont Neuf, the Eiffel Tower, the Arc de Triomphe, and the Notre Dame cathedral (which, in this version of Paris, are all lined up in a row), to me.

"Is that it?" I stir my cappuccino, wondering why I even bothered to order it from the cartoonlike *garçon* with the curlicue mustache, white shirt, and black vest, since it's not like I have any intention of drinking it.

She sighs, turning to look at me when she says, "Ever, can't you just relax and enjoy the view? When was the last time you were in Paris anyway?"

"Never," I say, rolling my eyes in a way she can't miss. "I've never been to Paris. And I hate to break it to you, Ava, but *this*—" I take a moment to gesture around, pointing at the Louvre, which is placed right next to Printemps department store, which is next to the Musée d'Orsay, "—is *not* Paris. *This* is like some cranked up Disney version of Paris. Like, you've taken a pile of travel brochures and French postcards, and scenes from that adorable cartoon movie *Ratatouille*, mixed them all together and *voilà,* created *this*. I mean, did you *see* the waiter? Did you notice how his tray kept tipping and twirling but never once fell? I doubt the *real* Paris has waiters like that."

But even though I'm acting like the biggest party pooper ever, Ava just laughs. Swinging her wavy auburn hair over her shoulder as she says, "Well, for your information, this is *exactly* as I remember it. Maybe these monuments weren't all lined up in a row, but it's so much nicer like this. I did attend the Sorbonne you know. In fact, did I ever mention the time when I—"

"That's great, Ava. Really," I say. "And I'd love to hear all about it if I wasn't *running out of time!* So, what I meant to ask was, what do you know about astrology or astronomy or whatever it is that involves the various moon cycles?"

She breaks off a piece of baguette and butters the side, saying, "Can you be more specific?"

I reach into my pocket and retrieve the folded-up paper I scribbled on right after my vision, squinting at her as I say, "Okay, what exactly is a new moon and when does it occur?"

She blows on her coffee, peering at me when she says, "The new moon occurs when both the sun and moon are in conjunction. Meaning that when you're looking at it from the earth plane, they both seem to occupy the same part of the sky. And because of that, the moon doesn't reflect the light of the sun, which also means it can't be seen because its dark side is facing the earth."

"But what does it *mean*? Is it symbolic of something?"

She nods, breaking off another piece of baguette when she says, "It's a symbol for new beginnings. You know, rejuvenation, renewal, hope—stuff like that. It's also a good time to make changes, drop bad habits—or even bad relationships." She gives me a pointed look.

But I just ignore that and move on, knowing she's referring to Damen and me, having no idea that I'm not just planning to end it,

I'm planning to *erase* it. Because as much as I love him, as much as I can't imagine a future without him, I truly believe it's the best thing for everyone. None of this ever should've happened. *We* never should've happened. It's unnatural, not right, and now it's my job to put it all back.

"So when does that happen in relation to the full moon?" I ask, watching as she covers her mouth when she chews.

"The full moon occurs around two weeks after the new moon. It's when the moon reflects the maximum amount of light from the sun, which, from the earth plane, makes it appear full. When in reality, it's always full since it's not like it goes anywhere. Oh, and as far as symbols go? You want to know that right?" She smiles. "The full moon is all about abundance, completeness, a sort of ripening of things into their full powers. And since the moon's energy is strongest at this point, it's also full of magick power."

I nod, trying to digest everything she just said, and forming the smallest inkling of understanding for why these phases are so important for my plan.

"All the moon's phases are symbolic of something." Ava shrugs. "The moon plays a powerful role in ancient lore and is said to control the tides. And since our bodies are mostly made up of water, some say it controls us too. Did you know that the word *lunatic* comes from the Latin word for moon, which is *luna*? Oh, and don't forget the werewolf legend—it's all about the full moon!"

Inwardly, I roll my eyes. There are no such things as werewolves, vampires, or demons—only immortals, and the immortal rogues who are determined to kill them.

"Can I ask why you're asking all this?" she says, draining the last of her espresso and pushing the cup aside.

"In a minute," I say, my words clipped, terse, far less conversational than hers. But unlike her, I'm not vacationing in Paris, I'm merely tolerating the view to get to the answers I need. "One last thing, what's so special about a full moon during *l'heure bleue*, or blue hour as it's called?"

She looks at me, her eyes wide, her voice breathless when she says, "Do you mean the blue moon?"

I shrug, remembering how the moon was so blue in the image it practically blended with the sky. Then figuring it was somehow symbolic of an actual blue moon with the way its color pulsated and shimmered, I say, "Yeah. But the blue moon specifically during the blue hour, what do you know about that?"

She takes a deep breath, gazing into the distance as she says, "The mainstream thought is that the second full moon in a month constitutes a blue moon. But there's another, more esoteric school of thought that says the *true* blue moon occurs when there are two full moons occurring not necessarily within the same month, but within the same *astrological sign*. It's regarded as a very holy day, one when the connection between the dimensions is very potent, making it an ideal time for meditation, prayer, and mystical journeys. It's said that if you harness the blue moon energy during *l'heure bleue*, then all sorts of magick can occur. The only limitations, as usual, are your own."

She looks at me, wondering what I'm up to, but I'm not ready to share that just yet. Then she shakes her head and says, "But just so you know, a genuine blue moon is very rare, only coming around every three to five years."

My stomach twists as my hands grip the sides of my chair. "And do you know when the next blue moon will occur?" While thinking: *Please let it be soon, please let it be soon!*

Feeling like I'm about to puke *and* keel over simultaneously when she shakes her head and says, "I have no idea."

But of course! The most important thing I need to know—is the one thing she doesn't know.

"Though I know how we can find out." She smiles.

I shake my head, just about to inform her that as far as I can tell, my access to the akashic records has just been revoked, when she closes her eyes and a moment later a silver iMac appears.

"Google, anyone?" She laughs, pushing it toward me.

thirty-eight

Even though I felt like an idiot the second Ava manifested that laptop (I mean, *duh*, why didn't I think of that?), we did get our answer fairly quick.

Though unfortunately, it wasn't the good news I was hoping for.

In fact, it was anything but.

Just when everything was coming together, seeming like it was destined to be—it all fell apart the second I learned that the blue moon, that rarest of full moons that only comes around every three to five years, which also just so happens to be my one and only window for time travel, has its next scheduled appearance—*tomorrow.*

"I still can't believe it," I say, climbing out of my car while Ava feeds the meter from a neat stack of quarters cupped in the palm of her hand. "I thought it was just another full moon, I didn't know there was a difference, or that they're so rare. I mean, what am I supposed to *do*?"

She snaps her wallet shut and looks at me. "Well, from what I can see, you have three choices."

I press my lips together, not sure I want to hear any of them.

"You can do nothing at all and just sit back and watch while everything you love and care about completely falls apart, you can choose to handle just one thing at the cost of all the others, *or* you can tell me just exactly what is going on here so I can see if I can help."

I take a deep breath and look at her standing before me, back in her usual outfit of faded jeans, silver rings, a white cotton tunic, and brown leather flip-flops. Always there, always available, always willing to help me, even when I don't realize I need it.

Even back when I was being dismissive (and if I'm gonna be honest—more than a little mean), Ava was right there, waiting for me to come around, never once holding my bad attitude against me, never once turning her back or shunning me in the way I shunned her. It's like she's been standing by all this time, waiting to step in as my psychic big sister. And now, she's pretty much the only one I have left—the only one I can count on—the only one who comes close to knowing the *real* me—including *most* of my secrets.

And in light of everything I just learned, I've no choice but to tell her. There's no way I can go it alone like I'd hoped.

"Okay." I nod, convincing myself it's not just the right thing to do, but the *only* thing to do. "Here's what I need you to do."

And as we head down the street, I tell her what I saw that day on the crystal. Managing to explain as much as I can while avoiding the *I* word—honoring my promise to Damen that I'll never divulge our immortality. Telling Ava that Damen will need the antidote so that he can get better, followed by his "special red energy drink" so he can rebuild his strength. Explaining that I'm faced with a choice between being with the love of my life, or saving four lives that were never meant to end.

So by the time we're standing outside the shop where she works, the shop I've passed many times before but swore I'd never enter—she looks at me, her mouth opening as if to say something, before clamping shut again. Repeating this scenario a few more times until she's finally able to mumble, "But *tomorrow*! Ever, can you leave that soon?"

I shrug, my stomach sinking when I hear it spoken out loud. But knowing I can't wait another three to five years, I nod with more assurance than I feel when I look at her and say, "And that's exactly why I need you to help me with the antidote, then find a way to get it to him along with the elix—" I pause, hoping I haven't aroused her suspicions, trying to recover when I say, "*—that red energy drink—* so that he can get better. I mean, now that you know how to get inside his house, I'm thinking you can find a way to, I don't know, spike his drink or something," I say, knowing it sounds like the worst plan *ever,* but determined to see that it works. "And then, when he's better—when the old Damen returns—you can explain everything that's happened, and give him the—the red drink."

She looks at me with an expression so conflicted I'm not sure how to read it, so I forge straight ahead. "I know it probably seems like I'm choosing against him—but I'm not. *Really* I'm not. In fact, there's a good chance that none of this will even be necessary. There's a good chance that when I go back to how I was, everything else will go back too."

"Is that what you saw?" she asks, her voice soft, gentle.

I shake my head. "No, it's just a theory, though I think it makes sense. I mean, I can't imagine it any other way. So all of this stuff I'm telling you now is just a precaution since it won't even be necessary. Which means you won't remember this conversation since it will be like it never occurred. In fact, you won't have any recollection of having known me. But just in case I'm wrong—which I'm pretty sure I'm not—but just in case I am, I need to have a plan in place—you know, just in case," I mumble, wondering who I'm trying to convince, me or her.

She grabs hold of my hand, her eyes full of compassion when she says, "You're doing the right thing. And you're lucky. Not many people get the chance to go back."

I look at her, my lips curving into a grin. "Not *many*?"

"Well, no one I can think of offhand." She smiles.

But even though we both laugh, when I look at her again my voice is serious when I say, "Seriously, Ava, I can't bear for anything to happen to him. I mean, I'd—I'd just *die* if I somehow found out that it did—and that it was my fault . . ."

She squeezes my hand and opens the shop door, leading me inside as she whispers, "Don't worry. You can trust me."

I follow her past shelves crowded with books, a wall of CDs, and an entire corner dedicated to angel figurines, before passing a machine that claims to photograph auras as we head for a counter where an older woman with a long gray braid is reading a book.

"I didn't realize you were on the schedule today?" She sets down her novel and glances between us.

"I'm not." Ava smiles. "But my friend Ever here—" She nods her head toward me. "She needs the back room."

The woman studies me, obviously trying to glimpse my aura and get a feel for my energy, then shooting Ava a questioning look when she comes away empty.

But Ava just smiles and nods in consent, signaling that I'm worthy of access to the "back room," whatever that is.

"Ever?" the woman says, her fingers creeping toward her neck, worrying the turquoise pendant that hangs at her collarbone.

A stone that, as I recently learned in my brief study of minerals and crystals on the iMac in Summerland, has been used for amulets meant to heal and protect for hundreds of years. And with the way she just said my name, and by the suspicious look on her face, it's not like I need to access her mind to know that she's wondering if she might need protection from me.

She hesitates, glancing between Ava and me, then focusing solely on me as she says, "I'm Lina."

That's it. No handshake, no welcoming hug. She just states her name and then makes for the door, flipping the sign that hangs there from *OPEN!* to *BE BACK IN 10!* Then motioning for us to follow her down a short hall with a shiny purple door at the end.

"Can I ask what this is about?" She rummages in her pocket for a set of keys, still undecided as to whether or not she'll be letting us in.

Ava nods at me, signaling that it's my turn to take it from here. So I clear my throat and cram my hand into the pocket of my recently manifested jeans whose hems, thankfully, still reach the floor. Retrieving the crumpled-up piece of paper as I say, "I um, I need a few things." Wincing when Lina snatches it out of my hand and looks it over. Stopping to lift a brow, grunt something unintelligible under her breath, and scrutinize me some more.

And just when it seems she's about to turn me away, she thrusts the list back into my hand, unlocks the door, and waves us both into a room that I didn't expect.

I mean, when Ava told me this was the place that would have what I need, I was more than a little nervous. I was sure I'd be thrust into some creepy hidden basement filled with all manner of strange, scary, ritualistic stuff, like vials of cat blood, severed bat wings, shrunken heads, Voodoo dolls—stuff like you see in movies or on TV. But this room is nothing like that. In fact, it pretty much looks like your average, more or less well-organized storage closet. Well, except for the bright violet walls punctuated by hand-carved totems and masks. Oh, and the goddess paintings propped against the overstuffed shelves sagging with heavy old tomes and stone deities. But the file cabinet is pretty standard issue. And when she unlocks a cupboard and starts rummaging around, I try to peek over her shoulder, but I can't see a thing until she's handing me a stone that seems wrong in every way.

"Moonstone," she says, noting the confusion on my face.

I stare at it, knowing it doesn't look like it should, and even though I can't explain it, something about it feels off. And not wanting to offend her since I've no doubt she wouldn't hesitate to evict me, I swallow hard, screw up my courage, and say, "Um, I need one that's raw and unpolished, in its absolute purest form—this one just seems a little too smooth and shiny for my needs."

She nods, almost imperceptibly, but still it's there. Just the briefest tilt of her head and curl of her lips before she replaces it with the stone that I asked for.

"That's it," I say, knowing I just passed her test. Gazing at a moonstone that's not nearly as shiny or pretty but will hopefully do what it's intended to, which is aid in new beginnings. "And then I'm gonna need a quartz crystal bowl, one that's been tuned to the seventh chakra, a red silk pouch embroidered by Tibetan monks, four polished rose quartz crystals, one small star—no, staur-o-lite? Is that how you say it?" I look at her just in time to see her nod. "Oh, and the biggest raw zoisite you've got."

And when Lina just stands there with her hands on her hips, I know she's wondering how all of these seemingly random items can possibly fit together.

"Oh, and a chunk of turquoise, probably like the size of the one you're wearing," I say, motioning toward her neck.

She looks me over, giving me a crisp, perfunctory nod, before turning her back and gathering the crystals. Wrapping them up so casually you'd think she was bagging groceries at Whole Foods.

"Oh, and here's a list of herbs," I say, reaching into my other pocket and retrieving a crumpled sheet of paper, which I then hand to her. "Preferably planted during the new moon and tended by blind nuns in India," I add, amazed when she just takes the list and nods without flinching.

"Can I ask what this is for?" she asks, her eyes on mine.

But I just shake my head. I was barely able to tell Ava, and she's a good friend. So there's no way I'm telling this lady, no matter how grandmotherly she may seem.

"Um, I'd rather not say." I shrug, hoping she'll respect that and get on with it since manifesting these items won't work, it's imperative they spring from their original source.

We look at each other, our gazes fixed, unwavering. And even though I plan to stand my ground for as long as it takes, it's not long before she breaks away and starts riffling through the filing cabinet, her fingers flipping past hundreds of packets as I say, "Oh, and one more thing."

Searching through my backpack for my sketch of the rare, hard-to-find herb that was oft used in Renaissance Florence. The final ingredient needed to bring the elixir to life. Handing it to her as I ask, "Does this look familiar?"

thirty-nine

With all of our ingredients gathered—well, everything but the spring water, extra-virgin olive oil, long white tapered candles (which, oddly, Lina was out of, considering they were pretty much the most normal thing I requested), orange peel, and the photo of Damen I didn't expect her to have—we return to my car.

And I'm just unlocking the door when Ava says, "I think I'll walk home from here since I'm just around the corner."

"You sure?"

She spreads her arms wide as though embracing the night. Her lips curving into a grin as she says, "It's so nice out, I just want to enjoy it."

"As beautiful as Summerland?" I ask, wondering what's brought on this sudden fit of happiness, considering how serious she was in Lina's back room.

She laughs, her head thrown back, her pale neck exposed, leveling her gaze on mine when she says, "Don't worry. I've no plans to drop out of society and move there full time. It's just nice to have the access when I need a little escape."

"Just be careful not to visit too much," I tell her, echoing the same warning Damen once gave to me. "Summerland's addictive," I add, watching as she hugs her arms to her body and shrugs, knowing

I've wasted my words since it's obvious she'll be back as soon and as often as she can.

"So, you've got everything you need?"

I nod and lean against the car door. "And the rest I'll pick up on my way home."

"And you're sure you're ready?" She looks at me, her face drawn and serious again. "You know, leaving all of this? *Leaving Damen?*"

I swallow hard, preferring not to think about that. I'd rather keep busy, focus on one task at a time, until tomorrow comes around and it's time to say good-bye.

"Because once something's done, it can't be undone."

I shrug, meeting her gaze as I say, "Apparently that's not true." Watching as she tilts her head to the side, her auburn hair blowing into her face before she captures the strands and tucks them back behind her ear.

"But what you're returning to—well, you realize you'll be normal again. You won't have access to such knowledge, you'll be completely unaware—are you sure you want to return to all that?"

I gaze down at the ground, kicking a small rock instead of looking at her. "Listen, I'm not gonna lie. All of this is happening so much quicker than I expected—and I hoped to have more time to—to finalize things. But ultimately—yeah, I think I'm ready." I pause, replaying the words I just said and knowing they didn't convey what I meant. "I mean, I *know* I'm ready. In fact, I'm *definitely* ready. Because putting everything back in its place and returning it to the way it should be—well—it feels like the right thing to do, you know?"

And even though I didn't mean for it to happen, my voice rose at the end, making it sound more like a question than the statement I intended it to be. So I shake my head and say, "What I meant was, it's absolutely, positively, one hundred percent the right thing to do." Adding, "I mean, why else was I granted access to those records?"

Ava looks at me, her gaze steady, unwavering.

"Besides, do you have any idea how excited I am to be with my family again?"

She reaches for me, hugging me tightly to her chest, whispering, "I'm so happy for you. Really I am. And even though I'm going to miss you, I'm honored to know you trust me enough to finish the job."

"I've no idea how to thank you," I murmur, my throat feeling tight.

But she just smooths her hand over my hair when she says, "Believe me, you already have."

I pull away and gaze all around, taking in this glorious night in this charming beach town, hardly believing I'm about to walk away from it all. Turning my back on Sabine, Miles, Haven, Ava—Damen—all of it—everything—as though it never existed.

"You okay?" she asks, her voice gentle and smooth as she reads my expression.

I nod, clearing my throat and motioning toward the small purple paper bag at her feet, the shop's name of MYSTICS & MOONBEAMS printed in gold. "You sure you've got it all clear, about how to handle the herbs? You need to keep them in a cool dark place, and you don't crush them or add them to the—*red juice*—until the very last day—the *third* day."

"Don't worry." She laughs. "What's not in here," she picks up the bag and clutches it to her chest, "is in here." She points at her temple and smiles.

I nod, blinking back tears I refuse to indulge, knowing this is only the beginning of a series of good-byes. "I'll stop by your house tomorrow and drop off the rest," I say. "Just in case you end up needing it, though I doubt that you will." Then I slide into my car, start the engine, and pull away. Heading down Ocean without waving good-bye, without once looking back. Knowing my only choice now is to look toward the future and focus on that.

• • •

After stopping by the store to pick up the rest of the items, I haul the bags up to my room and dump their contents onto my desk. Riffling through piles of oils and herbs and candles, eager to get to the crystals since they're going to require the most work. All of them needing to be individually programmed according to type, before being placed in the embroidered silk pouch and set outside where they can absorb as much moonlight as possible, while I manifest a mortar and pestle (which I forgot to pick up at the store, but since it's only a *tool* and not an actual *ingredient,* I figure it should be okay to just manifest one), so I can pulverize some of those herbs and get them all boiling in some (also manifested) beakers, before mixing in all of the other irons and minerals and colorful powders that Lina poured into small glass jars which she carefully labeled. All of this needing to be completed in seven precise steps that commence with the ringing of the crystal bowl that's been specifically tuned to vibrate to the seventh chakra so it may provide inspiration, perception beyond space and time, and a whole host of other things that connect with the divine. And as I look at the heap of ingredients piled high before me, I can't help but feel a small surge of excitement, knowing it's finally all coming together after loads of false starts.

To say I was worried about being able to find this stuff all in one place is putting it mildly. It was such an odd and varied list, I wasn't even sure if those items existed, which kind of made me feel doomed before I'd started. But Ava assured me not only that Lina could deliver but that she could also be trusted. And while I'm still not so sure about that last part, it's not like I had anywhere else to turn.

But the way Lina kept squinting at me, her gaze narrowing on mine as she gathered the powders and herbs, started to set me on edge. And when she held up the sketch I'd drawn and said, "What exactly are you practicing here? Is this some sort of alchemy?" I was sure I'd made a colossal mistake.

Ava glanced at me and was just about to step in when I shook my head and forced a laugh as I said, "Well, if you mean alchemy in its truest sense of mastering nature, averting chaos, and extending life for an indeterminate amount of time"—a definition I'd recently memorized after researching the term—"then no, I'm afraid my intentions aren't anywhere near that grand. I'm just trying out a little white magick—hoping to cast a spell that will get me through finals, get me a date for prom, and maybe even clear up my allergies, which are about to go haywire since it's nearly spring and I don't want my nose to be all red and drippy for prom pictures, you know?"

And when I saw how that failed to convince her, especially the part about the allergies, I added, "Which is why I need all that rose quartz, since, as you know, it's supposed to bring love, oh and then the turquoise—" I pointed at the pendant she wore. "Well, you know how it's famous for healing, and . . ." And even though I was prepared to go on and on, reciting the full list of things I'd learned merely an hour before, I decided to cut it right there and end with a shrug.

I unwrap the crystals, taking great care as I cradle them each in the palm of my hand, closing my fingers around them, and picturing a brilliant white light permeating straight through to their core, performing the all-important "cleansing and purifying" step, which, according to what I read online, is merely the first stage in programming the stones. The second is to ask them (out loud!) to soak up the moon's powerful energy so they can provide the service nature intended them for.

"Turquoise," I whisper, glancing at the door, making sure that it's closed all the way, imagining how embarrassing it would be for Sabine to barge in and catch me cooing to a pile of rocks. "I ask that you heal, purify, and help balance the chakras as nature intended you to do." Then I take a deep breath and infuse the stone with the energy of my intentions before slipping it into the bag and reaching for the next, feeling ridiculous and more than a little hokey, but knowing I've no choice but to continue.

I move on to the polished rose quartz, picking them up individually and infusing them with white light, before repeating four separate times, "May you bring unconditional love and infinite peace." Dropping them each into the red silk bag, watching as they settle around the turquoise before reaching for the staurolite—a beautiful stone believed to be formed from the tears of fairies, and asking it to provide ancient wisdom, good luck, and to help connect to the other dimensions, before moving on to the large chunk of zoisite, and holding it in both of my hands. After cleansing it with white light, I close my eyes and whisper, "May you transmute all negative energies to positive ones, may you aid in connecting to the mystical realms, and may you—"

"Ever? Can I come in?"

I glance at the door, knowing there's just an inch and a half of wood separating me from Sabine. Then I gaze at the pile of herbs, oils, candles, and powders, along with the rock I'm talking to in my hand.

"And please aid in recovery, illness, and whatever else it is that you do!" I whisper, barely getting the words out before I'm shoving it in the bag.

Only it won't fit.

"Ever?"

I shove it again, trying to jam it in there, but the opening's so small and the stone's so big it's not going to happen without ripping the seams.

Sabine knocks again, three firm raps meant to inform me that she knows I'm in here, knows I'm up to something, and that her patience is nearing its end. And even though I don't have time to chat, I'm left with no choice but to say, "Um, just a sec!" Forcing the stone inside as I run out to my balcony and drop it on a small table with the best view of the moon, before rushing back in and going into a full-blown meltdown when Sabine knocks again and I take in the state of my room—looking at it as she might see it, and knowing there's no time to change it.

"Ever? Are you okay?" she calls, with equal parts annoyance and concern.

"*Yeah*—I just—" I grab hold of the hem of my T-shirt and yank it over my head, turning my back toward the door as I say, "Um, you can come in now—I'm just—" And the moment she enters, I slide it back on. Faking a sudden bout of modesty, as though I can't bear for her to see me changing when I've never cared much before. "I'm—I was just changing," I mumble, seeing her brows merge as she looks me over, sniffing the air for the remnants of pot, alcohol, clove cigarettes, or whatever her latest teen-rearing book has warned her against.

"You got something on your—" She motions toward the front of my shirt. "Something—red that—well—that probably won't come out."

She twists her mouth to the side as I gaze down at the front of my T-shirt, seeing it marked by a big streak of red and immediately recognizing it as the powder I need for the elixir. Knowing its bag must have leaked when I see how it's spilled all over my desk as well as the floor underneath.

Great. Way to appear as though you were just changing into a clean shirt! I think, mentally rolling my eyes as she approaches my bed, perches herself on the edge and crosses her legs, her cell phone in hand. And all it takes is one look at the hazy reddish gray glow of her aura to know that the concerned look on her face has less to do with my apparent lack of clean clothes and more to do with me—my strange behavior, my growing secrecy, my food issues—all of which she's convinced lead to something more sinister.

And I'm so focused on how I might go about explaining those things that I fail to see it coming when she says, "Ever, did you ditch school today?"

I freeze, watching as she stares at my desk, taking in the mess of herbs and candles and oils and minerals and all kinds of other weird stuff she's not used to seeing—or at least not all grouped together like that—like they have a purpose—like the arrangement is far less random than it seems.

"Um, yeah. I had a headache. But it's no big deal." I plop onto my desk chair and swivel back and forth, hoping to distract her from the view.

She glances between the great alchemical experiment and me, and is just about to speak when I say, "Well, I mean, it's no big deal now that it's *gone*. Though believe me, it was at the time. I got one of my migraines. You know how I get those sometimes?"

I feel like the world's worst niece—an ungrateful liar—an insincere babbler of nonsense. She has no idea how lucky she is to be rid of me soon.

"Maybe it's because you're not eating enough." She sighs, kicking off her shoes and studying me closely as she says, "And yet, in spite of that, you seem to be growing like a weed. You're even taller than you were a few days ago!"

I gaze down at my ankles, shocked to see that my newly manifested jeans have crept up an inch since this morning.

"Why didn't you go to the nurse's office if you weren't feeling well? You know you're not allowed to just run off like that."

I gaze at her, wishing I could tell her not to sweat it, to not waste another second worrying about it since it'll be over with soon. Because as much as I'm going to miss her, there's no doubt her life will improve. She deserves better than *this.* Deserves better than *me.* And it's nice to know she'll soon have some peace.

"She's kind of a quack," I say. "A real aspirin pusher, and you know how that never works for me. I just needed to come home and lie down for a while. It's the only thing that ever works. So, I just—left."

"And did you?" She leans toward me. "Come home I mean?" And the moment our eyes meet, I know it's a challenge. I know it's a test.

"No." I sigh, staring down at the carpet as I wave my white flag. "I drove down to the canyon and just—"

She watches me, waiting.

"And I just got lost for a while." I take a deep breath and swallow hard, knowing that's as close to the truth as I can get.

"Ever, is this about Damen?"

And the moment my eyes meet hers, I can't hold back, I just burst into tears.

"Oh dear," she murmurs, her arms opening wide as I spring from my chair and tumble right in. Still so unused to my long gangly limbs, I'm clumsy and awkward and nearly knock her to the floor.

"Sorry," I say. "I—" But I'm unable to finish. A new rush of tears overtakes me, and I'm sobbing again.

She strokes my hair as I continue to cry, murmuring, "I know how much you miss him. I know how hard this must be."

But the second she says it, I pull away. Feeling guilty for acting as though this is just about Damen when the truth is it's only partly about him. It's also about missing my friends—in Laguna and in Oregon. And about missing my life—the one I've built here and the one I'm about to return to. Because even though it's obvious that they'll be better off without me, and I mean *everyone,* including Damen, that still doesn't make it any easier.

But it has to be done. There's really no choice.

And when I think of it like that, well, it does make it easier. Because the truth is, whatever the reason, I've been given an amazing, once in a lifetime opportunity.

And now it's time to go home.

I just wish I had a little more time for good-byes.

And when the thought of that brings a new rush of tears, Sabine holds me tighter, whispering words of encouragement, as I cling to her, held in the cocoon of her arms where everything feels safe—and warm—and right—and secure.

Like it's all going to work out just fine.

And as I burrow closer, my eyes closed, my face buried in the place where her shoulder meets her neck, my lips move softly, silently, saying good-bye.

forty

I wake up early. I guess since it's the last day of my life, or at least the last day of the life I've built here, I'm eager to make the most of it. And even though I'm sure I'll be greeted with a full-on chorus of the usual *Spaz! Loo-ser!* and the more recent *Witch!*, knowing it's the last time I'll be subjected to that makes all the difference.

At Hillcrest High (the school I'm returning to), I've got tons of friends. Which makes showing up Monday through Friday a lot more appealing, if not fun. And I don't remember ever once being tempted to ditch (like I am pretty much all the time here), and I wasn't depressed about not fitting in.

And to be honest, I think that's why I'm so eager to return. Because other than the obvious thrill of being with my family again, having a good group of friends who both love and accept me, and who I can be myself with—makes the decision that much easier.

A decision I wouldn't even stop to think twice about if it weren't for Damen.

But even though I can't quite wrap my mind around the fact that I'll never see him again—will never know the touch of his skin, the heat of his gaze, or the feel of his lips upon mine—I'm still willing to give it all up.

If it means reclaiming the old me and returning to my family—then there's really no choice.

I mean, Drina killed me so she could have Damen to herself. And Damen brought me back so he could have me to himself. And as much as I love him, as much as my whole heart aches at the thought of never seeing him again, I know now that the moment he returned me to life, he messed with the natural order of things. Turning me into something I was never meant to be.

And now it's my job to put it all back.

I stand before my closet and reach for my newest jeans, a black V-neck sweater, and my newish ballet flats—just like I wore in the vision I saw. Then I run my fingers through my hair, swipe on some lip gloss, insert the tiny diamond stud earrings my parents bought me for my sixteenth birthday (since they'll definitely notice if they're missing), along with the crystal horseshoe bracelet Damen gave me that has no place in the life I'm returning to, but there's no way I'm removing it.

Then I grab my bag, gaze around my ridiculously big room one last time, and head out the door. Eager to get one final peek at a life I didn't always enjoy and most likely won't even remember, but still needing to say some good-byes and set a few things straight before I'm gone for good.

The second I pull into the school parking lot, I start scanning for Damen. Searching for him, his car, anything, any little nugget, whatever I can get. Wanting to see as much of him as I can, while I can. And feeling disappointed when I don't find him.

I park my car and head to class, guarding against freaking out, jumping to conclusions, and overreacting just because he's not here yet. Because even though he's becoming increasingly normal as the poison slowly chips away at the progress of hundreds of years, from the way he looked yesterday—still gorgeous, still sexy, and not at all beginning to age—I'm guessing rock bottom is still days away.

Besides, I know he'll show up eventually. I mean, why wouldn't he? He's the undisputed star of this school. The best looking, the wealthiest, the one who throws the most amazing parties—or at least that's what I hear. He practically gets a standing ovation just for showing up. And tell me, who could resist that?

I move among the students, gazing at all the people I never even spoke to, and who barely spoke to me other than to yell something mean. And while I'm sure they won't miss me, I can't help but wonder if they'll even notice I'm gone. Or, if it'll all turn out like I think—I go back, they go back, and the time I spent here amounts to less than a blip on their screen.

I take a deep breath and head into English, bracing myself to see Damen with Stacia, but finding her sitting alone instead. I mean, she's gossiping with Honor and Craig as usual, but Damen's nowhere in sight. And as I pass her on the way to my seat, ready for just about anything she might toss in my path, I'm met only by silence, a stolid refusal to even acknowledge me, much less try to trip me, which fills me with dread and unease.

And after taking my seat and settling in, I spend the next fifty minutes glancing between the clock and the door, my anxiety growing with each passing moment. Imagining all manner of horrible scenarios until the bell finally rings and I bolt for the hall. And by fourth period when he still hasn't shown, I'm headed for a full-blown panic attack when I walk into history class and find Roman gone too.

"Ever," Mr. Munoz says, as I stand beside him, gaping at Roman's empty seat as my stomach fills with dread.

"You've got a lot of catching up to do."

I glance at him, knowing he wants to discuss my attendance, my missed assignments, and other irrelevant topics I don't need to hear. So I run out the door, racing through the quad and right past the lunch tables before I stop on the curb, gasping in relief when I see him. Or not *him,* but rather his car. The sleek black BMW he used to prize so much, that's now coated in a thick layer of dirt and grime and parked rather awkwardly in the no-parking zone.

Still, despite its filthy state, I gaze at it as though it's the most beautiful thing I've ever seen. Knowing that if his car's here, then he's here. And all is okay.

And just as I'm thinking I should try to move it so it doesn't get towed away, a throat clears from behind me and a deep voice says, "Excuse me, but aren't you supposed to be in class?"

I turn, my gaze meeting Principal Buckley's when I say, "Um, yeah, but first I just have to—" I motion toward Damen's poorly parked Beemer as though I'm doing a favor not just for my friend but for the sake of the school as well.

But Buckley's less concerned with parking violations and more concerned with repeat truancy offenders like me. And still smarting from our last unfortunate encounter when Sabine pleaded my case from expelled to suspended, he squints as he looks me over and says, "You've got two choices. I can call your aunt and ask her to leave work so she can come down here, *or*—" He pauses, trying to kill me with suspense even though you don't have to be psychic to know where this is going. "Or I can escort you back to class. Which would you prefer?"

For a moment, I'm tempted to choose option one—just to see what he'd do. But in the end, I follow him back to my class. His shoes pounding the cement as he leads me across the quad and down the hall before depositing me at Mr. Munoz's door where my gaze lands on Roman who's not only occupying his seat but shaking his head and laughing as I slink back toward mine.

And even though Munoz is used to my erratic behavior by now, he still makes a point of calling on me. Asking me to answer all manner of questions regarding historical events including those that we've studied and those that we haven't. And my mind is so preoccupied with Roman and Damen and my upcoming plans that I just answer robotically, *seeing* the answers he holds in his head and repeating them pretty much verbatim.

So when he says, "So tell me, Ever, what did I have for dinner last night?"

I automatically say, "Two pieces of leftover pizza and a glass and a half of Chianti." My mind is so ensconced in my own personal dramas it's a moment before I notice he's gaping.

In fact, everyone's gaping.

Well, everyone but Roman who just shakes his head and laughs even harder.

And just as the bell rings and I try to bolt for the door, Munoz steps before me and says, "How do you do it?"

I press my lips together and shrug as though I've no clue what he's talking about. Though it's clear he's not about to let it go, he's been wondering for weeks.

"How do you—*know stuff*?" he says, his eyes narrowed on mine. "About random historical facts we've never once studied—about *me*?"

I gaze down at the ground and take a deep breath, wondering what it could hurt to throw him a bone. I mean, I'm leaving tonight, and chances are he'll never remember this anyway, so what harm could it do to tell him the truth?

"I don't know." I shrug. "It's not like I *do* anything. Images and information just appear in my head."

He looks at me, struggling with whether or not to believe. And not having the time or desire to try to convince him, but still wanting to leave him with something nice, I say, "For instance, I know you shouldn't give up on your book because it's going to be published someday."

He gapes, his eyes wide, his expression wavering between wild hope and complete disbelief.

And even though it kills me to add it, even though the whole idea makes me want to hurl, I know there's something more that needs to be said, it's the right thing to do. Besides, what could it hurt? I mean, I'm leaving anyway, and Sabine deserves to get out and have a little fun. And other than his penchant for Rolling Stones boxers, Bruce Springsteen songs, and his obsession with Renaissance times—he seems harmless. Not to mention how it's not going to go anywhere anyway since I specifically saw her getting together with a guy who works in her building . . .

"Her name is Sabine," I say, before I have a chance to overthink it and change my mind. Then seeing the confusion in his eyes, I add, "You know, the petite blonde at Starbucks? The one who spilled her latte all over your shirt? The one you can't stop thinking about?"

And when he looks at me, it's clear that he's speechless. And preferring to leave it like that, I gather my stuff and head toward the door, glancing over my shoulder to say, "And you shouldn't be afraid to talk to her. Seriously. Just suck it up and approach her already. You'll find she's really nice."

forty-one

When I exit the room, I half expect to find Roman waiting for me with that same taunting gleam in his eye. But he's not. And when I get to the lunch tables, I know why.

He's performing. Orchestrating everyone around him, directing everything they say and do—like a bandleader, a puppet master, a big-top circus ringleader. And just as the hint of something nudges at the back of my mind, just as an inkling of insight begins to take shape—I see *him*.

Damen.

The love of every single one of my lives, now stumbling toward the lunch table, so unstable, so disheveled and haggard, there's no mistaking that things have progressed at an alarming rate. We are running out of time.

And when Stacia turns, makes a face, and hisses, "*Loo*-ser!" I'm stunned to realize the taunt is not meant for me.

It's directed at Damen.

And in a matter of seconds, the whole school joins in. All of the derision once reserved just for me is now directed at him.

I glance at Miles and Haven, watching as they add their voices to the chorus, then I rush toward Damen, alarmed to find his skin so clammy and cold, those once high cheekbones now alarmingly gaunt, and those deep dark eyes that once held such promise and warmth, now watery and rheumy and barely able to focus. And even though his lips are horribly dry and cracked, I still feel an undeniable longing to press mine against them. Because no matter what he looks like, no matter how much he's changed, he's still Damen. *My Damen.* Young or old, healthy or sick, it doesn't matter. He's the only one I've ever really cared about—the only one I've ever loved—and nothing Roman or anyone else does can ever change that.

"Hey," I whisper, my voice cracking as my eyes fill with tears. Tuning out the shrill taunts that surround us as I focus solely on him. Hating myself for turning my back long enough to allow this to happen, knowing he never would've let this happen to me.

He turns toward me, his eyes struggling to focus, and just when I think I've captured a glimmer of recognition—it's gone so fast I'm sure I imagined it.

"Let's get out of here," I say, tugging on his sleeve, trying to pull him alongside me. "What do you say we ditch?" I smile, hoping to remind him of our usual Friday routine. Just reaching the gate when Roman appears.

"Why do you bother?" he says, his arms folded, head cocked to the side, allowing his Ouroboros tattoo to flash in and out of view.

I grip Damen's arm and narrow my gaze, determined to get past Roman whatever it takes.

"Seriously, Ever." He shakes his head, glancing from Damen to me. "Why waste your time? He's old, feeble, practically decrepit, *and,* I'm sorry to say, but from the looks of things, not long for this earth. Surely you're not planning to waste your sweet young nectar on this dinosaur?"

He looks at me, blue eyes blazing, lips curving, glancing at the lunch table just as the shrill of taunts hits the next level.

And just like that *I know.*

The idea that's been nudging me, poking around the edges, and trying to get my attention, has finally been heard. And even though I'm not sure if I'm right, and knowing I'll have no choice but to slink off in shame if I'm wrong, I take in the crowd, my eyes moving from Miles to Haven to Stacia to Honor to Craig to every single kid who's just going through the motions, following along, doing what everyone else says and does without once stopping to question, without once asking *why*.

Then I take a deep breath, close my eyes, and focus all of my energy on them when I shout:

"WAKE UP!!!"

Then I stand there, far too ashamed to look now that all of their derision has switched from Damen to me. But I can't let that stop me, I *know* Roman's performed some sort of mass hypnosis, putting them into some kind of mindless trance where everyone's doing his bidding.

"Ever, please. Save yourself while you still can." Roman laughs. "Even I can't help you if you insists on continuing."

But I don't listen to him—can't listen. I have to find a way to stop him—to stop *them*! I've got to find a way to wake them all up, get them to snap out of it—

Snap!

That's it! I'll just snap my fingers and—

I take a deep breath, close my eyes, and yell as loud as I can:

"SNAP OUT OF IT!"

Which only results in my classmates going wild, their ridicule hitting the next level as a profusion of soda cans are hurled at my head.

Roman sighs, looking at me when he says, "Ever, *really*. I insist. You've got to stop this madness, *now*! You're making a bloody fool of yourself if you think that'll work! What're you gonna do next, slap all their cheeks?"

I stand there, my breath coming in short shallow gasps, knowing I'm not wrong, despite what he says. I'm sure he's got them spellbound, hijacked their minds by some kind of trance—

And then I remember this old documentary I once saw on TV, where the hypnotist brought the patient back not by slapping or snapping but by clapping on the count of three.

I take a deep breath, watching as my classmates climb on top of the table and benches, the better to pelt me with their uneaten food. And I know it's my last chance, that if this doesn't work—well—I don't know what I will do.

So I close my eyes, and yell:

"WAKE UP!"

Then I count from three to one and clap my hands twice at the end.

And then—

And then—nothing.

The whole school goes silent as they slowly come to.

They rub their eyes, blinking, yawning, and stretching as though awakening from a very long nap. Gazing around in confusion, wondering why they're on top of the table with the very same people they once deemed as freaks.

Craig is the first to react. Finding himself so close to Miles their shoulders practically touch, he bolts for the far end. Reassuring himself with the company of his fellow jocks, reclaiming his manhood with a punch on the arm.

And when Haven stares at her carrot sticks with a look of absolute disgust, I can't help but smile, knowing the big happy family is back to their normal routine of name-calling, eye-rolling, and snubbing each other in favor of their usual cliques, returned to a world where animosity and loathing still rule.

My school is back to normal again.

I turn toward the gate, prepared to take Roman down, but he's already gone. So I grip Damen tighter, easing him across the parking lot and into my car as Miles and Haven, the two best friends I've missed so much and will never see again, follow along.

"You guys know I love you, right?" I glance between them, knowing they'll freak, but it has to be said.

They look at each other, exchanging a look of alarm, both of them wondering what could've possibly happened to the girl they once pegged as the Ice Queen.

"Um, *okay* . . ." Haven says, shaking her head.

But I just smile and grasp them both to me, squeezing them tightly as I whisper to Miles, "Whatever you do don't stop acting or singing, it's going to bring you—" I stop, wondering if I should tell him how I just saw a flash of bright lights and Broadway, but not wanting to rob him of the journey by always looking ahead, I say, "It's going to bring you great happiness."

And before he can even respond, I've moved on to Haven, knowing I have to get this over with quick, so I can get Damen to Ava's, but determined to find a way to urge her to love herself more, to stop losing herself in others, and that Josh is worth hanging on to for however long it lasts. "You have so much value," I tell her. "So much to give—I just wish you could see how bright your star truly does shine."

"Um, gag!" she says, laughing as she untangles herself from my grip. "Are you okay?" She squints between me and Damen. "And what's up with him? Why's he all hunched over like that?"

I shake my head and climb inside, having no more time to waste. And as I back out of my space, I look out my window and say, "Hey, do you guys know where Roman lives?"

forty-two

I never imagined I'd be grateful for my sudden growth spurt and newly bulging biceps, but it's because of my new size and strength (not to mention Damen's emaciated state) that I practically carry him all the way from my car to Ava's front door in just a handful of steps. Supporting his body as I knock on her door, fully prepared to break it down if I have to, but glad when she answers and waves us both in.

I head for the hall as Damen stumbles along with me, pausing just outside the indigo door and gaping at Ava when she hesitates to open it.

"If your room is as sacred and pure as you think it is, then don't you think that will only help Damen? Don't you think he needs all the positive energy he can get?" I say, knowing she's conflicted about admitting the "contaminated" energy of a sick and dying man, which is just so ridiculous I hardly know where to begin.

She looks at me, holding my gaze far longer than my diminishing patience would prefer, and when she finally gives in, I barrel right past her, getting Damen settled on the futon in the corner and covering his body with the wool throw she keeps nearby.

"The juice is in my trunk, along with the antidote," I say, tossing her the keys. "The juice won't be any good for another two days, but he should be much better tonight, when the full moon rises and the antidote is ready. And then you can give him the juice later, to help rebuild his strength. Even though he probably won't even need it since it'll all reverse anyway. But still—just in case—" I nod, wishing I felt half as confident as I sound.

"Are you sure this'll work?" she asks, watching as I pull my very last bottle of elixir from my bag.

"It has to." I gaze at Damen, so pale, so weak, so—*old*. And yet, he's still Damen. Traces of his amazing beauty still present, marred only slightly by the acceleration of years resulting in his silver hair, his nearly translucent skin, the fan of wrinkles surrounding his eyes. "It's our only hope," I add, waving her away as I drop to my knees, the door closing behind me as I smooth his hair off his face and gently force him to drink.

At first he fights it, thrashing his head from side to side and keeping his mouth firmly closed. But when it's clear that I'm not about to give up, he gives in. Allowing the liquid to flow down his throat as his skin warms and his color returns. Emptying the bottle and gazing at me with such love and reverence, I'm overcome with joy just to know that he's back.

"I missed you," I murmur, nodding and blinking and swallowing hard, my heart bursting with yearning as I press my lips to his cheek. All the pent-up emotions I've fought so hard to keep in check all this time, now rushing to the surface, bubbling over, as I kiss him again and again. "You're going to be okay," I tell him. "You're going to be back to your old self very soon."

My sudden burst of happiness withering like a popped balloon as his gaze turns dark and sweeps over my face.

"You left me," he whispers.

I shake my head, wanting him to know it's not true. I never left him—he left me—but it wasn't his fault and I forgive him. I forgive him for everything he's ever done—or said—even though it's already too late—even though it doesn't really matter anymore—

But instead I just say, "No. I haven't. You've been ill. *Very* ill. But it's over with now and soon you'll be better. You just have to promise to drink the antidote when—" *When Ava gives it to you*—the words I can't bear to say, *won't* say, not wanting him to know that this is our last moment together—our final good-bye.

"All you need to know is that you're going to be fine. But you need to watch out for Roman. He's not your friend. He's evil. He's trying to kill you. So you must regain your strength so you can take him down."

I press my mouth to his forehead, his cheek, unable to stop until I've covered his entire face with my kiss. Tasting my own salty tears on the curve of his lips, as I breathe him in, hoping to imprint his scent, his taste, the feel of his skin, wanting to carry the memory of him wherever I go.

But even after I tell him I love him—even after I lie down beside him, pull him into my arms, and press his body to mine—even after I remain there for hours, lying right alongside him as he sleeps—even after I close my eyes and concentrate on melding my energy with his, hoping to heal him with my love, my essence, my very being, trying to impress some small part of myself onto him—even after all of that—the moment I move away, he says it again.

An accusation from his dream state, intended only for me.

"You left me."

Not realizing until I've said my final good-bye and closed the door behind me, that he's not referring to the past.

He's prophesying our future.

forty-three

I head down the hall and into the kitchen, my heart heavy, my legs wooden, and every step away from Damen just makes it worse.

"You okay?" Ava asks, standing at the stove, brewing some tea. As though all of those hours didn't just pass.

I shake my head and lean against the wall, unsure how to answer, unable to speak. Because the truth is, *okay* is pretty much the last thing I feel. Empty, hollow, bereft, awful, depressed—yes. But *okay*? Not so much.

But that's because I'm a criminal. A traitor. I'm the worst kind of person you could ever hope to meet. All of the times I tried to imagine that scene, tried to imagine how my last moment with Damen would be, I never once thought it would end like that.

I never once thought I'd stand accused. Even though I clearly deserve to be.

"You don't have much time." She gazes at the clock on her wall, then at me. "Would you like some tea before you leave?"

I shake my head, knowing I've a few things still to tell her, and a few more stops to make before I go for good.

"So you know what to do?" I ask, seeing her nod as she brings her cup to her lips. "Because I'm trusting you, Ava. If this doesn't work out in the way that I think, if the only thing that goes back is me, then you're my only hope." My gaze locks on hers, needing her to understand just exactly how serious this all is. "You've *got* to take care of Damen, he's—he doesn't deserve any of this, and—" My voice cracks as I press my lips together and avert my gaze. Knowing I've got to go on, that there's still more to say, but needing a moment before I can. "And watch out for Roman. He's good-looking and charming, but it's all a façade. Inside, he's evil, he tried to kill Damen, he's responsible for what he's become."

"Don't worry." She moves toward me. "Don't worry about a thing. I got the stuff out of your trunk, the antidote is in the cupboard, the juice is—fermenting, and I'll add the herb on the third day like you said. Not that we'll even need it, since I'm sure everything will go exactly as planned."

I look at her, seeing the sincerity in her eyes, relieved that at least I'm able to leave things in her capable hands.

"So you just get yourself over to Summerland, and I'll take care of the rest," she says, pulling me into her arms and hugging me tightly to her chest. "And who knows? Maybe someday you'll find yourself in Laguna Beach and we'll meet all over again?"

She laughs when she says it and I wish I could laugh along with her, but I can't. The weird thing about saying good-bye is that it never gets any easier.

I pull away, nodding in place of words, knowing that to say anything more will make me break down completely. Barely managing to eek out a "Thanks," before I'm already at the door.

"You've nothing to be thanking me for," she says, following behind. "But, Ever, are you sure you don't want to peek in on Damen, just one last time?"

I turn, my hand on the doorknob, considering, but only for a moment before I take a deep breath and shake my head. Knowing there's no use in prolonging the inevitable, and far too afraid to risk seeing the accusation on his face.

"We've already said good-bye," I say, stepping onto the porch and moving toward my car. "Besides, I don't have much time. There's still one last stop I need to make."

forty-four

I turn onto Roman's street, park in his drive, rush toward the door, and kick it right down. Watching the wood crack and splinter as it teeters from its hinges and swings open before me, hoping to catch him off guard, so I can punch all of his chakras and be done with him for good.

I creep inside, my eyes darting around, taking in walls the color of eggshells, ceramic vases filled with silk flowers, poster-sized prints of all the usual suspects—Van Gogh's *The Starry Night,* Gustav Klimt's *The Kiss,* and an oversized rendition of Botticelli's *The Birth of Venus* framed in gold and hanging right over the mantel. All of it appearing so surprisingly normal, I can't help but wonder if I've got the wrong house.

I expected grit, edge, a post-apocalyptic pad with black leather couches, chrome tables, an abundance of mirrors, and confusing art—something sleeker, hipper, anything but this chintz-ridden fuss palace that's nearly impossible to imagine someone like Roman living in.

I tour the house, checking every room, every closet, even under the bed. But when it's clear he's not home, I head straight for his kitchen, find his supply of immortal juice, and pour it straight down the drain. Knowing it's juvenile, useless, and probably won't make the least bit of difference, since the moment I go back everything will reverse itself again. But even if it adds up to no more than a minor inconvenience, at least he'll know that inconvenience came from me.

Then I riffle through his drawers, searching for a piece of scrap paper and a pen, needing to make a list of all the things I can't afford to forget. A simple set of instructions that won't be too confusing for someone who probably won't remember what any of it means, and yet still clear and concise enough to keep me from repeating the same horrible mistakes all over again.

Writing:

1. Don't go back for the sweatshirt!
2. Don't trust Drina!
3. Don't go back for the sweatshirt *no matter what!*

And then, just so I don't completely forget, and hoping it might trigger some sort of memory, I add:

4. Damen ♡

And after checking it over again (and again), making sure it's all there and that nothing's been missed, I fold it into a square, shove it deep in my pocket, and head for the window, gazing at a sky turned a deep sunless blue, with the moon hanging heavy and full just off to the side. Then I take a deep breath and head for the ugly chintz couch, knowing it's time.

I close my eyes and reach toward the light, eager to experience that shimmering glory one final time as I land on those soft blades of grass in that vast fragrant field. Aided by their buoyancy and bounce as I run, skip, and twirl through the meadow, performing cartwheels, back handsprings, and somersaults, my fingertips grazing over those glorious flowers with their pulsating petals and delicious sweet scent as I wind my way through those vibrating trees along the colorful stream. Determined to take it all in, to memorize every last detail, wishing there was some way to capture this wonderful feeling and hold it forever.

And then, because I have a few moments to spare, and because I need to see him one last time, need to be with him in the way that we used to, I close my eyes and manifest Damen.

Seeing him as he first appeared to me in the parking lot at school. Starting with his shiny dark hair that waves around his cheekbones and hits just shy of his shoulders, those almond-shaped eyes so deep, dark, and even, back then, strangely familiar. And those lips! Those ripe inviting lips with their perfect Cupid's bow, followed by the long, lean, muscular body that holds it all up. My memory so potent, so tangible, every nuance, every pore, is present and accounted for.

And when I open my eyes, he's bowing before me, offering his hand in our very last dance. So I place my hand in his as he tucks his arm around my waist, leading me through that glorious field in a series of wide sweeping arcs, our bodies swaying, our feet floating, twirling to a melody heard only by us. And every time he begins to slip from my grasp, I just close my eyes and make him again, resuming our steps without falter. Like Count Fersen and Marie, Albert and Victoria, Antony and Cleopatra, we are all the world's greatest lovers, we are all the couples we've ever been. And I bury my face in the warm sweet hollow of his neck, reluctant to let our song end.

But even though there's no time in Summerland, there is where I'm going. And so I run my fingers along the planes of his face, memorizing the softness of his skin, the curve of his jaw, and the swell of his lips as they press against mine—convincing myself that it's him—*really him!*

Even long after he's faded and gone.

• • •

The moment I head out of the field, I find Romy and Rayne waiting right by the edge, and from the looks on their faces I know they've been watching.

"You're running out of time," Rayne says, staring at me with those saucer-sized eyes that never fail to set me on edge.

But I just shake my head and pick up the pace, annoyed to know they've been spying, and tired of the way they keep butting in.

"I've got it all covered," I say, glancing over my shoulder. "So feel free to—" I pause, having no idea what they do when they're not bothering me. So I lift my shoulders and leave it at that, knowing whatever they're up to, it no longer concerns me.

They run alongside me, peering at each other, communicating in their private twin speak before saying, "Something's not right." They stare at me, urging me to listen. "Something feels terribly wrong." Their voices blending together in perfect harmony.

But I just shrug, not the least bit interested in cracking their code, and when I see those marble steps before me, I storm straight ahead, glimpsing the world's most beautiful structures, before rushing right in. The twins' voices silenced by the doors closing behind me as I stand in the grand marble entry, eyes closed tight, hoping I won't be shut out like the last time, hoping I can go back in time. Thinking:

I'm ready. I'm really and truly ready. So please, let me go back. Back to Eugene, Oregon. Back to my mom and dad and Riley and Buttercup. Please just let me return . . . and set everything straight again . . .

And the next thing I know a short hallway appears, leading to a room at the end—a room that's empty except for a stool and a desk. But not just any old desk, this is one of those long metal desks like the kind we had in the chem lab at my old school. And as I slide onto the seat, a large crystal globe levitates before me, flickering and flaring until it settles on an image of me, sitting at this same metal desk, struggling over a science test. And even though it's pretty much the last scene I ever would've chosen to repeat, I know it's the only opportunity I'll ever get to return. So I take a deep breath, press my finger to the screen—and gasp as everything around me goes black.

forty-five

"O—migod. I *totally* flunked that," Rachel groans, tossing her wavy brown hair over her shoulder and rolling her eyes. "I mean, I *barely* even studied last night. Seriously. And then I stayed up late texting—" She looks at me, her eyes wide as she shakes her head. "Anyway. All you need to know is that my life as we know it is over. So take a good look at me now because as soon as those grades are posted and my parents find out, I'll be grounded for life. Which means this is pretty much the last you'll see of me."

"Please." I roll my eyes. "If anyone flunked, we both know it's me. I've been lost in that class all year! And it's not like I'm going to be a scientist or anything. It's not like I'm ever going to *use* the information." I stop just shy of her locker, watching as she unlocks it and tosses a pile of books inside.

"I'm just glad it's over and that grades won't be out until next week. Which means I better live it up while I can. And speaking of—what time should I swing by tonight?" she asks, brows raised so high they're hidden under her bangs.

I shake my head and sigh, realizing I haven't told her yet and knowing she's gonna be mad. "About that . . ." I walk alongside her as we head for the parking lot, tucking my long blond hair behind my ear as I say, "Slight change of plans. My mom and dad are going out and I'm supposed to babysit Riley."

"And how is that a *slight* change of plans?" Rachel stops just short of the lot, her eyes scanning the rows of cars, determined to see who's riding with who.

"Well, I thought maybe after she goes to sleep, you can come over and—" But I stop, not bothering to finish since it's clear she's not listening. The second I mentioned my little sister, I lost her. Rachel's that rare only child who's never once fantasized about having a brother or sister. Sharing the spotlight just isn't her thing.

"Forget it," she says. "Little people have sticky fingers and big ears, you can't trust 'em. How about tomorrow?"

I shake my head. "Can't. It's family day. We're all heading up to the lake."

"See." Rachel nods. "That's exactly the kind of stuff you don't have to deal with when your parents split. In our house, family day is when we all meet in court to fight over the child support check."

"You don't know how lucky you are," I say, regretting the joke the second it's out. Because not only is it a total lie, but something about it leaves me feeling so sad and guilty I wish I could take it right back.

But it's not like Rachel was listening anyway. She's too busy trying to get the attention of the amazing Shayla Sparks, who's pretty much the coolest senior to ever walk the halls of this school. Frantically waving and stopping just short of jumping up and down and screaming like a groupie, hoping to get Shayla's attention as she loads up her sky-blue VW Bug with all her cool friends. Then lowering her hand and pretending to scratch at her ear as though she's not the least bit embarrassed when Shayla fails to acknowledge her.

"Trust me, that car's not so great," I say, checking my watch and gazing around the lot, wondering just where the heck Brandon is since he really should've been here by now. "The Miata drives better."

"Excuse me?" Rachel peers at me, her brows knit together in complete disbelief. "And since when have you driven either one?"

I squint, hearing the words repeat in my head and having no idea why I just said them. "Um, I didn't." I shrug. "I—I guess I must've read it somewhere."

She looks at me, her eyes narrowed as they work their way down my outfit, grazing over my black V-neck sweater and down to my jeans that are dragging on the ground. "And where'd you get *this*?" She grasps my wrist.

"Please. You've seen that like a million times already. I got it last Christmas," I say, trying to break free of her grip as Brandon comes toward me, thinking how cute he is when his hair falls into his eyes.

"Not the watch silly, *this*!" She taps the bracelet that's next to the watch, the one with silver horseshoes encrusted with pink crystal bits—the one that's not the slightest bit familiar though somehow manages to make my stomach go all weird when I look at it.

"I—I don't know," I mumble, wincing when I see her gape at me like I'm losing it. "I mean, I think my aunt might've sent it to me, you know, the one I told you about, the one who lives in Laguna Beach—"

"Who lives in Laguna Beach?" Brandon asks, slipping his arm around me, as Rachel glances between us, rolling her eyes when he leans in to kiss me. But something about the feel of his lips is so strange and unsettling, I quickly turn away.

"My ride's here," Rachel says, rushing toward her mom's SUV and calling over her shoulder to say, "Let me know if anything changes—you know, about tonight?"

Brandon looks at me, pulling me tighter against him until I'm practically fused to his chest, which only makes my stomach go weird again.

"If what changes?" he asks, oblivious to the way I squirm out of his arms, unaware of my sudden lack of interest, which is a total relief since I've no idea how to explain it.

"Oh, she wants to hit Jaden's party, but I'm scheduled to babysit," I tell him, heading toward his Jeep and tossing my bag onto the floor by my feet.

"Want me to stop by?" He smiles. "You know, in case you need help?"

"No!" I say, too forceful, too quick. Knowing I need to backtrack fast when I see the look on his face. "I mean, Riley always stays up late, so it's probably not a good idea."

He looks at me, his eyes grazing over me like he feels it too, the unidentified *big wrong thing* that hovers between us, making everything feel so dang weird. Then he shrugs and turns toward the road. Choosing to drive the rest of the way in silence. Or at least he and I are silent. His stereo is screaming full blast. And even though that usually gets on my nerves, today I'm glad. I'd rather focus on crap music I can't stand, than the fact that I don't want to kiss him.

I look at him, *really* look at him in the way I haven't done since I've gotten used to us being a couple. Taking in the swoop of bangs framing those big green eyes that slant down ever so slightly at the corners making him impossible to resist—except for today. Today it comes easy. And when I remember how just yesterday I was covering my notebook with his name, well, it just doesn't make any sense.

He turns, catching me staring and smiling as he takes my hand. Entwining his fingers with mine and squeezing them in a way that makes my stomach go queasy. But I force myself to return it, both the smile and the squeeze, knowing it's expected, what a good girlfriend does. Then I gaze out the window, holding down the nausea as I stare at the passing landscape, the rain-soaked streets, the clapboard houses and pine trees, glad to be getting home soon.

"So, tonight?" He pulls into my drive, muting the sound as he leans toward me and looks at me in that way that he has.

But I just press my lips together and reach for my bag, holding it against my chest like a shield, a solid defense meant to keep him away. "I'll text you," I mumble, avoiding his eyes as I glance out the window, seeing my neighbor and her daughter playing catch on the lawn, as I reach for the door handle, desperate to get away from him and into my room.

And just as I've opened the door and slipped one leg out, he says, "Aren't you forgetting something?"

I gaze down at my backpack, knowing it's all that I brought, but when I look at him again, I realize he's not referring to that. And knowing there's only one way to get through this without arousing any more suspicions from him or from me, I lean toward him, closing my eyes as I press my lips against his, finding them objectively smooth, pliant, but basically neutral, with none of their usual spark.

"I'll—um, I'll see you later," I mumble, hopping out of his Jeep and wiping my mouth on my sleeve well before I've even reached the front door. Rushing inside and heading straight to the den where I'm blocked by a plastic drum set, a guitar with no strings, and a small black microphone that's going to break if Riley and her friend don't stop fighting over it.

"We already agreed," Riley says, yanking the mic toward her. "*I* sing all the boy songs, and *you* sing all the girl songs. What's the problem?"

"The problem," her friend whines, pulling it even harder. "Is that there's hardly any girl songs. And you know it."

But Riley just shrugs. "That's not my fault. Take it up with Rock Band, not me."

"I swear, you are so—" Her friend stops when she sees me standing in the doorway, shaking my head.

"You guys need to take turns," I say, giving Riley a pointed look, glad to be presented with a problem I can handle, even though I wasn't consulted. "Emily, you get the next song, and Riley, you get the one after that, and then so on. Think you can handle that?"

Riley rolls her eyes as Emily snatches the mic from her hand.

"Is Mom around?" I ask, ignoring Riley's scowl since I'm pretty much used to it by now.

"She's in her room. Getting ready," she says, watching me leave as she whispers to her friend, "Fine. I get to sing 'Dead on Arrival,' you can sing 'Creep.' "

I pass by my room, drop my bag on the floor, then make my way into my mom's room, leaning against the archway that separates the bedroom from the bathroom and watching as she puts on her makeup, remembering how I used to love to do this back when I was little and thought my mom was the most glamorous woman on the planet. But when I look at her now, I mean, look at her objectively, I realize she actually is kind of glamorous, at least in a suburban mom kind of way.

"How was school?" she asks, turning her head from side to side, making sure her foundation is blended and seamless.

"Fine." I shrug. "We had a test in science, which I probably failed," I tell her, even though I don't really believe it went all that bad, but not knowing how to express what I really want to say—that everything feels strange, and uncertain, like it's off balance, lacking—and hoping for any reaction I can get out of her.

But she just sighs and moves on to her eyes, sweeping her small makeup brush over her lids and across the crease as she says, "I'm sure you didn't fail." She glances at me through the mirror. "I'm sure you did just fine."

I trace my hand over a smudge on the wall, thinking I should leave, go to my room and chill out for a while, listen to some music, read a good book, anything to take my mind off of me.

"Sorry this is so last minute," she says, pumping her mascara wand in and out of its tube. "I know you probably had plans."

I shrug, twisting my wrist back and forth, watching the way the crystals in my bracelet flicker and flare, glinting in the fluorescent light and trying to remember where it came from. "That's all right," I tell her. "There'll be plenty of other Friday nights."

My mom squints, mascara in hand, pausing in midstroke as she says, "Ever? Is that you?" She laughs. "Is something going on that I should know about? Because that hardly sounds like my daughter."

I take a deep breath and lift my shoulders, wishing I could tell her how something is most definitely going on, something I can't quite place, something that leaves me feeling so—unlike me.

But I don't. I mean, I can barely explain it to myself, much less her. All I know is that yesterday I felt fine—and today—pretty much the opposite of fine. Alien even—like I no longer fit—like I'm a round girl in a square world.

"You know I'm okay with you inviting a few friends over," she says, moving on to her lips, coating them with a swipe of lipstick before enhancing the color with a touch of gloss. "As long as you keep it to a minimum, no more than three, and as long as you don't ignore your sister."

"Thanks." I nod, forcing a smile so she'll think I'm okay. "But I'm kind of looking forward to having a night off from all that."

I head to my room and plop down on my bed, fully content to just stare at the ceiling, until I realize how pathetic that is and I reach for the book on my nightstand instead. Immersed in the story of a guy and girl so entwined, so perfectly made for each other, their love transcends time. Wishing I could climb inside those pages and live there forever, preferring their story to mine.

"Hey, Ev." My dad pokes his head into my room. "I've come to say both hello and good-bye. We're running late, so we gotta leave soon."

I toss my book aside and race toward him, hugging him so tight he laughs and shakes his head.

"Nice to know you're not too grown up to hug your old man." He smiles, as I pull away, horrified to find that there are *actual tears* in my eyes, and busying myself with some books on a shelf until I'm sure the threat is long past. "Make sure you and your sister are packed and ready to leave. I want to be on the road nice and early tomorrow."

I nod, disturbed by the strange hollow feeling invading my gut as he leaves. Wondering, not for the first time, just what the heck is going on with me.

forty-six

"Forget it. You're not the boss of me, Ever!" Riley shouts, arms folded, face scowling, refusing to budge.

I mean, who would've guessed that a ninety-pound twelve-year-old could be such a force of nature? But no way am I giving in. Because the second my parents left and Riley was watered and fed, I sent Brandon a text, telling him to come by around ten, which is any minute now so it's imperative I get her to bed.

I shake my head and sigh, wishing she didn't have to be so dang stubborn, but fully prepared to do battle. "Um, I hate to break it to you," I say. "But you're wrong. I *am* the boss of you. From the moment Mom and Dad left until the time they return, I am one hundred percent the boss of you. And you can argue all you want, but it won't change a thing."

"This is so *unfair*!" She glares. "I swear, the second I turn thirteen there's going to be some *equality* around here."

But I just shrug, as eager for that moment as she. "Good, then I won't have to babysit you anymore and I can get my life back," I say, watching as she rolls her eyes and taps her foot against the carpeted floor.

"Please. You think I'm stupid? You think I don't know Brandon's coming over?" She shakes her head. "Big deal. Who even cares? All

I want to do is watch TV—*that's it.* And the only reason you won't let me is because you want to hog the den with your boyfriend so you can make out on the couch. And that's exactly what I'm gonna tell Mom and Dad if you don't let me watch my show."

"Big deal. Who even cares?" I say, delivering a pitch-perfect imitation of her. "Mom said I could have friends over, *so there.*" But the moment it's out, I can't help but cringe, wondering who's the child here, her or me?

I shake my head, knowing it's just another empty threat, but not willing to take any chances, I say, "Dad wants to leave early, which means you need to get some sleep so you're not all grumpy and cranky in the morning. And for your information, Brandon's *not* coming over." I smirk, hoping it'll mask the fact that I'm a horrible liar.

"Oh yeah?" She smiles, her eyes lighting up as they focus on mine. "Then why'd his Jeep just pull into the drive?"

I turn, peering out the window, then glancing at her. Sighing under my breath as I say, "Fine. Watch your show. Whatever. See if I care. But if it gives you nightmares again, don't come crying to me."

"C'mon, Ever, what's your deal?" Brandon says, his expression crossing the border from curious to annoyed in a matter of seconds. "I waited over an hour for your little sister to go to bed so we could be together and now you start acting like *this*. What gives?"

"Nothing," I mumble, refusing his gaze as I readjust my top. Peering at him from the corner of my eye as he shakes his head and buttons his jeans—jeans that I never asked to be *unbuttoned* in the first place.

"This is ridiculous," he mutters, shaking his head and fastening his belt. "I drive all the way over here, your parents are gone, and now you're acting like—"

"Like what?" I whisper, wanting him to say it. Hoping he can sum it up in just a few words, define just what it is that I'm going through. Because earlier, when I changed my mind and sent him the text asking him to come over, I thought it would put everything back to normal again. But from the moment I answered the door, my first instinct was to close it again. And no matter how hard I try, I can't figure out why I'm feeling this way.

I mean, when I look at him, it's obvious how lucky I am. He's nice, he's cute, he plays football, he's got a cool car, he's one of the most popular juniors—not to mention that I liked him for so long I could hardly believe it when I learned he liked me. But now everything's different. And it's not like I can force myself to feel things that I don't.

I take a deep breath, fully aware of the weight of his stare as I toy with my bracelet. Turning it around and around, trying to remember just how it got there. Aware of something niggling at the back of my mind, something about—

"Forget it," he says, getting up to leave. "But I'm serious, Ever. You need to decide what you want pretty soon, because this . . ."

I gaze at him, wondering if he'll finish the sentence and wondering why I can't seem to care either way.

But he just looks at me and shakes his head, grabbing his keys as he says, "Whatever. Have fun at the lake."

I watch as the door closes behind him, then I move to my dad's recliner, grab the afghan my grandma knit for us not long before she died, and pull it up to my chin and tuck it under my feet. Remembering how just last week I was telling Rachel I was seriously considering going all the way with Brandon, and now—now I can barely stand for him to touch me.

"Ever?"

I open my eyes. Riley's standing before me, her bottom lip trembling, her blue eyes on mine.

"Is he gone?" She glances around the room.

I nod.

"Will you come sit with me, while I try to fall asleep?" she asks, biting down on her lip, giving me that sad puppy dog look that's impossible to resist.

"I told you that show was too scary for you," I say, my hand on her shoulder as we head down the hall, getting her all tucked and settled before arranging myself right around her. Wishing her the sweetest of dreams and smoothing her hair off her face as I whisper, "Don't worry. Go to sleep. There's no such thing as ghosts."

forty-seven

"Ever, you ready? We need to leave soon! We don't want to hit traffic!"

"Coming!" I shout, even though I'm not. I just continue to stand there, right smack in the middle of my room staring at a crumpled piece of paper I'd found in the front pocket of my jeans. And even though it's written in my hand, I've no idea how it got there, much less what it means. Reading:

1. Don't go back for the sweatshirt!
2. Don't trust Drina!
3. Don't go back for the sweatshirt *no matter what!*
4. Damen ♡

And by the fifth time I read it, I'm still just as confused as the first. I mean, what sweatshirt? And why am I not supposed to go back for it? Not to mention, do I even know a Drina? And who the heck is Damen, and why is there a heart by his name?

I mean, *why* did I ever write such a thing? *When* did I ever write such a thing? And what could it possibly mean?

And when my dad calls again, followed by the sound of his footsteps storming up the stairs, I toss the paper aside, watching it land on my dresser before falling to the floor, figuring I'll sort it all out when we return.

As it turns out, the weekend was good for me. Good to get away from my school, good to get away from my friends (and boyfriend). Good to spend time with my family in a way that we don't get to do all that often. In fact, I feel so much better now, that as soon as we get back to civilization, back to where my cell can access a signal—I'm going to text Brandon. I don't want to leave things the way we had. And I really believe that whatever weird thing I was going through is now past.

I grab my backpack and toss it over my shoulder, ready to leave. But as I glance around our campsite one last time, I can't shake the feeling that I've left something behind. Even though my bag is packed and everything appears to be clear, I continue to stand there, my mom calling my name over and over, until she finally gives up and sends Riley.

"Hey," she says, pulling hard on my sleeve. "C'mon, everyone's waiting."

"In a minute," I mumble. "I just have to—"

"Have to *what*?" She smirks. "You have to stare at the smoldering embers for another hour or two? Seriously, Ever, what's your deal?"

I shrug, toying with the clasp on my bracelet, having no idea what my *deal* is, but unable to shake the feeling that something is wrong. Well, maybe not *wrong* exactly, more like *missing* or *undone*. Like there's something I'm supposed to be doing that I'm not. And I just can't decide what it is.

"Seriously. Mom wants you to hurry, Dad's worried about hitting traffic, even Buttercup wants you to get it together so he can stick his head out the window and let his ears flap in the breeze. Oh, and I'd kind of like to get home before all the good shows are over. So, what do you say we move it, okay?"

But when I don't move it, when I don't do much of anything, she sighs and says, "You forget something? Is that it?" Eyeballing me carefully before glancing over her shoulder toward our parents.

"Maybe." I shake my head. "I'm not sure."

"You got your backpack?"

I nod.

"You got your cell phone?"

I tap my backpack.

"You got your brain?"

I laugh, knowing I'm acting strange and ridiculous and freaky as hell, but then after the last few days you'd think I'd be used to it by now.

"You got your sky-blue Pinecone Lake Cheerleading Camp sweatshirt?" She smiles.

"That's it!" I say, my heart beating frantically. "I left it by the lake! Tell Mom and Dad I'll be right back!"

But just as I turn, Riley grabs hold of my sleeve and pulls me right back. "Chillax." She smiles. "Dad found it and tossed it in the backseat. Seriously. So can we go now?"

I glance around the campsite one last time, then follow Riley to the car. Settling into the back as my dad pulls onto the road and a muffled chime comes from my phone. And I've barely dug it out of my bag, barely even had a chance to read it, before Riley's peering over my shoulder, trying to peek. Forcing me to turn so abruptly, Buttercup shifts, shooting me a look that lets me know she's not happy. But even after all that, Riley still tries to see. So I roll my eyes and do what I always do, I whine, *"Mom!"*

Watching as she flips a page in her magazine without missing a beat, automatically saying, "Stop it you two."

"You didn't even look!" I say. "*I* wasn't doing anything! Riley won't leave me alone."

"That's because she *loves* you," my dad says, meeting my eyes in the rearview mirror. "She loves you *so much* she wants to be around you *all* of the time—she just can't get enough of you!"

Words that send Riley clear to the other side of the car, pressing her body against the door as she shouts, "Gag!" Then swinging her legs to her side as far as she can, upsetting poor Buttercup all over again. Shivering dramatically, as though the thought is just way too disgusting to bear, as my dad catches my eye and both of us laugh.

I flip my phone open, reading the message from Brandon that says: *Sorry. My bad. Call me 2nite.* And I immediately respond with a smiley face, hoping that'll tide us over until I can work up enough emotion to send something more.

And I've just leaned my head against the window and am about to close my eyes when Riley turns to me and says, "You can't go back, Ever. You can't change the past. *It just is.*" I squint, having no idea what she's talking about. But just as I start to ask, she shakes her head and says, "This is *our* destiny. *Not* yours. Did you ever stop and think that maybe you were supposed to survive? That maybe, it wasn't just Damen who saved you?"

I stare at her, my mouth hanging open, trying to make sense of her words. And when I glance around the car, wondering if my parents heard too, I see that everything is frozen. My dad's hands are stuck on the steering wheel, his unblinking eyes staring straight ahead, while the page of my mom's magazine is stuck in midflip, and Buttercup's tail is caught at half-mast. Even when I gaze out the window, I notice how all the birds are caught in midflight, while the other motorists are paused all around us. And when I look at Riley again, her intense gaze on mine as she leans toward me, it's clear we're the only ones moving.

"You have to go back," she says, her voice confident, firm. "You have to find Damen—before it's too late."

"Too late for *what*?" I cry, leaning toward her, desperate to understand. "And who the heck is Damen? Why are you saying that name? What does it even mean—"

But before I can finish, she's already rolling her eyes and pushing me away as though none of it happened.

"Jeez, stalk much?" She shakes her head. "I mean, seriously, Ever. *Boundaries!* Because regardless of what *he* thinks," she points toward our dad, "I have absolutely no interest in *you*."

She rolls her eyes and turns away, singing along to her iPod, her voice raspy, warbled, croaking out a Kelly Clarkson song in a way it was never intended. Oblivious to my mom who smiles and chucks her lightly on the knee, oblivious to my dad, gazing at me through the rearview mirror, our smiles meeting at the exact same moment, sharing a joke meant only for us.

Still holding that smile as a huge logging truck pulls out in front of us, slamming into the side of our car, and making the whole world go black.

forty-eight

The next thing I know I'm sitting on my bed, mouth wide open in a silent scream that never had a chance to be heard. Having lost my family for the second time in a year, left with only the echo of Riley's words:

You have to find Damen—before it's too late!

I spring from my bed and bolt for my den, going straight for the minifridge and finding the elixir and antidote gone. Unsure if it means I'm the only one who went back in time while everyone else stayed the same, or if I'm picking up right where I left off—with Damen in danger and me running away.

I sprint down the stairs, moving so fast they're like a blur under my feet, having no idea what day it is, or even what time, but knowing I've got to make it to Ava's before it's too late.

But just when I hit the landing, Sabine calls out, "Ever? Is that you?"

And I freeze, watching as she comes around the corner, wearing a stained apron with a full plate of brownies in hand.

"Oh, good." She smiles. "I just tried your mom's recipe—you know the ones she always used to bake? And I want you to try one and tell me what you think."

I freeze, unable to do anything but blink. Forcing a patience I don't really have when I say, "I'm sure they're fine. Listen, Sabine, I—"

But she doesn't let me finish. She just cocks her head to the side and says, "Well, aren't you at least going to try one?"

And I know this is not just about seeing me eat, it's also about wanting approval—*my* approval. She's been questioning whether or not she's fit to look after me, wondering if she's in some way responsible for my behavioral problems, thinking that if she'd only handled things better, none of this would've happened. I mean, my brilliant, successful, high-performing aunt, who's never lost a single court case—wants approval from *me*.

"Just one," she insists. "It's not like I'm trying to *poison* you!" And when her eyes meet mine, I can't help but notice her seemingly random choice of words, wondering if it's some sort of message, pushing me to hurry, but knowing I have to get through this first. "I know they're probably not nearly as good as your mom's, because hers were the undisputed best, but it *is* her recipe—and for some reason I woke up early this morning with this overwhelming urge to make them. And so I thought—"

Knowing she's capable of going into a full-on opening argument in her pursuit to convince me, I reach toward the stack of brownies. Going for the smallest square, figuring I'll just eat it and run. But when I see the unmistakable letter *E* carved right in its center—I *know.*

It's my sign.

The one I've been waiting for all along.

Just when I'd given up hope, Riley pulled through. Marking the smallest brownie on the plate with my initial in the exact same way that she used to do.

And when I look for the largest one and see an *R* carved onto it, I definitely know it's from her. The secret message, the sign she promised, right before she left me for good.

But still, not wanting to be some crazy delusional person who finds secret meaning in a plate of baked goods, I glance at Sabine and say, "Did you—" I point at my brownie, the one with my initial carved into its middle. "Did you put that there?"

She squints, first at me, and then at the brownie, then she shakes her head and says, "Listen, Ever, if you don't want to try it, then you certainly don't have to, I just thought—"

But before she can finish, I've already plucked it off the plate and plopped it into my mouth, closing my eyes as I savor its chewy sweetness, immediately immersed in the feeling of *home*. That wonderful place I was lucky enough to revisit, no matter how short a time—finally realizing it's not relegated to just one single place, it's wherever you make it.

Sabine looks at me, her face anxious, awaiting my approval. "I tried them once before, but for some reason they didn't turn out nearly as good as your mom's." She shrugs, gazing at me shyly, eagerly awaiting my verdict. "She used to joke that she used a secret ingredient, but now I wonder if that might've been true."

I swallow hard, wiping the crumbs from my lips, and smiling when I say, "There *was* a secret ingredient." Seeing her expression fall, wondering if that means they're no good. "The secret ingredient was *love,*" I tell her. "And you must've used plenty, because these are awesome."

"Really?" Her eyes light up.

"Really." I hug her to me, but only for a moment before I'm pulling away. "Today's Friday, right?"

She looks at me, her brows merged. "Yes, it's Friday. Why? Are you okay?"

But I just nod and flee out the door, knowing I've even less time than I thought.

forty-nine

I pull into Ava's drive, and park my car sloppily—back wheels on the cement, front wheels on the grass, moving toward the door so quickly I barely acknowledge the stairs. But just as I reach it, I take a step back—something feels weird, off, strange in a way I can't quite explain. Like it's too *quiet,* too *still.* Even though the house appears just as I left it—planters on either side of the door, welcome mat in place—it's static in a way that seems eerie. And as I raise my knuckles to knock, I've just barely tapped it when it opens before me.

I head through the living room and into the kitchen, calling out for Ava and noticing how everything is just as I left it—teacup on the counter, cookies on a plate, everything in its usual place. But when I peek in the cupboard and see that the antidote and elixir are missing, I'm not sure what to think. Not knowing if it means that my plan worked and it wasn't needed after all, or if the opposite is true, and that something's gone wrong.

I race toward the indigo door at the end of the hall, eager to see if Damen's still there, but I'm blocked by Roman who stands right before it. His face widening into a a grin as he says, "So nice to have you back, Ever. Though I told Ava you would be. You know what they say—you can't go home again!"

I take in his deliberately tousled hair that perfectly frames the Ouroboros tattoo on his neck—knowing that despite my advances, despite my waking the school, he's still the one in charge around here.

"Where's Damen?" My eyes rake over his face, my gut twisting tight. "And what've you done with Ava?"

"Now, now." He smiles. "Don't you worry 'bout a thing. Damen's right where you left him. Though I must say I can't believe that you left him. I underestimated you. I had no idea. Though I can't help but wonder how Damen would feel if he knew. I bet he underestimated you too."

I swallow hard, remembering Damen's last words: *You left me.* Knowing he didn't underestimate me at all, he knew exactly which path I'd choose.

"And as for Ava." Roman smiles. "You'll be happy to know that I've *done* nothing with her. You should know by now that I only have eyes for *you,*" he murmurs, moving so fast I've barely had a chance to blink when his face is mere inches from mine. "Ava left on her own accord. Allowing us our privacy. And now that it's just a matter of—" He pauses to glance at his watch. "Well—seconds really, until you and I can make it official. You know, minus all the nasty guilt you would've felt had we hooked up sooner—before he'd had a chance to *pass.* Not that *I* would've felt guilty, but you strike me as the sort who likes to think of yourself as good and pure and well intentioned and all that rubbish, which, truth be told, really is a bit too maudlin for my tastes. But I'm sure we'll find a way to work through all that."

I tune out his words as I plan my next move. Trying to determine his weakness, his kryptonite, his most vulnerable chakra. Since he's blocking the very door I need to get through, the door that leads to Damen, I've no choice but to go *through* him. Though I need to be careful with how I proceed. Because when I do make a move, it needs to be swift, unexpected, right on target. Otherwise, I'm in for a battle I may never win.

He lifts his hand to my face and caresses my cheek, and I slap it so hard the crunch of his bones pierces the air as his crumpled fingers wobble and dangle before me.

"Ouch." He smiles, shaking his hand as he flexes his instantly healed digits. "You're a feisty one, aren't you? But you know how that only turns me on, right?" I roll my eyes, feeling his cold breath on my cheek as he says, "Why do you continue to fight me, Ever? Why do you push me away when I'm all you have left?"

"Why are you doing this?" I ask, my stomach twitching as his eyes darken and narrow, displaying a complete absence of color and light. "What did Damen ever do to you?"

He tilts his head back, peering at me when he says, "It's real simple, darlin'." His voice suddenly changing, dropping the British accent and adopting a tone I've never heard from him before. "He killed Drina. So I'm killing him. And then everything's even. Case closed."

And the second he says it, I *know.* I know exactly how I'll take him down and get behind that door. Because along with the *who* and the *how,* I've now got the *why.* The elusive motive I've needed all this time. And now the only thing standing between Damen and me is one solid punch to Roman's navel chakra, or sacral center as it's sometimes called—the center of jealousy, envy, and the irrational desire to possess.

One solid blow and Roman is history.

But still, before I take him down, I've one more thing to do. So I look at him, my gaze fixed and unwavering when I say, "But Damen didn't kill Drina. *I* did."

"Nice try." He laughs. "Pathetic, a bit maudlin like I said, but I'm afraid it won't work. You can't save Damen that way."

"But why not? If you're so interested in justice, an eye for an eye and all that—then you should know that *I'm* the one who did it." I nod, my voice taking on new urgency and strength. "*I'm* the one who killed that bitch." Watching as he sways, ever so slightly, but still enough for me to notice. "She was always hanging around, completely obsessed with Damen. You must've known that, right? That she was totally fixated on him?"

He winces. Neither confirming nor denying, but that wince is all I need to keep going, knowing I've hit the sore spot. "She wanted me out of the way so she could have Damen to herself, and after months of my trying to ignore her and hoping she'd go away, she was dumb enough to show up at my house and try to confront me. And—well—when she refused to back down and went after me instead—I killed her." I shrug, relaying the story with a lot more calm than I felt at the time, making sure to leave out my own ineptitude, cluelessness, and fears. "And it was so *easy.*" I smile, shaking my head as though reliving the moment all over again. "Seriously. You should've *seen* her. It's like, one moment she was standing before me all flaming red hair and white skin—and the next—*gone*! And by the way, Damen didn't show up until the deed was already done. So, as you see, if anyone's guilty, it's *me* and not him."

My gaze is on his, my fists ready to strike, moving right into his space when I say, "So, what do you say? You still wanna date me? Or would you rather kill me instead? Either way, I'll understand." I place my hand on his chest and push him hard against the door. Thinking how easy it would be to just lower it a few inches, jab really hard, and be done with all this.

"*You?*" he says, the word more like a question, a crisis of conscience, than the accusation he meant it to be. "You and *not* Damen?"

I nod, my body tensed, poised for fight, knowing nothing will keep me from getting into that room, and raising my fist as he says, "It's not too late! We can still save him!"

I freeze, my fist hovering at the halfway mark, unsure if I'm being played.

Watching as he shakes his head, visibly distressed when he says, "I didn't know—I thought for sure it was him—he gave me *everything*—he gave me *life—this life*! And I thought for sure that he—"

He moves around me and flees down the hall, calling, "You go check on him—I'll get the antidote!"

fifty

The first thing I see when I burst through the door is Damen. Still lying on the futon, looking as thin and pale as he did when I left him.

The second thing I see is Rayne. Huddling by his side, pressing a damp cloth to his face. Her eyes growing wide when she sees me, her hand held up before her as she shouts, "Ever, *no*! Don't come any closer! If you want to save Damen, then stop right there—do *not* break the circle!"

I gaze down, seeing some grainy white substance that looks just like salt, formed into a perfect ring that keeps the two of them in and me out. Then I look at her, wondering what she wants, what she could possibly have in mind cowering beside Damen and warning me away. Noticing how she looks even odder outside of Summerland with her ghostly pale face, tiny features, and large coal-black eyes.

But when my gaze shifts to Damen, watching as he fights and struggles for each breath—I know I have to get to him, no matter what she says. It's my fault he's like this. I abandoned him. Left him behind. I was stupid, and selfish, and naïve enough to think that everything would work out okay just because I wanted it to, and that Ava would stick around to pick up the pieces.

I step forward, my toe landing just outside the border as Roman rushes in from behind me and shouts, "What the bloody hell is *she* doing in here?" His eyes wide with shock as he gapes at Rayne, still crouching beside Damen from behind the barrier.

"Don't trust him!" she says, her eyes darting between us. "He knew I was here all along."

"I didn't know any such thing! I've never even seen you before!" He shakes his head. "I mean, sorry darlin', but Catholic schoolgirls just ain't my thing. I prefer my women a little more feisty, like Ever, here." He reaches toward me, trailing his fingers down the length of my back, chilling my skin in a way that makes me want to react—but I don't. I just take a deep breath and try to stay calm. Focusing on his *other* hand—the one that's holding the antidote—the key to saving Damen.

Becausc in the end, that's the only thing that matters—everything else can wait.

I snatch the bottle and unscrew the top. And I'm just about to penetrate Rayne's circle of protection when Roman puts his hand on my arm and says, "Not so fast."

I pause, glancing between them, Rayne looking me right in the eye when she says, "Don't do it, Ever! Whatever he tells you, do *not* listen. Listen only to me. Ava dumped the antidote and ran off with the elixir not long after you left, but luckily I got here just before *he* did." She gestures toward Roman, her eyes like angry points of the darkest night. "He needs you to break the circle so he can get in, because he can't get to Damen without you. Only the worthy can access the circle, only those with good intent. But if you step in now, Roman will follow, so if you care about Damen, if you truly want to protect him, you have to wait until Romy gets here."

"Romy?"

Rayne nods, glancing between Roman and me. "She's bringing the antidote, it will be ready by nightfall since it needs the full moon's energy to be fully complete."

But Roman just shakes his head, laughing as he says, "What antidote? I'm the only one with the antidote. Hell, I'm the one who made the poison, so what the hell does she know?" And when he sees the confusion on my face, he adds, "I really don't see how you have much of a choice. If you listen to this one"—he flicks his fingers toward Rayne—"Damen *will* die. But if you listen to me, he *won't*. The math's rather simple, don't you think?"

I look at Rayne, watching as she shakes her head and warns me not to listen to him, to hold out for Romy, to wait for nightfall, which is still hours away. But then I gaze at Damen beside her, his breath becoming more labored, the color drained from his face—

"And if you're trying to trick me?" I say, all of my attention now focused on Roman.

Holding my breath as he says, "Then he dies."

I swallow hard and stare at the floor, unsure what to do. Do I trust Roman, the rogue immortal who's responsible for all of this in the first place? Or do I trust Rayne, the creepy twin with her covert double-talk and an agenda that's never been clear? But when I close my eyes and try to concentrate on my gut, knowing that it's rarely wrong, even though I often ignore it, it's frustratingly still.

Then looking at Roman when he says, "But if I'm *not* tricking you, then he *lives*. So I really don't see how you have much of a choice—"

"Don't listen to him," Rayne says. "He's *not* here to help you, *I* am! *I'm* the one who sent you the vision in Summerland that day, *I'm* the one who showed you all the ingredients required to save him. You were shut out of the akashic records because you'd already made your choice. And while we tried to show you the way, while we tried to help you and stop you from leaving, you refused to listen, and now—"

"I thought you didn't know my business?" I narrow my gaze. "I thought you and your creepy sister couldn't access—" I pause, glancing at Roman, knowing I have to tread carefully with what I'm about to say. "I thought you couldn't *see* certain things."

Rayne looks at me, her face stricken, shaking her head as she says, "We never lied to you, Ever. And we never misled you. We *can't* see certain things, that's true. But Romy's an empath and I'm a precog, and together we get feelings and visions. That's how we first found you, and we've been trying to guide you ever since, using the information we sense. Ever since Riley asked us to look after you—"

"Riley?" I gape, my stomach swirling with nausea. *How could she be involved in any of this?*

"We met her in Summerland and showed her around. We even went to school together, a private boarding school she manifested, which is why we wear this." She motions to her plaid skirt and blazer, the uniform she and her sister always wear. And I remember how Riley always dreamed of going to boarding school, saying it was so she could get away from me. So it makes sense that she'd manifest one. "Then, when she decided to—" she pauses, glancing at Roman before she continues, "to *cross over,* she asked us to look after you if we ever saw you around."

"I don't believe you," I say, even though I have no reason not to. "Riley would've told me, she would've . . ." But then I remember how she once said something about meeting some people who showed her around, and I wonder if she was referring to the twins.

"We also know Damen—he—he helped us once—a long time ago . . ." And when she looks at me, I'm just about to fold when she says, "But if you could just wait a few more hours until the antidote's complete, then Romy will be here and . . ."

I glance at Damen, his emaciated body, his pale, clammy skin, his eyes appearing sunken, his breath ragged, every inhale and exhale progressively weaker—and I know there's only one choice to make.

So I turn my back on Rayne and look at Roman when I say, "Okay, just tell me what to do."

fifty-one

Roman nods, his eyes on mine as he removes the antidote from my grasp and says, "We'll need something sharp."

I squint, not quite understanding. "What're you talking about? If that's *really* the antidote like you say, then why can't he just drink it? I mean, it's ready, right?" My stomach twisting under the weight of his gaze, so steady and focused on mine.

"It *is* the antidote. It just requires one final ingredient to make it complete."

I suck in my breath, knowing I should've known better, that it couldn't be that easy when Roman's involved. "What is it?" I say, my voice as shaky as I feel inside. "What kind of game are you playing?"

"There, there." He smiles. "Not to worry. It's nothing too complicated—and it certainly won't take *hours*." He shakes his head at Rayne. "All we need to get this show on the road is just a drop or two of your blood. That's it."

I stare at him, not comprehending. I mean, how could that make the slightest bit of difference between life and death?

But Roman just looks at me, answering the question in my head when he says, "In order to save your immortal partner, he must consume an antidote containing a drop of his true love's blood. Believe me, it's the only way."

I swallow hard, far less afraid of shedding blood than being played a fool and losing Damen for good.

"Surely you're not worried that you're not really Damen's one true love—*are you*?" he asks, his lips curving the tiniest bit. "Perhaps I should call Stacia instead?"

I grasp a pair of nearby scissors and aim them toward my wrist, and I'm just about to plunge when Rayne screams, "Ever, *no*! *Don't* do it! It's a trick! Don't believe him! Don't listen to a word he says!"

I look at Damen, seeing the labored rise and fall of his chest moving so slow and ragged now there's no time to waste. I know in my heart that he has only minutes left, not hours. Then I bring the scissors down hard, watching as their sharp pointy tip penetrates my wrist, nearly splitting it in two. Shooting a geyser of blood straight into the air, before gravity takes over and pushes it down. Hearing Rayne scream, a wail so piercing it cuts through the sound of everything else, as Roman crouches beneath me, collecting my blood.

And other than feeling faint, and the slightest bit dizzy, it's only a matter of seconds before my veins are fused and my skin is all healed. So I grab the bottle, ignore Rayne's protests, and break through the circle, pushing her aside as I drop to my knees, slipping my fingers under Damen's neck as I force him to drink. Watching his breath grow fainter and fainter—until it stops completely.

"NO!" I cry. "You *can't* die—you *can't* leave me!" I force the liquid down the length of his throat, determined to bring him back, return him to life, like he once did with me.

I hold him to me, willing him to live. Everything around us completely shut out as I focus on Damen, my one true soul mate, my eternal partner, my only love, refusing to say good-bye, refusing to give up hope. And when the bottle is empty, I collapse onto his chest, pressing my lips against his, filling him with my breath, my being, my *life*. As I murmur the words he once said to me: "Open your eyes and look at me!"

Over and over again—

Until he finally does.

"Damen!" I cry, a flood of tears streaming down my cheeks and onto his face. "Oh, thank God, you're back! I missed you so much—and I love you—and I promise I'll never *ever* leave you again! Just—just please forgive me—please—"

His eyes flicker open as his mouth tries to move, forming words I can't hear. And when I lower my ear to his lips, so grateful to be with him again, our reunion is cut short by a series of claps.

Slow, steady claps coming from Roman who's now standing behind me. Having penetrated the circle as Rayne cowers in a far corner of the room.

"Bravo!" he says, his face mocking, amused, as he glances between Damen and me. "Well done, Ever. I must say, that was all very—*touching*. It's not often one bears witness to such a heartfelt reunion."

I swallow hard, my hands shaking, my stomach beginning to ping, wondering what he could possibly be up to. I mean, Damen's alive, the antidote worked, what else could there be?

I glance at Damen, watching the steady rise and fall of his chest as he falls back to sleep, then I gaze toward Rayne who's looking at me with widened eyes and an expression of disbelief.

But when I look at Roman again, I'm sure he's just enjoying a last chance at fun, a pathetic show of bravado now that Damen is saved. "So, you want to go after me now? Is that it?" I say, fully prepared to take him down if I have to.

But he just shakes his head and laughs. "Now why would I want to do that? Why would I want to rid myself of a whole new brand of fun that's only just begun?"

I freeze, panic building inside me, but trying not to show it.

"I had no idea you'd be so easy, so predictable, but then again, that's love, right? It tends to make one a little bit crazy, a tad bit impulsive, even irrational, don't you think?"

I narrow my eyes, having no idea what he's going on and on about but knowing it can't be good.

"And yet, it's amazing how quickly you fell for it. No sales resistance at all. Seriously, Ever, you just sliced yourself open with virtually no questions asked. Which goes back to my original point, never underestimate the power of love—or, in your case, was it guilt? Only you know for sure."

I stare at him, a horrible understanding growing inside me, knowing I've made a grave mistake—that I've somehow been played.

"You were just *so* desperate to trade your life for his, *so* willing to do anything to save him—that it all went so seamlessly, so much easier than I ever expected. Though truth be told, I know just how you feel. In fact, I would've done the same thing for Drina—if only I'd been given the choice." He glares at me, his lids so narrowed his eyes are like angry slivers of darkness. "But, since we already know how that ended, I suppose you'd like to know how this ends too, right?"

I glance at Damen, ensuring he's still okay, watching him sleep as Roman says, "Yes, he's still alive, don't worry your pretty head about that. And just so you know, he'll most likely remain that way for many, many, *many* years to come. I have no plans to go after him again, so don't you fret. In fact, it was never my intention to kill either one of you, regardless of what you might've thought. Though, in all fairness, I suppose I should warn you that all this happiness does bear a cost."

"What is it?" I whisper, staring at Roman, having no idea what he could want besides Drina who's already gone. Besides, whatever the cost, I'll pay it. If it means getting Damen back, I'll do what it takes.

"I see I've upset you," he coos, shaking his head. "Now I've already told you that Damen will be fine. In fact, more than fine. He'll be raring to go and better than ever. Just look at him, would you?

See how his color's returned, how his form's bulking up? Very soon he'll be right back to that handsome, strapping young lad you've convinced yourself that you love so damn much you'd do *anything* to save him, no questions asked—"

"Get to the point," I say, my eyes on his, annoyed by the way these immortal rogues always insist on making every single moment about *them*.

"Oh no." He shakes his head. "I've waited *years* for this moment, and I will *not* be rushed. You see, Damen and I go way back. Back to the very beginning, in Florence, where we met." And when he sees my expression, he adds, "Yes, I was a fellow orphan, the youngest orphan, and when he spared me from the plague I looked to him like a father."

"Which would make Drina your mother?" I say, watching his gaze harden before relaxing again.

"Hardly." He smiles. "You see, I loved Drina, I'm not afraid to admit it. I loved her with all of my heart. I loved her in the same way you think you love him." He motions toward Damen, who's returned to the way he was when we met. "I loved her with every ounce of my being, I would've done anything for her—and I never would've abandoned her like you did with him."

I swallow hard, knowing I deserve that.

"But it was always about Damen. *Always. About. Damen.* That's all she could focus on. All she could see. Until he met you—the first time—and Drina turned to me." He smiles briefly, but it quickly fades when he says, "For *friendship,*" practically spitting the word. "And *companionship.* And a big strong shoulder to cry on." He scowls. "I would've given her anything she wanted—anything in the world—but she already had everything—and all she wanted was the one thing I couldn't give her, *wouldn't* give her—Damen. *Sodding.* Auguste." He shakes his head. "And unfortunately for Drina, Damen only wanted *you.* And so it began—a love triangle that lasted four hundred years, each of us relentless, driven, never once giving up hope, until I was *forced* to—because *you* killed her. Guaranteeing we'd never be together. Guaranteeing our love would never be known—"

"You knew I killed her?" I gasp, my stomach twisting into a horrible knot. "This *whole* time?"

He rolls his eyes. "Well, *duh*!" He laughs, performing a perfect imitation of Stacia at her brattiest. "I had it all planned, though I must say, you really threw me for a loop when you abandoned him like that. I underestimated you, Ever. I truly did. But even so, I held on to my plans, I told Ava you'd be back."

Ava.

I look at him, my eyes wide, not sure I want to know what happened to the one person I thought I could trust.

"Ah, yes, your good friend Ava. The only one you could count on, right?" He nods. "Well, as it turns out, she gave me a reading once, quite a good one too I might say, and well, we kept in touch. You know she practically fled town the moment you left? Took all the elixir too. Left Damen alone in this room, vulnerable, defenseless, just waiting for me. Didn't even stick around long enough to see if your little theory was true—figuring you were long gone, so, either way, you'd never know the difference. You know, you really should be more careful about who you trust, Ever. You shouldn't be so naïve."

I swallow hard and shrug. There's nothing I can do about it now. I can't take it back, I can't change the past, the only thing I can change now is what happens next.

"Oh, and I loved how you kept peering at my wrist, searching for my Ouroboros tattoo." He laughs. "Little did you realize we wear them wherever we choose, so I chose my neck."

I stand there silently, hoping to hear more. Damen didn't even know there were immortal rogues until Drina went bad.

"I started it." He nods, his right hand over his heart. "I'm the founding father of the Immortal Rogue tribe. While it's true that your friend Damen gave us all the first drink, when the effects began to wear off, he left us to age and wither, refusing to give us more."

I shrug and roll my eyes. Granting someone over a century's worth of living is hardly what I'd call selfish.

"And that's when I started experimenting, learning from the world's greatest alchemists until I'd surpassed Damen's work."

"You call that a triumph? Turning evil? Taking and giving life at will? Playing *God*?"

"I do what I have to." He shrugs, inspecting his nails. "At least I didn't leave the remaining orphans to shrivel. Unlike Damen, I cared enough to track them down and save them. And yeah, every now and then I recruit someone new. Though I assure you there's no harm done to the innocent, only to those who deserve it."

Our eyes meet, but I quickly look away. Damen and I should've seen this coming, shouldn't have assumed Drina was the end.

"So imagine my surprise when I show up here only to find this—little—urchin—huddling with Damen in her little magick circle, while her creepy twin runs around town, trying to piece an antidote together before nightfall." Roman laughs. "Quite a successful search too, I might add. You should've waited, Ever. You shouldn't have broken the circle. Those two deserve far more credit than you were willing to give them, but then, as I said, you do have a tendency to trust the wrong ones. Anyway, meanwhile back at the bungalow, I just kicked around here, waiting for you to show up and break the protective seal, like I knew you would."

"Why?" I gaze at Damen, then over at Rayne, still huddled in the corner, too frightened to move. "What difference does it make?"

"Well, it *is* what killed him." He shrugs. "He could've lived for days had you not broken through like that. Lucky for you I had the antidote on hand to bring him back. And even though there's a price, a huge hefty price, what's done is done, right? And now there's no going back. *No. Going. Back.* You understand that better than any of us now, don't you?"

"Enough," I say, my hands curled into fists. Thinking I should get rid of him now, eliminate him for good. I mean, Damen's safe, Roman's not needed, so what harm could it do?

Except that I can't. It's not right. I mean, Damen *is* safe. And I can't just go *eliminating* people just because I deem them no good. I can't abuse my power that way. Much is expected to those given much, and all that.

I relax my fists, unfolding my fingers as he says, "That's a wise choice. You don't want to do anything too rash, even though soon you'll be tempted. Because you see, Ever, while Damen's going to be fine, perfectly fine and healthy and basically everything you could ever want him to be, I'm afraid that's just going to make it all the more difficult when you realize you can never be together."

I look at him, my fingers shaking, my eyes blazing, refusing to believe him. Damen's going to live—I'm going to live—so what could possibly keep us apart?

"Don't believe me?" He shrugs. "Fine, go ahead, consummate your love and find out. It's not like I care. My loyalties to Damen ended centuries ago. So I'll have absolutely no qualms when you jump his bones and he ends up dead." He smiles, his eyes right on mine, and when he sees the incredulous look on my face, his smile grows into a laugh. A laugh so large it reaches toward the ceiling and shakes the walls of this room, before it settles all around us like a blanket of doom.

"Have I ever lied to you, Ever? Go ahead, think about it. I'll wait. Haven't I been truthful all along? Oh, sure I may have saved a few of the smaller, insignificant details for last, which, though it may be quite naughty of me, really does add to the fun. But now, it seems we've come to the point of full disclosure, so I'd like to make it clear, crystal clear, that the two of you can *never* be together. No DNA exchange whatsoever. And in case you still don't get what that means, then allow me to spell it out by stating that no bodily fluids of any kind may ever be exchanged. And just in case you need a translation of *that,* well, it means you can't kiss, lick, spit into each other's mouths, share each other's elixir—oh, and of course, you also can't do what's yet to be done. Hell, you can't even cry on his shoulder over the fact that you can't do what's yet to be done. In short, you can't do *anything.* Or at least not with each other. Because if you do, Damen will die."

"I don't believe you," I say, my heart racing, my palms slick with sweat. "How is that even possible?"

"Well, I may not be a doctor or scientist by profession, but I did study with some of the greats back in the day. Do Albert Einstein, Max Planck, Sir Isaac Newton, or Galileo mean anything to you?"

I shrug, wishing he'd stop name-dropping and get on with it already.

"So, in the simplest terms, allow me to say that while the antidote alone would've saved him by stopping the receptors from multiplying additional aged and damaged cells, the moment we added your blood, we made sure that any future reintroduction of your DNA will only cause them to go active again, thereby reversing the entire process and killing him. But we don't need to go all Science Channel here, just know that you can never be together again. *Never.* Understood? Because if you do, Damen dies. And now that I've told you—the rest is up to you."

I stare at the ground, wondering what I've done, how I could've been stupid enough to trust him. Barely listening when he says, "And if you don't believe me, then go ahead, hop on board and give it a try. But when he keels over, don't come crying to me."

Our eyes lock, and just like that day at the lunch tables at school, I'm sucked inside the abyss of his mind. Feeling his longing for Drina, her longing for Damen, his longing for me, my longing for home, and knowing it's all resulted in *this*.

I shake my head, wrenching myself from his grip as he says, "Oh, look, he's waking! And looking as gorgeous and hunky as ever. Enjoy your reunion, darlin', but remember, don't enjoy it *too* much!"

I glance over my shoulder, seeing Damen beginning to stir, stretching his body and rubbing his eyes, then I lunge for Roman, wanting to hurt him, destroy him, make him pay for all that he did.

But he just laughs and dances out of my way, heading for the door and smiling as he says, "Trust me, you don't want to do that. You just might need me someday."

I stand before him, shaking with rage, tempted to plunge my fist into his most vulnerable chakra and watch him vanish forever.

"I know you don't believe it now, but why don't you take a moment to think about it. Now that you can no longer cuddle with Damen, you're about to become very lonely, very quickly. And since I pride myself on being the forgiving type, I'd be more than willing to fill your void."

I narrow my eyes and raise my fist.

"And then—there's the small, inconsequential fact that there just may be an antidote to the antidote—"

His eyes meet mine as I suck in my breath.

"And since I created it, only I would know for sure. So, the way I see it, you eliminate me, you eliminate any hope of the two of you ever being together. Is that a risk you're willing to take?"

We stand there, the two of us joined in the most hideous way, our eyes locked, unmoving, until Damen calls my name.

And when I turn, all I see is *him*. Returned to his usual splendor as he rises from the futon and I rush to his arms. Feeling his wonderful warmth as he presses his body to mine, gazing at me in the way that he used to—as though I'm the most important thing in his world.

I bury my face in his chest, his shoulder, his neck, my entire body thrumming with tingle and heat as I whisper his name again and again, my lips moving across the cotton of his shirt, summoning his warmth, his strength, wondering how I'll ever find the words to confess the horrible thing that I've done.

"What happened?" he asks, his eyes on mine as he pulls away. "Are you okay?"

I glance around the room, noticing Roman and Rayne are both gone. Then I peer into his deep dark eyes as I say, "You don't remember?"

He shakes his head.

"None of it?"

He shrugs. "The last thing I remember is Friday night, at the play. And then after—" He squints. "What is this place? Surely this isn't the Montage?"

I lean into his body as we head for the door. Knowing I have to tell him—sooner rather than later—but wanting to put it off for as long as I can. Wanting to enjoy the fact that he's back—that he's alive and well and we're together again. Heading down the steps and unlocking my car as I say, "You were sick. *Very* sick. But now you're better. But it's kind of a long story, so—" I shove the key in the ignition, as he places his hand on my knee.

"So where do we go from here?" he asks, as I shift into reverse.

Feeling his gaze as I take a deep breath and pull onto the street, determined to ignore the much larger question in his question, when I smile and say, "Anywhere we want. The weekend starts now."